RAYNE &
DELILAH'S
MIDNITE
MATINEE

ALSO BY JEFF ZENTNER

The Serpent King

Goodbye Days

RAYNE & DELILAH'S MIDNITE MATINEE

JEFF ZENTNER

CROWN

New York

MAY 2019

Text copyright © 2019 by Jeff Zentner
Jacket art copyright © 2019 by Simon Prades

All rights reserved. Published in the United States by Crown Books for Young Readers, an imprint of Random House Children's Books, a division of Penguin Random House LLC, New York.

Crown and the colophon are registered trademarks of Penguin Random House LLC.

Visit us on the Web! GetUnderlined.com

Educators and librarians, for a variety of teaching tools, visit us at RHTeachersLibrarians.com

Library of Congress Cataloging-in-Publication Data
Names: Zentner, Jeff, author.
Title: Rayne & Delilah's Midnite Matinee / Jeff Zentner.
Other titles: Rayne and Delilah's Midnite Matinee
Description: First edition. | New York : Crown, [2019] | Summary: Told in two voices, Josie and Delia struggle with growing up and growing apart as they face tough decisions about their post-high school futures and the fate of their weekly cable television show.
Identifiers: LCCN 2018049011 | ISBN 978-1-5247-2020-9 (hardback) | ISBN 978-1-5247-2021-6 (glb) | ISBN 978-1-5247-2022-3 (ebook)
Subjects: | CYAC: Best friends—Fiction. | Friendship—Fiction. | Television programs—Production and direction—Fiction. | Change—Fiction.
Classification: LCC PZ7.1.Z46 Ray 2019 | DDC [Fic]—dc23

Printed in the United States of America
10 9 8 7 6 5 4 3 2 1
First Edition

Random House Children's Books
supports the First Amendment and celebrates the right to read.

For Tennessee and Sara, my salvations

For Jessi Zazu (1989–2017)
and all young women
who make things together,
who burn bright

Josie

Here's the thing with dreams—and I'm talking about the kind you have when you sleep, not the kind where you're finally learning to surf when you're fifty: they're carefully tailored to the only audience who will ever see them, which is you. So I'm not big on telling people about my dreams for that reason.

That said, there's this recurring dream I have. It comes around every couple of months or so, but I wish it were more often because it's awesome, and when I wake up from it, I lie there for a few moments, wishing I could reenter it. In this dream, I'm at a familiar place. Often it's my grandma's house.

Her house was tiny. It always smelled like quilts and oatmeal cookies and that musty odor when you first turn on a window-unit air conditioner after winter. It had a cellar that smelled like cold dirt even during the summer, where she kept store-brand cans of creamed corn, jars of home-pickled dilly beans, and two-liter bottles of Diet Coke. In my dream, I descend into the cellar. I find a door leading to a passageway. I go in. I follow it for a long way; it's cool and dark, and I'm not afraid. Eventually it opens into this grand, palatial, brightly lit marble room. There are columns and fountains, and the air smells like flowers. I push forward and find room after room. It's all grand and glorious, beautiful and perfect. It's not what you would expect to find.

But there it is, and for those few minutes (I've heard that dreams are never more than five minutes long, which I totally don't believe, but whatever), you get to experience the most unexpected grandeur, running like a rabbit warren under my grandma's little house in Jackson, Tennessee.

And then I wake up, the thrill of possibility and discovery drifting upward off me like steam. It's such a delicious feeling. *Just stay a little longer,* I say. But it doesn't.

Yet another reason it sucks to tell people about your dreams is that then they suddenly become amateur dream interpretation experts: [Nondescript German psychiatrist voice] *Well, you see, when you were riding that bicycle made out of fish sticks while wearing an adult diaper, it symbolizes . . .* That you're afraid of failure. That you're filled with seething rage. That you're afraid to become such a grown-up that you no longer call fish sticks "fish dicks." Who knows?

But dreams are their own universe. They exist in you, and you're the God of that universe, so no one can tell you what they mean. You have to figure it out, assuming dreams have any meaning at all, which I think they only sometimes do.

This dream, though—the one about finding all the hidden rooms—I think it does mean something. I think it means there's something great inside me, something extraordinary and mysterious and undiscovered.

That's a thing I tell myself. It's a thing I believe.

Delia

I love mediocre people. The ones who try their hardest to make something beautiful, something great, something that someone will remember and talk about when they're gone—and they come up short. And not by a little bit. By a *lot*. They're my people. We laugh at them, but you really have no choice in this life but to believe with all your heart that you're extraordinary. You have to hold this conviction against all evidence to the contrary. Living is too sad otherwise.

I wonder sometimes if I'm really the mediocre person I think I am, because probably one of the deals with being mediocre is you don't realize you are. In fact, I bet you've got to think you're *better* than everyone else to attain full mediocrity. Some of these movies Josie and I watch? They must be the product of a megalomaniacal mind. Any self-awareness at all would keep them from being put out into the world. Bad monsters. Nausea-inducing (and not in the good way that you want from a horror movie) camera work (bonus points for obvious attempts at "artiness"). Bizarre, tossed-off romantic subplots that are often more terrifying than the threat at the heart of the movie. Nightmarish musical interludes (the more whimsical and unrelated to the plot or theme of the movie, the more unnerving). Abrupt, anticlimactic endings that look like the money ran out before the story did.

I feel this obligation to bear witness to all of it and give others the chance to also. A duty, I guess. *Here, this is the work of my brothers and sisters in garbage. Remember them and what they tried to do.*

I also love mediocre people because we're always getting left behind. When someone leaves you, maybe you get a reason and maybe you don't. I don't know which is better. If you get a reason, I guess you can work on improving or something. So that the next time you don't get left behind. That probably works better with boyfriends and girlfriends than with dads. You only get one dad, and if he scoots, it sorta doesn't matter if you get a reason because it's not like you can work on it for your next dad.

I don't know why Dad left. I don't think it's because either Mom or I was mediocre. He loved mediocrity as much as I do. At least I think he did. All the movies were his. Or his and Mom's.

Someday I want to ask him why.

Josie

"New pants?" I ask as Delia gets in my car.

"Yep. Seven bucks on Ebay, not including shipping from Slovenia."

"Leather?"

"For seven bucks?" Delia starts sniffing the air like a blood-hound. "It reeks in here."

"Whatever, weirdo," I say.

"It's, like, kerosene-y and skunky."

I sniff so hard I get light-headed. "Nope. Nothing here."

"Is it Buford?" Delia says, casting a glance at the back seat, where my basset hound, Buford T. Rutherford B. Hayes, is sprawled like a tan garbage bag of dog Jell-O, looking doleful. Looking maybe even a bit more full of dole than usual, sensing he's being scapegoated.

"Buford is innocent before God, Delia Wilkes. How dare you? And why would he smell kerosene-y and skunky?"

"Because he has, you know, flaps. And he's farty."

"Well, one, I gave my farty, flappy dog a bath like a day ago. And two, I know his bouquet, and it's not so chemical-y."

Delia sniffs again, harder, closing her eyes. "So you *can* smell it."

"Yes, Hannibal Lecter, I can now," I say. "My car smells like a gas station that hosted a skunk orgy. I get it."

Delia says nothing but lifts one of her black-vinyl-clad legs to her nose. She sniffs a couple of times, drops her leg, and looks out the window silently. Guiltily, if we're being honest. A tiny smile tugs at the corners of her mouth.

I pounce. "Oh *ho ho!* What did you discover?"

"Nothing." The corners of her mouth lift a little higher.

"Has the stink hunter become the stink hunted?"

"I want you to know that this smell is not issuing forth from my ass."

"*Issuing forth?* Who says that?"

"I'm just saying, my ass is clean."

"Mmm-hmmm."

"Don't give me a skeptical mmm-hmmm. These pants didn't smell when I opened the package yesterday. It's like a heat-activated funk."

"Mmm-hmmm." The AC in my Kia Rio definitely isn't keeping up with the late-April heat. It feels like spring stumbled while carrying a load of summer in its arms.

"Seriously," Delia says. "How do you de-reek vinyl pants? Run through the car wash while wearing them?"

"Are you even sure they're vinyl as opposed to skunk leather?" This whole situation is so quintessentially Delia. If you told me that Delia had ordered a pair of pants off Ebay for seven bucks, I would *assume* that they'd arrive smelling like cyborg sweat. It's the kind of luck she has. One time she found a spider in a banana. As in, she opened the banana and boom—spider.

We pull up to a red light. The driver next to me gives me a long stare. Fair enough. It's not every day in Jackson, Tennessee,

6

that you see two girls dressed like vampires—wearing red-lined black capes—driving down the street. We're both also sporting some dramatic makeup because we don't have time to apply it at the studio. Arliss runs a *very* tight ship.

"By the way," I say, "don't you owe someone an apology?"

"Sorry for accusing your car of smelling."

"No." I turn back to Buford and nod. He glances up with a hangdog expression. I think the word *hangdog* was invented to describe expressions like Buford is giving me, because he literally looks like a dog that's melting off a hanger. "Him."

Delia turns back and grabs Buford by the jowls and scratches his head and neck vigorously. "Oh, aren't you a good boy and not a stinky boy. Auntie Delia's sorry for saying that you smelled like a skunk soaked in kerosene when it was Auntie Delia all along."

He whimpers and lays his head back down on the seat. He hates us both. I mean, we basically torture him . . . but in a loving way? Is that a thing? He's like four hundred in dog years, and he's profoundly over our nonsense. He never signed up for this.

I try to tell him *Mama loves you* with my eyes. "Can you even imagine the assault you've been mounting on poor Buford's nose?" I say to Delia. "His sense of smell is a million times better than ours."

"He's fine. He probably likes it. Dogs eat their own puke." Delia's phone buzzes. She pulls it out like it's a live cicada in her pocket, stares at it for a couple of seconds, and puts it away with a faint sigh. Probably her mom having some weird deal. By now, I know better than to ask. But I do anyway. "Your mom?"

Delia usually has an air of nervous good cheer before we film, but the good-cheer part flickers from her face like a lightbulb not screwed in all the way, leaving just the jittery energy. "Waiting on an important email."

Delia is not the important-email type. "College stuff?" (She's also not the college type. More like community college, which is where she's going.)

She shakes her head. "My dad."

"He get in touch with you?"

"I saved up and hired a PI to track him down."

"Seriously? You walked into a PI's office like an old-timey dame?"

"No, I emailed her like a new-timey dame. She's supposed to get back to me today."

"Do you not have an aunt or an uncle or something who knows where he is?"

"His dad died when he was a kid. His mom died when I was like three. I think he has a couple of half siblings that not even he knew. We're not in touch with any of his aunts or uncles. I'd have had to hire a PI to track *them* down."

"Wow. So . . ." I'm pretty surprised, honestly. Delia isn't what you'd call a go-getter. Her grades suck. She skips class a bunch. Starting this show was the most motivation she's ever displayed. Tracking down a long-lost dad is *very* proactive for her.

"Yeah. But talking about it is making me nervous. I'm not a TV natural like you. I gotta concentrate."

A few seconds of charged silence tick by.

"Speaking of doing TV professionally, get this: my mom tells me she's been in touch with this friend from law school who works for Food Network, and apparently they have offices in Knoxville, and she told her that she could get me an internship." Even as the words leave my mouth, I regret them. Just because a segue is natural doesn't mean it's a great idea. That's probably a good thing to keep in mind if I want to make it in TV.

Delia stares at me. "When would you . . . ?" She trails off.

"I don't even know if I want to do it. It's TV and it might be a good start to my career, but I'm not sure about Food Network."

"So it would be—"

"During the school year."

"But aren't you still planning on going to UT Martin?"

"Yeah." I feel a strange twinge of something as I say it. I can't quite identify what it is. Like I'm lying, but I'm not.

"But you still haven't committed to UT Martin. Like formally."

"I have. But I also committed to UT Knoxville."

"Is that even allowed? Committing to two schools?"

"I mean, I think it's definitely frowned upon. But the deadlines were coming up and my mom wanted me to see what she could do with the internship thing before I really committed to a school. So now I have until fall to cancel on one of them."

"If you don't go to school around here, we can't do the show."

"What if you came to Knoxville with me?" I should cut this off. I can sense Delia's panic. This is a terrible time to be discussing this. Not that there's a great time.

"We already know Knoxville public access isn't into the show. We've tried like fifty times to get them to syndicate us." Her voice is rising and brittle.

"What if I came home on breaks and we recorded a bunch of episodes?"

"No way would Arliss be up for that. And my work schedule wouldn't allow it."

There's a moment of awkward silence.

"We're a team," Delia says. "We're way better when we do the show together. I need you."

"Okay, I told you. I'm going to UT Martin. Don't freak out." I'm pretty sure I'm not lying to Delia, but I'm not 100 percent sure. More like 95 percent. Or 94 percent. Or 94.7 percent.

"I'm not freaking out."

She is unequivocally freaking out.

The light turns green. I give the driver next to me a curt nod before driving off. He stares straight ahead.

Delia

And now I'm kind of freaking out on top of my stressing over the PI. Thinking about even the slimmest possibility of Josie leaving is exactly the thing I don't want to be doing right now. And . . .

"Oops." I clap a palm to my heavily made-up forehead.

"What?"

"We gotta stop at Dixie Cafe and get some chicken livers for Buford's segment."

"DeeDee."

"I forgot! I was preoccupied with the PI thing!" And more recently with the *best friend possibly betraying me by leaving* thing.

"That is in the opposite direction. If we're late . . ."

"I have no idea if the twins' friend's dog will cooperate without the chicken livers."

"You know Arliss."

"I know Arliss."

Josie hits the brakes and makes a U-turn, drawing a honk. "We need some energetic bongo music to play when we have to drive really fast because you've forgotten something."

"I'll text Arliss and tell him we're running late."

"Because he's super good about checking texts."

"I'll tell him we're bringing him dinner."

"You're paying," Josie says.

We drive with the chicken livers like they're going to be transplanted into several very important chickens, barreling up to the TV Six studio—Jackson, Tennessee's only truly local television station.

Arliss Thacker stands outside the back door of the studio, smoking. He squints at us like we pulled up on a parade float celebrating the word *moist*, hitting your funny bone, phlegm, and leaning your seat back on airplanes. He consults his watch with conspicuous deliberation and concentration.

"He hates us so much," I murmur.

"Do you blame him?"

"Oh, I one hundred percent do not."

Josie fumbles with her sticky seat belt. "We've only brought him misery."

"Probably."

"No, I definitely know because he told me. He literally said to me once, verbatim: 'You two have only ever brought me misery.'"

"Sounds right."

Josie gathers the lacy black skirts of her gown and gets out, whistling for Buford to follow her, which he does with the resigned reluctance of a man going to a public colonoscopy, waddling behind her flappily. She carries the Styrofoam container of pulled pork, squash casserole, and fried okra that we got Arliss.

I go around to the back of Josie's Kia, grab our plastic tub full of props, and heft it, starting toward the door on Josie's heels. The tub begins to slip. "Hey, Arliss, could you—"

Arliss is a big guy—a honey-baked ham of a man who looks like a biker—but he never offers to help us haul stuff in. He actually reminds me of Buford. That spiritual kinship is probably why Buford is the only one of us he's ever happy to see.

He squats to scratch Buford behind the ears, ignoring Josie even after she wordlessly hands him the dinner container. "What have I told y'all about load-ins?"

"That you've done enough for ten men's lifetimes." I recall Arliss saying he used to be a bass player for some country band in the nineties. He's pretty tight-lipped about his past, which has led to rampant speculation on Josie's and my part.

"I said that I've done enough for a *hundred* men's lifetimes." He stands to let Buford pass, takes one last long drag off his cigarette, flicks the butt to the ground, and grinds it out with his boot heel.

"Right," I grunt, and the tub slips from my grasp and tumbles to the ground as I climb the concrete steps. The lid pops off, and puppets and plastic candelabras spill out.

Josie returns to help me.

"I was actually hoping y'all wouldn't show. You had two more minutes," Arliss says, leaning back against the open door.

"But then how would you spend your Friday night?" I ask.

"By not missing you at all and doing something more fun like eating a frozen chicken potpie and thinking of all the ways I've disappointed the people who love me."

"What would TV Six show at eleven on Saturday night instead of *Midnite Matinee*?" Josie asks, tossing our Frankenstein puppet, Frankenstein W. Frankenstein, into the tub.

Arliss shrugs. "Mormon Tabernacle Choir? *Hunting and Fishing West Tennessee with Odell Kirkham*? Dead air? Who cares? I'd go with the dead air, personally."

"What would they show in Topeka, Macon, Greenville, Des Moines, Spokane, Fargo, and Little Rock?" Josie asks.

"Whatever the people in those cities like to ignore or watch while they're too high to operate Netflix."

I pick up the tub and walk in. The studio is well insulated from the outside. It's cool and dark and has the warm, metallic smell of electronics combined with the mustiness of a basement. It takes my eyes a moment to adjust. Arliss has displayed rare initiative by already having our antique red velvet chairs set up in the corner where we film. I pull our faux-brick cloth backdrop out of the tub, unfold and unroll it, and start tacking it up. It gives a dungeon-like appearance. Oh, don't worry, we've gotten letters from viewers about how this is unrealistic for the old New Orleans house where our characters supposedly live. People have a lot of free time, apparently. Especially the kind who pay for postage to "well, actually" a public access show.

Josie sets our plastic electric candelabra on the thrift-store table between our chairs and plugs it in, then sets a plastic skull next to it and clips a plastic raven to the back of her chair. She begins her vocal warm-ups. *Tip of the tongue, top of the teeth. Tip of the tongue, top of the teeth. Topeka bodega Topeka bodega Topeka bodega. Many mumbling mice are making midnight music in the moonlight, mighty nice.*

I finish tacking up our backdrop and hang the nylon spiderweb with a rubber black widow that occupies the top right corner of our set. I accidentally put it up on the left side once. We got letters about that. Multiple letters.

Arliss looks on glumly, dinner box in one hand, shoveling squash casserole into his mouth with the other, Ritz cracker

14

crumbs cascading onto his Chris Stapleton T-shirt and resting on the swell of his beer gut.

I pull a white lab coat and a pair of goggles from the tub and extend them to Arliss. He just stares, unblinking, and takes another bite. I roll my eyes, pull an envelope from my pocket, and hand it to him.

"Don't roll your eyes." He belches into his closed mouth, buries his fork in the remnants of his squash casserole, and takes the envelope delicately between his index and middle fingers, like it's a secret message he's going to tuck away in his décolletage. Still with the one hand, he opens it and counts. "Twenty, thirty, forty, forty-five . . . fifty."

"We good?"

He folds it and stuffs it in his back pocket. "Good as we ever are."

"All right, Professor. Get dressed." I hand him the lab coat and goggles.

He turns, tosses the remains of his box into a nearby garbage can, and takes his costume. He grunts as he puts on the lab coat and pulls the goggles over his head, resting them on his brow. "This is the worst job I've ever had, and I've had some bad ones."

"So you've said." I check my phone. My adrenaline flares like lighting a stove burner after leaving the gas on too long. I have a new email. I click on it, and it's junk. A sharp wave of disappointment neutralizes some of the adrenaline, but I still have to wait for the thudding of my heart to subside.

Josie

Someone pounds at the back door. Arliss goes to answer.

"It's the twins," I call after him. "They're supposed to have their friend with another basset with them."

Arliss grunts in acknowledgment and opens the door. He steps aside to let them pass.

Colt and Hunter McAllen are frequent guests on *Midnite Matinee.* They don't particularly love the kind of horror movies we show. They're not great friends with Delia and me. They're *emphatically* not geniuses. But they share one shining, redeeming trait that makes them perfect guests: they're willing to do dumb stuff, no questions asked. It occurred to us to invite them onto our show after they got suspended for riding dirt bikes down the halls of our school. From there, it was no great leap to put on black spandex skeleton costumes and plastic skull masks and, for no compensation of any sort, dance with the most utterly joyous, unfettered abandon you can imagine. Putting on the skeleton costumes is, for them, like putting on a mantle of courage. And they have *zero* skill as dancers. But they'll just go for it. Anything. They'll try doing splits. Hunter almost took out half our set once attempting a backflip that he only halfway landed. Which is an apt metaphor for our show, I guess.

"What up, JoHo?" Colt goes for the high five.

I let him flap in the breeze. Guess how much I enjoy being called JoHo. "Let's see the dog."

In the darkness of the hallway behind him, I hear a jingling of dog tags and a yip. A smallish beagle trots up to me excitedly, followed by his owner.

Reflexively, I kneel to pet the dog, scratching him behind the ears. "Hey! Aren't you a sweetie!" Then I stand, turn, and face the twins. "What is this?" I ask in a low voice (I guess so the beagle won't get his feelings hurt).

"The dog you asked for," Hunter says.

"I told y'all we needed a basset hound."

"Yeah," Hunter says.

"So this is a beagle. I say bring me a basset hound; you two Bill Nyes bring me a beagle."

"I think it would be 'Bills Nye,'" Delia says, joining us. "Nice beagle, guys. I thought we asked for a basset hound." She hands Colt and Hunter their costumes.

"I told them Tater was a beagle," the beagle's owner says. "They said it was fine."

"Beagles and basset hounds are the same thing. Just that beagles become basset hounds," Hunter says with an air of un-earned authority.

"What are you *talking about*?" Delia's face is incredulous. "That's not even *sorta* how it works."

"Yep. Like how cats become raccoons," Colt says.

"In the wild," Hunter adds.

I don't know where to begin. "I—wait—cats become—no, hang on. One thing at a time. You thought beagles get older and shorter and saggier and their ears get longer and we start calling them basset hounds?"

"We're not dog scientists, y'all," Colt says. "Hell."

"It's just our opinion," Hunter says.

"That beagles become basset hounds?" Delia asks. "That is your opinion?"

"Yep," they say together.

"Well, that's not how opinions work," I say.

Hunter shrugs.

"Like, science wins over opinions," I say.

"That's *your* opinion," Hunter says.

"Just to be clear," Delia says. "You two live in a world where animals spontaneously change species and animals within the same species become other types of animals?"

"Our cousin seen it happen," Hunter says.

"By the way, let's just go with what y'all are saying and assume that beagles magically transform into basset hounds at a certain point in their lives—I can't believe I'm doing this, good lord. *This* particular beagle has pretty obviously not yet made the change to basset hound, right?" I say like I'm speaking with a very young child.

Hunter and Colt would probably look sheepish at this point, but their faces already have a sheeplike quality.

"So even in your deeply strange worldview, y'all blew it," I continue.

Hunter and Colt look at each other, their exchanged glances saying *You wanna field this?*

"Did y'all literally split a single brain when you were in the womb and each one of you ended up with half?" I ask.

This sends them into gales of laughter. They love it when I insult them. They must have some weird crush or something. I think it's why they're so easily persuaded to relinquish their dignity for free on a public access show. They start trying to thwap each other in the nuts.

I turn from them to the beagle's owner and finally get a good look. There wasn't enough light in the hallway to see him well. His face is nothing special, but one of his eyes has a faint purple bruise encircling it and he has a Band-Aid slightly below the bridge of his nose.

The owner raises his hands in surrender. "All they told me was that they needed to use Tater. But I came along to help because they don't know much about dogs."

"They don't know much about dogs? *Oh, really?* Let me ask you something: did you have any expectation that your beagle would transform into a basset hound?"

"Nope. That's not how it works."

"I am so glad to hear you say that." I walk quickly back to the tub, pull out a dog-sized skirt and blouse, and hand them to Tater's owner. "Dress him."

"Bet you didn't expect your life to turn out this way, buddy," Arliss says to Tater's owner before turning to Delia, who hands Arliss a VHS tape and a typed sheet with segment cues mapped out.

I face Tater's owner and motion at my eye and my nose. "What's with this . . . dude?"

He extends his hand. "Lawson Vargas."

I shake his hand. "Josie Howard. Who threw you through a plate-glass window?"

"I fight MMA. Got kinda banged up in a match a little while ago."

"Good times. You're not gonna MMA us or anything, are you?"

He smiles. His face is kind when he smiles and becomes a lot more interesting. "Naw."

I raise my finger to tell him to hold on. I walk back to the tub and return with a black robe and a *Scream* mask. "Okay, Lawton—"

"Lawson. It's fine."

"Right. Sorry. Lawson. You're gonna dance with your idiot goofball friends." I shove the robe and mask into his hands.

He accepts them tentatively. "I'm not a dancer."

"And Tater isn't a basset hound, but oh! See how I don't care."

"I can't."

"You can roundhouse-kick people in the throat, but you can't dance?"

"Different skill sets."

"This show has a very limited pool of resources. We use whatever we have at hand, and you are at hand. Plus, you need to be punished for not owning a basset hound and not having smarter friends."

He looks at the costume he's holding and smiles a lopsided smile of concession.

He actually does have a nice face, I guess, upon reflection. He should try to get kicked in it less.

Delia

I hand Arliss the VHS tape with my dad's writing scrawled on it in Sharpie. "I bet you didn't know that the dude who directed *A Christmas Story* also directed a horror movie in the early seventies called *Children Shouldn't Play With Dead Things.*"

Arliss eyes the tape like I've handed him a revolver and told him to kill his grandmother or be killed. "So that's our dreck of the week."

"For a seventy-thousand-dollar movie, it's actually pretty decent."

"*Arliss Shouldn't Help Make This Show.* Get it?" Arliss says.

"You wanna know what it's about?"

"I do not."

"So this theater troupe goes to this island off the coast of Florida, where there's a graveyard. And they're led by this hippie doofus who's full of hot turds, and he suggests they do this weird ritual and raise a corpse from the dead, but—"

"Lemme guess: children shouldn't play with dead things?"

"You might enjoy this one."

"So far, we're zero for however many episodes we've done in the last year and a half."

I hand him a sheet where we've mapped out the time cues and where to cut in the segments so he doesn't have to watch the movie. Also a CD. "This is new intro music that our friend Jesmyn composed and recorded for us."

"We'll get letters."

"Always."

"Let's get this show on the road. I have a very important date with not being here."

"Arliss? That movie was my dad's, and—"

"I know, they all are."

"Yeah, but . . . this is one of the ones he and I actually watched together, so . . ."

"It's special. I'll be careful," he says, suddenly quiet and sober, looking me in the eye. Arliss has always treated my growing up without a dad with more respect and gentleness than he affords anything else.

"I'd hate if he ever came back and—"

"I'll treat it with ten times the care that went into the making of the actual movie."

"Do twenty times." I turn to Josie, who has apparently just handed the poor beagle owner a costume. He's blushing. "You ready, Rayne?"

"Ready, Delilah."

• • •

I don't know who watches *Midnite Matinee* or why.

I mean, I have some idea from letters we get. Here's my guess: it's lonely people. People who don't have a lot going on in their lives, because they have time to sit at home on a Saturday night (that's when we air in most markets, including our home market) and flip through channels. People who aren't rich, because if they were, they'd have more entertainment options. People who aren't hip, because if they were, they'd seek out higher-quality entertainment options. People who don't truly love to be frightened, because if they did, they'd find actual scary movies. People who prefer their awful movies straight, with no commentary, because otherwise they'd watch old episodes of *Mystery Science Theater 3000*. People who still write letters.

It's a very niche crowd.

Most of all, I think it's people who love to be reminded that sometimes you do your best and you come up short, but there's still a place in the world for people like that. People like them. It might be 11:00 on a Saturday night on a public access station in Topeka, Kansas, but it's a place. It's comforting to know that you don't have to be excellent to not be completely forgotten. Maybe it's people who feel like the world is leaving them behind.

Maybe it's people who simply want to remember a time when they were happier and their lives were easier. That's why I would watch.

Josie

We do the best we can. I figure because TV is what I want to do with my life, I might as well do it right. Also, Arliss gives us exactly two takes before he deems it "good enough for access" (short for "public access") and then it airs in all of its broken glory. We hear this phrase a lot.

We discovered this the hard way one night when both Delia and I were loopy from lack of sleep and hopped up on sugar and caffeine, and I accidentally said "grost" instead of "ghost" during the second take on a segment. We tried to keep it together. Delia shuddered with silent laughter, turning red, her hand over her mouth and nose, tears streaming from her eyes. I tried to keep talking, but my voice started to wobble and tip like a drunk tightrope walker, and we both lost it completely. For a solid minute, we laughed so hard we couldn't breathe, making a "cut" motion across our necks while Arliss glowered at us, shaking his head grimly, mouthing *Good enough for access*. This only made us laugh harder. The segment ended with both of us in fetal position on the floor, racked with laughter. It aired like that. Good enough for public access, indeed. Yeah, we got letters.

Delia removes her septum piercing. We fit our vampire fangs over our canines, perform last-minute touch-ups on each other's makeup, and take our seats.

Arliss gets the lighting right and stands behind the camera, counting down on his raised fingers. "And we're rolling in five . . . four . . . three . . . two . . . one."

"Goooooooooood evening, boys and ghouls, zombies and zombettes, witches and warlocks, this is *Midnite Matinee,* and we are your hosts, Rayne Ravenscroft . . ."

"And Delilah Darkwood," Delia says.

"How are you doing tonight, sister?"

"Well, sis, I'm feeling pretty great considering I'm two hundred years old."

"You don't look a day over a hundred and eighty." We pause. Arliss will insert a rim-shot sound effect here. "So, Delilah, what do we have for our viewers this week?"

We both pause. This is where Arliss will insert a peal of thunder sound effect.

The twins and Lawson stand behind Arliss as he works the camera. The twins look deathly bored. Or merely vacant. Hard to tell with them. Lawson, however, wears a childlike expression of wonder, as though he's watching the filming of a show about people getting punched in the nuts or whatever MMA guys enjoy watching. I guess if you've never seen a TV show being filmed, even ours is impressive.

I get it. I'd be lying if I said I didn't get a rush every time I was on this side of a camera. Ever since I was old enough to remember, I've been fascinated by strangers on TV. How they're beamed out to the world and become part of people's lives. How they connect with millions. I knew I wanted that. Aside from a hot two weeks when I was nine and I wanted to be a marine biologist, I've never wanted to be anything else.

It's nice to know your thing.

Delia

"Folks, tonight's movie is the 1972 classic *Children Shouldn't Play with Dead Things,* directed by none other than Bob Clark, who you may remember from a little film called *A Christmas Story,*" I say.

"You'll shoot your eye out, kid!" Josie says.

"That's the one, Rayne! Boy, you've seen a lot of Christmas movies for a two-hundred-year-old vampire."

"I'm a Christian vampire, Delilah." (We'll get letters for that one.)

"Anyway, folks, this movie is a little different, as you'll soon see. No leg lamps, Red Ryder BB guns, or Ovaltine here. Instead, we have a motley crew of actors wearing some pretty amazing seventies garb, who go to an island off the coast of Florida, where they perform a ritual to raise the dead. And it goes . . . well . . . watch and see." We pause for Arliss to insert a *boing* sound or a descending slide whistle.

"I bet it's called *Children Shouldn't Play with Dead Things* for a reason. So, Delilah, if children aren't supposed to play with dead things, can they play with us?"

"What do you mean, Rayne?"

"Well, we're technically *undead.*"

"Good point! The movie's title specifically says *dead* things, not *undead* things."

"So I guess children *can* play with us!"

"Sure," I say. "Of course, we'll suck their blood if we get the chance, so it still might not be the best idea."

We leave space for Arliss to insert more comical sound effects. We know our show is goofy. We're working within a tradition here. Elvira. *Tales from the Crypt.* Vampira. Svengoolie. Zacherle. Dr. Gangrene. Your humor has to be a mirror of the movies you show: it can't be too good. It can't be too mean-spirited. You can poke fun at the films, but you have to fundamentally respect them and honor that your show might be the first and last time people see that movie—something that someone poured their heart and soul into.

Arliss keeps track of the time, and he gives me the signal to wrap up the intro.

"All right, wolf men and wolf ladies. Without further ado . . . *Children Shouldn't Play with Dead Things.*"

We let several seconds of silence pass so there's time to fade out on us and fade into the movie. I spend these seconds doing what I always do: praying that he sees. Somehow. Some way. Somewhere. Topeka, Macon, Greenville, Des Moines, Spokane, Fargo, Little Rock. Wherever he is. I can't tell you what I hope he does if he sees. I don't know if I want him to regret leaving. If I want him to come back. If I want him to be proud.

All I know is that I want him to see.

Josie

Arliss claps. "What's next?"

I nod at the twins and Lawson. "Doggy wedding, and then dance party so these guys can leave."

Tater the beagle looks decidedly unhappy to be wearing a skirt and blouse. Behind me, Buford whimpers as Delia pulls his suit on him. We also make him wear a bat costume sometimes. He hates it.

"Is Tater okay with us taking him for this segment?" I ask.

"He's pretty chill." Lawson kneels beside us and scratches Tater's tummy. Lawson smells like bodywash from neon orange bottles that are all AXE XXXXXXTREME ATOMIC FRESH-BLAST MOUNTAIN ICE ODORPUNCH and also menthol-y kicked-in-the-face bruise medicine, with top notes of WD-40. It's not an appealing-sounding combination, and yet it works, strangely.

I lead Tater by the collar over to the set. Delia has the container of chicken livers in one hand and Buford's collar in the other. Buford whines at the suit he's wearing and tries to get at the chicken livers. His normally sad eyes always convey utter despair at these times. *Kill me,* they plead. *Even if it's painful.*

Delia and I get set up on the floor, and Arliss takes his place behind the camera.

"This segment goes after a part in the movie where the acting troupe digs up a corpse in a suit and takes it back to this cabin on the island, and then they stage a wedding between the corpse and the leader of the troupe," Delia says.

Arliss stares and blinks.

"Oh, and we'll need you to perform the dog wedding," I say.

His face grows stonier.

"I know," Delia says. "Your life is very hard."

"Tight shot on the dogs," I say.

Arliss fiddles with the camera. "Not my first rodeo, sweet pea. Rolling in . . . five . . . four . . . three . . . two . . . one."

I grip Buford behind his front legs and make him gesture (I hope PETA never sees this). I speak in a deep, comically broad Southern accent. "Why, I say, aren't you the most lovely creature? My name is Colonel Buford T. Rutherford B. Hayes. What's yours?"

Delia holds Tater by his front legs and makes him cover his mouth with a paw coyly. She giggles and speaks in a high-pitched, equally horrific Sookie–from–*True Blood* Southern accent. "Why, sir! How you do flatter! My name is . . ." Delia looks to be racking her brain. "What name did we decide on for her?" she whispers in her normal voice.

Delia can never keep our character names straight in skits. "Magnolia P. Sugarbottom," I mutter back, trying not to move my lips, like a ventriloquist.

"Magnolia P. Sugarbottom," Delia says, returning to Sookie voice.

I put the container of chicken livers on the floor and use Buford's paw to slide it over to Tater. "Ms. Sugarbottom, I own the largest chain of chicken liver restaurants in the world, and I offer you some of my finest chicken livers in exchange for your paw in holy matrimony."

Tater whines and licks at the container. "Colonel, I would be honored to be Mrs. Magnolia P. Rutherford B. Hayes. Do you promise that you can handle me at my worst, so that you deserve me at my best, which is also quite, quite bad?"

"Ms. Sugarbottom, I promise."

"So you know, Colonel, I'm super hard to deal with almost always. I'm really a giant pain in the rear."

"I will love and cherish you anyway and apply a healing salve to my buttocks."

"Then I shall wed you this very moment, Colonel, before you can change your mind."

I make Buford wave to the camera. "Wonderful! Simply wonderful! Oh, Professor? Professor Von Heineken?"

One guess how Arliss picked the name Professor Von Heineken. He put exactly as much work and thought into it as he puts into every aspect of the show.

Arliss pulls his goggles down over his eyes and ambles onto the set, looking exactly as happy as you'd expect a grown man forced to perform a dog marriage on public access television would look. He'll cut in some wedding music that Jesmyn recorded for us.

Arliss clears his throat. He's supposed to do a German accent, but he always forgets. (We get letters; he doesn't care.) "Okay, uh, do you, Buford, take . . ."

"Magnolia," Delia says. Arliss is even worse at remembering character names than Delia is.

"Yep. Her. To be your lawfully wedded wife, so help you God?"

"For as long as you both shall live," Delia says.

"For as long as you both shall live, so help you God?"

"Professor! You gotta get the words right or it's not legally binding," I say.

"Oh *no,*" Arliss says. "Anyway, I now pronounce you . . . dog and dog wife, I guess. You may sniff the bride's butt or really whatever you're into. Just go nuts. Who cares?"

Delia and I clap and push Buford and Tater at each other. They whimper and turn their heads. We let them go. Tater runs off set. Buford sort of melts to the floor like a scoop of ice cream licked off the cone onto hot asphalt. Arliss slinks back to the camera. We clap until we see Arliss signal that he's not focused on just the dogs anymore.

I make a great show of wiping my eyes and sigh. "I always cry at weddings, Delilah."

"Me too, Rayne. I love happy endings. But, viewers at home, to see if our friends—the children who play with dead things—have a happy ending, stay tuned!"

"And cut!" Arliss walks from behind the camera, grabs the container of chicken livers, opens it, pops two in his mouth, drops a couple on the ground for Buford, who looks the most excited he's looked all day, and takes a couple to Tater, who eats them out of his hand.

"I've never attended a dog wedding before," Lawson says to me as I come off set, leading Tater by the collar.

"And?"

"It was very romantic. I always hoped Tater would find the right someone."

This guy is a massive goofball, but a good sport. "You ready for your big dance scene?" I ask.

"I have no idea what I'm doing."

"Dude, none of us do."

"Come on. You're amazing." He nods at Delia, who's handing a CD to a decidedly glum Arliss. "Y'all are both great. But you especially."

I start to respond, but Arliss cuts me off. "Dance party. Let's go."

I wave for the twins and Lawson to come. The twins whoop and pull their skeleton masks into position and run on set, shoving our chairs and end table aside to make room. They jump in place, slapping the sides of their heads, psyching themselves up.

Lawson does a couple of quick stretches followed by a few high kicks. Nothing else about him is that impressive, but he moves well—quick and strong. "That's good," I say. "Incorporate some of the karate moves."

Delia and I take our positions; the twins and Lawson are just off set, out of the shot.

Arliss goes over to the light switch and cues up the music on the laptop and speakers we've set up. "This music is royalty free, right?"

"Yep," I say. "And you better believe it sounds like it."

Delia and I stand there for a moment to give Arliss a space to fade us in.

"Wow, Delilah, this movie sure is a spooky romp!" I say with exaggerated cheer.

"Yes, it is, Rayne. I think—"

Arliss begins flicking the lights on and off. Delia and I look around wildly. Arliss will insert a spooky cackle sound effect.

"Delilah?" I say, voice quavering theatrically.

"Rayne?"

"I think we're about to take a trip . . . *to the bone zone!*" We say the last part in unison. We pull our capes around ourselves and retreat off separate sides of the set. Arliss begins flickering the lights to simulate dance floor lights and starts the music. Imagine the most low-rent, dollar-store dance music you can. Nope, worse. It's filled with weird air-horn sounds and sped-up chipmunk voices and this flatulent bass that sounds like stomping your bare foot in a bucket of dead fish. Given the choice, I would prefer to listen to the screaming of the damned.

Lawson hesitates. The twins shove him onto the set, where he stands frozen for a second while the twins take formation behind him. The twins begin dancing wildly. Pelvic thrusts. Pantomiming drawing revolvers from invisible holsters, shooting them, and blowing away the smoke. They jump at each other and chest-bump. Lawson finally gets into the groove a little bit, but then all at once he starts this series of alternating high, strong kicks. The twins whoop and holler encouragement. We make (what I assume is) eye contact, because he kicks harder and higher, jumping and spinning, when I give him a thumbs-up. He's doing great, especially considering he's wearing a black robe and a mask.

He's clearly an inspiration because behind him, one of the twins cups his hands for the other twin to step on to try the backflip again. The flipping twin over-rotates, lands on his heels, falls, and rolls backward off camera. Someday one of them is going to crack open his head and flood the studio with whatever noxious gas is inside.

Lawson looks back, motions for the remaining twin to move, and then executes a textbook backflip, landing perfectly and doing a jumping spin kick. We cheer silently.

Delia

There's no reason Dad shouldn't love our show the way he loved the Dr. Gangrene, Zacherle, and Svengoolie episodes he watched while I was growing up. I mean, we have people doing karate moves and *backflips*. We're not terrific, but we're un-terrific in the ways he always loved.

Lawson comes off set flushed and glowing. He nods quickly to me, and then looks to Josie for approval. She gives him a thumbs-up, and he beams.

Another dude who loves Josie. Color me shocked. I'd comfortably estimate that of guys who meet Josie and me simultaneously—and who are in the mood for love—approximately one hundred percent go for Josie. Almost all have been guys I didn't care about at all, like Lawson. But I choose Josie over any dumb boy, and plus, I'm used to rejection. Maybe that's what they see in me. Even more than Josie's flawless teeth and Scarlett Johansson voice and long, curly hair that's the color of a jar of dark honey in front of a candle and the couple of inches of height she has on me, I think it's that they can see there's nothing with her they need to fix. No baggage. Whereas with me? Mechanic's special. No one wants the sad girl. Whatever.

"All right, next segment," Arliss says. He turns to the twins and Lawson and motions with his thumb toward the door. "Leave."

They drop their costumes in the tub.

"Can I stay and watch?" Lawson asks. He keeps glancing in Josie's direction. "I've never seen a TV show filming."

"Nope. Too distracting. This job requires tremendous concentration and care," Arliss says, his voice dead.

"But we were here during—"

"*Too. Distracting.*"

"Okay. Sorry."

The twins scurry for the door. They've never once been interested in staying a minute longer than necessary.

Lawson waves. "It was nice to meet y'all. Good luck with the show. When's it on?"

"Saturday nights at eleven," I say.

"Cool. Bye, Delia. Bye, Josie," he says. "I guess we're in-laws or something now that our dogs are married, right?" He blushes and laughs awkwardly.

"Sure," Josie says, straight-faced.

Lawson starts toward the door, giving a whistle. "Come on, boy." Tater trots after him. As Lawson opens the door to leave, he turns once more and waves clumsily to Josie. She gives him an *okay this is really the last one* wave. Then he's gone.

"I'm ready whenever y'all are done teenaging," Arliss says.

"Whatever," Josie says. "*You're* teenaging."

"You are." Arliss does a mocking, coquettish wave.

"I was being polite."

"Polite would be not wasting my time with sassmouth so I can get to what I really want to be doing with my Friday night, which is sitting on my back patio with my dog and listening to the new Jason Isbell album."

While they're talking, I see my phone light up, buzz, and skitter in a semicircle on one of the chairs off set. I run over and check it, my guts quivering. Nothing. A coworker texting to ask if we can swap shifts next week. There's nothing in this world worse than a phone notification that's not for the thing you need.

"It does too sound boring to a normal person, right, DeeDee?" Josie calls to me.

I put my phone back down. "What? Sorry."

"Arliss's Friday-night plans sound super boring, and we're way more fun."

"For sure."

Arliss snorts. "I've had pieces of popcorn stuck in my teeth that I enjoyed more than doing this show. All right," he says with a clap. "Let's roll."

"We love you, Arliss," I say. I'm not lying. Try as he might to push us away, Josie and I both think he's terrific and want to be his friend, even though he hates us. The more he doesn't want to be our friend, the more we want to be his. If coolness is doing your own thing and not caring what anyone else thinks about it, then Arliss is pretty cool.

"I warned y'all once about sassmouth," Arliss says.

• • •

I don't remember exactly when we started roasting some of our letter writers, but I know that it came out of necessity to keep our sanity. As two young women working in a field whose audience contains its fair share of middle-aged dudes with endless appetites for inconsequential minutiae, we get explained at a lot. *Actually, the basis for the Dracula lore is blah blah blah . . . Actually, in Lovecraft's mythos yakity yak yak . . . Actually, Frankenstein was the name of the doctor, not the monster herka derka diddly dee.* That last one we get *constantly.* Arliss inserts an old-timey car horn *aoooooogah* sound now after we read one. We have a bit planned for the next time we get one of those.

Still annoying but somewhat more flattering (because at least they're paying attention) are the letters complaining about the continuity errors in our show's universe: *On the episode that aired on June 21, Delilah said that you were both 200 years old, but two months later, in August, Rayne made reference to your being 250 years old. Which is it?* (Who-gives-a-pair-of-shorn-yak-nuts years old is the answer, by the way.)

And then there are the pervs. Use your imagination. No, really. Almost anything you can conceive of. And more, if you have a bad imagination. We don't read their letters on air. We should really give them to the cops. We used to yell at them on the show, until we figured out that some of them were getting off on that too. It's fun being a girl. Josie gets it the worst.

Most of the letters come to the show's email address or our Facebook page, and we print them to read on the show. Sometimes, though, people mail stuff to us at the station. We've gotten animal bones; DVDs of movies people thought we should see; DVDs of movies people thought no one should see, therefore we should see; DVDs of movies people made themselves; and so on. I have, taped up in my bedroom, a fan art drawing someone from Fargo did.

We drape a black blanket between our chairs, where Arliss

will crouch with the Frankenstein W. Frankenstein puppet and hand us the mail. (The second "Frankenstein" is pronounced Frahn-ken-shteen. You better *believe* we get letters.)

Arliss sets a box of letters behind the drape, fits the puppet on his hand, and kneels with a grunt so that only his puppet arm is visible. "We're rolling." When Arliss helps us with a segment, he just points the camera at the set and lets it roll.

Josie and I take our seats, sit quietly for a few seconds to give Arliss room to fade us in, and then start.

Josie kicks us off as usual. "Welcome back, vampire bats and black cats, it's time for our favorite segment and yours . . . the mailbag! Where we hear from you out there in TV land! Oh, Frankenstein? Frankenstein W. Frankenstein?"

Arliss raises the puppet and speaks in a high, hoarse voice. "Whattya want? I was sleeping and dreaming about never having to do this again." Arliss has the most fun when we let him play himself.

"Frankenstein!" I say. "It's always so nice to see you!"

"Well, it sucks to see you!"

"All right, all right. Let's get to the letters, you old grump," I say.

We do a couple run-of-the-mill thank-you letters with a pause after each for Arliss to insert the sound of applause.

Arliss dips his hand below the drape, comes up with a letter in Frankenstein's arms, and hands it to me.

I clear my throat to read. "This one comes to us from . . . Chad? Chad in Macon. Hi, Chad! He writes:

> Dear *Midnite Matinee*, I generally enjoy your show, but I must take issue with your use of the name

Frankenstein for a puppet who is clearly intended to be Frankenstein's Monster. This may seem like a minor quibble, but I believe that it is important to treat texts—especially such vital ones of the horror canon—with scrupulous accuracy. Yours truly, Chad.

I leave a beat before speaking so Arliss can insert the old-timey car horn sound effect. "Well, Chad. Here's the thing: imagine what you care about least in this entire world."

"It could be anything," Josie says. "The state of the Malaysian economy."

"The process by which shoelaces are manufactured."

"The size of the possum population in Cleveland."

"Imagine those things you care so little about. We care even less that you've got your undies in a twist over our puppet's name."

"Hang on, Delilah, let's ask Frankenstein if he cares that we call him Frankenstein instead of Frankenstein's Monster."

Arliss pops up his hand. He's always game for crapping on our insufferable letter writers. "Yeah? What?"

"Do you care if people call you Frankenstein instead of Frankenstein's Monster?" I ask.

"I don't care even one little bit, and I think anyone who does needs to get out more."

I toss the letter over my shoulder. "Well, there you go, Chad. Maybe you can go get a snack or go pee every time Frankenstein is on our show." I wait a beat for Arliss to insert a crowd-booing sound effect.

"Okay, next letter. Frankenstein?"

Arliss hands Josie a letter.

"All right, viewers, this one comes to us from Troy in Spokane. Hi, Troy! He says:

Dear Rayne and Delilah, I wanted to say that I'm a big fan of *Midnite Matinee* and I've been watching for almost all the time that your show has been airing on my local station. I love your senses of humor and the fun little skits you guys do during the movie. You always crack me up. Stay cool and keep up the good work. Love, Troy.

Josie turns over the letter. "Oops, there's more.

PS: I had this weird idea for a funny skit you guys could do. Maybe some time you could crush raw eggs with your bare feet and then—

Arliss pops his hand back up. "Uh-oh! Abort! Abort! Heading to Weirdville!"

"Oh, Troy," Josie says, shaking her head, lowering the letter to her lap, a note of dawning understanding in her voice.

"Troy, Troy, Troy. We were *rooting* for you," I say. I kinda saw it coming. I've developed a sort of pervert sixth sense. It's not so much the stuff our letter writers are into. Who cares about that? To each their own. It's that maybe just don't tell two high school girls about it, especially when they didn't ask.

"You blew it, Troy. You blew it by being gross," Josie says.

"You're a creep, Troy," Arliss says.

"I think we need to *scream* these letters a little better, Frankenstein. Get it?" Josie says, winking broadly.

40

"Like 'screen' but 'scream' because we can't resist a horror-related pun," I say, returning her wink, after leaving a beat for Arliss to insert a rim shot or booing.

"Should we do one more letter?" I ask.

Arliss pops up. "Nope. Frankenstein's good at this point."

"All right, then," Josie says. "I guess that settles it."

She starts telling our viewers where they can send their non-weirdo letters, when, out of the corner of my eye, I see my phone light up and jitter around. Adrenaline clangs in my ears like a fire alarm. I swear, if it's not the email I'm waiting for, it will validate my theory that you are never, ever more popular than when you're expecting an important email.

Josie

We cut and Delia dashes to her phone, her face slick and pale with queasy anticipation. She picks it up, checks, and disappointment registers. Her shoulders fall. My heart hurts for her. She's visibly dejected as we film the show's farewell segment.

As we come off set, Arliss reaches into the box of letters and tosses a glossy mailer at me before starting to wind up cables. "Here, this came for y'all a couple months back. Forgot to give it to you."

I pick it up off the floor. It's an advertisement for ShiverCon, a convention for makers of horror films, horror hosts, and film buffs. It's the biggest con of its kind. This year it's being held in Orlando. We've never gone, even though we'd like to—Delia more so than me. I debate whether to even show this to her. It might just bum her out, since we probably can't go. Work schedules, money, etc. She removes the choice from me.

"What's that?" she asks.

"A thing for ShiverCon."

"Lemme see."

I hand it to her, kneel, and scratch Buford behind the ears. He gives me an even, slightly reproachful gaze, like *It'll take you a while to work off this debt.* "I know, Bufie Bear, I know. But you've been a very good boy today." I start helping Buford out of his little suit.

"Hey, Jack Divine's going to be speaking at ShiverCon," Delia says, reverence and awe in her voice.

"That name means nothing to me," I say. "Hey, do you know if Lawson gave us back the outfit Tater was wearing?"

"Jack Divine was, like, a big horror host named Jack-O-Lantern in LA in the seventies. He directed and produced a bunch of low-budget horror movies, but he was best known as a producer and director for SkeleTonya's show all through the eighties and early nineties, when she was on USA Network. You at least know SkeleTonya."

"Goth Dolly Parton vibe?"

"That's her. She's a big deal at cons and stuff."

"SkeleTonya is awesome," Arliss says, brushing past us. "I watched her when I was a teenager."

"Arliss, why have you never told us you're capable of finding pleasure in things?" I ask.

"Don't mistake my not finding pleasure in this show specifically with not finding pleasure in things generally."

"It would be so cool to meet him," Delia murmurs. "We should go. Try to talk to him. Give him one of our DVDs."

"You two make a great team," Arliss says. "Because you"—he points to Delia—"kinda suck at TV but know everything about every dumb horror movie and show. And you"—he points to me—"are pretty good at TV but seem to know jack about horror movies."

He's not wrong. That is exactly why Delia and I make a good team.

"I'm pretty sure Lawson accidentally walked out with our costume still on Tater," I say.

"I'm fairly certain he did, but not accidentally," Delia says.

"You don't think he's pulling some rom-com meet-cute shenanigans, do you?"

"You saw how he waved."

"Oh, brother."

"He was nice, at least. And entertaining on camera. Work your charms with him and get him back on the show. Maybe he can karate-chop some bricks or something."

"Hey," Arliss says, "I almost forgot. Josie, you need to record a quick sponsorship spot for Disc Depot."

"Did they give you copy for me to read?"

"You've been inside Disc Depot. Take a wild guess whether they lovingly prepared you some excellent copy."

"What should I say?"

"I love Disc Depot. I could do it," Delia says.

"They requested Josie specifically. Look, you're not accepting the Nobel Prize. You're plugging a used CD, DVD, and video game store that smells like incense burned in a shoe, has walls covered in Bob Marley and Jim Morrison posters, and pays us seventy-five bucks to sponsor a public access show for nerds and weirdos."

"I'm serious," Delia says, eyes fixed on the flyer like it's a holy tract. "We should go and try to meet Jack Divine. He might be able to take our show to the next level."

"We'll talk in the car," I say.

I sit on set and wing the ad. It'll mostly be my voice cut in with still photos of the inside of Disc Depot. I call them the best spot to buy pre-owned music, movies, and video games in all of west Tennessee. I don't know this to be true or even believe it myself, but it's probably fine.

. . .

Arliss grunts farewell as we leave the dim and cool of the studio into the dark and humid night.

"We had more DVD and T-shirt sales than last week. Between that and the new sponsorship money from Disc Depot, we had a pretty good week," Delia says, opening my passenger door.

"What does 'more DVD and T-shirt sales than last week' mean?" I ask, helping Buford into the back seat.

"Like one more of each."

We laugh.

"I thought the show went well," Delia says. "Like we're improving."

I start my car and pull out. "From when we started? Worlds better." Our first shows might generously be described as "fever dream–like."

Delia holds up the ShiverCon flyer. "So that's why I'm saying we should try to go to this and meet Jack Divine. We gotta put ourselves out there. What's the saying? 'Shoot for the moon because even if you miss, you'll land among the stars.'"

"That's not that inspirational, if you think about it. 'Shoot for the moon because even if you miss, you'll go drifting off into the black icy void of space, where you'll die alone and no one can see your shame.'"

"I like your version better."

"When is ShiverCon?" I ask.

45

"Last weekend in May. After graduation."

"I gotta check. I feel like I have something."

"Check."

"What would we do? Roll up to Jack Divine and be like, 'Hey, come out of retirement or whatever and make us famous'?"

"Maybe a little slicker than that, but basically."

"Doesn't stuff like this happen through agents or managers or something?"

"You tell me. You're the one who wants to go into TV professionally."

"Pretty sure it does. Pretty sure it doesn't happen from people working it at cons."

Delia shrugs. "Maybe not. But we should try. Jack Divine is a big deal. We just got done marrying two dogs and talking to a puppet. We gonna embarrass ourselves?"

"It isn't even so much embarrassment. It's . . . is this even what we want for the show?"

"What? To take it to the next level? Get into more markets? Get more viewers? Of course. It's what I want. Do you not?"

"Sure. Obviously." I realize even as I'm saying it that I don't really know the answer to that question because I haven't thought about it.

"If you want to do TV for a living, why not keep going with what we started? If he made us as big as he made SkeleTonya, there's your career right there."

There's your career. Something about that feels strange. But Delia's voice is drenched in yearning. "Can this dude even still make something like this happen?" I ask.

"Why not?" Delia replies.

"Because he was big before we were even born. That's probably like a century in TV years."

"He definitely can't help us if we don't even try."

We pull up to a stoplight, and I reach back to scratch Buford's belly. I want to change the subject. "Isn't it funny how people are like 'My dog is my best friend' and yet we still don't make them wear pants? It's like, 'Hey, dude, I can see your best friend's butthole at this moment.'"

"I know, right? Also those bumper stickers that are like, 'Who rescued whom?' You did, lady. You rescued the dog. You're the one with opposable thumbs and a car to drive to the shelter. You can take credit."

A few moments of silence pass. I hesitate, but I ask anyway because the air gets heavy with Delia's anxiety as soon as every moment of levity subsides. "So, did you hear back from the—"

"No."

"Weren't you supposed to have heard something by now?"

"Yeah." Delia checks her phone again, as if for emphasis. "Text from Arliss. He says: *This movie is far worse than I was led to believe.*"

"What're you going to do if you do hear something? Like say the PI gives you an address and phone number and stuff? Then what?"

Delia laughs ruefully. "Honestly? I don't even know. I think having them would make me feel . . . like I had power over something, maybe?"

We fall silent again for a while, passing fast-food joints and auto parts stores. Something's begun to gnaw at me. Rubbing like a shoe that doesn't quite fit. It's like when you get that weird anxiety that you think you could trace back to something specific you remembered or heard, but you can't quite retrace your steps in your mind. Maybe I'm picking up Delia's energy.

"Don't let him hurt you again."

"Who? My dad?"

"Yeah."

"I thought you were talking about Arliss for a sec. Because of his text."

We laugh.

"Could you imagine?" I say. *"Delia. Protect your heart from Arliss. Guard it away and do not let him betray you again."*

"I certainly shan't allow Arliss to break my heart. I'm so distracted tonight. Sorry."

"Understandable."

We near Delia's trailer. I feel her nervousness congealing. "Are you good? Do you want me to hang with you?" I ask. I know Delia's a survivor, but it doesn't stop me from always wanting to save her.

"I'm fine. I'm going to help Mom clean the house. It's kind of a dump because neither of us has had time."

I doubt very much that Delia's mom hasn't had time. But I don't say anything. Delia's really protective of her mom.

We pull up in Delia's driveway. Her mom's palm- and tarot-reading sign is illuminated and casts a soft white glow on their patchy lawn. Delia hops out and retrieves the tub from the trunk. "Good show tonight," she says to me.

"You too," I say. "Good luck with the PI thing."

"Yeah. Check your schedule and see if you could do Shiver-Con. I'm serious."

"I know. You have our next movie picked out?"

"Not yet. Got a couple ideas. Bye, Buford!" Delia waves to Buford, who looks up, regards her woefully, and slumps back down when he sees that no treat is forthcoming. "Okay, later," she says to me.

"Call or text if the thing happens and you're freaking out."

"Will do."

I watch her lug the tub to her front door, walking at a slant in the pale light of the sign. That's Delia in general: walking at a slant under the weight she carries.

I hope she's going to be okay. I really do. With some people you can't tell. It's hard when you care deeply about someone who has a lot of bad luck. You wonder how long you can stand between them and fate.

Delia

I've come to believe that everyone gets five or six perfect days in their life. Days with not a single wrong note or thorn, days that ripen like a peach in your memory as years pass. Every time you go to bite it, it's juicy and sweet.

I've had one. I was seven and it was October and my birthday. I opened presents that morning. It seemed like I got twice as many as any year before. I'd heard my parents talking about a bonus my dad received at work. I got books and comics and toys. At the time it seemed like enough to make a wall around me.

My dad and I spent the morning playing Mario Kart. I won again and again and again. I couldn't lose. It didn't occur to me at the time that he was letting me win, but it does now. My mom wasn't around during all this. I don't remember what she was doing. Maybe making my cake. Maybe she was still in bed. She was going through one of her dark times, and when that happened, she didn't get out of bed much. It must have been one of her bad days. She couldn't simply decide not to have one of her bad days on my birthday. My dad said he wanted a daddy-daughter day. Maybe Mom was why.

But even without her and just my dad, it was still a perfect day.

We played Mario Kart until we got hungry, and then he took

me to Cicis for pizza. He challenged me to a contest of who could eat more. He told me I could eat whatever I wanted, so I think I got one slice of cheese pizza and then six slices of dessert pizza. I won this game too. Again, I suspect he let me win.

After seemingly hours of feasting like depraved Roman emperors (who were at Cicis for some reason), we returned home. With great ceremony, Dad began picking out videos. These were the forbidden fruits. The ones he and Mom watched only after I was asleep. The scary ones. The ones he'd promised I could watch when I was old enough. On that birthday, I was old enough.

We're not talking Rob Zombie or *The Texas Chain Saw Massacre* here. For my first foray into horror, we watched a bunch of episodes of *Dr. Gangrene*. The gentle, silly humor of the segments interwoven with the movie diluted to a manageable degree what few frights the cheesy movies held. Still, I spent hours in a haze of delicious adrenaline, tension and release, snuggled up tight to my dad. He smelled like dryer sheets and cigarette smoke. We sat like that for hours, gorging ourselves on Reese's Peanut Butter Cups, gummy worms, and grocery-store-brand grape soda, my favorite.

I loved every second. I knew even then something was writing itself onto my heart, changing me. Making me.

I dozed off at some point. I don't know how sleep overcame the excitement of the day and all the sugar I'd eaten. I finally crashed, I guess. I woke up and I was in our front yard and it was crisp and dark. We didn't have Mom's palm-reading sign then. The air smelled like the sweetness of fallen apples right before they turn. I felt the sky yawning above me. But I wasn't afraid because I could still smell my dad too, and I was in his embrace.

I didn't feel small because somehow all that emptiness above me made me feel large and protected.

"Look up, DeeDee," he whispered in my ear, and I could feel the scrape of his stubble on my cheek. "The sky is amazing tonight."

I did, and it was. The stars seemed to dance, there were so many of them, turning the black of the sky to a deep blue. I felt like if my dad let me go, I would fall upward into them, weightless.

"You cold?" he whispered. "Wanna go back inside?"

I shook my head.

"When did you get so big?" he asked. "But you're still my baby as long as I can hold you."

I gazed heavenward. The moon was bright too. Almost full. It turned the vapor of my breath silver. I shivered.

He kissed me on the cheek. "Happy birthday, baby doll." He took me back inside and put me in my bed and stroked my face until I fell asleep again.

For the next year, almost every night, we watched his shows together. Horror hosts showing terrible movies and doing goofy skits. We watched even on *his* bad days—the days when, like Mom, he couldn't get out of bed. He didn't seem to have as many as Mom, but he had his too.

Mom got worse. To my seven-year-old self, it didn't seem like they were fighting an unusual amount. But then again, I had no point of comparison. By my eighth birthday, he had left. He never told us why. I guess he was doing worse than I thought.

I wish I could have hated him. It would hurt to cling to that, like gripping a thorny branch. But it'd be something more solid than what I had—the memory of love.

And because I won the genetic mental-health lottery, I had

52

plenty of bad days too. Like the ones Mom and Dad had. For years and years.

I almost didn't make it.

But instead of not surviving, I got on some medication that made me feel right, and then I started making a dumb show on TV Six with my best friend, and that was something I could hold on to.

. . .

I go around to the back door and open it quietly because I saw Candy Tucker's Dodge Challenger parked in our gravel driveway, which means my mom must be doing a reading. The smoky spice of incense hitting my nose confirms this. I set down the tub by the door and pad through our kitchen, the sink filled with unwashed dishes and mounds of unopened mail on the table.

"DeeDee?" my mom calls from the living room. "You don't need to tiptoe, we're all done in here."

"I got a new man," Candy calls out in her bourbon-sanded alto. "Needed your mama to tell me if he was worthless like the last one. And the one before him. And the one before him."

I enter our candlelit living room. Shadows dance on the knickknacks, paintings, photos, and thrift/antique store arcana that cover nearly every horizontal and vertical surface. "And?"

"Looks gooooood!" Candy says with a salacious grin. Behind her my mom makes a pained "mmmmmmm" expression and flashes me the "so-so" sign. Candy gives a long, hacking, wet cough.

"He's a lucky guy," I say.

"Tell that to my last three husbands," Candy says, rising

from the small table where my mom does her tarot readings. "I been meaning to catch your show, honey, but it seems like I'm never home when it's on."

Candy Tucker is decidedly not the *stay home watching public access on a Saturday night* type. Say what you will about her lack of romantic success thus far; she is a firm believer in taking control of her own destiny in matters of the heart.

"It might not be your thing. We have a niche viewership."

"Oh, I'm sure I'll love it. I think the world of you and your mama." She pats me on the cheek in a whiff of Febreze and cherry car freshener. "Bye-bye, Shawna, I'll see you when I see you," she says to my mom, giving her a hug and a quick peck on the cheek before fishing her dragon-shaped vape pen from her purse.

We wait until we hear the roar of her engine starting before we say anything.

"It's bad, huh?"

Mom facepalms and shakes her head. "I told her the truth. Said, 'Look, Candy, there are promising signs, but I'm not seeing a lasting relationship here.'"

"And Candy heard: 'There are promising signs—'" I keep moving my mouth but don't say anything.

"Pretty much."

"Job security for you, at least."

"Pretty much."

"I'm starving. There anything to eat?"

"I ordered pizza earlier. It's in the fridge." Mom follows me into the kitchen. Under the harsh fluorescent kitchen lights, she looks a lot more spent than she looked in the more forgiving candlelight of the living room. "How was the show tonight?"

"Good. The Idiot Twins brought one of their friends who's like a karate expert and he did some cool stuff during Dance Party."

"Idiot Twins?"

"Colt and Hunter. Also, they told us they knew someone with a basset hound for the dog wedding. So they show up with the karate expert and his dog, which is a beagle. And guess what their explanation was? 'We thought beagles turn into basset hounds when they get older.'"

"Bless their hearts."

I pull the cleanest-looking plate off the pile of unwashed dishes, rinse it, put a couple of slices of pizza on it, and put it in the microwave. "Bless them indeed."

My phone, which I had somehow managed to forget for a few minutes, buzzes. I yank it from my pocket so fast I almost rip the vinyl. (If that's indeed what these pants are made of. I'm having doubts.)

Josie: My Instagram keeps recommending videos of turtles having sex. Why.

Me: OMG HAHAHAA (I HATE YOU RIGHT NOW BTW)

Josie: WHY DO YOU HATE ME? IS IT BECAUSE UR JEALOUS OF HOW SENSUAL INSTAGRAM THINKS I AM?

Me: I haven't heard back on the Thing. I thought you were the Thing.

Josie: Awwww. Sorry boo.

Me: It's ok.

Josie: How are you?

Me: Meh.

Josie: I feel you. Seriously though, why does IG think I want to watch turtles boning.

Me: I DO NOT KNOW OK. IT'S A MYSTERY. NOW I SERIOUSLY CANNOT DEAL WITH MY PHONE BUZZING AND IT NOT BEING THE THING.

Josie: Ok DeeDeeBooBoo, love u. Let me know when you know about the Thing.

Me: Def will. Love u, JoJoBee.

I pull my pizza from the microwave, excavate myself a space at the table, and sit. I start picking letters off the top of one of the stacks and opening them. "Mom?" I say, reading a bill.

"What is that?"

"From the power company. Says this is our final notice."

"Thought I paid that."

"Clearly you did not unless I misread and in this context 'final notice' means 'Hey, we *finally noticed* that you do a phenomenal job of meeting your financial obligations, so we just wanted to say great job!'"

"Oops."

"Yeah, *oops.* Where's the checkbook?" I've known how to write a check since I was eight. It was not a skill I was happy to acquire. It made me feel like an orphan every time I had to be the mother to my mother.

Mom walks back to her room, returns with the checkbook and a pen, and hands them to me. I start writing the check.

"*Boing,*" Mom says.

I stop. "What does that mean? Is this check going to bounce?" I ask without looking up.

"Kidding. It shouldn't."

"It's funny because financial ruin!" Her joke would be a lot funnier if our utilities hadn't been cut off in the past for bouncing checks. But the right corner of my mouth pulls upward in spite of myself.

"I got my paycheck from Target a little while ago, and Candy paid me tonight in cash. Oh! And I sold another piece from my Etsy store!"

"Which one?"

"The necklace with the mouse skull."

"Blessed are the spooky weirdos."

If this check bounces, I will feel even more guilty about having paid a PI several hundred dollars to track down my dad.

I finish writing the check, put it in the envelope that came with the bill, and study Mom's face. "Hey," I say gently. "You okay?"

She sighs. "I've been having bad days lately. Can't get out of bed."

"I noticed. You taking your medication?"

She looks away and taps the table, like she can run out the clock.

"Mom. I'm not just going to forget that I asked you a question."

"I'm on hiatus."

"You don't go on *hiatus* from taking mental health meds."

"I was feeling better."

"You were feeling better *because of the medication.*"

She lifts her hands in surrender. "My prescription ran out."

"So you get it refilled."

"Wanna watch a movie? They put the Rob Zombie version of *Halloween* on Netflix."

"Mom. Are you listening to me?"

"Yes. Okay."

"Okay what?"

"I'll refill my prescription and start taking my meds again." Her face is wan and tired.

"Thank you." I take a bite of pizza, pull another letter off the stack, and open it.

"We can go through that later. Get your dinner and let's watch *Halloween.*"

I'll say this for my mother: she's very good at making me feel less lonely in this world, even when she has no energy to take care of herself. But I need to make sure I'm being heard. "I do not want to have to bathe with baby wipes because our water's been cut off because, like, our water bill is sitting—"

My phone buzzes.

Josie

I walk in the front door, Buford jingling behind me, and follow the sound of the TV to the living room, where my dad sits, with no particular light of interest in his eyes, watching a show about sharks. My mom's curled up next to him, reading. My younger sister, Alexis, sits cross-legged on the end of the couch, texting or Snapchatting. Buford slinks over to his bed in the corner, refusing to make eye contact with anyone.

I squeeze in between my mom and Alexis, who huffs in annoyance.

"Hey, Jo," my mom says. "How'd filming go?"

"You need to wash your face," Alexis says.

"You need to go put on vampire makeup like me. Your face is too plain."

Alexis hmphs and goes back to her texting.

Mom stink-eyes us. "Josephine, Alexis, I hope y'all are not going to ruin my peaceful Friday night with bickering."

"She's the one—" I start.

Mom puts down her magazine and gives me the look I imagine she gives her jailbird clients when she is thoroughly not having even a little bit of it. "How often do I care who started what?"

"Never," I grumble, then slump back and start texting Delia to tell her that Instagram thinks I love watching turtles hump.

"My question earlier was not rhetorical," Mom says. "How was filming?"

"Fine," I mutter, not looking up from my phone. "We mostly didn't screw up."

"This the episode that's gonna make you a star?" Alexis also fixates on her phone.

I delicately reach over with the toe of one of my witchy black stilettos and kick her phone out of her hands.

Alexis mewls indignantly. "Mom."

"When I become famous, I'm going to have my bodyguards do that. You'll be on your phone and they'll come up and be like *boop* and kick it out of your hands. And I'll watch and laugh," I say.

"I'm so sure you're gonna make enough money doing your corny show on channel six to hire anyone."

"I'm mo mure you're gonna mew mew mew to mire manyone," I say in a high-pitched voice.

Dad uncrosses his arms from over his belly. "All right, now. I'm going to start taking away phones and car keys if this fussing at each other doesn't stop. Y'all heard me?"

"Yes," Alexis and I say in unison.

"We were having a perfectly pleasant evening until you two started in," Mom says.

"Well, I was having a perfectly pleasant evening until I saw Alexis, so she's obviously the problem."

"I don't care that you're eighteen. I'll send you to your room," Mom says.

I read Delia's reply to my text. *Oopsie.* I shouldn't have texted her with trivialities while she was expecting a big email.

"Although," my mom continues, "Alexis has made a worthwhile point, in a roundabout way."

I roll my eyes. "I *am* going to my room. You don't even need to ask." I begin to rise.

"Your mother is talking to you," my dad says.

I slump down and stare at the TV.

"I know you have fun with it, but you need to consider that doing a low-production-value show on public access is not the fast track to a career in television," my mom says.

"I never said it was."

"You have an opportunity to get experience at Food Network, a national station." She turns to my dad. "Brian, turn it to Food Network. I want it playing while I make my point."

My dad picks up the remote and changes the channel. Guy Fieri, that graffitied bulldog, is alternating between jamming swollen sandwiches in his mouth with both ring-bedecked hands and hollerin' in ecstasy.

"Mom, I'm not interested in Food Network. Besides, I wouldn't actually be on TV there. Here, I am."

"Whether you're interested in ultimately making a career at Food Network is beside the point. You need real experience at a real channel, and you have that chance in a city where you've gotten into college."

"Jo," my dad says, "we're not trying to be hard on you. We want what's best for you and your goals."

"I'm working on my goals. In fact, Delia and I want to go to ShiverCon at the end of May for a meeting with a big producer."

"What's ShiverCon?" my mom asks.

"It's a big convention for people who are into horror films and TV. Lots of important people will be there."

"We've planned a family trip to Atlanta on the last weekend in May to visit Aunt Cassie," my dad says.

I knew I had something. Cassie is my favorite relative, a TV addict like me.

Out of the corner of my eye, I catch a glimpse of Alexis smirking. "Dang, Alexis. Sitting there all smiling." I try to kick her phone again, but she's ready this time and pulls it out of reach.

"I wasn't even smiling at you. Chill."

"Okay, Josephine," my mom says. "I can tell you're hungry from the way you're acting. There's tilapia and pasta salad in the fridge. Go."

"Fish is nasty," I mutter, rising from the couch. "I'll be in my room."

I'm happy for the excuse to exit. I don't like talking about the Food Network thing. It's not that what my parents are saying doesn't make sense. It's that . . . I don't even know. Something inside me tells me it's not right. I'm not especially interested in hashing out what that is with my parents while Alexis the Unsullied Princess sits there grinning.

I go upstairs, lock the bathroom door, set my phone beside the sink, and start washing off my makeup. My phone buzzes and skitters on the tile counter with an incoming text. I dry my hands and quickly pick it up to check, assuming it's Delia. It's not.

(731) 555-7423: Hi, Josie, this is Lawson Vargas from earlier. I got your number from the twins. I realized I accidentally left with your dog costume on Tater. Can I bring it by?

Oh, boy. We got a slick one. Delia called it. I want to text her, but it's probably not safe yet, since she hasn't said anything.

Me: It's cool, just give it to the twins when you see them again.

Lawson: I don't see them very often because we don't hang out much.

Points to Lawson for that, I guess. I make eye contact with myself in the mirror and shake my head. What's the one thing I know about this guy so far? That he doesn't give up. Hence the spectacular kicking technique and flexibility. Hence the battered face.

Me: Tonight?

Lawson: If you're home.

I consider telling him I'm not home and to drop it on the front porch. But that seems too cold. He did put on a great show to help us. Plus, it would be healthy for Alexis to witness a boy wanting so badly to see me on a Friday night.

Me: When?

Lawson: I can come by now.

Of course you can, Lawson. Of course you can. I text him my address. *At least you have a nice face.*

Delia

My stomach is a fist. I stand and pick up my phone but I almost have to sit again, my legs tremble so violently. I'm already a pretty pale person, but I can sense myself taking on a ghostly green cast.

"DeeDee? You don't look great," Mom says, her voice sounding distant and submerged.

I shake my head. "I'm fine," I say in what I recognize to be a profoundly unfine voice. "I gotta go to the bathroom." I totter away on gelatinous legs.

"I hope I didn't leave out that pizza too long," Mom calls after me.

I slip inside our cramped bathroom, its counters perpetually piled deep with beauty products and hairstyling implements with tangled cords, shut the door and lock it, and sit on the toilet, shaking and trying to breathe down the adrenaline. When I finally feel less dizzy, I lift my phone and read.

Ms. Wilkes, sorry for not getting back to you sooner.
I was tied up on a stakeout. I've managed to track
down someone who I believe is your father—

My heart pounds. I close my eyes and lower my phone. I wanted her not to be able to find him. I wanted him to be gone forever so all I would have is one perfect day and an October night sky filled with stars and the bright moon. I wanted to not have to make any decisions. But I also didn't want any of that and I wanted to find him. Even if I put my few perfect memories at risk. I swallow hard and keep reading.

A Derek Armstrong lives at 685 Herbert Street in Boca Raton, Florida. About five years ago, he legally changed his name from Dylan Wilkes. Information from public records roughly matches his description: 5'9", blue eyes, Caucasian. I couldn't find a phone number, but I came up with an email address: derekarmstrong1982@gmail.com. I can keep digging if you want to be more certain, but I'd need another payment of $300 up front.

I'm looking at my father's name, but it isn't his name. *My father and I don't have the same last name anymore. He changed it so that we wouldn't.* Even his name is a broken promise. Dylan Wilkes is dead. There's only Derek Armstrong now. *Why would he change his name? Is he in trouble? A spy? Just really intent on never being found?*

I wanted him to be dead so that he *couldn't* have tried to make contact with me all these years. His being alive makes it a choice. I press my hands to my eyes, and warm tears well between my fingers. My emotions churn and seethe. I can't even begin to untangle the ball of twisted sensations I'm having. My body is telling me crying is the right response. And yet, even in the privacy of the bathroom, I try not to, as if the universe only allots you a finite number of crying jags, so you have to make each one count. It's dumb. But still. Sometimes if you fake being strong, you start to believe yourself.

"DeeDee? Everything all right?" Mom calls.

"Yep," I call back in as cheery a voice as I'm able to muster (not particularly cheery). But speaking out loud causes my composure to start slipping from my grasp like a greased rope, and I begin weeping as quietly as I can. The toilet seat is cold and hard under my gasoline-skunk-scented legs.

At least I'm dignified.

Josie

I've been waiting for about ten minutes when a black pickup slows, stops, and parks in front of my house. He must have *hauled*. I'm guessing he doesn't live nearby because he doesn't go to my high school. I hurry downstairs and go outside as Lawson steps out of his truck. He's traded his T-shirt and jeans for an untucked button-down shirt, khakis, and gleaming white sneakers. He carries himself like he dressed up for me. There really *is* something endearing about him, but no.

Lawson, holding the dog costume, squints as I approach. "Whoa, I almost didn't recognize you. I've only ever seen you with vampire makeup and fangs."

"Sorry to scare you."

"No, no. I mean, I think you look great." His face reddens. "Really pretty," he mumbles.

"You didn't need to do this. I don't have, like, a dog costume emergency going."

"No, I know. I just—I didn't want to forget." He hands me the costume. "By the way, I wanted to tell you again—you're amazing on TV. You seem like a pro."

"Well, thanks. It's what I want to do, so . . ."

"Like as your career?"

"Yeah."

"I'd watch." He fidgets and scratches at the ground with a toe like a chicken. He seems to be gathering himself for something.

"Tomorrow night. Eleven on channel six. But your episode will be on next week."

"Oh, I won't be able to watch myself. Too embarrassing."

"But you don't mind getting karate-kicked in front of people?"

"That's different. When I'm in the moment, I'm too busy to get embarrassed about that."

"Huh. Well, thanks again for bringing this by and for helping with the show. Tell Tater I said hi." I start back inside. I hope he got what he wanted out of our brief visit.

"Josie?" he calls.

I turn.

"Do you maybe wanna go get something to eat?" There's a nervous tremor in his voice. It occurs to me that he's probably got more jitters asking me out right now than when facing imminent bodily injury.

"Uh . . ." I wonder how long I can say "uh" before it gets unseemly. I'm doing some quick math in my head. *Yes, I am hungry because tilapia doesn't float my boat. Yes, I am in the mood for some social interaction because Delia is tied up. No, I do not want said social interaction with my family. Yes, I would like to get away from them. But . . . But . . .* This Lawson dude is sweet but very not my type. And I don't even really have a type. Just not fightjock; I know that for sure. I guess I wouldn't be committing to marry him.

It would be fun too to spend some time being looked at the way Lawson looks at me. And I really need to wrap up this "uh," which has been going on for a while. "Okay. You gotta come inside and meet my mom and dad, though. Rule."

He beams. "That's cool."

"Okay." I lead him inside. He follows me into the living room. "Mom, Dad, this is Lawson—" I start to grab for his last name but realize I've forgotten it. "He and I were going to get something to eat."

Lawson comes from behind me to shake my parents' hands. "Sir, ma'am, it's nice to meet you. I'm Lawson Vargas." He even gets Alexis. "Hey. You Josie's other sister?"

"I'm her only sister," Alexis says.

Lawson looks confused. "What about Delia?"

Alexis looks at him quizzically and laughs. "Josie and Delia look nothing alike."

"You thought that because we play sisters on the show," I say.

"That and because you guys talk the same and have a bunch of the same mannerisms," Lawson says.

"We get that a lot," I say.

Alexis assesses Lawson. "Why's your face all messed up?"

I roll my eyes. "Alexis? Could you not?"

"I don't mind," Lawson says.

"Mind or not, that's not how we talk to a guest, is it, Alexis?" Mom says the last part with steel, and her eyes focus on Alexis like she's trying to burn an ant with a magnifying glass.

"Am I not allowed to be curious?"

"You are, while still being polite," Mom says.

"I was wondering too, to be honest," Dad says.

"It's fine. I practice mixed martial arts, and I had a tough sparring match. Took a couple hits."

69

My dad nods, clearly weighing the relative virtues of athletics against the vices of violence. "Kickboxing?"

"Yes, sir. Sorta."

My dad stands and puffs himself up. He's an accountant and a giant teddy bear, but he fancies himself as very intimidating and stately. "All right. Here are the rules: curfew is midnight. Not midnight and one minute. Midnight. Second rule, and most important, is that my daughter is the boss while you're out. That means if you want to do something she doesn't want to do, she wins and you don't get to do the thing you wanted to do, no matter what it is. The third rule is that there are no exceptions to the rules. Any questions?"

"No, sir, those sound like good rules."

My dad sits back down, a look of serene magnanimity on his face, like some merciful potentate who just forgave a villager for killing one of his royal stags. "All right. What are your plans?"

"We're going to get something to eat," I say.

"Good idea, because she is in a *mood*. Y'all have fun," Alexis mutters.

I fold my arms and give her an acid glare that says, *At least I'm not sitting at home on a Friday night.*

I can't lie—there was a part of me that hoped my dad would scare him off. Leaving the house for a free meal and to kill boredom might not end up being worth sitting through an hour or two of excruciating small talk with someone with whom I have absolutely nothing in common.

Outside, Lawson opens the passenger door for me, and I hop up into his truck. He has one of those Black Ice air fresheners with a winged skull printed on it. It smells like cologne you'd buy in a comically huge jug, the kind that's meant not to make someone smell good but to overwhelm your nose with something different from what the wearer would ordinarily smell like. It makes his truck smell exactly like I'd expect an MMA guy's truck to smell like.

Lawson starts his truck and plugs the aux cable into his phone. The musical equivalent of a Realtree-camo Yeti cooler blares.

I shake my head and cover my ears. "Oh, nope. No. Can't."

"Not a Florida Georgia Line fan? Hang on, I'll find something else." He fiddles with his phone. Thomas Rhett starts playing.

"Nope."

"Okay." He cues up Sam Hunt.

"Strike three." I unplug his phone and start to plug in mine to cue up some Florence and the Machine, but a text interrupts me.

Delia: Literally sobbing on the toilet.

Me: Oh DeeDee. Hugs.

Delia: I maybe found my dad.

Me: OMG.

Delia: Yep.

Me: Where?

Delia: Florida.

Me: Of course Florida. You ok? Wanna talk?

"So where do you want to go?" Lawson asks.

I hold up a finger. "Sorry, hang on a sec. Delia's having an issue."

Delia: I'm processing. Maybe in a while? What are you doing?

Me: You won't believe who I'm with now.

Delia: GTFO.

Me: Oh yes.

Delia: The Idiot Twins' friend?

Me: Oh yes.

Delia: I TOLD YOU.

Me: Wanna hear something adorable?

Delia: Always.

Me: He thought we were sisters.

Delia: Haha, everyone thinks that.

Me: Seriously. Anyway, he wanted to buy me dinner and I'm hungry and wanna get out of the house, so <shrug>.

Delia: Have fun.

Me: I'll try. I think I'll mess with him a little.

Delia: Solid plan. Report back. Love u, JoJo.

Me: Love u, DeeDee.

I lay my phone in my lap. "Okay. Sorry."
"No worries. Where are you in the mood to go?"

"I don't know. I've never been to a restaurant before."

Lawson looks at me, searching my face for some sign I'm joking. I summon my best acting abilities and play it totally straight, staring forward serenely.

"Seriously, though."

"I am. Never been to a restaurant. I'm excited to try one. Heard good things."

"You have *never* been to a restaurant?"

"Haven't gotten around to it yet."

"Are you for real?"

"Completely."

"Come on."

"Swear."

He stares. "You're—Wow. I'm responsible for taking you to your very first restaurant?"

"I've heard you don't have to cook your own food and someone brings it to your table?"

"*Never*? How can that be?"

I shrug.

"Is it like a religious thing?"

I nod solemnly.

"But your religion lets you dress like a vampire and be on TV?"

I nod solemnly.

Lawson turns and looks forward, shaking his head slightly, incredulously. "Man," he murmurs. He turns back to me. "I don't want to make you go against your religion."

I fold completely. I can't do it anymore. Peals of laughter. "I'm sorry. Sorry. Yeah, I've been to a restaurant. I don't care where we go. No fish."

A smile slowly spreads across Lawson's face like spilled syrup. "You're very convincing."

"I try."

"Applebee's?"

"Come on, now. Applebee's is the country music of restaurants."

"What?"

"I mean, it sounds like it was named after some racist Southern governor. Like H. Barton Applebee or something."

"Olive Garden?"

"Also has a dumb name. Garden full of olives. Ridiculous. I'm pretty sure olives grow on trees."

"I kinda wish you really hadn't ever been to a restaurant before."

Delia

I think it would probably help head off questions if I looked pale and sickly upon coming out of the bathroom. As I wash off what's left of my vampire makeup after crying, I see this presents no problem.

"You okay, DeeDee?" Mom asks, brow wrinkled.

"We got some fried chicken livers from Dixie Cafe for a segment with Buford and I ate a couple of the leftovers, and maybe it was a mistake."

Mom feels my forehead. "You're all clammy, but I don't think you have a fever. Maybe go lie down?"

"Yeah. If I feel better, we'll watch a movie." I wonder for a hot minute how my mom would react if I told her I'd been trying to track Dad down. I'm guessing not great, or else she'd have tried herself. Of course, I can't be totally sure she hasn't. I somehow know the news would hurt her deeply.

I sense her watching, quiet behind me.

I go into my room and shut the door. It's cramped with piles of clothes, comics, graphic novels, books, but most of all, VHS tapes. Hundreds. Titles scrawled on them in black marker in my dad's slapdash writing. They take up every square inch under my creaky bed.

I slump onto the floor, still reeling. I had no emotional plan

75

for if I *actually* found him. All I wanted was some closure that I didn't have to dig up from within myself. I stare at the message from the PI for a while, my dad's email address glowing in it like a blinking red light on a far-off radio tower.

As though my fingers have their own agenda, separate from my mind's, I begin typing.

Dear Dad,

Actually, I don't know if I'm allowed to call you that anymore. Or if I want to. Or if you want me to. But I don't know what else to call you. It looks like you don't even have the same name anymore. I guess if you wanted me to call you anything at all, you wouldn't have changed it. I'm a little bummed out with the name you picked, by the way. There's nothing wrong with the name Derek Armstrong, but you definitely could have picked one with more flair. Of course, maybe that was the point. To avoid being noticed.

I don't know why I'm writing this. I don't know what to tell you. I could say I miss you, but that's not as true as that I used to miss you. I could say I'm not angry with you, but that's not as true as that I'm not angry with you anymore.

Mom is better now. I don't tell you that because I think it'll make you come back. I just think you should know. She got on some medication that helps stabilize her moods, and it works pretty well for her as long as she takes it, which is most of the time. She got on it after you left. I don't think she wanted to, but she knew she had to. I guess if you left to try to get her to do something about it, it worked.

It turns out that I inherited brain chemistry or something from you guys, and I had a lot of bad days too after you left. I'm better about taking my medication than Mom is.

I'm about to graduate, and then I'm going to Jackson State Community College. I work about twenty hours a week at Comic Universe. I'm not dating anyone, and I don't have a ton of friends, especially since Jesmyn, one of my best friends, moved to Nashville, but it's fine. I mostly hang out with Mom and my best friend, Josie.

Speaking of Josie, there's something I'm excited to tell you. She and I are horror hosts on our own show called *Midnite Matinee* on TV Six here. Every Saturday night from 11:00 p.m. to 1:00 a.m. You can stream it on the TV Six website. We're doing pretty great. We're already syndicated in Topeka, Macon, Greenville, Des Moines, Spokane, Fargo, and Little Rock. Which I guess means you probably haven't seen us by accident like I hoped you would, since you live in Florida. Or at least I think you do.

We use the movies you left behind. I wonder sometimes if you miss those too. I wonder if you miss them most of all. I've taken good care of them if you ever want them back. You know where to find us. We still live in the same place we did. Money's always been tight. It probably was when you were here. I can't remember ever being rich.

Like I said, I don't know why I'm writing this. I don't know what I hope to gain. I don't even know if this is you. If it's not you, maybe delete this and give your daughter (if you have one) an extra hug and tell her how lucky she is.

No, actually, I lied. I do know why I'm writing this. It's because I hope you'll watch my show. I hope you'll see that you left me with something I love and will always love. I hope you'll be proud of me.

I type *Love, Delia* but scrap it. I try *Sincerely, Delia* but ax that too. I give "Your daughter, Delia" a shot.

I delete the whole email.

I cry as quietly as I can for a little while, and then walk out to join my mom, because I dislike feeling any more abandoned than absolutely necessary.

Josie

"Dude, shut up," I say.

"What? I'm for real," Lawson says.

"No, you are not. That is nonsense." I get out of his truck and shut the door.

He follows suit. "Why?"

"Because pancakes"—I say *pancakes* with somewhat more contempt than even I think is due—"are not anybody's favorite food. They're never more than someone's fifth favorite food. It'd be like if toast was your favorite food. It's not allowed."

"You're messing with me, like you were about never having been to a restaurant."

"Not this time."

"They're delicious."

"They're disks of cooked flour that you put butter and liquid sugar on."

"I know what they are."

"Sorry. You have to pick a new favorite food."

"I can't just pick a new favorite."

"Brown flour Frisbees with cow grease and sugar sludge."

Lawson claps his hands over his ears. "No! I can't listen to you ruin pancakes for me. You don't hate pancakes."

"No, I don't. They're my eleventh favorite food, which is where they should be for a normal person."

"I can't believe you called butter 'cow grease.' I'm gonna need a minute to recover."

"That went too far. I'm not proud."

Lawson looks up as he opens the door of Five Guys for me. "Now that's a Friday-night sky."

This turn for the poetic catches me off guard. Unless this is some weird joke. He does love pancakes and have a gross air freshener and listen to crappy music. "Do what now?" I ask.

"A Friday-night sky. You ever notice that you only see some kinds of skies on certain nights? That's a Friday-night sky."

I stop, look up, and study the sky for a moment. "Looks like a normal sky to me."

"Friday-night skies feel . . . more hopeful. They always smell good too."

"You're smelling french fries."

"I swear. You never noticed Friday-night skies?"

"No." This is not entirely true. As he's been carrying on about them, I realize that I've noticed Friday-night skies too. But it's not a terrific idea to agree with a dude too much at first, in my opinion. Better to see sooner than later how they handle your thinking differently than they do. Not that I'm envisioning a bunch of other dates with this guy. But habit's habit.

We order cheeseburgers and approximately a laundry basket's worth of fries and sit. I brace myself for awkward conversation. At times like this I try to imagine I'm the host of my own talk show and I have to interview awful celebrities and seem really engaged and make it entertaining for my public. Good practice for my TV career someday.

"All right. Come clean," I say. "You left with my dog costume on purpose."

He laughs nervously. "What? No!"

"Mmmmmmmmmm-hmmm."

"No, for real."

"Mmmmmmmmmm-hmmm."

"I genuinely left on accident with the costume and got out to my truck and then I remembered."

"But you didn't turn around and walk a hundred feet back to the building."

"I figured your camera guy probably locked it."

Arliss probably did. "You couldn't have just left it by the back door?"

"It might've gotten stolen."

I fold my arms. "Stolen."

He shrugs.

"Because that is *definitely* a thing that happens in our society: dog costume theft. It's reached epidemic levels."

"You never know."

"You legitimately sometimes know. You really do occasionally know."

"People will sell anything to buy drugs."

"That is a true statement that still makes you zero percent less ridiculous."

He grins the grin of the busted. "I don't get to eat like this much," he says, holding up a fry appreciatively like a fine cigar.

"Because of training or whatever?"

"Yeah, my life is sorta one chicken breast and protein shake after another."

"You hate joy."

81

"Makes me a better fighter. That brings me joy."

"Mr. Dedication up in here."

"Speaking of dedication, I wanted to ask you at the studio, but I didn't get a chance. How'd you end up doing a TV show?"

I finish a big bite of cheeseburger. "Delia and I have this mutual friend from school, Jesmyn. Actually, she moved to Nashville, but anyway. Delia was friends with her first. So I was in one of our school's musicals with Jesmyn, and we started talking, and I told her I wanted to go into TV someday."

"Acting or—"

"I wanna be like Mindy Kaling and write and be on my own show."

"How long have you wanted to do that?"

"Like, my whole life. I can't remember when I didn't. I used to make movies when I was little on my mom's digital camera."

"I interrupted, sorry. You were saying about you and Delia?" Lawson says.

"So Delia grew up watching shows like ours with her dad. And she'd mentioned to Jesmyn that she wanted to start doing a horror show on public access, but she needed someone to do it with because she was scared to do it alone. She originally asked Jesmyn, but she's more of a musician, so Jesmyn sent Delia my way."

"Obviously it worked out."

"In the beginning, I was just doing it to be on TV. Honestly, it surprised me what good friends we became. We didn't have tons in common at first other than the show. But now we've influenced each other in a bunch of ways."

"How so?"

"Mmm . . . for one thing, I would *never* have gotten into cheesy horror movies if it weren't for her. I always liked horror movies, but not the kind we show. And I guess she's picked up my sense of humor."

"And you guys talk alike."

"Apparently so."

Talking about Delia has reminded me to check in on her. She might give me a graceful out to the evening. I mean, I'm having fun, it's fine, whatever, but still. I take a big bite so I don't have to talk, and I text her.

Me: Why is it totally ok to melt cheese on scrambled eggs but you can't on boiled eggs?

A few seconds pass.

Delia: OMG you're right. The thought of melting cheese on boiled eggs makes me wanna vom.

Me: First off you gotta make the boiled eggs hot and that is the grossest thought.

Delia: It IS. Hot boiled eggs would feel very off-putting. Is Law-man making you eat eggs for dinner???

Me: Nah, I was just thinking about it because I'm eating a cheeseburger and thinking about stuff we melt cheese on.

Delia: Sorry, I'm still thinking about hot boiled eggs and trying not to yak.

"That Delia?" Lawson asks.

"Oh . . . yeah. Sorry." I put my phone down. I didn't notice him looking at me.

"You had this little smile on your face while you were texting."

"She and I are always cracking each other up. You have friends like that? The Idiot Twins?"

"The Idiot—" he says quizzically, and laughs. "Oh, Hunter and Colt? I'm barely friends with those guys."

"Kudos. How do you even know them?"

"Scout camp when we were kids. They used to go out in the lake and one would fart in the water and the other would try to catch the bubbles in his mouth."

I snort involuntarily and clap a hand over my mouth before I can spray him with bits of bun, meat, and cheese. "Yeah, that is *real* gross."

"It's somehow way nastier than smelling it, even though both involve taking it into your body."

"Let's make a deal right now that we're never, ever going to use the phrase 'taking it into your body' with reference to a fart ever again, because I find that *very* upsetting."

Our shudders subside, and we eat for a while in silence. It's not a tense silence, but it's not an easy one either.

Lawson finally breaks it. "So what's next for you? We graduate soon, right? You a senior?"

I sigh. "Yeah, senior. I applied to a few schools. I'm planning on going to UT Martin so I can stay close to Jackson. It'll make it easier for Delia and me to keep doing the show. But . . ."

"But what?"

I wave it off. "Nothing."

"You sounded like you wanted to say something else."

"No, it's that my parents are pressuring me to go to UT Knoxville instead. My mom knows a lady who works at Food Network, and they have an office in Knoxville—"

"For real? In Knoxville? Weird."

"I know, right? Travel Channel has its headquarters there too, apparently. Anyway, she could get me an internship, but I don't know."

"Sounds like a cool opportunity."

"Maybe you should be hanging with my mom right now instead. Y'all would get along."

"I'm just saying."

"I'm *on* TV here. That's gotta be better than getting coffee for . . . Alton Brown's secretary or whatever."

Lawson pops a french fry in his mouth. "I don't know. Maybe. Maybe not."

"You know something I don't?" I put only the thinnest of veils on my irritation. I did not sign up for an awkward quasi-date with some dude I barely met and who listens to bad music, only to get the same lecture my parents could give me.

He shrugs. "I know when you fight, sometimes the position that seems the best isn't. You gotta think long term. Give up something now to get something better later."

"Well, thanks for that helpful advice. It's definitely never occurred to me to think more than several hours into the future."

"I'm not trying to piss you off."

"Who's pissed?"

"I can hear it in your voice."

"You've known me for how long now?"

"Long enough."

"Anyway, Delia would be super bugged if I left. This show is like her whole world. I don't think she'd be able to do it by herself."

Another silence. This one is definitely strained.

I break it. "What about you? What are you doing when you graduate?"

He nods, considering the question. "College at some point, but I want to take a year off to work and train really hard. I'll be in my fighting prime in a few years, and I want a shot at going pro. I really like my coach and my gym here, so I'm sticking around."

"How long have you been at it?"

"Well, I started Tae Kwon Do pretty early before moving into Muay Thai—"

"What's that?"

"Muay Thai? It's this Thai kickboxing style where you use your whole body to put force into kicks and strikes."

"Oh, like the way I eat pizza."

"I got into that and Brazilian jujitsu when I was fourteen, which is when I started fighting MMA."

"Why MMA, of all things?"

"I have three older brothers and a bunch of older cousins."

"Ah."

"Yeah. Got my ass whupped a lot. Lovingly. But a loving ass whupping is still an ass whupping."

"Couldn't find a less painful thing to be passionate about than mixed martial arts?"

"Lots of less painful things. But nothing worthwhile."

"What's so magical about it? Why do it?"

He starts to speak and stops. He blushes. Then he looks me

86

in the eyes and says, "I want to be a champion." I'm taken aback by the quiet, unarmored confidence with which he expresses an otherwise pretty cheesy sentiment. So much so that I don't even have anything clever to say in response.

He senses this and continues. "I want to be the best."

"As opposed to a champion who gets his ass beat constantly and is the worst?" I knew it wouldn't take me long to recover my game. "They give you this big trophy with a boot kicking an ass and on the ass it says 'You.'"

"You're funny," he says.

He's clearly sincere. I can already tell he's not the ironic or sarcastic type. I've had boyfriends who were nothing but irony and sarcasm, and it grated after a while. Especially how they always thought they were funnier than me (they weren't) and wouldn't laugh at my jokes (which were funny).

So he gets a sincere smile from me. "You think?"

"I think."

"You have better taste in comedy than in music."

"Hey, now."

"Here's what you love." I pump my fist. *"Don't you dare say that my hat ain't fancy,"* I sing in my best bro country singer voice. I was in show choir and I've been in some of the school musicals, so I'm not a terrible singer.

Lawson starts grooving along with my singing. "I'm into it."

"And you better not say that my boots ain't prancey and my buckle ain't sassy and my Skoal can ain't classy."

Lawson grins. "This is my jam right here."

"And you best not say that my jeans ain't too tight and my truck ain't too high," I finish with a slow flourish and jazz hands.

Lawson claps and whistles. "Encore!"

I shake my head. "This is my life. Freestyling country music."

"I'll be your bodyguard when you get famous."

"If I were famous for making country music, I'd want someone to kill me as soon as possible."

"I bet we could make a country fan out of you."

"I bet nope, never."

"You like cheesy movies. I bet you could start loving cheesy music."

"You even admit it's cheesy!"

"I only admit *you* think it is."

"Dude, you would legit have your work cut out for you. Trust me on that."

We chat about nothing in particular and laugh for a little while. Lawson has an endearing mix of quiet confidence—maybe from his fighter side—and sweet nervousness, like a kid who's excited to ride a roller coaster that scares him—maybe from being around me. It's fun. More than I thought it would be, for sure. I do thoroughly enjoy the way he looks at me.

If we had more in common, I'd maybe want to do it again sometime. Maybe.

We pull up to my house. "Okay, dude, I had a good time. Thanks." I put up my hand for a high five, which he dutifully gives.

"I like being around you." (Sweet nervousness.)

"Cool," I say with considered nonchalance.

"I'd like to do this again sometime." (Quiet confidence.)

Oh joy. He's not going to take the hint. I imagine what would happen if I suddenly pretended to die. Just slumped in my seat, tongue lolling out, my head flopping at an improbable angle, my eyes open and glassed over. Until he laid my body on the front lawn and drove off (although he's definitely more the *carry me to my door and ring the doorbell and deliver my corpse to my parents with an apology* type).

He's still looking at me expectantly, awaiting a response. *Great.* I know I'm about to cut hard and deep, but he wasted so little time trying to get me to go out with him, I feel like it's in order. "I—Okay. I'll be totally straight with you."

"Please."

"We don't have a lot in common, true?"

"Maybe, maybe not. That's what I wanted to find out."

"I can tell we don't have much in common."

"After only an hour or two?"

"It's obvious."

"All right."

"You don't think it's obvious?"

"No. Not to me."

"Well, it is to me. So we can be friends, cool, no big deal. But I'm not looking for anything more than that."

"Is it because I'm—"

I hold up a hand to halt him. "I don't care that you love punching people."

"I was gonna say 'a country music fan.'" He gives me a slight, sad smile. It's a nice smile. This is not as easy as I hoped.

"Oh."

"Shoulda let you pick the music."

I blush. "It really is because I'm not feeling a relationship with anyone right now."

"That's fine. We can be friends." His voice is soft, and he averts his eyes. But otherwise, he takes the hit very well. I'm a little surprised, in fact. I sorta wanted him to be a tad more broken up about it. Maybe MMA fighters also train in emotional resilience. I'm picturing Lawson with a grizzled old man in a porkpie hat standing in his corner while he's fighting, screaming about the importance of self-care.

"I'm totally down to be friends. I just didn't want to lead you on," I say.

"All good. So, guess I'll see you later?" There's no bitterness in his voice. No sarcasm. No hint of a sense of thwarted entitlement. I've had a more pleasant time telling this dude I *wouldn't* date him than I had actually *dating* some of my exes.

"Yeah." I open my door and start to get out.

"You need a dancer for the show next week?"

I pause halfway out of the truck. "We can always put you to work. You good with wearing a skeleton costume?"

"What's dignity worth anyway?"

I laugh. "Right? Okay, bye for real. Thanks for dinner."

"No problem. Bye." There's a melancholy in his eyes. He has nice eyes.

I feel him watching to make sure I get into my house safely. I turn and wave as I go inside, and he waves back before driving off.

Why do I suddenly feel like he and I were grappling, and I was winning, and without my even noticing, he gained the upper hand? More importantly, why am I so unbothered by it?

I go to my room, flop on my bed, and stare out the window. Friday-night sky. Look at that.

Delia

Mom and I recline on opposite ends of the couch with our legs entwined between us, our standard movie-watching position. My phone buzzes. I should ignore it so that I'm not texting during the movie, but I'm too anxious and wound up tonight to let anything go.

Josie: What's up? You good?

Me: I'm okay. I feel weird. Watching a movie with Mom. Oh, btw, my dad changed his name, no biggie.

Josie: ARE YOU SERIOUS.

Me: Yep.

Josie: Is he on the run from the law or something?

Me: Or he's a secret agent. I hope it's that and he wasn't just trying to make sure I'd never find him. How was your trip to Corntown with karate guy?

Josie: It wasn't bad. It was fine.

Me: ???

Josie: I had to be all "we're not gonna get together" at the end.

Me: Oof.

Josie: I needed to tell him sooner than later. He was throwing vibe.

Me: You're not feeling it, you're not feeling it.

Josie: He liked my jokes though.

Me: That's big. I read this great essay on Dollywould about how lots of guys don't like girls who are funnier than them.

Josie: Right?? Or who are funny at all. Speaking of, wanna hear something hilarious I was gonna tell you earlier?

Me: Duh.

Josie: I've never read Frankenstein.

Me: Um, how am I just NOW learning this? Tell me what you think it's about.

Josie: Uhhhhh, the doctor builds a Frankenstein in his basement and the Frankenstein wants a girlfriend so he goes bonkers and tears up the countryside and whatnot until the villagers kill him with pitchforks. The end.

Me: NOPE.

Josie: Close?

Me: Literally LOL, you are so not even close. OMG let's do a segment on the show where you tell what you think Frankenstein is about.

Josie: [selfie of her flipping me off]

Me: Cooooooooome ooooooooon

Josie: Speaking of the show I told Karate Kid he could come help next week.

Me: LEADING HIM OOOOOOOOON.

Josie: Totally not!!!!

Me: JK. We'll figure something out for him to do.

Josie: Maybe he could break boards or something?

Me: I literally can't imagine any show on television that wouldn't be improved by a martial arts demo break. I gotta go, I'm watching a movie with my mom and being rude.

Josie: K, talk later. Love you, DeeDeeBooBoo.

Me: Love you, JoJoBee.

"You gonna watch this movie with me or text Josie?"

"I already told her I was being rude." I lean over with a soft grunt and toss my phone gently onto the coffee table.

"This isn't as good as the original," Mom murmurs, staring at the TV.

I grab another Twizzler from the big plastic jar Mom set on the floor beside the couch. "Do you think Rob Zombie's ever like, 'Please, Mr. Zombie was my father's name. Call me Rob'?"

"I bet Zombie isn't even his real name."

"Maybe he changed it for the stage like some actors do. Like he used to be Robin Zombiertalli or something."

"Natalie Portman used to be Natalie Hershlag," Mom says.

"Is that true?"

"I swear."

"How do you even know that?"

"I don't remember."

The movie ends. Mom picks up the remote and turns off the TV, and we sit motionless for a few moments, listening to our trailer tick and settle around us.

I sit up and stifle a yawn with the back of my hand. I'm proud of how well I pretended like everything was fine. "I'm going to bed."

"Wait," Mom says.

I look at her.

"You gonna tell me why you seem off tonight?" she asks. Sometimes I wonder if her gift is just being really empathetic and attuned to what people are feeling. Feeling the pain of others might partially account for how much of my childhood she spent sad.

"I'm fine. Just tired."

"Your energy is all wrong," Mom says. "First you're jittery and nervous, and then you run off to the bathroom and you're there for fifteen minutes, and when you come out, you seem sad. Is it a guy?"

"Yes. I'm in love with a cool hunk named Chadford, but he doesn't love me."

"Wanna tell me what's going on?"

It's like when you don't think you're hungry. But then you pass a pizza place and get a whiff and you realize you're not only hungry, you're hungrier than you've ever been in your life. *Yes. I do want to tell you what's going on. No one would understand better than you. But I can't. I can't. I can't. I can't.*

"Are you in some kind of trouble?" Mom's voice is gentle but urgent.

"Trouble? Like—"

"I don't know, DeeDee. I read tarot cards and palms, not minds."

"No."

"Then?"

Maybe she'll be okay. Maybe enough time has passed that she'll be fine and it won't hurt too much. Maybe.

I draw a deep breath and hold it before speaking. My blood is thrumming, a headache emerging at the base of my skull. "I . . . might have tracked down Dad." The words no sooner leave my mouth than I realize what an atrocious time it is to spring this on her, especially with her currently spotty medication consumption.

It takes a moment for the news to register, but I see the hurt spreading on Mom's face like a drop of blood blooming on white cloth.

"DeeDee?" Her voice implores me to be making some awful joke. Scolds me for it. Begs me to say, *Just kidding!*

"I saved my money and hired an investigator."

"Why?"

I can't tell if "why" is a question or a rebuke. "She came up with an address for a Dylan Wilkes in Boca Raton, Florida. He's changed his name to Derek Armstrong." I wait a couple of beats before adding, stupidly, as though Mom might've forgotten who Dylan Wilkes was, "She maybe found Dad."

Mom's face turns ashen, and she sags into herself. She hasn't been good for a few weeks, but tonight she rallied. That's done. She says nothing for so long it scares me. I can hear the ticking of our cuckoo clock, which doesn't keep time, nor does the cuckoo work. It just ticks.

"Mom?"

"Why?" She shakes her head slowly, as if watching a building burn on TV. "Why on earth?"

"I don't know." This is true.

Mom's eyes well. She quickly wipes them and puts her fist to her trembling lips. "DeeDee." Her voice cracks and dissolves.

"I'm sorry."

"I almost *drowned* when he left. On top of everything else, I was suddenly a single mom. It almost killed me. I thought I wouldn't make it. It rips my heart up even *talking* about it." She says this in a near-whisper.

"I had to find out."

"And you did. So now what?"

"I don't know." I'm damming back tears and my throat aches like I've swallowed an ice cube that was slightly too big for my esophagus.

"Contact him? Dig everything back up?" A tear leaves a shiny streak down Mom's cheek.

"I said I don't know." I'm crying now too. "I want to know why."

"You want to know *why*? I can answer that. Because things got tough here, and it was easier to run out on both of us than deal with the hard reality. Because he only thought about himself."

"Did he tell you that?"

"Isn't it obvious?"

"What if there's more to it than that?"

"What could there be?"

"I don't know. I don't know what to think."

"I do. I think I needed to never think about him again. That's what. There's not a day that goes by that I don't, but still. You have any idea what it's like to love and hate someone so much?"

"You aren't the only one he hurt."

"Here we're struggling to pay the bills, and you're paying someone who-knows-how-much to open old wounds. You have to let this drop. You can't keep digging."

I sit still and don't say anything.

Mom presses. "Promise me you will stop."

I wipe my eyes with the backs of my hands, break eye contact, look away, and nod slightly.

She rises from the couch. "I can't. I need to go to bed."

"Mom."

She raises her hand for me to stop talking.

"Mom."

She keeps her hand raised. "DeeDee. Please." She's not sharp or angry anymore, but exudes the sort of weariness she did during her worst days, when she seemed to hope her heart would simply stop beating.

She blows out the candle that was the only light we were using and walks to her room tenuously, like she's balancing on her head the sloshing bowl full of whatever's been allowing her to keep it together for the last almost-decade. From her room, the sound of hushed sobbing, the kind coming from a wellspring that can't be capped, try as she might.

I sit in the dark stillness of our puny living room, the red ember of the candlewick gradually dimming and then dying, white smoke curling off it. Encircling me are the baubles and trinkets we've used to line our little nest. I've never thought of them as talismans against sadness, but maybe that's exactly what they are.

Josie

I have this belief that humans who are connected in some way can feel what the other is feeling, even over distances. Don't ask me how it works; I couldn't tell you. All I know is I'm not surprised when I get a text from Delia, because I can sense something's up with her.

Delia: Can you talk? I'm not good.

Me: Of course. Hugs, BB.

Delia: I told my mom I maybe found my dad.

Me: And?

Delia: Her reaction was NOT great.

Me: Aw, baby girl. What can I do?

Delia: I don't know. Distract me somehow.

Me: K. What if you could fly, but you had to be naked. Would you? Discuss.

Delia: What about like a swimsuit bottom.

Me: Nope. Butt ass naked. Nothing on bottom.

Delia: Can I fly high enough so people can't see my business?

Me: No. You can only fly 50 feet high max.

Delia: Can I fly super fast? So my butt crack is just a pink blur?

Me: You can fly 50 miles an hour max.

Delia: Can I fly at night?

Me: No. Full daylight. The goods will be on display.

Delia: Going for it.

Me: Yeah?

Delia: Flying sounds way fun, and flying with no pants would probably feel nice. And the stigma of being caught in public with no pants on would probably be canceled out by the coolness of flying.

Me: We discuss important stuff.

Delia: Thank you for being you.

Me: You know I love you, BooBear.

Delia: Good, because my mom and dad both hate me now.

Me: Your mom loves you more than any mom has ever loved a kid and your dad left for some reason but not because he hated little kid you. Trust.

Delia: How do you know?

Josie: If I were your dad I would love you and tell dad jokes like "Hi, tired, I'm dad" if you said you were tired and wear khakis and polo shirts and wear my phone on my belt like I'm Batman.

Delia: Now I'm crying laughing. I'm gonna get dehydrated.

Me: You need sleep.

Delia: For real. Ok, I'm gonna go. Pre-production at my house tomorrow?

Me: Yep. You already got a movie picked out?

Delia: Werewolf in a Girls' Dormitory. It's an Italian movie from 1961 that features werewolves killing girls by what sounds like humping them.

Me: Nice.

Delia: And the audio is total garbage. Voices don't match lips at all.

Me: Here for it.

Delia: I get off work at 5. Come over at 6. I'll let you get back to your Project Runway.

Me: Love you, DeeDeeBooBoo.

Delia: Love you, JoJoBee.

Delia

I sleep like a rock skipping across a pond. That shallow sleep where your mind still screams at you so loudly it keeps waking you up. Where you're never quite certain whether you've been sleeping.

I'm not sure if I'm awake or asleep when my brain finally makes the connection. *Florida is where ShiverCon is happening. Florida is where my dad maybe lives.* Now I'm definitely awake, my heart churning in my chest like a washing machine. I grab my phone and look it up: Orlando is 196 miles from Boca Raton, where my dad lives. I could make it. This is maybe fate telling me something: *Meet with Jack Divine. Enlist his help in taking* Midnite Matinee *to the next level. Make it the thing that'll stop Josie from going to Knoxville to try to get her career started. Find my dad. Ask him why. Maybe bury something that's been clawing at my heart like a cat in a sack.*

If I have the courage to do it.

Josie

I've had dates before that were fine, with perfectly nice guys, and I've never given them a moment's thought afterward. But something keeps turning in my mind as I watch *Project Runway*, a show about people sacrificing and striving and working so hard to be the best at something. It's the way Lawson talked about wanting to be a champion. He may be a complete dork in every other way, and we may have nothing else in common, but that set something humming inside me.

I wonder if he has dreams about vast hidden rooms at his grandma's house. I almost text him to ask him, but immediately think better of it.

I guess you don't need to like the same music or have the same favorite food for someone to know your secret heart.

Delia

"I know I say this every time, and you'd think I'd be used to it by now, but this movie really is garbage," Josie says, catching a piece of kettle corn before it can fall down her shirt.

"I warned you," I say, picking up the remote and pausing our ancient VCR.

"I mean, it is *upsettingly* bad."

"Isn't it amazing that we live in a time when we have access to crappy art?"

"Like?"

"Like think how you've never seen a horrendous Renaissance painting. Not every artist in the Renaissance was Michelangelo, right?"

"Ah. True."

"There must have been some Renaissance painters that were disasters. Where are their paintings?" I shift position on the couch.

"They probably got burned for firewood or something."

"I wish there was a museum of crappy Renaissance art. I would totally go."

"The little placards would be all 'Please note Rigatoni's—' "

I giggle and spray kettle corn shrapnel. "*Rigatoni?* He's both a dismal painter and literally named after *pasta?*"

"No, rigatoni pasta is named after him. He had to invent rigatoni because his paintings sucked. His pasta was his true master-piece."

"It *is* good pasta. You were saying?"

"'Please note Rigatoni's rendering of the human form . . . or at least we're pretty sure that's the human form. It could also be a shaved dog walking around on its hind legs. Who honestly knows?'"

I start the video again, and we watch for a while. I cover a yawn, hit pause, and lean forward over the coffee table to type on my laptop. "We should do a segment where our voices and lips don't match up, like in the movie."

"It'll require Arliss to do some work, but I'm into it."

"He can offset the audio recording for that part. Should be easy. And we'll make it up to him by cutting his Professor Von Hein—" Another yawn.

"You get any sleep last night?"

"Maybe an hour and a half uninterrupted."

"Thinking about your dad situation?" Josie gets up to take the kettle corn bowl to the kitchen.

"Dump that in the sink," I call after her.

"If I leave it, it'll be there the next time I come over." She runs water in the bowl and starts scrubbing.

She's not wrong. "Yeah. Mostly the dad situation."

"That sucks."

"What makes it even worse is it's sent my mom spiraling. She went off her meds at some point, and she's been doing bad lately. I had to literally drag her out of bed this morning before I went to work."

"Dude." Josie comes back in the living room and sits cross-legged on the couch next to me.

"Yeah. Super fun trying to haul someone who won't talk to you out of bed."

"She needs to get back on her meds."

"Well, yeah. But she's seriously the worst sometimes."

We stare at the paused TV screen for a moment before Josie picks up the remote with a long sigh. "Might as well get this janky-ass—"

I put my hand on the remote. "Hang on." I knew I wanted to talk to Josie about this at some point tonight, but I'm taking even myself by surprise. Sleep deprivation. "I really think we need to go to ShiverCon. If we can get something going with Jack Divine, it could take us places."

"I forgot to tell you. We're going to Atlanta to visit my aunt that weekend."

"JoJo. This is, like, an amazing opportunity."

"DeeDee, visiting Cassie gives me *life*. You haven't experienced joy until you've stayed up all night bingeing *Scandal,* eating espresso gelato, and talking smack with my aunt."

"I know, but listen."

"I'm listening. What?"

"Your aunt will always be there. We have one chance to meet Jack Divine."

"I *know* I'll have a good time with Cassie. We have *no* idea if Jack Divine will even give us the time of day."

"If he doesn't, he doesn't, but at least we tried. And if we don't try, the show keeps plugging along pretty much how it is. And if the show keeps going how it is, you're—" I can't finish the thought. I don't want to say it out loud. I might give the universe ideas.

"I'm what?"

"I don't know. You're going to keep getting pressure from

106

your parents to go to UT Knoxville." I hesitate and then mutter, "You're gonna go."

"I told you yesterday. I'm going to UT Martin. I'll keep doing the show. That's my plan."

She says it emphatically, but somehow it doesn't reassure me. It feels like she's gripping tight to a slick bar of soap that could suddenly shoot from her hand.

"And what if our show doesn't take off?" I ask. "Sooner or later you'll have to move on if you want a career in TV."

"We can cross that bridge when we come to it."

I chew on the inside of my cheek, a nervous habit when I'm stressed. "I want to cross the bridge now. Riding on Jack Divine's back." My voice has taken on an urgent pitch. I know I sound desperate, and that's never good when you want something, but it's hard to hide the desperation.

"DeeDee."

"JoJo. Plus, I've heard there are lots of creepy dudes at cons, and I don't want to be alone."

I try to project calm confidence as I don't want this to seem like as quixotic a mission as it is. I'm not sure I'm succeeding.

But still, Josie says, *"Okay.* I'll talk to my parents."

"I know you're reluctant."

"I'll drive down and visit her another time. But you're coming when I do because my dad will hate it if I go alone."

"Deal."

We stare at each other for a second. Josie wordlessly reaches behind her, grabs a sofa pillow, and bops me in the face with it. I silently sit there and take it. We laugh.

Josie unpauses the movie. "The werewolf in this movie truly does sound like he's humping people to death."

"I think it's kinda hot."

"Part of me wants to explore that further, but I'm really afraid of what I'll find."

As we watch, I start thinking about my dad. I wonder what he's doing while I'm watching one of the artifacts of our short life together. I think how someday, I want to be good enough—*enough* enough—that no one who's held me in their arms under an October night sky ever wants to abandon me.

The end credits roll.

Josie turns to me and says, "Do you think cave people let their cave kids draw garbage drawings on the walls of the cave?"

Josie

"Arliss seems to be in a way better mood than usual," I whisper to Delia.

On set, Arliss, dressed as Professor Von Heineken (he voluntarily did it for this segment, another rare wonder), stands braced, holding a wooden board in both hands, the camera rolling behind him. Lawson, dressed in his Tae Kwon Do outfit (he told me what it's called but I forgot) and a skeleton mask, does a spin kick and breaks the board cleanly in half. Arliss whoops.

"All this time, the key to his heart was people breaking stuff with kicks," Delia says.

"Okay," Arliss says to Lawson as they set up several boards between cinder blocks. "When you break the boards, look right into the camera and yell, and I'm going to do a tight zoom, like in an old martial arts movie."

"You gotta keep working it with Lawson," Delia whispers. "He makes the show more interesting, and he transforms Arliss into less of a dickhead."

"By the way, did you notice how Lawson was dressed when he arrived tonight?" I ask.

"Kind of. I thought he was trying to look cool for the show."

"No! Because why do that if he knew he was going to wear his Tae Kwon Do outfit?"

"*Excellent point.*"

"Remember how he dressed last time?"

"Vaguely. Didn't he sort of dress like a basic dude?"

"Exactly, which is why you can't even remember. Like he buys everything from American Eagle or whatever. So *this* time—"

Delia giggles. "He's wearing these obviously brand-new black skinny jeans and black Vans and—"

"A black leather *cuff.*"

"You're *right.* He's *totally*—"

"Shhhhhhh!"

Delia lowers her voice. "*He's totally dressing to impress you.*"

"Isn't it so funny?"

"*It's adorable.*"

"Like what if he was wearing a spanking new fedora from Target too?"

"The leather cuff is the fedora of the wrist."

"You should tell him where you got your stinky vinyl pants," I say. "He might be in the market."

We crack up as silently as we can, hands over our mouths, clutching at each other. I bury my face in Delia's arm. Arliss and Lawson are too busy to notice. At least I hope so. Lawson's been throwing bashful little sidelong glances in my direction all night.

"Quiet on set!" Arliss hollers, briefly back to his old self. "Shut your asses."

But this just makes us cackle harder, so we run outside, sit on the back steps, and laugh loud and long, the sticky humidity taking only minutes to make our vampire garb cling to our backs like leaves on wet pavement. At some point, we're not even laughing at the original thing anymore; we're laughing at how much we're laughing.

"He is in *luhhhhhve*," Delia says.

"We should go back in," I say, wiping tears.

"It's pretty cute how much he wants to French you."

"Delia! Ew!"

"By the way, did you ask your parents about going to Shiver-Con?" Delia's tone goes abruptly from teasing to anxious.

"No."

"*What?*"

"I'm going to. Chill."

"Okay, you gotta do it soon."

"I will."

"Promise."

"I just said I would." Then after a pause, "I meant to tell you, your pants smell better. I mean, not *better*, but, you know, less bad. They didn't make my car stink this time."

Delia pulls her knee to her nose and takes a long sniff. "Yeah, I think the fumes needed to evaporate, maybe."

"Or they've killed off our smell buds or whatever's in your nose."

"I'm going to email Jack Divine and try to start a dialogue."

"*Start a dialogue?*"

"I don't know! Start the ball rolling. How's that?"

"'Dialogue' sounds smarter. What are you gonna say?"

"I gotta track down his email first."

"Then what are you going to tell him?"

"Haven't gotten that far yet. Maybe send him some clips."

"Plan it out, so you don't ramble."

"I don't ramble. Rude." But Delia gives that lopsided smile she reserves for when she knows she's been justifiably roasted.

"No, when you get nervous, you do."

"I'm going to tell him we want to meet him at ShiverCon and discuss possible next steps."

"Just be normal. Don't be weird and businessy."

"I won't."

"Don't use phrases like 'synergy' and 'step up to the plate.'"

"I don't even know what synergy is."

"And don't tell him 'we' until I know for sure if I'm coming."

"Then ask."

We hear Arliss bellowing. We spring to our feet and run inside. He's counting down from some number, and he's on four. I assume when he gets to zero, he's walking away whether the show is finished or not.

・ ・ ・

"Well, folks, that's it for another episode of *Midnite Matinee*. We hope you dug the movie!" Delia says.

"And thanks to our special guest, uh . . ." I suddenly realize we forgot to give Lawson a stage name.

Delia jumps in. "Kickin' Kenny."

"Kickin' Kenny! I doubt we'd have come up with anything better even if we'd thought about it. And don't forget to tune in next week for more chills . . ."

"And thrills!"

We smile, wave, and then wait until Arliss yells, "Cut." Lawson stands behind Arliss, beaming. He has apparently pleased Arliss enough not to be kicked out the minute he's done with his scene.

We start taking down the set.

"How'd it look tonight?" I ask Arliss as he approaches, winding up a microphone cable.

He draws in a breath and belches, "Real," then draws in another breath and belches, "Bad."

"Well, thanks for that," I say.

Lawson, still wearing his Tae Kwon Do getup but with his new Vans, starts helping Delia unpin the spiderweb.

"Good job," Delia says to Lawson. "We might need to make you a regular."

"We'll reimburse your board costs," I say.

"Oh, it's no big deal. They're cheap."

"Good, because I was kidding."

Delia tosses the candelabra and plastic skull in a bin and clamps down the lid. "Lemme see your keys, JoJo."

I hand her my keys and she walks outside, lugging the bin.

Arliss finishes fiddling with the camera. "I gotta take a dump. Don't break anything or have sex while I'm gone." He stalks away.

I wrinkle my nose. "Gross, Arliss. Gross," I say to his back.

Lawson half smiles. "Jeez, I'm standing right here."

"You know which part of what he said I was referring to," I say with an eye roll.

"I watched the show last week, by the way." He picks up our end table.

"Oh yeah? You can stick that in the corner. As long as it's out of the way."

"Yeah. Well, I watched y'all's parts. I had a hard time with the movie itself."

"Lightweight."

"Technically I'm a welterweight."

"Uh-oh! That some fighter guy humor? Huh? You busting out some fight material on me?"

He grins. "Maybe." He stands beside me while I arrange the chairs and table in the corner. He smells like laundry detergent and clean, bleached cotton. It's a nice smell. "So you had some nutty letters tonight. Are all your letter writers such weirdos?" he asks.

"No, lots of really normal, well-adjusted people love to watch public access shows starring two high school girls from Jackson, Tennessee."

"I didn't know you were allowed to say 'Opinions are like buttholes; everyone has one, but it's best to keep it to yourself' on public TV."

"Public *access* TV. There's a massive difference. Also, most of the people who worry about that sort of thing aren't paying attention to us. But good memory."

He walks over and picks up a stray splinter from one of his broken boards. "It was a memorable phrase."

I wonder where Delia is. I thought it would be suddenly tense and awkward when Arliss left Lawson and me alone, but it isn't. Lawson isn't being weird at all, the way some guys act when you say you just want to be friends. It's pretty refreshing.

"Doesn't it hurt when you break boards?" I ask.

"Nope."

"Seriously? Are you pretending to be tough?"

"There's a secret to it."

"Are you allowed to reveal it to someone who isn't a member of the Sacred Brotherhood of the Broken Board?"

He raises a finger, walks over to his duffel bag, and grabs a spare board. He hands it to me. "Hold."

"Dude, I'm not going to hold this while you break it. Too scary."

"Nope. Not gonna break it. Here, hold it like this." He positions my hands on the board. His fingers are surprisingly gentle for how strong they are. He maneuvers the board so I'm holding it square toward him, in front of my chest.

He taps on the board. "If you aim for the board itself, you'll hurt yourself. You have to focus your energy on a point beyond the board." He reaches over and taps at the space between the board and my chest. "And then—" He coils back and strikes. I barely have time to flinch. Just before he hits the board, he stops and flicks it with his finger.

I squeal and drop the board, giggling. "You freaked me out, jackass."

He reaches out as quickly as he struck, catching the board before it hits the floor. "We promised Arliss we wouldn't break anything."

"Also that we wouldn't have sex."

"We're good on that too." Lawson smiles and reddens. "We've done nothing to spoil Arliss's dump."

An awkward silence follows. I break it by pointing at the general area of his groin (such a gross word). "So you're a black belt."

"Since I was ten."

"For *real*? Dedication."

"Never been afraid of commitment."

"Clearly." *Slick little plug for yourself, by the way, Mr. Vargas.* "How did you get into martial arts?"

"My whole family used to watch reruns of *Walker, Texas Ranger*. And I loved it when Walker would kick butt."

"As opposed to *what*? When Walker would hold forth on quantum physics? When he would write haikus? When he

115

would interpret Bach on the harpsichord? That show is an infomercial for Chuck Norris kicking people through plate-glass windows in slow motion."

"So you've seen it."

"Have you not learned yet that my having seen something does not speak well for the quality of it? Yes, I've seen it. It's bad even by my standards."

"I mean, it's not gonna win any Oscars, for sure."

"For multiple reasons. First off, it's not on the air anymore. Second, TV shows aren't eligible for Oscars; they're eligible for Emmys. And third, there's no Emmy category for Best TV Show That Exists Solely to Show the Protagonist Kicking People Comically High into the Air."

"That didn't happen that much."

"I've seen two episodes, and it happened on both."

Lawson looks over the set. "You got everything? We good in here?"

"I think so."

We start walking toward the door. Arliss would probably love it if we were gone when he returned.

We're halfway to the door when I realize I don't have my phone. There are no pockets on my gown, so I'm always misplacing it on set. *"Gah."*

"What?"

"My phone."

"Lost it?"

"Yeah. You have my number in your phone?"

"Yep."

"Call it for me."

I walk back into the studio as Lawson dials. There's a buzzing on the floor behind some of the chairs used for studio audiences. I guess I set it on one of those chairs and it fell behind. I pick it up and answer. "Pizza Trough. What kind of pizza do you want?"

Lawson doesn't miss a beat. "Wow, I don't know, what kind of pizza do you have?"

"We're featuring our new Poultry Lover's pizza."

"Oh, tell me about that."

"It's a pizza piled high with succulent chicken, duck, turkey, goose . . . What's another kind of bird?"

"Pheasant."

"And pheasant. With a scrambled egg–stuffed crust and a zesty egg yolk dipping sauce."

"Huh. I like all those things, and yet that pizza sounds weird and gross."

"Did I mention that the crust is made out of pancake?" I start to walk back toward the door.

"Wait," Lawson says. "Stop walking but don't hang up. I wanna ask you something."

I stop. "Depends on if we're still pretending I'm a representative of Pizza Trough."

He laughs, a jitter in it. "No. I was gonna ask you over the phone because I'm nervous and I hadn't planned on doing this. I have a fight next Saturday night, and I was wondering if you wanted to come?"

"I can actually hear you speaking right now even if I hold the phone away from my ear."

"I know."

"Next time you want to ask me something like this, we should put a blindfold on you. Same thing," I say.

"I swear it's easier for me this way."

"You had no trouble asking me to dinner last week."

"This is different."

"You seem less scared about actually engaging in hand-to-hand combat than me watching."

"Yeah."

"Normally Delia and I use Saturday nights to get ready for next week's show." I get ready to really lean on this as an excuse, but then . . . I don't feel like it.

"It's cool if you can't make it." His voice contains equal parts disappointment and relief.

"But we could do show prep another night."

"Awesome. I'll text you where it's at." He sounds like he's speaking through a smile.

And just to be a butthead: "I like your new clothes. They look sharp."

"What? No. I've had them for a while."

"No, you have not."

"Have!"

"You *just* got them."

"No."

"You sound really busted right now. Why would you be weird about clothes being new if they weren't new?"

"Okay, fine. They're new."

"So let's try this again." Now *I'm* speaking through a smile. "I like your new clothes."

"Thanks. I maybe hoped you would."

"I know."

Delia

I wedge the bin into the back seat of Josie's car. I figure Josie and Lawson will be along shortly, so I pull out my phone and call my mom to see if she wants me to stop and pick up something for dinner.

"Hello?" Her voice is thick and woolly with sleep. *That ain't good.*

"Mom? Are you at work? Why do you sound like you just woke up?"

"What time is it?"

"Seven-thirty. At night."

"Oh damnit. Oh lord."

"Mom."

"I fell asleep."

"Oh, no kidding?"

"I have no energy."

"Please get up and go into work or call them or something."

"Okay."

"I am *really* going to need you to get back on your meds. I am so serious right now."

"I will."

"Don't tell me that just to get me off your back."

Mom's voice is somehow both petulant and plaintive. "I was fine until you started digging things up with your dad."

My blood rises. "Oh. *Whatever.* Blame this on me."

"I'm just saying."

"Well, stop saying. This is happening because you started feeling better and you thought, 'Welp, time to quit taking the things that made me feel better.'" Intellectually, I know it can't help to get pissed at her. But . . .

Mom starts in about something, but I can't deal.

"You know what? I gotta go. I gotta help Josie with our stuff. Later." I hang up. It's such a scary, lonely feeling when Mom gets this way. What I wouldn't give for a few consecutive years where my life didn't feel so precarious. Where my mom could always be my mom.

The studio door opens and Josie and Lawson exit, laughing. Lawson says something to Josie that I can't quite make out before he splits off to go to where he's parked, his new clothes bundled under his arm. He steals a last furtive glance at Josie before getting in his truck.

It triggers a strange mix of jealousy and urgency. The world—in whatever form it decides to take—is so hungry for some people, it can't help but try constantly to lure them away from wherever they are by promising even more. I wonder if people like that—people like Josie—are harder to leave behind. They must be. Wouldn't that be nice?

Josie and this show are the two good things I have that I can count on. The world has taken more from me before. It won't hesitate to do it again.

"Did Arliss say anything before you left?" I hand Josie her keys.

"He said, 'I gotta take a dump,' and as far as I know, he's still in there."

I grimace. "He has the charm of a wet bus seat. Thanks for that mental image, by the way."

"Said the girl who's memorized every Wikipedia page on every serial killer."

"We both know that Arliss pooping is a way grosser thought than any torture murder."

"Hey, not to change this terrific subject, but next Saturday, you wanna go with me to see Lawson kick people in the face?" Josie gets in and starts the ignition.

"What time?"

"I don't know. Nighttime. Fightin' time. Nighttime is the right time for fight time."

"What about show prep?"

"Can you do it earlier in the day?"

"I'm working."

"What about another night?" Josie looks over her shoulder and backs out of her parking space.

"We always do it Saturday nights."

"Don't you think it sounds kinda fun to go see a cage fight?"

I shrug and try to appear noncommittal.

"You love the bizarre, and I *know* you will sit through literally anything," Josie says. "This'll be like the show *Spartacus* but with fewer dongs." She pauses. "Probably."

"Do you say '*fewer* dongs' or '*less* dongs'?"

"I think 'fewer' is correct."

"I can never keep it straight," I say.

"Are we still talking about dongs or—"

"Whether it's 'less' or 'fewer' that's correct."

"Ah. Anyway, I bet you'll love the cage fight."

"I don't love anything as much as Lawson loves you."

"Trying to change the subject," Josie says in a singsong voice.

"*Whatever.* We were just talking about whether it's more correct to say 'fewer dongs' or 'less dongs.' That's not a subject that's off-limits to change. Besides, I'm not wrong about Lawson."

"You are in fact not wrong."

"It's pretty adorable how he looks at you."

"It kind of is. Now enough changing the subject."

I sigh loudly. "I'll go. Fine."

"I mean, he's so sweet and goofy, I want to see if he's a kind and gentle kickboxer."

I check my phone. "Can I bring my mom to the fight and sign us up for a round?"

"Uh-oh."

"Yeah, uh-oh. I called a little while ago to see if she wants me to bring home dinner and she's in bed, which is sort of a problem because she's not really supposed to be *in bed* so much as she's supposed to be *at work.*"

"I'm no expert in what constitutes good performance at your mom's job, and yet I feel comfortable saying that that's probably not considered good performance."

"Sure, sure, yeah, no. Nope."

"It's probably actually considered bad performance."

"I think that is a fair characterization of being in bed when one is supposed to be at work."

"Your mom is a trip. I mean . . ."

"I have been *begging* her to get back on her meds because she's a manageable level of flaky when she's on them. She can function." The air in Josie's car is stagnant, so I roll down my window. The breeze that blows in is humid but cool and green-smelling, in that hopeful way of spring. It almost feels like it's mocking me with its cheery, verdant optimism.

"Do you need me to help you hold her down and force-feed her? I legit will."

"How about if she loses her job and we become homeless, you let me come live under your bed in your dorm at UT Martin?"

"What about her?"

"She can do whatever. I don't care," I mutter.

"You don't mean that."

"It gets exhausting mothering my mother."

"I hear you," Josie says. "But let me just say that having a mother who is *always* a mother is overrated."

"Trade you."

"I totally would. Remember how after you found out Devin had hooked up with Kylie Miller, she let you stay home from school, forged a doctor's note, made you fried cheesecake bites, and rented *The Room* to cheer you up?"

The memory makes me smile in spite of myself. "Remember how she accidentally put windshield washer fluid where the oil is supposed to go in our car and made the engine melt so we had to eat peanut butter sandwiches for dinner for a month and a half?"

"Remember when Principal Ward brought your mom in for a parent meeting after you got caught ditching too many times and she called him Principal Wardhog to his face?"

"Remember when she tried to pet a possum that had gotten under our porch?"

"Your mom isn't perfect, but she's pretty great."

"It's different when you have to live it," I say.

"She's always in your corner."

"Let's change the subject." Josie's right, and it's making me sad coming up with arguments against my mom's awesomeness. Venting about her to Josie allows me to let it go and also enables me to see my mom's good side again.

"Fair enough," Josie says. "Wanna stop at Books-A-Million on the way home?"

"I wish, but I gotta get home and ride my mom's ass."

We drive in silence for a while.

"You rocked tonight, by the way," Josie says.

"I practiced my lines at work and did some vocal warm-ups before you picked me up."

My heart revs with a quick surge of excitement. It feels like the kind where you're sitting there and out of nowhere, this rogue wave of contentment and joy washes over you. Maybe it's connected to something you're looking forward to that day. A package. A three-day weekend. A movie. A reassurance. It's always something small. And the wave is gone as soon as it comes, but in that moment, it's glorious. Like maybe *everything* will be okay. For a second it washes away every care and your heart is clean before the worries come flooding back.

"Look at *you*. Upping the game for Jack Divine!" Josie says.

"Pretty much. And for us. Upping the game in general."

We stop at a red light, and Josie looks deep in thought.

"What?" I ask.

"What what?"

"You have your obviously-thinking-about-something look."

She waves it off. "I've been formulating a theory."

"Tell me."

"I'm not sure it's ready for sharing."

"You do realize we were *literally* just exposing a bunch of people to *Werewolf in a Girls' Dormitory*, right? Like, the ship of only sharing things that are ready for sharing has *sailed*."

"So my theory is that all men have either a fox face or a tiger face."

"A fox face or . . ."

"For example, Benedict Cumberbatch—fox face. Ryan Gosling—fox face. Channing Tatum—tiger face. Idris Elba—tiger face."

I nod slowly, testing the theory in my head. "So it's not just good-looking guys get tiger and ugly guys get fox."

"No. Foxes are cute. But they have different faces from tigers."

"This theory is both amazing and completely useless."

"There's some very important work going on in this car. We are advancing science here," Josie says.

"Okay, Lawson?" It might be my imagination, but Josie's face turns rosy.

"I don't know," she says.

"Oh, really?"

"Haven't thought about it."

"Not even a little? As you were formulating the theory?"

Josie sort of shrugs and gives a *why should I have been thinking about the guy who clearly adores me* frown. "I guess I'd say . . . tiger," she murmurs. "Yeah. Tiger."

"*Yeah. Tiger,*" I say in a gauzy, dreamy voice.

"That is *not* how I talk."

"It so is. Lawson and Josie, sittin' in a tree—"

"Oh yeah? Well, Delia and the Idiot Twins, sittin' in a tree—"

125

"K-i-s-s-i-n-g," I sing.

"S-u-c-k-i-n-g," Josie sings over me.

We both crumble into laughter and we're barely able to catch our breath before we get to my dark and empty house.

. . .

Jack Divine's website looks super homemade. I don't love that, but hey, our website is a free homemade WordPress site, so we can't talk. Plus, there are all sorts of stories about people in showbiz who hate technology. I read somewhere that Jack White doesn't have a cell phone. It's fine. It probably would have intimidated me if Jack Divine's website was *too* good. I like that he's okay with unpolished things. I poke around until I find a contact email address.

Dear Mr. Divine:

I have to breathe through a jolt of adrenaline that feels like leaning up against a hot car. I start typing again after it subsides.

My name is Delia Wilkes. My friend Josie Howard and I host a show called *Midnite Matinee* on TV Six, the public access station in Jackson, Tennessee. We show old horror and sci-fi movies like you did when you were doing *Jack-O-Lantern's Fright-Day Night Revue*. We're already syndicated in seven other markets, and we haven't even been on the air for two years.

We're huge fans of yours. I grew up watching

your show with my dad. Josie and I are going to be at ShiverCon next month, and we were hoping we could meet you.

This is stupid. You're nobodies, says the cartoon devil Delia that appears on my shoulder. *This is how you make the show good enough that Josie won't leave,* says the cartoon angel Delia that appears on my other shoulder. *This is how you keep the best thing in your life going and make it better. This is how you don't get left behind.*

We'd maybe like to talk to you about possibly working together.

I delete the line. I try again.

We'd like to talk to you about working together.

It feels so presumptuous. But I don't want to sound too tentative either. I start to delete it but change my mind, mainly because I have nothing better to replace it with. *This sucks.*

Here are a couple of links to YouTube videos showing clips of our show. We know we have room to improve, but we feel that we need someone with the experience to help take the show to the next level and reach more markets.

The clips aren't my favorite and each only has about 350 views, but I don't know how to capture better clips from the show. At least these are convenient.

If you're interested in seeing more, please send me an address and I can send you a DVD with a couple of episodes of the show.

Sincerely,
Delia Wilkes (aka Delilah Darkwood)

I hold my breath for a beat or two before letting it out in a rush and hitting send. *Don't get your hopes up*, I tell myself. *Nobody with a website that janky checks email very often.* It feels very strange to be sending a message to someone I used to watch on TV with Dad. Sorry, I mean *Derek Armstrong*.

Me, to Josie: Ok, I emailed Jack Divine. Fingers crossed.

Josie: Cool. What did you say?

Me: We were big fans and wanted to meet him at ShiverCon. Sent him a couple of YouTube clips. Asked if we could send him a DVD with episodes.

Josie: Nice. Sounds like you weren't too weird.

Me: Nope. Now you gotta ask your parents about ShiverCon.

Josie: I will. What if Divine says no?

Well, Josie, if he says no, I still need to go and track down one Derek Armstrong, so . . .

Me: I think we should still go. Maybe someone else there can help us.

Josie: If we don't know if he's going to help us, I'd rather visit my aunt.

Me: But I really wanna go and I can't afford to if you don't drive. I don't have money for a plane ticket or whatever.

Josie: DeeeeeeeeDeeeeeeeee.

Me: If you want a career in TV we gotta start doing stuff like this.

Josie: I mean, let's feel out the vibe.

Me: I never know exactly what it means when you say that.

Josie: It means there's maybe a vibe, and we're going to feel it out.

Me: Ok it seems like you're literally just saying words when you say that.

Josie: It's hard to define.

Me: I noticed. BTW Jack Divine's website is hilariously low rent.

Josie: Uh-oh.

Me: I think it's fine? It kinda makes him seem more legit in a weird way?

Josie: If you say so. K, I gotta go eat. Love you, DeeDeeBooBoo.

Me: Ask about ShiverCon. Love you, JoJoBee.

• • •

I turn on the TV and idly drift until I land on a half-finished showing of *Jason X* on the Syfy channel. I've seen it a couple of times, but I can't resist. It's like *Alien*, if *Alien* were written on an Arby's napkin in a Camaro doing donuts in a parking lot.

I have a gray uncentered feeling of unease. Like when you know you've forgotten something important, but you can't remember what it was. And you try to tell yourself that it must not have been that important if you forgot it, but you can't quite persuade yourself. I keep checking my phone, as though Jack Divine is going to answer an email from a random high school girl on a Friday night—or at all.

And then my brain makes a connection. Emailing Jack Divine reminded me of my dad. And if I'm brave enough to randomly email Jack Divine, then I'm brave enough to randomly email my dad. Maybe.

Dear Dad,

I didn't know whether I should call you Dad or Derek Armstrong the first time I tried to email you. Of course, I never had to decide because I chickened out and didn't send it. This time I'm calling you Dad whether you like it or not. You're still my dad, no matter how much you don't want to be anymore.

In my first email, I told you about the stuff that's going on in my life, but I'm not sure I feel like telling you all that yet. I don't want the good stuff in my life to make you feel any less guilt (if you even feel any) for leaving. Instead, I'm going to tell you about my first birthday after you left.

A little while ago, I was thinking about my last birthday with you here. It was one of the best days of my life. My first birthday after you left? Not so much. It was pretty thrown together. We had it at Chuck E. Cheese's. Mom was doing really bad then, and we got invites out at the last minute. We invited seven kids from my class, but only two came. I remember I cried later because I was humiliated. Mom looked so exhausted, I told my friends she had the flu. I was embarrassed by that too, even though now I know she was doing the best she could. I tried to have fun and laugh and play the games, but all I could think about was how empty and sad my life felt. I could tell it was super obvious to my friends. We got home, and Mom locked herself in her bedroom. I sat in the living room with my two presents and wondered if I would ever be happy again.

But I'm happy now. Mostly. I have some good things in my life. My best friend Josie and I are horror hosts on our own show on TV Six here. It's called *Midnite Matinee*. We're already in seven markets outside

Jackson. I promised myself I wasn't going to tell you the good things in my life, but I can't help it. I'm too proud.

I don't expect you to ever respond to this. In fact, I'm not even sure I'm going to send it. The more I type, the less I feel like it. I guess if you're reading this, I decided to send it. But here's a promise: one day I'm going to show up in your life and make you look me in the eye and tell me why you left. You owe me that, at least.

Your daughter,
Delia

Delete.
Cry.

Josie

Me: How tall does someone have to be before they have to explain to people why they're not a basketball player?

Lawson: I don't know. Why?

Me: Because after I dropped Delia off, I saw someone who was at least 6'8" but he didn't look at all like a basketball player.

Lawson: If I saw someone who was 6'8" I would definitely wonder why they didn't play basketball if they didn't.

Me: It would suck to be 6'8" and really want to be an accountant or something.

Lawson: It might be an advantage for making really tall spreadsheets.

Me: Haha.

Dad is giving me the look, so I slip my phone under my leg and take another bite of lasagna. Lawson has just passed the Random Josie Observations test. To pass this test, you must never, ever question the validity of one of my random observations but only engage with it on its own terms. This was a crucial test for Lawson to have aced if he wanted to be my friend. My phone buzzes under my leg, and I sneak a quick peek.

Lawson: It was really nice to see you tonight. That always makes me happy.

I appreciate his profound lack of chill about me. It's flattering.

"Josie's checking her phone," Alexis says.

Dad renews the look. "Josie."

I kick Alexis under the table. "Dude, seriously. You're basically a stack of rats standing on each other's shoulders and wearing a hoodie and sweatpants."

She mewls in protest (sounding not unlike a stepped-on rat, if I'm being honest).

"We've warned you several times specifically about comparing Alexis to a stack of rats in human clothing," Mom says.

"Well."

"Well nothing," Mom says. "You know Alexis finds that upsetting."

"I wouldn't need to do it if she weren't such a snitch."

Dad points with his fork and talks with his mouth full. "She wouldn't need to snitch if you didn't do stuff for her to snitch about."

"That's victim-blaming," I say.

Mom snorts. "Please."

Silence passes, punctuated by the scraping of forks on plates. Alexis, blessedly, asks to be excused and leaves; we squint at each other as she goes, and I mouth, *Eat me.*

Dad leans back in his chair. "So how was filming tonight?"

"Good. That guy Lawson you met last week helped us again."

"What did he do?"

"Broke a bunch of boards. He's way good at Tae Kwon Do."

More silence, the scraping of forks on plates. My dad starts to push back from the table, and I suddenly realize I have a golden opportunity. My parents are full and seem reasonably content, my fight with Alexis has probably subsided in their minds, and she isn't around.

"Hey, so, question," I say nonchalantly. *No big deal, Mom-bro and Dad-bro, just chillin' here.*

My parents fix their gazes on me.

"Remember what I was telling you about ShiverCon? How Delia and I thought it would be a good idea to go?"

"That's the thing happening the weekend of our family trip to visit Aunt Cassie, right?" Mom asks, a suspicious timbre in her voice.

"Yeah . . . so, Delia and I have been talking and we really, really think we need to go down there and try to meet this TV producer. And . . . network."

Dad leans forward. "Who will then . . ."

"Get our show to a wider audience. Hopefully."

"And what makes you think he'll be able to do that?" my mom asks.

"I mean, he was a big-time producer in the nineties. Like for the kind of show we do."

"The nineties were before you were born," Mom says. "I'm not a showbiz expert, but that strikes me as a long time."

"People have comebacks."

Dad gets up, goes to the fridge, and gets a Diet Coke. "How do you know he's even interested in a comeback?"

"He's going to be speaking at ShiverCon. They probably wouldn't have invited him if he weren't still important in that world. And he probably wouldn't do it if he weren't still interested in show business."

"People do stuff for lots of reasons," Dad says.

"But more to the point," Mom says, "this was going to be our last family vacation before you went to college. Once you get to college, things'll be different."

"Not *that* different." I slump in my chair and fiddle with my fork. Buford sidles up to me with a jingle of tags, his sad eyes hopeful for some scraps. I scratch him behind the ears.

"We want you to come with us on this trip," Dad says.

"And I *want* to come, but this is a great opportunity for us."

"You already have a great prospect with that internship at Food Network," Mom says. "Have I mentioned that Tamara created the slot especially for you? It's not even part of the normal internship program. That's the only reason you haven't missed out on the chance already."

I faux-gasp. "*What?!* You hadn't mentioned that already like fifteen times."

"No need to be cute, Jo," Dad says. "We're having a grown-up conversation here."

I sit up straight again, sensing an opening. "Isn't part of being a grown-up doing things on your own? This internship offer is something that *you* got for me. I want to find my way in life for myself. I want to *earn* what I get." I work to keep from smiling as I see this land on my parents. I pull Buford's face to mine and give him a kiss. "Yes, we do, don't we, Bufie Bear? We like to earn what we get!"

My parents fidget and trade quick *well, this IS how we raised her* looks.

"Is this even what you really want?" Dad asks. "To keep doing this show, but on a higher level?"

"Yes!" I know it's key that I sell this part and I try, but I break eye contact at the last second.

Mom seeks my eyes. "Jo."

"What? I want to be on TV. I have since I was little. And now I have a chance to do it with something *I* helped create."

Mom and Dad say nothing.

I fill the silence. "This is *my* future. Why can't I be, like, the author of my own destiny?"

"Where is this conference again?" Dad asks.

"Florida. Orlando."

Dad drums his fingers on the tabletop. "You're planning on getting down there how?"

"Drive."

"Staying where?" Mom asks.

"A hotel. Near the conference center."

"I assume all of this costs money?" Dad asks.

I shrug and nod.

"Hundreds of dollars," Dad says.

"That you don't have," Mom adds.

I look up at them with pleading eyes. "I have some money saved up. My birthday money."

They frown and stare.

"Delia's going to be splitting the costs with me."

Dad slurps at his Diet Coke and stifles a belch. "You want us to let you blow your savings for the privilege of skipping out on the family trip we want you to go on?"

"It sounds bad when you say it like that," I say. "More like pay hundreds of dollars so I have a chance to make a career out of something I helped create."

More frowns. More stares.

I return their gazes with the sweetest, most imploring one I can muster. "I've been *so* good in high school. Instead of, like, smoking pot and hooking up, I've been spending Friday and Saturday nights working on this show. That should count for something."

Mom and Dad each draw a long contemplative breath through their nose. Finally, Mom speaks. "What's the plan for the show if this producer can't or won't help you?"

"We keep doing it and look for the next chance to take it up a notch."

"Your dad and I need to talk about this, but if we say yes, we're going to want something in return."

"Okay."

"If it doesn't work out with this producer, you have to promise you'll give the Food Network internship a shot."

"Mom." My heart plummets and starts racing simultaneously. "I'm eighteen."

"You are eighteen. And we're paying for your college and insurance, so think hard about how independent you really want to be."

"We don't want you putting all your eggs in one basket," Dad says.

I think about Delia. She'll die if I make this promise. But she'll die if I don't go. I get really envious sometimes of disloyal people. I bet life is easier when you don't have to worry about emotional attachments.

I slump in my chair and look at the floor. "Eggs in one basket. That's such a dumb phrase. It only works in a world where all the chickens have gone extinct and you can't just, you know, go get some more eggs and everything's fine."

My parents wait, knowing I'm stalling.

"And what would even make chickens go extinct? Foxes couldn't do it all. Even if they teamed up with the coyotes. Like a fox-coyote alliance. It'd have to be some gross chicken disease. Like chicken Ebola or something. And then do you even want to eat those eggs? That's the question you gotta ask yourself."

Judging from my parents' stony expressions, I'm absolutely slaying with this bit. I know I'm being muscled, but I'm conflicted enough that I don't have the fight in me that I otherwise would.

"Okay, fine," I say quietly. A cold stab of remorse pierces me in the solar plexus. I'm selling out Delia. Maybe. *But if I didn't make this promise, my parents would lean on me not to go, so I'm actually a really good friend, right? This is what Delia would want, right?*

"You promise?" Dad asks.

"Yes. That's what 'okay, fine' means." I scratch Buford's tummy vigorously and speak right in his face. "Doesn't it? Doesn't it, Bufie Beans? Who's a good boy? Who knows what 'okay, fine' means? *You do.*" He winces and tries to leave, but I grab him in a hug with one arm and keep scratching his belly.

"We're trying to support you, Jo. We're not pushing you to go to law school or become a computer programmer. But we want you to chase your dreams in the most effective way," Dad says.

I stop scratching Buford and let him hobble away. I stare at the table and listen to the distant bright chitter of Alexis talking with her friends. *I'm sure Delia would love knowing that she's considered an inconvenience to the realization of my dreams.*

I feel like I've just signed a deal with a benevolent devil who paid for my braces and who's paying for my car insurance and health insurance and college.

I ambush Buford on my way back to my bedroom. I give him a huge hug, from which he struggles to free himself, and I say, "Who's the worst friend, Bufie Buns? Huh? *Who is the worst friend to Auntie Delia?* Is it me? It's me!" He looks at me evenly with his sad, brown, judgmental eyes. "Oh, whatever," I say. "Like you're a perfect friend. Remember the time you betrayed me by pooping on the stairs and I slipped in it with my bare feet and fell down and twisted my ankle and had to go to the ER? Yeah, I think you do remember. The truth hurts. The truth hurts."

He just looks at me.

. . .

Me: Ok, talked with the parents. ShiverCon is happening.

Delia: !!!!!!!!!!!!!!!!!!!!!!!!!!!!! Were they chill about it?

Me: SUPER CHILL. They were like "do whatever, brah." Chill is their personal brand.

Delia: Wait really???

Me: Please, are you kidding?

Delia: Haha I don't know.

Me: You really do actually kinda know at this point.

Delia: Ok fine. Wanna hear something hilarious?

Me: I like how you still give me the opportunity to say "no, I hate hilarious stuff."

Delia: I still haven't asked my mom if I can go.

Me: OH. HILARIOUS THAT YOU RODE MY ASS REPEATEDLY FOR SOMETHING YOU DIDN'T DO YOURSELF. You are SUCH a butthole.

Delia: IKR??? She's going to say yes.

Me: YOU DON'T KNOW THAT.

Delia: I really do actually kinda know at this point.

Me: What are you doing right now?

Delia: Just got done watching Jason X on Syfy.

Me: Haha that movie is like Alien for dumb people.

Delia: OK I WAS LITERALLY THINKING ALMOST THAT EXACT THING.

Me: GTFO!

Delia: SWEAR.

Me: We should, like, do a TV show together.

Delia: Ha, K.

Me: What if Jack Divine makes things happen for us? What if we blow up and become rich?

Delia: I would buy an old-timey motorcycle and sidecar and have a trained chimpanzee sidekick ride around with me everywhere.

Me: And he's wearing goggles???

Delia: We both are. And he's smoking a pipe and wearing a tuxedo.

Me: AMAZING.

Delia: Your turn.

Me: I'm gonna pull out a stack of twenties and make it rain in super inappropriate places, like elevators and public restrooms.

Delia: Nice. I won't let money change me.

Me: Me neither. I'll be the same person I've always been: someone who intends to become absolutely horrible at the first hint of money and fame.

Delia: Hahahahahahahahahahaha. I'd buy my mom a nicer house than our dumpy trailer for sure.

Me: I'd pay for Alexis's college, but the catch would be that I get to choose where she goes. So enjoy your Bible college in Arkansas or whatever.

Delia: We should do something nice for Arliss.

Me: Let's hire two 18-year-old girls for him to grump at all the time.

Delia: He's gonna miss us.

Me: I would.

Delia: I'll miss him.

Me: Same.

Delia: BTW when I typed "Arliss" just now, it autocorrected to "Ass IRL."

Me: This world is filled with truth and beauty and magic.

· · ·

I'm catching up on my shows, but I keep zoning out. I thought texting with Delia would help with the restlessness and anxiety from my negotiation with my parents, but it didn't. It actually kinda made me feel worse.

Take two.

Me: What are you doing?

Lawson: Staring at a tall, cool protein shake. Working up the will to drink it.

Me: Mmmmmmmmmm. Stop making me jealous.

Lawson: Yeah, I'm trying to pretend it's a milkshake.

Me: I think milkshakes are weird.

Lawson: Please don't say you hate milkshakes too.

Me: No, but it's weird drinking melted ice cream with a hamburger. Admit it. If it was called a large melted ice cream, people wouldn't get them.

Lawson: You had to mention a hamburger. Making weight is super fun.

Me: What's making weight?

Lawson: To be able to fight in my weight class, I have to come in under a certain limit. I'm a welterweight, so max 170 pounds.

Me: I assume they check and they don't just have a mean person look at you and tell you it looks like you've put on weight.

Lawson: Yep, before the fight we have a weigh-in to officially confirm.

Me: So no pancakes for you.

Lawson: Haha, nope.

Me: Too bad because I'm sitting in bed right now eating a giant stack of them.

Lawson: Oh yeah?

Me: Giant. Like 16 pancakes. Smeared with butter and sticky fake maple syrup. I'm eating them with my hands and wiping my hands on my sheets. I'm gonna roll around in them when I'm done.

Lawson: Hahaha stop.

Me: NEVER. I CAN'T GET ENOUGH OF THIS DELICIOUS SWEET FLOURY PASTE IN MY MOUTH. MMMMMMMM BABY.

Lawson: I'm actually pretty grateful that you're grossing me out right now.

Me: I know. So assuming you make weight or whatever, what am I looking for at this fight of yours?

Lawson: I'm gonna try to hit the other guy until he's knocked out, or the ref or ring doctor stops the fight. Or try to submit him, which is where you get him in a jujitsu hold so he taps out. And I'm going to try to avoid any of those things happening to me.

Me: Can you try to make him tap out with emotional pain? Get him down and whisper that he'll never impress his mother? That his friends consider him ridiculous?

Lawson: LOL. Oh, and if neither fighter gets knocked out or submitted, it goes to a decision from the judges, who award points. The only thing worse than winning by decision is losing by decision.

Me: Who are you fighting on Saturday?

Lawson: Kody "Hollywood" Clemmons.

Me: Hang on, where is Hollywood Clemmons from?

Lawson: Dyersburg, Tennessee.

Me: Oh, so pretty much Hollywood. What's your fighting nickname?

Lawson: Don't have one.

Me: Too bad "Hollywood" is taken because you've been on TV like twice now.

Lawson: True.

Me: Lawson "Lawman" Vargas.

Lawson: Hahahahaha no way.

Me: Lawson "Lost in Translation" Vargas.

Lawson: That one doesn't even make sense.

Me: Because "Lawson" sounds like "Lost in" and I love the movie Lost in Translation.

Lawson: Haven't seen that.

Me: WHAT. FIX THAT.

Lawson: I'll only watch it with you.

Me: Fine, Lawson "The Punchin' Pancake" Vargas.

Lawson: No.

Me: Lawson "The Beaglemaster" Vargas.

Lawson: We need to get to know each other better so you have more material for names.

This is a perfect place to leave him hanging. I'm feeling a lot better. I start to get back into my show, but this weird impulse compels me to see if there are any of Lawson's fights on YouTube. There's only one, and it has twenty-seven views. He looks a lot younger. The fight isn't super interesting. A lot of circling around each other, cautiously punching and kicking. I guess looking for holes in the other's defense. An opening. His opponent is bigger than him.

For a while, they grub around on the ground. I think the official term is "wrasslin'." Lawson looks like he's losing. Then, suddenly, they're a tangle of frantically wriggling arms and legs. Lawson emerges from the tangle, pulling his opponent's arm between his legs, which are over his opponent's chest, pinning him down. A couple of seconds like that and suddenly Lawson jumps up and starts running circles around the ring, arms outstretched in victory. His opponent kneels, head bowed, looking dejected. Lawson runs to the side of the cage thingy they're fighting in, pulls himself to the top, and starts high-fiving and hugging three guys who look like they could be his older brothers.

He drops back down and hugs his now-standing opponent and whispers something in his ear. They pat each other on the back and head and shake hands as best they can with gloves on. Then the referee announces Lawson as the winner and raises his arm high. Lawson's face is incandescent with joy, beaming, triumphant.

I watch the video a few more times because it's something to do, and also he does have a very nice face.

Delia

"Hang on, you actually *told* Royce Kiser that that dream meant he was terrified of impotence? You didn't just think it in your mind?"

My mom pulls open the glass door of the Goodwill. "What was I supposed to do? Lie?"

"Royce Kiser, who parades around downtown in cargo shorts and camo Crocs, carrying an assault rifle and one of those huge yellow flags with the snake that says 'I hate Mondays' or whatever?"

" 'Don't Tread on Me.' "

"What?"

"That's what's on the snake flag."

"Oh, I thought you were literally saying not to tread on you, and I'm like, 'Fine, I won't.' How'd he react?"

"Guess."

"Badly."

"It's like you inherited my gift of vision."

"Royce's always carrying that gun around probably helped your diagnosis."

Eau de discarded treasures fills our nostrils. It's my favorite smell that's not, strictly speaking, terrific or pleasant. "I wonder what makes thrift-store smell. Like chemically."

Mom shrugs and pulls out a blouse, studying it for rips and stains. "Mold? Bacteria?"

You'd think our acknowledgment of thrifted items possibly being saturated with mold and bacteria would put us off, but you would be wrong. Thrifting is Mom's and my holiest sacrament, along with watching horror movies and going to chain restaurants and ordering only more appetizers than we can eat. Our love for thrifting is greater than any microorganism. Our work schedules and school make it tough for us to go, but we were both free and clear tonight. And bonus, Mom is having one of her good days.

I nod at the blouse. "What do you think?"

"Eh. Too similar to one I have."

"Shame they can't figure out how to infuse good smells with the persistence of thrift-store funk," I say, pressing a dress sleeve to my nose.

"You mean if they could separate out the thrift-store mold or bacteria and hand it some pumpkin spice smell and go, 'Here, hold this instead.'"

"We can put a man on the moon, right?"

"Actually, I was listening to the news the other day on my way to work, and they said America can't put people into space anymore."

"Really?"

"Yeah, apparently the Russians have all the rocket ships."

"That's weirdly depressing."

"I know."

"I mean, I wasn't super invested in, like, my country's ability to put people on the moon, but still."

"It sounds like we need to make up for it by producing synthetic thrift-store mung that smells good."

"Oh my lord, did you just say 'mung'?"

"I did."

"Mom. That is so gross."

"You deserve it for all the times you've grossed me out, Miss Never-Heard-a-Disgusting-Nature-Fact-She-Could-Keep-to-Herself."

"Did I ever show you that YouTube video of how much slime a hagfish can make?"

"No."

"Remind me to show you."

"You know what? I am totally fine never seeing it."

We drift through the store, aimless like vultures hoping to glide into the scent of some new roadkill. After Dad left, this is where we brought everything he left behind. His movies were all we kept. I wanted to hang on to some of his old clothes that still had his smell on them, but Mom said that would only make things worse. I think she was right.

I see a promising pair of pants, pull them out, and look at the tag. I wrinkle my nose and mutter, "Old Navy."

"They always fool you. Their stuff looks good at a thrift shop."

"Thrift stores should be called Older Navy at this point."

"Why bother? Pay three-ninety-nine at the thrift store for something that cost five-ninety-nine at Old Navy."

I pull out a red sundress. "Hey! This might be a cute graduation dress."

Mom gives me a look.

"What?"

"My daughter is not graduating from high school in a thrift-store dress."

"I went to high school in thrift-store clothes."

"Exactly."

"I never minded."

"I'm not letting my only daughter get married in a used dress, and I'm not letting you graduate in a used dress."

I smile, glad for the pushback. Mom never has the energy for it when she's down. I hope she's back on her meds and they've started working again. "I'm still hanging on to the dress."

"Knock yourself out."

"For a while there I didn't think I would finish high school."

"Why do you think I'm being such a hard-ass about this? I just had an idea, actually."

"Spill."

"We should get tattoos together to celebrate your graduation."

"Seriously?"

"Why not? You're eighteen now."

"What should we get?" I've been fascinated with Mom's tattoos ever since I was little. I used to draw on my arms in washable marker to be like her. She has a skeleton key on her left wrist, my name on her right wrist, an Edward Gorey drawing on her right upper arm, with an Edgar Allan Poe quote underneath. Dad had tattoos too, but I liked Mom's better.

"Let's think about it. Something meaningful to both of us."

Another spark of life. Mom's good days are really good.

We drift out of the clothes into the home and kitchen section. Mom gasps and grabs an old-timey plate from a lower shelf. "DeeDee!"

It shows two kids fishing—a boy and a girl. Both have comically oversized heads and huge, vacant dead eyes. It looks like something a serial killer in a Russian prison would have painted.

"Okay, that is *upsetting*," I say.

"I *know*," Mom says gleefully.

"I'm so terrified by things that are supposed to be cute from the days when stuff only needed to be more cute than smallpox scars and dying of dysentery."

"We're obviously bringing this home with us."

"I mean, why wouldn't we want our house to look like the Sawyer house from *Texas Chain Saw Massacre*." My phone buzzes. I pull it out and glance at it. The hot metallic tang of adrenaline makes my heart feel like it jumped into a too-hot bath. "Holy balls," I murmur.

My phone almost slips from my grasp in my haste to open the email. I catch it from falling and pray I didn't accidentally delete it. I jam the dress I'm considering buying under my arm and read.

DEAR MISS WILKS

MR DIVINE THANKS YOUR FOR YOUR MESSAGE! HE IS A VERY, BUSY , MAN BECAUSE OF HOW MANY PEOPLE LOVE HIS WORK BUT HE IS WILLING TO MEET WITH YOU AT SHIVER-CON, TO TALK ABOUT YOU'RE SHOW . . . ,THIS IS HIS ASSISTANT AND MY NAME IS CELESTE ST. JAMES. I LOVE TO ANSWER HIS EMAIL'S..

I feel like I've gotten off a roller coaster. My heartbeat gallops in my ears. If the floor of the Goodwill weren't so covered in mung (thanks, Mom), I'd want to sit down and catch my breath. I don't necessarily love the jankiness of the email (like I didn't love Jack Divine's low-rent website), and his assistant's name sounds like the name of a porn star, but still. It's a positive response from Jack Divine.

"I think I could wear this with . . . DeeDee? Hey."

I glance over. Mom has meandered back to the clothes and is holding a short, black, lacy dress up to herself.

"Sorry, what?"

"Rude. Checking your phone while I'm talking to you."

"What were you saying?"

"Never mind."

"No, it's just that—do you remember *Jack-O-Lantern's Fright-Day Night Revue*?"

"Vaguely?"

"Dad and I watched it together."

"Okay."

"You remember SkeleTonya."

"I *loved* SkeleTonya. Still do." Mom scrutinizes the dress top to bottom.

"So anyway, the guy who was Jack-O-Lantern also produced and directed SkeleTonya's show. Guy named Jack Divine."

"That name sounds made up."

"Probably. Anyway, he's going to be at ShiverCon in Orlando at the end of May, and he wants to meet with Josie and me about the show."

"Your show?"

"Yes!"

Mom gasps. "This is huge, DeeDee!"

"I know! This could be a big break for us!"

"So obviously you're going to have to go down to Orlando."

"We'll take Josie's car."

"Will it make it?"

"I hope."

"I'd let you use ours, but I'll have to work, probably."

"Ours isn't in much better shape than Josie's."

"True. So I guess this trip won't be free?"

"No. Convention costs. Hotel costs. Gas. Food."

"We maybe ought to make that sundress your graduation dress after all."

"I told you I'm cool with that."

"And the tattoos might have to wait."

"I've managed all this time without one."

Mom smiles, squeezes my arm, pulls me close, and lays her head on my shoulder. She smells like Suave shampoo, rose essential oil, and grocery-store incense. "I'm so proud of you. You built this with your own two hands."

"I had a lot of help from Josie. I couldn't do it without her."

"Yes, you could."

"It wouldn't be as good."

"It'd be different, is all."

I keep flipping through things I've already looked at, excitement subsiding slowly to a manageable level, a low simmer. Mom meanders back toward the books and plates. I start to text Josie with the good news, but instead I stop and watch Mom. The sun is setting through the dusty plate-glass windows at the front of the store, making our little Temple of Discarded and Cast-Off Things glow golden. It's illuminating her face and hair like she was painted by an artist who is tired of never selling a painting and has resorted to painting things everyone loves.

I've always thought she was beautiful. Even when she was exhausted from crying, and not sleeping, or sleeping too much. Even when I knew she didn't feel beautiful, she was.

I wish I could see myself the way I see her. I have her nose. The curve of her full upper lip. Her muddy hazel eyes that she says are green but aren't. Her hair that's the right color of brown that it takes black or red dye well (and we both seesaw between each color).

I join her by the books and plates. "Mom?"

"DeeDee?"

"What do you want most out of life?"

Mom looks at me and laughs. "We just making small talk now?"

"I'm serious."

"I'll let you know if we see it here."

"Mom."

"What prompted this?"

"I'm thinking about what if I were in a position to give you anything you wanted."

Her lips purse in thought. "I guess . . . to be happy. That's all. Be with the people I love. Live a good life. Watch horror movies with my daughter. It'd be nice if it were a little easier to pay the bills while all that was going on. But happiness is what I want."

"I want you to have all of that. I'm going to give it to you if I make it big."

Mom puts her arm around me. "You're already doing a great job."

She smiles and I smile back, making a mental note to store this day away in my memory. It wasn't a perfect day, but it's worth hanging on to.

155

Josie

If the color neon green had a smell, it would be composed of the odor of nervous boys jacked up on adrenaline, beer, and industrial disinfectant. And that's exactly the scent hanging in the air of the main auditorium of the Carl Perkins Civic Center as Delia and I enter OCTAGON VALOR XTREME 16. (I added the XTREME part. It fit.) Testosterone fogs the large space, leaving an oily film on everything.

We immediately stick out for not wearing too-tight T-shirts with unimaginably ornate and bedazzled crucifixes, raptors, old-timey warrior helmets, swords, vaguely Japanese imagery, and skulls splayed across them like they were blasted there with a shotgun full of silver paint. Peppered in and around the images are words like ARMAGEDDON, VENGEANCE, VENOM, HONOR, and WARRIOR. They follow the design philosophy of "more is more." These T-shirts tend to be paired with jeans sporting entirely too much stitching on the back pockets. I wonder if that's so the wearer always has extra thread handy for the impromptu suturing of a fight wound.

Then there are the terrible tattoos snaking up arms: barbed wire loops around biceps, tiger and koi sleeves, pat inspirational sayings (THAT WHICH DOES NOT KILL YOU MAKES YOU

STRONGER; THE MORE YOU SWEAT IN PRACTICE, THE LESS YOU BLEED IN BATTLE), and ghoulish portraits of what I can only assume are children and deceased relatives.

"This is so goofy," Delia says, taking in the scene.

"It's as cheesy and weird so far as I was hoping it would be," I say.

"I can't believe Lawson thrives in this culture."

"I mean, I can. He seems really into honor and such."

"Is honor something you can be *into*?"

"Why not?"

"It sounds weird. *The knights were very into honor.*"

"Sounds fine to me."

Delia shrugs. "I guess. But it kinda sounds like the knights dabbled in honor."

"Like they would do some honor on the weekends?"

"You have an honor boat you take out on Sundays to go waterskiing."

As we make our way to seats as close to the octagon as we can find, I scan the crowd for the guys I saw in the YouTube video, who I thought were Lawson's brothers.

"I do kind of love this," Delia says. "I'm excited for the gratuitous violence we're about to witness."

"Oh, that's the part I thought you would like the best," I say.

"I'm really responding most of all to the general cheesiness."

We're not the only girls in attendance, but men heavily outnumber women. Our fellow attendees treat us with a mix of exaggerated chivalry—like we're maidens at a joust—and the expected catcalls. It's nicer than what I anticipated, which was only catcalls.

157

"Are you so excited to see Lawson fight?" Delia asks.

I'm careful to inject studied nonchalance into my voice, lest Delia get the wrong idea. "Yeah, it'll be cool. He does such great work with boards, it'll be exciting to see what he can do with a rib cage."

"I hear roundhouse kicks are doing *amazing* things with the human face these days."

"Speaking of, I'm gonna let him know we made it."

Me: Yo dude, we're here.

Lawson: You came!!!!

Me: I said I would, doofus!!!

Lawson: People don't always do stuff they say.

Me: I'm big on promises. Are you psyched?

Lawson: Little nervous. The guy I was gonna fight had to drop out with an injury, so they subbed in a new guy who's got a better record and might be harder to beat.

Me: Aww you'll do great.

I nearly say "I've seen you fight," but no need for that right now.

Lawson: I gotta go do some stretching and warm up. I'm glad you came! I'll look for you!

Me: Cool. We'll talk after? When you've won?

Lawson: For sure.

The fifty-something, pasty, wilted-corncob-looking guy sitting next to Delia has slipped in to engage her in conversation. Delia emits some pheromone that attracts weirdos. There was this dude at school who liked her, and she told him jokingly that she'd go to a dance with him if he'd pee his gym shorts on purpose during PE, and he did and got sent home. (She didn't go to the dance with him.)

"No," Delia says to the guy, who has a face even a mother would admit, in all candor, was not her best work, and whose gray goatee looks like a bedraggled mouse humping his chin. "I'm saying that if I were to eat something at any time of the day, I would eat it at breakfast. A salad is something I will not eat, no matter what time of day it is. Therefore, I will not eat it for breakfast. Pizza is something I will eat. Therefore, I'll eat it for breakfast." Delia casts a *rescue me* look in my direction.

"You and your friend can come to Buffalo Wild Wings with us after. Our treat," Corncob says, nodding at Delia and me and then back at his son (?) and/or friend (?), who looks like a sub sandwich that was dipped in Elmer's Glue and then propped up in front of a fan through which someone had tossed handfuls of hair clippings.

"We are literally in high school for like two more weeks," Delia says.

Corncob shrugs and gives a grunt that somehow says, *The only time I've ever willingly read something was to look up age-of-consent laws.*

"Also we're a super-specific kind of vegetarian where we don't eat any kind of animal's wings," I say. "No bird, bat, cockroach. No kind of wings."

"I ain't ever heard of that," Corncob says.

"Also we have to do some production work for our TV show after," Delia says with a delicious air of casual haughtiness.

"Y'all are on TV," Corncob says like he's the one telling us.

"Yep," Delia says.

"What's your show called?"

"Midnite Matinee."

"What's it about?"

"We show old horror and sci-fi movies."

Corncob shakes his head. "I don't believe you."

"Well, guess what?" Delia says. "We don't believe that you're really going to Buffalo Wild Wings."

"Yeah, you're not allowed in because the last time you were there you both got chicken bones stuck up your noses and they had to call nine-one-one because you kept blacking out from lack of oxygen," I say.

"One of you passed out from wing poisoning and your face landed in the ranch dressing trough and you almost died by ranch drowning," Delia says.

"No," Corncob says.

"Never happened," Hairy Sandwich says.

"Oh yeah? Prove it right now," I say.

"Right now. Do it, prove it," Delia says. "Photographic evidence."

"We go to Buffalo Wild Wings all the time. We ain't lying," Hairy Sandwich says.

"And yet you can't prove it," Delia says.

I can see her scanning the room for new seats. But it's pretty full. That's also the upside to this situation. There are so many people around, we don't even have to pretend to be nice to these two clowns.

"Also, FYI, both of you guys' tattoos look like they were done while you were sitting in a canoe," I say, praying in my heart for some deliverance from these thirsty idiots. And just like that, as if my will caused the universe to turn on its axis, a tuxedoed announcer makes his way to the middle of the octagon with a microphone. The lights go out, except for inside the cage. Spotlights sweep the room chaotically.

"Laaaaaaaaaaaadies aaaaaaaaaand uhhhhh gentlemen. Welcome to Ahhhhhhctagon uhhh Valorrrrrrrrrrr Sixteeeeeeeeeen." The crowd goes bonkers, hooting and hollering for blood.

"Toniiiiiiiiight's fights will consist of three five-minute rounds, which will be scored by our judges. And now, without further ado, lehhhhhhhhhhhhhhhht's ruhhhhhhhhhhhmble!"

Delia winces as Corncob and Hairy Sandwich stick pinkie fingers in their mouths and give piercing whistles and make what sound like hog calls.

The fights begin. We're into it ironically at first, but then start genuinely having fun trying to top each other yelling stuff. We get looks, but so what?

"Make him feel like every day is Monday!" Delia shouts.

"Embarrass him in front of everyone he's ever loved!" I shout.

"Dip your hands in his blood!" Delia shouts.

"Send him back to school to get his degree in computer science!" I shout.

"Show him how angry you are that stuff that's supposed to smell like green tea doesn't smell like green tea!" Delia shouts.

"Okay, that one was a stretch," I say.

Corncob and Sandwich, meanwhile, really bring the creativity with "Whup his ass!" "Beat his ass!" and to change things up, "Kick his butt!" And occasionally, "Git some! Hoo-whee!"

"Being here is making me realize that I like almost everything," Delia says.

I test her assertion in my mind. "Is that true? I'm trying to think of a thing you don't like, and I'm coming up empty. Hallmark movies?"

"Love them."

"Malls."

"Love. It's weird to me to be super resistant to things that are designed specifically to be liked. There are so many other ways to use your energy. Just enjoy stuff that's fun. And the mall is fun."

"Outlet malls."

"Love even more than normal malls."

"Okay, I give up. Wait!" I cast Corncob and Hairy Sandwich an obvious side-eye.

"Got me there."

There's a bizarrely exciting monotony to the fights. Plenty of circling each other, testing for openings, lots of what looks like cuddling on the ground, punctuated with jackhammer explosions of action. Delia's and my tolerance for sitting through badly plotted movies—which is what we'd otherwise be doing at this time on a Saturday night—serves us well.

Finally, the fight immediately before Lawson's ends with a submission.

"Lawson's up!" Delia says, as if I forgot.

I nod, watching the entrances where the fighters have been coming and leaving. My nerves are suddenly alive with jitters. I don't want to see him get hurt. I somehow put out of my mind that that was a possibility.

"What?" Delia asks.

162

"Nothing."

"You had a weird expression."

"No, I—Hey!"

The announcer has made his way to the middle of the octagon with his microphone. "Laaaaaaaadies and gentlemuhhhhhhn, we have come to our welterweight bout. In the red corner, at one hundred seventy pounds, with a record of nine and oh, fighting out of Memphis, Tennesseeeeeeeeee, Noooooooooooooah 'Niiiiiiiightmaaaaare' Puuuuuuuurdue."

A fighter in a hoodie with the hood up emerges to some terrible heavy metal that sounds like it was written for a U.S. Army commercial and makes his way toward the ring, punching and feinting. My heart sinks. He looks twice Lawson's size. Aren't they supposed to be the same weight? He whips off his hoodie and tosses it to his coach or whatever. He looks like he's made out of steak and veins draped over a sledgehammer. He's covered in creepy tattoos. I heard somewhere once that clowns are supposed to do their makeup with soft, rounded edges so as not to frighten kids (we can leave aside the question of whether that's ever successful). His ink is lots of spikes and teeth and blades and pointy things that look unwelcoming. Like the human version of a reptile that advertises its venomousness with garish colors. And speaking of, his hair and beard are dyed in blond and black streaks. He has the arrogant half smirk of someone who knows you're using the bathroom after him and leaves the toilet seat up on purpose.

I want Lawson to punch him in that smile for me.

Steak 'n' Veins does a slow lap around the ring, pumping his fists, punching the air.

"Aaaaaaaaaaaaaaaand in the blue corner, at one hundred

sixty-nine pounds, with a record of three and oh, fighting out of Jaaaaaaaaackson, Tennessee ... Laaaaaaaaaawson 'Lahhhhhhhhhhst in Translation' uh Vaaaaaaaaaaargas!"

I squeal involuntarily and turn to Delia.

Her face shines like she already knows. "Are you serious?!"

"I was *totally* joking when I suggested it to him."

"Hey, it's no dumber than any of the other fighter nicknames."

She's right. One of the fighters was nicknamed "Hot Dog." And if we're being honest, "Nightmare" is pretty on the nose.

"No Light" by Florence and the Machine starts booming through the arena. It makes my heart feel swoopy, like suddenly remembering on Thursday night that you have a three-day weekend.

I snap back to meet Delia's eyes again. "Okay."

"All right. But seriously."

"But seriously. I did *not* tell him to pick that."

"What*ever.*"

"There he is!" I stand. Delia stands with me.

Lawson emerges, doing a bouncing sort of strut, shaking out his arms. He's wearing a stiff, new-looking ball cap and a T-shirt—his clothing choices are peak Lawson, no attempts here to impress me. His face is pure titanium resolve.

I cup my hands to my mouth and shout, "Go, Lawson!"

It somehow catches his attention, and our eyes meet. He allows the hardness of his face to soften into the faintest hint of a fearless smile. He raises a gloved hand and points in my direction before bounding up into the ring, handing his hat to his coach (?), and whipping off his shirt.

He's bigger now than he was in the video I saw. Honestly,

164

I've never been super impressed by muscles; in fact, I find them sort of comical and eye-roll-y, like *Wow, I bet you're fascinating to talk to. Tell me more about creatine.* All of my past boyfriends have been either much more wiry or much more teddy-bear-like. But . . . he has a nice body.

"Lawson looks like he works out," Delia says, reading my mind.

"I gotta think it helps with the punching?"

"That one your boyfriend?" Corncob asks.

"My friend," I say. "But mostly none of your business."

"Nightmare's gonna beat his ass."

"Nightmare's gonna beat your face's ass," I say.

"That don't make no sense," Hairy Sandwich says.

"You know what doesn't make any sense? Literally your face. Your face does not make sense," Delia says.

Hairy Sandwich starts to gabble something.

"Hey, I know," I say. "Let's play the not-talking-to-each-other game. Let's see who wins that."

"We don't wanna talk with y'all. Y'all ain't as pretty as you think," Corncob says.

"Awesome, then you'll probably win," Delia says.

Lawson and Steak 'n' Veins, who's several inches taller than Lawson, square off, staring each other down. Neither blinks. Steak 'n' Veins eyes Lawson the way my mom eyes me when I track in mud. Lawson returns his caustic stare with yet more serene confidence. It's a nice look on him. Objectively speaking.

The ref finishes conferring with the two. A woman in Daisy Dukes and a neon-pink bikini top struts a lap around the ring, holding a sign with a "1" on it. Lawson puts up his gloves to touch gloves with Steak 'n' Veins the way the other fighters have

165

done. Steak 'n' Veins turns his back on the gesture. Even though I've seen very few fights, this seems like a clear dick move. Anger mixes with my surging adrenaline as the fighters circle each other warily. I'm suddenly petrified of seeing Lawson get hurt. I forget I'm still standing until Delia sits down beside me. I wipe my sweaty palms on my legs.

The fight begins. Steak 'n' Veins immediately comes on strong, attacking hard. But Lawson avoids his punches and returns a few of his own. Steak 'n' Veins charges at Lawson and narrowly avoids a high kick to the side of the head. He takes Lawson to the ground and gets on top of him, and they start that weirdly intimate tangled embracing the fighters do, throwing short punches and elbows at each other's heads and faces.

It's both thrilling and terrifying to see Lawson in his element. It's hard to watch, but at the same time, I can't look away. I'm trying to reconcile the goofy, sweet guy I've been on a sorta date with and the calculating warrior I'm watching.

Lawson slips out from under Steak 'n' Veins and jumps to his feet, and the two square off again. Lawson throws a kick and knocks him off-balance. He charges and forces Lawson to retreat with a flurry of punches. So on and so forth.

Time spills out like ketchup from a bottle, but the bell finally rings, ending the first round. The fighters go to their respective corners and get water and pep talks.

I've been clenching my fists for the last five minutes. I breathe and relax back into my seat. I feel like *I've* been fighting.

"You nervous for Lawson?" Delia asks.

"I mean, yeah, but he seems to be doing fine."

"I'm thoroughly enjoying this. We might have to start a

second show where we watch MMA fights and comment on them."

"If Jack Divine doesn't leave us too busy, I'm in." Cold guilt runs through me as I say it. I have the urge to confess the promise I made my parents, to get it off my chest. But now isn't the time—she's having too much fun. I would be too, were I not so worried about Lawson.

"I was mostly kidding," Delia says. "But a little bit not."

"Heard anything else from Jack Divine?"

"No. But I wasn't expecting to. We sort of left it at 'We'll talk at the con.'"

"Should we, like, try to get a firmer plan down for what we'll be talking about?"

"I'm afraid of bugging him. We probably don't want to come across as too needy."

The break ends, and Lawson and Steak 'n' Veins meet in the middle of the octagon again. My heart resumes its hurried patter.

"Put him away, Nightmare!" Hairy Sandwich yells.

"Knock his ass out!" Corncob yells.

"Go, Lawson!" I yell.

Maybe he heard me, because Lawson goes on the attack. Steak 'n' Veins absorbs the force of the assault, somehow remaining standing. He grapples his way behind Lawson and grabs him around the torso in a sort of bear hug. He leaps backward, taking Lawson with him, slamming Lawson's head and upper back onto the mat. The crowd goes *bonkers,* drowning out the sound of my involuntary gasp.

"*Suuuuuuuuuuuuuplex,*" Corncob hoots in Delia's face. "*Suuuuuuuuuuuuuplex, come git you some.*"

167

Her face puckers and she turns away, fanning in front of her nose. "Your breath seriously smells like you have a raccoon graveyard inside your body."

I wasn't in the mood for these clowns even before they were rubbing Lawson's getting hurt in my face. "Your breath smells like you ate a bowl of dog turds with a spoon made of cat turds," I snap.

He shrugs matter-of-factly. "I had some garlic bread from Little Caesar's in my truck and ate it before I came in."

"You just keep garlic bread in your truck?" Delia looks at him like he told her his favorite drink is warm milk with a handful of cat hair thrown in.

"It's truck bread. If I need a snack."

"Truck bread isn't a thing. That's gross. You're gross," Delia says.

"Joke's on you because it's delicious. Gets crunchy like chips."

I lean over to Corncob and hiss, "Shut up. You're making the arena stink. Shut up."

I turn my attention back to Lawson, who's back on his feet, visibly dazed and unsteady. He parries a flurry of blows from Steak 'n' Veins. My heart feels like it's under a board that someone is stacking books on. I'm so far forward in my seat, I'm barely sitting. My thighs are burning. "*Come on, come on, come on,* Lawson, come on," I murmur urgently, over and over.

Almost as if he can hear me, Lawson dodges a knee strike, takes a couple of steps backward, and delivers a ferocious kick directly to the side of Steak 'n' Veins' head. Steak 'n' Veins stumbles back and lands on his tailbone. The crowd's reaction is almost as explosive as after Steak 'n' Veins' suplex.

I jump out of my seat and scream, "Go, Lawson!" I turn to

Corncob and point in his face. *"Kick in the heeeeeeeeeaaaaaaaad.*
Kick in the heeeeeeeeeeaaaaaaaaad." I chant it a few more times,
Delia joining in.

Lawson tries to capitalize on Steak 'n' Veins' fall, but Steak
'n' Veins manages to tangle him up on the ground so he can't get
in a clean punch.

The second round ends, and the third round begins. Both
fighters are obviously tired. They spend a lot of time circling
each other, moving more slowly. During one of the grab-ass
interludes on the ground, Steak 'n' Veins catches Lawson over
the right eye with a lucky elbow, opening a cut. Blood starts
streaming down Lawson's face. The sight turns my stomach into
a balloon animal.

I don't know how he's doing this—down there, all alone,
injured, bleeding, fighting through the humiliation of being
slammed on the ground in a giant room filled with shouting
people. In front of me. After he invited me. He's made of something different from every other guy I've known in my life. He's
made of something solid and warm that feels nice to run your
hand over, like a wooden banister in an old building.

For the last few minutes of the fight, I sit completely still and
watch him the way you watch an animal you don't want to scare
off. It's like I'm worried any wrong move on my part will throw
him off for that split second and cause him to catch an unlucky
punch or kick.

"Hey," Delia whispers, startling me.

"Huh?" I keep my eyes fixed on the octagon.

"You're way pale."

"I can only handle the sight of blood when I know it's red
corn syrup."

169

"And also probably when it's not on your friend."

"That helps for sure."

The bell ending the match finally rings. Lawson moves toward Steak 'n' Veins to shake his hand, but Steak 'n' Veins turns his back and stalks to his corner. That guy is a serious nut sack, if you ask me.

This has been one of the longer fifteen-plus minutes of my life. I'm not sure how I feel. I don't regret coming—I know that much. I guess maybe it's like watching childbirth or something. You're not gonna be all *That was so fun to watch you suffer and see stuff that's supposed to be inside your body outside your body,* but you're glad you were there for them.

Lawson and Steak 'n' Veins stand in the middle of the ring with the referee between them, gripping each of their hands.

"Helluva fight," someone behind us says.

"Can't believe Nightmare couldn't seal the deal," Hairy Sandwich whines. "That's weak. Going to a decision."

"Laaaaaaaadies and gentlemen, we haaaaaave a decision from our judges. Judge Collins scores the fight thirty to twenty-nine for the red corner."

I can't remember who's what corner, but from Corncob and Hairy Sandwich's quick hisses of "Yes," I gather Steak 'n' Veins is red. Lawson's face is expressionless. No hint that he's bothered or worried. They cleaned the blood off his face and closed his cut when he went back to his corner after the fight ended.

"Judge Hamlin scores the fight thirty to twenty-nine for the blue corner."

A quick trumpet blast in my heart. I grab Delia's knee. "Come on, Lawson. Come on," I murmur.

"Aaaaaand Judge Patten scores the fight thirty to twenty-nine for the red corner. The winner! By split decision! Noooooooooooooah 'Niiiiiiiightmaaaaare' Puuuuuuuurdue!"

The ref lifts Steak 'n' Veins' arm skyward for a moment before Steak 'n' Veins breaks his grip and starts running laps around the octagon, pounding on his chest. He jumps up and straddles the top of the octagon wall, pointing at the crowd, face agloat. He's acting like he knocked Lawson out with one punch ten seconds into the fight, instead of winning by one point or something.

Hairy Sandwich and Corncob jump out of their seats and pump their fists like they themselves won a strenuous physical contest instead of sitting in chairs while failing in their gambit to get two high school girls to join them at a chain wing restaurant.

Lawson lifts his eyes over the faces of the crowd. I know he's not looking at anything in particular; he just doesn't want to look anywhere near the ground. Pain grays his face. He's clearly struggling to be brave in defeat, but it's obvious how much he's hurting. It's heartbreaking. It's like watching a hawk stumble along the ground with a broken wing. Not that I've actually seen that. But I can't imagine it's an inspiring sight.

Then I remember that my being here is probably making this ten times worse. Cold guilt seeps in like water when you accidentally step in a puddle in socks. It's exactly as pleasant a sensation too.

I watch him leave the octagon, walking without any of the verve with which he entered, trying to hold his head high while not looking anywhere near me.

I need to do something for him.

Delia

"He looks *bummed*," I say.

Josie nods, watching him exit.

"I'd be," I continue. "And, like, I super don't care about winning stuff."

Josie nods again, still not looking at me.

"So what should we—"

"I wanna try to say hi real quick," Josie says. "He looks like he needs a hug."

"You giving out hugs?" Hairy Sandwich asks.

He's barely landed on the *s* in *hugs* when Josie goes, "*Noooooooooo,* we are *not.*"

"Not even one of those hugs where we pat you on the back really hard so it's obvious we don't like you," I say.

"You're maaaad," Hairy Sandwich says in a singsong voice. "You're mad because your boyfriend lost."

Josie draws a quick breath through her nose. "Okay, one? Not my boyfriend. But whatever. Two? He has the balls to go in the ring and actually fight, while you two armchair warriors sit and watch. So between you guys? He *always* wins."

"I could take him," Corncob says.

"Nope. You could *not.* He would beat you up very, very badly and humiliate you," Josie says. "He would take your gross truck bread and stomp all over it."

I stand. "We saw Lawson. Let's go," I say to Josie.

Josie stands and says to Corncob and Hairy Sandwich, "Sitting next to you two is as fun as holding in a fart in class."

"Ain't supposed to hold in farts. Bad for your liver," Corncob says.

"That's not correct," I say.

" 'S my opinion."

Josie just stares at him for a second. "A. Not how opinions work," she says finally. "B. If you take nothing else from our brief encounter, let it be this: you *can* hold in farts. You can do it for a very long time, and it's fine. I'm no expert in human anatomy, but I know that the body's fart tubes are not connected to the liver. So, for the benefit of everyone who loves being around you, if any, please—hold them in."

And with that, we leave.

As much as I was genuinely enjoying myself (in spite of our neighbors), I was only really having fun while Josie was having fun.

• • •

In the corridor where we wait, we can hear the whoops and cheers of the final bout. I look at Josie and notice for the first time how *great* she looks tonight. She's absolutely nailed the *not trying to look good but accidentally looking really good except it's no accident* thing.

"This is where he's coming out?" I ask.

"That's what he said in the text," Josie says. "He'll be a sec, though. He said he's supposed to stay until the final fight is over."

"You sure he wants to see us?"

"No. But I want to see him."

She seems nervous and unsteady. I don't see her like that often.

So we wait. People mill around us. A roar from the arena inside as the final bout ends. A few minutes later, Lawson emerges, wearing his new clothes, carrying a duffel bag. His hair is wet. He walks slowly and with a slight limp. He holds his head high in the way of someone who's being trained in it, like he's been told to imagine a book balanced on top of his head. Butterfly bandages close the cut over his eye. A mustard-colored bruise blooms fresh on one of his cheekbones. He sees us and twists his mouth upward into a sort of thin, pained half smile. He looks like he wishes we weren't there.

Josie cocks her head and returns his half smile. "You were awesome," she says as he finally gets within earshot. It was a very long walk.

"Thanks," he says quietly, eyes to the floor. "Not awesome enough, I guess."

"Whatever, dude. Those judges are dumb." She steps forward and gives him a long, slow hug, obviously taking care not to hit any tender spots. He unenthusiastically accepts the hug with one arm, not setting down his bag.

"Super dumb," I say. "I thought you won."

He nods. Not in agreement, but in acknowledgment of what I said.

I don't know him well, but I've been around him enough to feel the warm, buoyant, good-natured energy he exudes. That's

174

all gone. There's a bare patch on the floor where it used to be, like after you move a refrigerator.

"Thanks for coming," he murmurs. "But I really wanted you to see me win."

"Aw. You're . . . still a winner in my book," Josie says, playing it totally straight.

Josie and I look away from each other because we both know that if we make eye contact after she laid down some Velveeta cheese like that, we're going to start busting up, as we do at the most inappropriate moments. Like the time at a school assembly when one of the PE teachers was giving us a pep talk and we realized he was basically plagiarizing the lyrics to "All Star" by Smash Mouth. We got detention for that one.

Lawson is about to respond, when three big guys who look vaguely Lawson-esque—thick black hair and similar facial structure—and who dress like Lawson, pre-Josie-impressing fashion awakening, rush up and start hugging him and mussing his hair and generally grab-assing. He half-heartedly fends them off. "Stop. Quit, guys. Damn. For real. Knock it off."

The largest and oldest-looking one has a large tattoo of crossed American and Mexican flags on his forearm, above "USMC." "Careful of his eye," he says. "Bust it back open, he'll bleed like a damn faucet all over your truck on the way home."

"You got robbed, little bro," another says.

"'Bout took Purdue's head off with that kick," the third says.

"You fought with heart, bro. That's what matters. You ain't defeated. Just gotta get back in the octagon," the second says.

"Come on. Let's get. Mom and Dad are waiting. Gotta prove to Mom you're still alive," the first says, assuming a fighting stance and playfully swatting at the back of Lawson's head.

Lawson bats him away and looks at us apologetically. "My brothers."

Josie nods. "I figured from the 'Mom and Dad' part."

"Great fight, Vargas!" a passerby yells. Lawson waves.

"You gonna introduce us to your young lady friends?" one of the brothers asks.

"Josie, Delia, these are my brothers, Connor, Wyatt, and Trey."

Hey, how you doin', what's up? they say. We nod.

Lawson sighs. "Okay. I better go. Like they said, gotta show my mom I pulled through." He still doesn't make eye contact with Josie.

She reaches out and grabs his forearm gently. "Hey," she says softly.

Lawson looks at her. His eyes are a well of hurt. He tries to smile but comes up short, averting his eyes. He limps away, his brothers romping around him. We give them enough of a head start that we know we won't run into them in the parking lot and have to face the dreaded double goodbye.

"Well, that was awkward," Josie says, unlocking her car. Someone whistles at her. She shoots them a caustic look. "I mean, I almost feel guilty we came."

"He was glad you did."

"I guess." Josie backs out until a jacked-up Dodge pickup honks at her, and we're on our way.

• • •

It's uneasily silent; I can tell Josie is mulling. I decide to test the waters. "You wanna pick up some snacks for pre-production?"

Josie hesitates. "Would you be totally pissed if we did pre-pro another time?"

Yes. "Why?" I try to sound nonchalant.

"I feel like I should swing by and try to cheer up Lawson."

"He seemed like he wanted to be alone."

"He seemed like he wanted to *seem* like he wanted to be alone, but actually he wanted someone to come cheer him up."

"He has his family."

"I get the sense he feels a little differently about me than his three brothers."

"Just go tomorrow."

"Haven't you ever tried to sleep on a night when something really crappy has happened to you? It sucks."

"You're literally asking *me* if I've ever tried to sleep when something crappy has happened to me?"

"See? You know."

Something in my chest feels like it's pinching me. Drawing me into myself. Making me small inside. "I also know that we *always* do pre-pro on Saturday night. It's our thing."

"DeeDee. We can do it another time. Tomorrow."

"JoJo. That's totally not the point. The point is: this is a thing we do, it's our job, and you wanna ditch out to go cheer up a dude you just met because he barely lost his fight." I know in my heart I'm being super unchill. But I can't help it. The pinching in my chest worsens.

"*So* not fair. He's my friend—*our* friend, honestly—not some dude I just met."

"This isn't even about him. It's about a lack of dedication."

Josie gives a clipped laugh. "You *cannot* be serious right now."

177

I shrug.

"Lack of—Dude, I have worked on this show with you *religiously*. We have done legitimately dozens of episodes. And I don't even—" She cuts herself off.

"What? You don't even what?"

"Nothing."

"No, just say it. You don't even like doing this show with me."

"That is not *remotely* what I was about to say."

"Sure."

"DeeDee."

"What were you going to say?"

"I don't even know. Geez, it was a half-formed thought. Cut me some slack."

I slump in my seat and look out the window. "Whatever. Do what you gotta do."

"Can you please be cool about this?"

"Yessiree!" I say in my most obnoxious faux-cheerful voice.

"If the shoe was on the other foot, you'd be really grateful."

"What, like if I had been defeated in hand-to-hand combat and you came to visit me?"

"Exactly."

"I'd want to be alone, probably."

"Whatever, DeeDee."

We get to my trailer. Mom's sign is illuminated in the front yard. The pinching in my chest has become a vise grip. I feel like I'm watching something I dropped in the bathroom bouncing right before it's inevitably going to fall right into the toilet. I've been a total clown dildo. But I think Josie has too, a little.

I get out.

"Are you cool?" Josie asks.

"Yeah. Whatever."

"DeeDee, we can do pre-pro another time. I kinda gotta go comfort Lawson now if I want to be a good friend."

"It's fine. Go."

"Love you, DeeDeeBooBoo."

"What are you even going to do over there?"

"I was thinking about making him some pancakes. They're his goony favorite food."

"You've never cooked even one thing."

"I've cooked pancakes! How dare you?"

"You should go get that premade batter they have in squeeze bottles at the grocery store. That'd be hilarious."

"Wait, are you serious? They sell pancake batter in bottles?"

"Yep."

"Obviously it's gross, right?"

I shrug. "I'm guessing it's not terrific?"

"How amazing would it be to carry one of those bottles in your water bottle carrier while you're out biking, and you stop to talk to some people, and while you're talking, you just casually squirt some in your mouth and swish it around."

I laugh in spite of myself. "And there's like extreme energy pancake batter with B vitamins and caffeine and whatnot."

We both laugh for a second or two, and it feels good.

"Love you, DeeDeeBooBoo."

"Love you, JoJoBee."

"I'm sorry for ditching out."

"It's cool. Let me know how the squeeze-bottle pancakes are." I shut my door and walk to my trailer. I'm not mad anymore, just sad.

Josie drives away, leaving me behind.

• • •

Mom is sitting on the couch, one leg tucked under her, a bare foot resting on the coffee table, a bottle of nail polish in each hand. "DeeDee! You need me to clear out? I wasn't sure when you'd get home."

"No." I collapse onto the couch next to her.

"Where's Josie?"

"Not here."

"I got that part. I thought y'all were prepping the show."

"We were supposed to."

"And?".

"Now we're not."

"Y'all okay?"

"Fine. What're you watching?"

"Don't know. *Forensic Files* or something. Did y'all have a fight?"

"I said we were fine."

"I pick up on your energy, DeeDee."

I sigh loudly. "Sorta, okay? We sorta had a fight. But we're good."

Mom holds up the bottles. "Green or purple?"

I stare at the TV. "Purple."

"You didn't even look."

"Every time I see someone with green toenails, I'm like, *What happened there?*"

"It's a cute shade. Nice springtime color."

"They're your toes."

"I'm gonna do purple. Want me to do yours when I'm done?"

"Sure." I hook the toe of one of my Chuck Taylors on the

heel of the other one and push it off. Then I do the same with the other foot.

Mom shakes the bottle, leans forward, and starts to work on her toes. She works for a while before asking, "How was the fight?"

"Actually pretty fun. We couldn't see super great, and we sat next to a couple of old nasty pervs, but otherwise . . ."

"How pervy are we talking about?"

"They didn't try to grope us or anything."

"Better not have. I'd cut their nuts off." Mom's never been Ms. Motivation, but she's always found the moxie to be protective of me. Which I appreciate. "Weren't you there to see your friend?" she continues.

"More Josie's friend. He's in love with her."

"How'd he do?"

"Good but still lost. Barely."

"Bummer."

"He took it hard."

"Well, yeah. Is that why Josie isn't here?"

"She's going to see him, even though he didn't ask and I bet he'd rather be alone."

Mom wipes off an errant smudge of nail polish with a cotton ball soaked in nail polish remover. I've always liked the sharp burn of it in my nostrils. "That's sweet of her."

"What? To ditch me?"

"Not to ditch you, but it doesn't sound like she's doing that."

"What do you call it, then?"

"Her friend needs her, and she's going to him."

"It would be cool if you'd take my side."

"DeeDee, I'm always on your side." She finishes one foot and blows on it.

181

"Not so much this time." I slump farther into the couch, leaning my head away from Mom.

Mom reaches down, pulls one of my feet onto her lap, and starts painting. "What do you want me to say? I'll say it. Want me to say, *That little bitch, Josie. I'll pull all her hair out?*"

"No."

"That doesn't feel good to hear."

"Not really."

We sit in silence for a few minutes while Mom paints and the TV drones. She used to work at a nail salon, so she takes the task seriously. Outside, lightning splashes blue-white across the sky, and thunder rumbles like a distant dump truck driving over a pothole. I shouldn't love thunderstorms as much as I do. Our trailer isn't the best place to be during a tornado. But I've always loved storms. When my friend Jesmyn lived here, I would make her watch them with me. She thought it was dumb at first, but then she came to love it as much as I did.

Of course, Jesmyn moved and left me behind. We don't talk nearly as much as we used to. She has a cool boyfriend now who takes up all her time, and pretty soon she'll be going to Carnegie Mellon, where she'll find even more cool friends to take up her time.

"Mom," I say softly.

"What, baby?" Mom murmurs, focusing.

"Why does everyone I love leave me behind?" My voice quavers.

Mom stops and looks at me. Her eyes are deep and soft. She caps the bottle of nail polish and sets my foot on the coffee table, careful not to smear anything. (She is still a professional, after all.) She gently pulls me upright, to her, and cradles my head on her shoulder. "Oh, sweetie."

I weep quietly for a moment or two.

"I thought maybe this wasn't just about Josie," Mom says, her voice muffled in my hair.

I shake my head. "What's wrong with me? Why am I so broken?"

Mom holds my face in both hands and turns it to hers. "You're not broken. There's nothing wrong with you."

"If that's true," I say, my voice snagging in my throat, "why do people keep leaving?" Someday I'd love to know why the people with the least to lose are always losing the little they have.

She pets my hair. "I don't know, sweetie. But I know it's not because there's something wrong with you."

"Then people should stay with me."

"I won't ever leave you. Hear me?"

I nod.

"Never," she says.

I nod.

"Ever."

I gather the pieces of myself and take a deep breath, ragged at the edges. I lie back again and put my foot in Mom's lap so she can finish.

"Did Josie say something about leaving?" Mom asks, her voice distant in concentration.

"No. But, like, the danger is there. Creeping on my life from the bushes."

"Gimme your other foot. Careful you don't smear the one I just did."

"Is this what my life is going to be?" I give my mom my other foot.

"What? Having to be careful you don't smear nail polish?" A roll of thunder, a camera flash of lightning.

"No. Sitting at home alone on Saturday nights. Rinse and repeat until I die."

Mom half smiles. "I won't take offense at that."

"You know what I mean. Obviously I'm not alone at *this* moment."

"I think you're going to have a wonderful life filled with lots of people who love you."

"Be nice if a few stuck around," I mutter.

"I've seen that for you. I've told you that before."

"I know, but—"

"You doubt my gift?" Mom tries to sound lighthearted, but I can tell she's hurt.

"I mean . . ."

"DeeDee! You think I'm conning people?"

"No. Just, I wish your gift worked better on our own household." My voice trails off. I try to say the last part sweetly. But it never really helps to say something hurtful to someone sweetly, because all it tells that person is that you *know* you're saying something hurtful.

Mom deflates, and she smiles sadly. She doesn't say anything for a few seconds, looking like she's trying to appear deep in scrutiny as she paints. Finally, she says in a quiet voice, "Yeah. I wish that too."

"Mom."

"It's fine. No, you're right." Lightning. Thunder. "I didn't know it was supposed to storm tonight."

"See what I mean?" We both laugh even though it's not that funny.

"There," Mom says, resting my other foot gently on the coffee table and blowing on my nails. "Pretty, pretty."

I wiggle my toes. "Now *this* gift of yours I do believe in."

"Ouch."

"Kidding."

I half watch the TV and simmer in my feelings. Now I'm wondering why Josie didn't invite me to go to Lawson's with her.

Mom finishes and props her feet up next to mine. We have the same feet. We share shoes all the time. She hugs my arm and rests her head on my shoulder.

I rest my head on top of hers. "Mom," I say quietly.

"Hmm?"

"You're a good last-person-in-the-world-to-stay-with-me."

She squeezes my arm tighter. "My gift wasn't wrong when it came to your dad."

"You knew?"

"Not that he'd leave. Only that something wonderful would come from being with him, and I was not wrong. I was not wrong at all."

We sit like that in silence. Mom reaches up a couple of times to brush tears off her cheek.

She's the only person who doesn't ever make me feel like I love them more than they love me.

Outside it begins to rain hard, pummeling the windows in heavy pulses, like the air has a heartbeat. One of those dark green spring rains that won't let up for two days, stripping blossoms from the trees, making morning feel like dusk, and you wonder if you'll ever see the sun again.

Josie

Naturally I messed up the first three or four pancakes I tried to make. But I'd planned for this and had several bottles of batter. At least my parents were at a movie and Alexis also wasn't home to ask questions. I really didn't feel like explaining why I was making pancakes on a Saturday night. I tried one of the pancakes, and it wasn't horrible. Anyway, it's the thought that counts.

I get Lawson's address from the Idiot Twins. I thought about asking Lawson, but I want this to be a surprise. Also, there's a tiny part of me that hopes he won't be home.

He lives on the other side of town from me, but Jackson isn't huge, and I get there quickly. I dash to the front door. The wind is picking up, and it looks like it's going to storm. I have a plastic bottle of Mrs. Butterworth's in one hand (fake maple syrup kinda yiks me out because every time I eat it, I sweat fake maple syrup smell for days, but Lawson seems like a Mrs. Butterworth's guy) and a plate of warm pancakes covered in plastic wrap in the other. I stand at the front door for a second, feeling weird. It's late on a Saturday night to be delivering anything unexpected to anyone, much less a stack of pancakes.

Still, I came all this way, so I ring the doorbell. I didn't sell my dignity by buying squeeze bottles of pancake batter for nothing.

A woman who looks like she could be Lawson's mom answers the door. "Hi?" she says uncertainly. Rightly so.

"Hi, sorry, I know it's getting late. I'm Josie Howard. Friend of Lawson's. I was at the fight earlier. I brought these over to cheer him up. I'm not a weirdo." *Nailed it. Nothing like assuring someone you're not a weirdo to put them at ease that you're not a weirdo.*

The woman's face spreads easily into a wide smile. Lawson has her smile. It's a nice smile. "Oh! Lawson mentioned you! Nice to meet you! Aren't you sweet? Come in, come in. Sorry about the house. I'm Lawson's mama, by the way."

"I thought maybe." I follow her inside. Lawson's house is modest and comfortable, and clearly his mom has won the war for its decorative soul. It has "special meal" smell mixed with the chemical tang of Glade apple-scented plug-ins. Whooping spills out of the living room, drowning out the sound of some game. Lawson's mom steps in, and I follow.

"Boys, this is Lawson's friend Josie."

I peek my head in and give a little wave.

"Hi," I say to the man who looks like Lawson's dad. "Hi again," I say to his brothers. They nod politely. "We met at the fight," I explain to Lawson's mom.

"I'm Lawson's dad, Arturo. I go by Art." He speaks with an accent and has a warm and kind face. A nice face. Like Lawson's.

I step inside and shake his hand. "Josie Howard."

"Lawson expecting you?" one of the brothers—Connor, Wyatt, or Trey—asks.

"No."

"Don't be surprised if he ain't any fun to hang out with,"

187

Connor, Wyatt, or Trey says. "Don't judge him based on to-night."

"You think Law's gonna be sad to see a pretty girl carrying a stack of pancakes?" Connor, Wyatt, or Trey says. "Buddy, he ain't whupped that bad." They all laugh raucously.

I blush.

"Y'all behave," Lawson's mom says with a heretofore unseen firmness, eyebrows raised.

We climb the stairs. I look at the family pictures lining the landing. "You're sorta surrounded in this family, huh?" I say.

"On all sides. Boys, boys, boys everywhere. But"—she leans in, a conspiratorial tone in her voice—"I always win. Even if they don't realize it."

She knocks on a closed door. "Lawson, honey?"

"What?" he calls.

"Can I come in? You got company."

"Yeah." He says it after a beat's longer hesitation and more reluctance than I would have liked.

She opens the door, and over her shoulder, I see Lawson re-clining on his bed, paperback in hand, ice pack covering one eye. Tater is snuggled up next to him.

My heart does a strange little swoop when I see him. Like when a bird is flying along really fast and it stops beating its wings for a second and does that glide-and-dip thing. *Um, okay, I guess, heart. Stop being goofy.*

We make eye contact and he tries to get up quickly, but he's obviously sore and moves deliberately, like an old man. I never noticed before how fluidly and gracefully he moved normally, until seeing him like this. "*Josie?* Git, Tater." Tater jumps down from the bed and exits.

"Tater!" I bend down and scratch Tater's neck with my free hand as he's leaving. "Hey, dude," I say nonchalantly, standing and holding out the plate of pancakes. "I brought you your favorite food out of all the possible foods on earth." I punctuate this with a little eye roll.

"How'd you know where I lived?"

I blush again. This really is bananas, what I'm doing. "I . . . got your address from the twins. Wanted this to be a surprise." I'm keenly aware of Lawson's mom, still standing there. *What she must think of me right now. The Pancake Stalker.*

"I am surprised," Lawson says, not unhappily (or happily).

"Anyway, I just came to drop these off."

"It was a good surprise." He sounds like he's saying this for his mom's benefit.

"I'm gonna grab y'all some milk and another plate and silverware," Lawson's mom says, and leaves.

The air between us is thick and stiff.

"So. Hi," I say.

"Hey."

"I met your dad. He seems really nice."

"He's cool."

"So he's named Arturo, and his sons are named Connor, Wyatt, Trey, and Lawson?"

Lawson gives the barest hint of a smile. "My mom, who's a seventh-generation Tennessean, made a deal with my dad: she names the boys; he names the girls."

"She's four for four, and your dad—"

"Big loser. Just like me."

"Oh, come on. You lost by like one point."

"Still."

"You doing all right?" I ask.

"Yeah." He motions at the book he's left tented on his bed. "Doing some reading. Distracts me." He's having trouble making eye contact, like back at the arena after the fight.

I take in his room for the first time. It's a hundred times neater than any dude's room I've ever been in, and it's filled with books.

"You're a legitimately huge reader," I say, walking over to one of his bookshelves. They skew heavily toward sci-fi and fantasy.

He sits back on his bed. "I contain multitudes."

"What're you reading?"

He holds up the book. "Last book in the Bloodfall series. You read them?"

"I'm into the show."

"The books are better."

"Always."

Lawson's mom comes back in, balancing a couple of plates, a couple of glasses of milk, some silverware, and a little crock of butter. She arranges them on Lawson's desk. "All right. I'll leave you two to your feast." She exits again.

I unwrap the pancakes. "They're probably soggy. Sorry. I'm a pancake-delivery rookie."

Lawson comes over to me, puts a couple on his plate, and starts buttering them. "I'm sure they're great."

"Maybe? Anyway, I'll leave you alone."

"What? Why?"

"You seem like you want to be alone."

"No. I mean, I don't want to be around most people, but . . ." He finally makes eye contact. He really does have nice eyes.

There's an intelligence in them I guess I haven't noticed before, when he wasn't in a room surrounded by books.

A clap of thunder makes us both jump, and rain starts battering the windows.

"Besides, it might be dangerous to drive right now."

"I feel weird that I ambushed you."

"I won't lie, I'm a little embarrassed to be showing my face in front of you." He pours some syrup on his pancakes, grabs a knife and fork, and sits on the edge of his bed.

"You have no reason to be."

"I invite you, thinking you're going to watch me win, and instead I lose." His voice cracks. He stares at his plate. Then, as suddenly as the rain started, his face collapses like a baby's when he figures out a stranger is holding him, and he begins weeping, his shoulders shaking, his body too small to contain what's overfilling his heart. He tries to catch himself, but it all slips out.

I'm stunned for a second, but I recover. "Hey. Oh. Hey, hey." I go to him, take the plate from his hands, and set it on the desk. Both hands now free, he presses his palms to his eyes. I sit beside him and put my arm around his shoulders. He has nice shoulders. I pull him toward me, until he rests his head between my cheek and my shoulder. His hair smells coconutty, like shampoo that comes in a huge bottle your mom buys on sale. He keeps trying to collect himself, but more spills, like when you attempt to pick up a bunch of stuff you've dropped, but every time you get a grip on one thing, something else falls.

"Hey," I murmur. I'm definitely in uncharted waters here. I don't know what to say. "It's okay. It's cool," I say over and over. It's legit like that scene in *Good Will Hunting* where Will starts flipping out and Robin Williams's character is like, "It's not your fault." I stroke his hair. He has nice hair. Maybe I don't need to say anything to fix this. Maybe I can't. Still, I try saying *It's not your fault* once. Nope.

I stretch out and gently kick the door shut with my toe. My read of the Vargas family dynamics is that it would be best if Lawson's brothers didn't see him crying. I hold him until his sobs subside.

He wipes his eyes with the back of his hand and draws a stuttering breath. "If I weren't already embarrassed enough."

"Dude. No. I get it."

"Men don't cry."

"Sure they do."

"I've never lost before."

"I'm not surprised. You fight like someone who seldom loses."

"I dreamed of going undefeated for my whole career. Now that's never going to happen. I can never get that back." He starts to fold back into himself.

"Honestly, I don't think I'd even wanna root for a fighter who had never lost."

"Why?"

"It's like, *Ohhhhhh, look at me, I'm little Mr. Perfect. I never lose. I'm really boring because all I do is drink fancy milkshakes made out of horses and punch trees. Ohhhhhh, I'm so cool.*"

A pale glimmer of a smile flickers across Lawson's face. An ember of light returns to his eyes. "I should've punched more trees and drunk more horse shakes."

"How many horse shakes were you knocking back a week?"

"One or two."

"Oh."

"On a good week."

"Yeah, that's not enough."

"*Now* you tell me."

"What was your tree-punching regimen like?"

"Terrible."

"Talk numbers."

"Maybe an hour a day."

"Not nearly enough."

"Obviously." He's unambiguously smiling now.

"You need motivation."

"I do."

"I'm going to give you some motivational sayings to re-member."

"Let's do this."

"Ready?"

"I think so."

"Because these are going to be very motivational."

"I think I'm ready."

"Should I put something in front of the window so you don't accidentally jump out in excitement?"

"Maybe. We'll see. Okay, hit me." He pounds his chest a few times with a bruised fist.

"Ready? *Pain . . .*"

"I'm listening."

"*Is the feeling . . . of winning . . . entering your body.*"

"Oh, that's good."

"Right? I know. Next. *Those who don't work hard . . . for a long time . . . will have . . . a hard time . . . for a long . . . time.*"

"That's deep."

"Yeah. I'm literally just inventing these right now."

"I would never know that."

"One more?"

"Oh yeah."

"How are your motivation levels?"

"On the charts, but barely. Almost off."

"Get ready, then, because this next one will send them *flying* off."

"I'm ready."

"Weakness . . . is the strength . . . of the weak man who loves to lose . . . but strength . . . is the strength of the strong man who hates to lose. . . ."

"Wow. *Wow.*"

I hold up a finger. "Not finished. *And winning . . . is the strength of the winning man who loves to win . . ."*

"Amazing."

I hold up a finger. "Still not done . . . *And loves to crush the weak man and the strong man in his mighty fists. For though I walk through the valley of the shadow of death . . ."*

Lawson slowly stands, grimly assumes a fighting stance, and does a high kick. He manages to play it straight for a couple of seconds before cracking up.

"Your pancakes are getting cold." I retrieve his plate off the desk and hand it to him.

"I cannot believe you made me pancakes."

"I truly struggled with affirming your gooniness."

He takes a bite. His eyes roll back. "Mmmmmmmmmm."

"Oh, please."

"Do you have any idea what's involved in cutting weight for a fight?"

"Eating lots of celery?"

"I *wish* I got to eat lots of anything. Celery is a decadent treat when you're cutting weight. No lie, these pancakes taste like heaven. And I just ate dinner too."

"Let me try one bite."

He holds out a piece on the end of his fork, and I gently grab it off with my teeth. It's not terrible. Good job, plastic-squeeze-bottle batter. I watch, pleased with myself, as Lawson digs in.

He pauses between bites. "I did everything right." His voice is abruptly forlorn again. "I suffered to make weight. I trained hard. I was mentally ready, you know? I could *see* myself winning. I couldn't see anything *but* winning."

I grab for the rope with which he's lowering himself down the well. "At least you didn't lose in a blatantly cartoonish way, right?"

He looks at me.

I continue. "I mean, what if you'd gotten hit and you flew into the air and did two backflips and then landed in such a way that your nose went right up your butt."

"I don't think that can happen. I've never once seen that happen."

"Oh, I have. Last week, in fact."

He peeks out over the edge of the well. "Oh, really?"

"Last week I was at another MMA fight and that exact thing happened."

"Wow. It seems like I would've heard about that."

"Especially because the dude it happened to had to go to the hospital for butt-inhalation poisoning."

"Man. I heard you can die from that."

"Oh, he *did* die. He was like—" I flop back on Lawson's bed with my eyes crossed and my tongue lolling out.

195

He laughs, and I lie there, fake-dead. And while I do, I realize something: I never feel pressure to be someone I'm not when I'm around him. I never feel like I need to hide any part of who I am. Being around him feels like waking up on a Saturday morning when the whole day ahead of you is free and you've slept the perfect amount, and your bed is the most ideal temperature, it's like you're part of an experiment in human comfort. It's so easy. So effortless.

Then, as if reading my mind: "I like you," he says softly after his laughter subsides. "I like being around you."

"I like you," I say softly. "I like being around you." And it's true.

We gaze at each other for a second. "You have a piece of pancake on your mouth." I reach up and rub a crumb from his mouth with my thumb. He has nice lips.

"You have a piece of pancake on *your* mouth," he says, and gently rubs his thumb across my top lip, letting it linger there. His touch makes a warmth bloom below my stomach, as if molten, raspberry-scented chocolate has replaced my bone marrow.

All right, then. You might've given my brain some advance warning, body. But it's fine.

"Wait, you have some pancake on your face," I murmur. I lean forward and stroke his bruised cheek with my hand and his lips with my thumb. His lip feels slightly swollen. Somehow my hand knew he would be fun to touch before my brain did, but my brain has finally caught up.

"I do? That's embarrassing," Lawson murmurs. "On my face?"

Our eyes lock.

"All over it. I kept wanting to say something." I continue stroking his cheek.

He scoots a little closer. I reciprocate.

"Wow. Get it all."

"Oh, I will." Now I'm sitting so close to him, I can feel the warmth from his body. I'm having a lot of fun touching him.

"Don't stop until you do. I don't want to be walking around with pancake on my face."

"I don't know how that happened."

"Me neither." Our faces are very close.

And speaking of not knowing how things happen, now we're kissing, and his hands are in my hair and on the back of my head and he's pulling me into him. *It's fine. Friends do this. They suddenly kiss and kiss and think they're going to stop but instead they keep going with even more intensity. It's fine.*

He tastes sweet, like a carefree and joyous morning spent watching cartoons.

I'm not sure how long we go at it. Kissing bends time into itself. A kissing minute is equal to years of normal life. After a while we pry our lips apart and lock eyes. He has long eyelashes. They're quite nice.

"Hey," he says softly, smiling.

"Hey," I say, smiling.

"I've wanted to do that since the first time I saw you." He reaches out and brushes a lock of hair behind my ear, and then caresses the spot between my ear and my jaw. He's impossibly gentle for someone so strong. It's hard to imagine him punching anyone.

"I know."

"That obvious?"

"Very obvious."

"I think maybe this is brightening my night more than the pancakes," he says.

"Dude, I better beat pancakes."

"One of us deserves to win a fight tonight."

"I dug your prefight walking-out music, by the way."

"I hoped you would."

"I liked your new combat nickname too."

"I hoped you would." He reclines onto his bed and pulls me on top of him. I go very willingly.

He kisses my neck and behind my ear, his hands on my lower back. It's leaving me breathless, honestly, but I manage to say, "How much would it have sucked if I'd shot you down?" I sit up, cross-legged.

He sits up and faces me. "Whatever, you started kissing *me*," he whispers as he kisses me behind my ear. In his voice, there's the swagger and confidence that make him a great fighter, and I'm lying if I say I don't enjoy it tremendously.

"Why are you so cool all of a sudden?" I say, playfully pushing his chest.

He smiles with one side of his mouth. "What do you mean?"

"You're this sweet guy who really loves pancakes and listens to Miranda Lambert and reads fantasy books. I didn't expect you to kiss like a cool guy."

"You saying I'm not cool?"

"I'm saying you kiss like a cool guy."

"What if I told you I've had some practice?"

"Well, la-dee-dah, lover boy!"

He laughs. "This'll shock you, but there are girls who like guys who work out a lot. Even if the working out has nothing to do with impressing them."

I give him another lighthearted push. "You calling me an MMA groupie?"

"Not even a little bit."

"Because I'll karate you."

"Don't karate me."

"I know karate. I'm good at it." I rear back. "Hiiiiiiya!" I karate-chop his chest. Listen, it's a very nice chest.

He laughs and catches my arm and pulls me closer. "I know kiss fu."

I snort-laugh involuntarily. "Good *lord*. *That* is why I'm shocked you're good at kissing. You are a goof." I start laughing again, but he cuts me off with a kiss. It's a pleasant surprise.

We pause. He goes to kiss me again, but I stop short, teasing him. "Who's more fun to be all tangled up in? Me or Nightmare Purdue?"

"That's who you're jealous of? Not the other girls?"

I shrug.

"You're more fun."

"Yeah?"

"No contest. First-round knockout."

"Second victory of the night for me!"

He goes to kiss me but stops. "I just want to look at you for a second. You're beautiful."

"Don't forget funny."

"And funny."

I sigh and press into him. We kiss some more.

Lawson breaks the kiss after days (or months?). "I'm going to win a fight in front of you someday." The joking is gone from his voice. So is the despondency of earlier.

"I believe you." I fix a piece of his hair knocked wayward by our rumpus.

"I really want that. I want you to see me as a champion."

"I know."

Finally—thoroughly flushed, my hair a mess, a dull ache in my lower pelvis, and my lips swollen—I have to leave. I go to open his door. He moves behind me as nimbly as his aching muscles will allow, as though to help. But instead, he pushes me gently but firmly against the door, kissing my neck from behind, his hands on my stomach and hip. He pulls me back into him. "Come here," he whispers. "Just stay forever."

I close my eyes and lay my head on his shoulder and let him keep running his lips down my neck. Then I spin to face him, and we start kissing again. He presses me into the door. I dissolve. I am unmade. Taken apart.

"Thanks for making me pancakes." There's no defeat left on his face. Only purest victory.

This whole thing rolled over me like the storm raging outside. Thunder pounding in my rib cage like something that wants to escape, that's too small for the space it's in. The air between us is alive with bolts of arcing blue electricity.

• • •

Me: You awake, DeeDeeBoo?

Delia: Yes even though I'm so tired.

Me: You mad at me still?

Delia: I was never mad at you ya goober. Just bummed we couldn't do pre-pro. But I hung with my mom and she gave me a pedi and it was chill.

Me: Ok cool because I have some kinda big news.

Delia: Can I guess???

Me: You'll never guess.

Delia: Oh I daresay I will.

Me: OH DARE YOU SAY???

Delia: YES I DARE. YOU AND LAW-MAN TOTALLY FRENCHED.

Me: DEEDEE!!!!!!!!

Delia: TELL ME I'M WRONG.

Me: YOU ARE IN FACT NOT WRONG, CHARLOTTE HOLMES.

Delia: SCREAMING. KNEW IT.

Me: How????

Delia: Um literally it was the easiest thing imaginable to guess.

Me: WHYYYYYYYYYYY.

Delia: He's ALWAYS looked at you with The Look and when you were watching him fight, you returned The Look.

Me: Sigh. RIP to my chill.

Delia: SO. HOW WAS IT???

Me: I MEAN HE KISSES LIKE A COOL GUY.

Delia: Do tell!!

Me: He seems to . . . know how his body works.

Delia: OOOO LALA.

Me: And he's good at moving around someone else's body.

Delia: LOL @ "someone else's body" like whoever could that be, pray tell?

Me: Hahahahaha. Anyhoo.

Delia: So is this a thing now?

Me: I guess??? I DEF WANT MORE. DID NOT SEE THAT COMING.

Delia: Ok but you gotta stop dryhumping long enough to do pre-pro tomorrow.

Me: Oh 1,000%. I'm super sorry again for ditching out tonight. Law-man needed cheering up.

Delia: "Cheering up" LOL. Loving these euphemisms.

Me: He's a big reader btw. Who knew?

Delia: That's hot.

Me: He was reading a Bloodfall book when I got there.

Delia: NICE. Good taste.

Me: It was a sexy surprise.

Delia: How awesome is this storm btw?

Me: So awesome. This rain is bonkers.

Delia: Even if you'd come over tonight I probably would have made you watch the storm with me and we wouldn't have gotten any work done.

Me: Truth.

Delia: Wanna know what I find so romantic btw while we're on the subject?

Me: ???

Delia: You know how pythons are taking over the Everglades?

Me: EEEEEK WHAT.

Delia: Yep. I guess people released pets or something?

Me: That is HORRIFYING.

Delia: I know right? So imagine someone had to release a boy python and someone had to release a girl python and somehow they found each other in that huge swamp.

Me: AW. I hate snakes more than I hate having cramps but that is romantic.

Delia: Is Lawson staying in Jackson after graduation?

Me: I think so. I think he wants to keep training with his same coach or whatever.

Delia: Nice. Well, I'm having a hard time keeping my eyes open. Congrats once more on frenching.

Me: Hey, I'm sorry again for ditching you tonight, love.

Delia: All good. But to punish you I'm picking out a real doozy of a movie.

Me: Haha I deserve it.

Delia: We're gonna do "The Werewolf vs. the Vampire Woman."

Me: THAT. SOUNDS. TERRIBLE.

Delia: Yeah, it was made in 1971 and it looks like they went to a porn set and handed the actors costumes and were like "here put these on when you're done boning and we're gonna make another movie real quick."

Me: Omg.

Delia: Yep. And the script reads like they wrote it while the actors were changing. Ok, gonna go sleep. Love you, JoJoBee.

Me: Love you, DeeDeeBooBoo.

• • •

I'm still too amped up to sleep, and it doesn't help when Lawson texts me.

Lawson: Thanks again for the "pancakes."

Me: I guess "pancakes" are my favorite food now too.

Lawson: Your "pancakes" are the best I've ever had.

Me: I should make you "pancakes" again soon.

I lie and stare at the ceiling, ignoring the show that burbles from my laptop speakers, and feel him fade from my lips. My whole body is still crackling like a bonfire.

I keep running through the last part of Delia's and my text conversation. Before we started talking about the movie. A different feeling is beginning to creep through the euphoria and is winding itself around my stomach (like one of those pythons that apparently now infest the Everglades). I guess Lawson is staying in Jackson. That sucks. That's another thing to think about. I'd love it if I could avoid making my own life more complicated than it needs to be.

Delia

Dear Dad,

Yeah, I called you Dad. You don't know this, but I've struggled for a while with what to call you. Sounds like you struggled a bit with that yourself. But I'm calling you Dad because you did in fact make me, so you're my dad no matter what. I guess I could call you "Father," but that makes me sound like I'm a hedgehog on some gently whimsical and badly drawn European kids' show.

Anyway, graduation was last night. You also wouldn't know this, but graduating from high school wasn't a given for me. Mom was there. She looked great in her new dress. My friend Jesmyn and her boyfriend, Carver, drove down from Nashville to be there.

When I walked across that stage, it felt amazing to have finished something. It felt good that I didn't quit and run away when things were hard.

Afterward, Jesmyn, Carver, my best friend Josie, her boyfriend Lawson, and I went back to our house. We talked and laughed until it got really late.

We watched one of your movies, *The House on*

Haunted Hill. Jesmyn and Carver helped Josie and me get ready for our show. I guess now is a good time to mention that I have a show on TV Six here in Jackson. It's called *Midnite Matinee.* I'm a real-life horror host. Just like we used to watch together. My show's even syndicated in a bunch of cities. But not yours.

We taped the show tonight, actually. We roped Jesmyn and Carver into it. Jesmyn is an amazing piano player, and she performed this creepy Bach song on her keyboard with the organ sound effect. We made Carver and Lawson dance. They're both terrible.

Afterward, Carver asked why we don't do our show on YouTube. I guess he had a friend who was big on YouTube. I told him that Josie wants to work in TV someday. I said I was specifically interested in TV because I grew up watching TV horror hosts. I didn't tell him that you introduced me to them and then I watched your tapes after you left.

But the real reason we did public access and not YouTube is I'd figured you didn't watch YouTube. You left me hundreds of VHS tapes written on with black Sharpie. I don't think you're a YouTube guy. I wanted you to be flipping through channels one night and see me there on your TV. And I wanted you to be proud of me and regret leaving me.

Boy, is the way I feel about you complicated. I love you for all the things you did. And I hate you for the one thing you didn't do, which was stay.

Carver and I somehow got on the subject of losing people. His three best friends died right before he started senior year, so I guess he thinks about it a lot. I do too. I didn't say this, but I think it might be harder to lose someone the way I lost you because you chose to be dead to me. Even though you're out there alive somewhere, living a new chapter of your life.

I wonder a lot how and why. How you left so much of yourself behind all at once. Why you did.

Next week we're going to ShiverCon in Orlando, and we're going to meet Jack Divine. He produced and directed SkeleTonya back in the day. I've watched all your SkeleTonya tapes. We're hoping he can help us make the show bigger. I'm scared if we can't make the show bigger, Josie will leave to pursue her goal of being on TV professionally. Another person leaving me behind.

And while we're in Orlando, maybe I'll be brave enough to drive to your city and show up on your front porch and ask you why you left. Maybe I'll figure out what's wrong with me that you were able to leave me behind so easily and never look back.

I look a lot different now. Hope you recognize me.

Your daughter,
Delia

By the end I'm crying so hard I have a hard time seeing the screen. I guide the cursor over the "send" button. I sit and chew on my thumbnail. I take lots of deep, trembling breaths.

I delete.

Josie

"I have some issues with the name Books-A-Million," I say.

Lawson holds the door of Books-A-Million open for me. It feels like walking into a cavern, from the floral late-May heat. "Why?" Lawson asks.

"Because it's supposed to be a play on the phrase 'thanks a million,' but 'books' doesn't sound like 'thanks.'"

"Maybe."

"No. *Definitely*. What other 'blank a million' phrase have you ever heard?"

Lawson ponders.

"I see you thinking," I say. "Stop wasting your energy and admit I'm right."

"'Banks' sounds like 'thanks.' You could name a bank 'Banks-A-Million.'"

"Meh."

"Come *on*. It's perfect! Million, like how banks have millions of dollars."

"Yeah, no, I definitely got it. Okay, one, I would *never* trust my money to a banking institution that used a pun name. Two, each bank is just one bank. At least at Books-A-Million there are lots of books. Multiple books."

"There are lots of dollars at banks. Millions."

"But no synonym for 'dollars' rhymes with 'thanks.'"

Lawson deftly dodges a table that snuck up on him while he was listening to me talk. "You are tough to win over."

"The way it should be. You see the book you want?"

"Not yet."

"Do they have it?"

"I guess it's possible Books-A-Million decided not to carry the new G. M. Pennington Bloodfall prequel because they're tired of making money."

"Oh ho ho! Is that sarcasm I detect? Huh? Comedian?" I start poking him in the ribs. "You a funny guy?"

He giggles and fends me off. "Stop. That tickles."

"Clever guy?" Poke poke.

He grabs my hands and spins me around and pulls me backward into him. "Maybe," he murmurs into the side of my neck, dragging his scratchy jaw down it. It gives me the same feeling as jumping a little higher on a trampoline than you expected to.

I pull away from him, not because I particularly want to, but because I don't want to be "that couple" at a bookstore. "What about a fight gym called Spanks-A-Million?"

"What are you talking about?"

"You know. Spanking. Fighting."

"Spanking's not a form of fighting. There's no spanking in MMA."

"Yes, there is."

"I would know."

"Then how come when I went to your fight, one of the fights ended in an absolutely devastating spanking?"

"Liar."

210

"I'm not. One fighter put the other fighter over his knee and spanked him until he cried and said he wanted to stop fighting."

"How'd I miss that?"

"Same way you missed this." I turn around slowly, holding his book like a game show host.

His face gleams. *"Yes!"* He reaches for it. I pull it away. He reaches again. I pull away. He stands with his arms at his sides, looking crestfallen in the way of someone whose spoon fell into their soup. I extend the book to him. He reaches for it. I pull it away and boop him on the head with it.

"Too slow."

He feigns deep sadness and turns, his shoulders slumped.

"Awwww, here." I come around in front of him and hand him the book. We laugh. When he takes the book, our hands touch and he lingers for a beat or two longer than necessary.

We stroll the aisles, browsing. This is our first bookstore date, and I'm deeply enjoying the look on Lawson's face. There's an unguarded softness to it. He keeps turning his (extremely thick) book over and over in his hands. *Where did you come from, you surprising boy? How did this happen?*

"Where do you think Bermuda is, by the way?" I ask.

He looks at me like I asked him if we should drop our pants and start pulling books off the shelves using our butt cheeks. *"Bermuda?"*

"Yep."

"Why?"

"Because."

"Random."

"Just guess."

He goes for his phone. I grab his hand. "No cheating."

"Uh. Like by the Bahamas."

"Nope."

"By Jamaica."

"Nopers."

"Where?"

"There's seriously no place on earth that's less where you think it is than Bermuda."

"Can I cheat already?"

"Now you can."

He gets out his phone and looks. "What?!"

"I *know.*"

"It's like in the middle of the Atlantic Ocean."

"I know!"

"It's basically on the same longitude or latitude or whatever as North Carolina."

"Yep."

"That blows my mind."

"The world is a magical place, dude." *Filled with things you weren't expecting.*

I pull a book with an interesting cover off the shelf and leaf through it.

"You wanna get something for your drive this weekend?" Lawson asks. "Orlando's far."

"Nah, Delia and I'll talk and listen to music."

"What is it you're doing down there again?"

"Going to ShiverCon. Meeting with this big TV producer and director named Jack Divine."

"That's amazing."

"I hope so."

"What?"

"Nothing."

"You sounded sad there."

"No." Every time I think about what's at stake from this meeting, it makes me nervous and sad. I guess my voice betrayed me.

"So this TV guy might make you guys big time?"

"Hopefully. Or at least bigger than we are now."

"I hope you'll still let me on the show to break boards even if you become huge."

"I mean, obviously."

We meander through the store. We aren't even looking at books anymore. We're just being together. Our hands brush and we smile at each other, maybe each thinking the other did it on purpose.

"Do you . . . wanna come?" I blurt out. *Hey, mouth, check in with brain first next time?*

He turns to me with a look of pleased incredulity. "What, like, to the con? In Orlando?"

"If it's okay with Delia. I gotta check with her. But yeah."

"Where would I stay?"

"Delia's mom got us a hotel room. You could stay there with us." My heart churns in my chest like a turbulent spot in a river. I'm sweetly adrenaline-sick in my lower belly. "If your parents would be down. It'd be totally innocent."

"Yeaaaah, my mom's religious enough that she might not be down."

"She left us alone in your room with the door closed."

"True, but I guarantee she thought there'd be no way I'd want to get romantic right after I lost a fight."

"*Get romantic?* That phrase stresses me out so much."

"Whatever. Insert any phrase you want." Before I can speak, he sees how he left himself open. He raises a finger. "Don't."

"What? I wasn't gonna." (I absolutely was gonna.)

"You were gonna." Lawson appears to be running calculations. "I could tell my parents I'm going to a training workshop in Orlando and staying with some other fighters."

"It'd be nice to have some muscle. I've heard cons aren't always cool places for women."

"So, like, your bodyguard."

"Basically."

"Who you're having an affair with."

"Gross!"

"Too far?"

"Just."

"Your bodyguard who you kiss."

"I'll reluctantly allow that. So?"

"So."

"You wanna come?"

"Hell yeah, I do. If Delia's cool with it."

"Drop me by her work on our way back and I'll ask her."

We pay for Lawson's book and walk out of the cool of the store into the sultry dusk heat of the parking lot. It smells like warm tar and french fries. The sun is setting orange in the pollen-hazed sky.

Lawson suddenly falls quiet. The sort of silent that calls out, that demands an explanation.

"What?" I pinch at his arm playfully.

He smiles a little, wistfully, and shakes his head.

"Come on! What?"

Same smile, still looking away from me. "There's something I want to tell you, but you can't joke."

He has a vulnerable timbre in his voice. Things are going great between us, but it's way early for him to be telling me he loves me. I'm definitely not ready to hear it or say it. My heart quickens. "Okay." *Fingers crossed it's not that.*

He takes a deep breath, like he's steeling himself for a punch. "I've never had someone I could go to the bookstore with. My brothers used to give me tons of grief for loving to read, and I guess I didn't have the right friends? Anyway." He looks at me and back down. "It's good when your life starts turning out how you want it to. When you get the right people in it."

I'm deeply relieved not to be dealing with a premature *I love you.* I measure my response carefully, making sure there's no hint of teasing. I don't say anything for a second but grip his biceps and rest my head on his shoulder as we walk. He rests his head on mine. He smells like icy, clean, neon-blue deodorant.

Finally, I say, "I've had boyfriends who liked to go to the bookstore, but mostly so they could pretend to be smarter than me and brag about all the Kurt Vonnegut and Charles Bukowski they've read."

"Who and who?"

"You can't imagine what a relief that question is."

"No guy who tries to make you feel dumb deserves you."

"Extremely agree."

"Bet I can plank longer than any of them." Lawson plays it as a joke, but there's a territorial edge to his voice that I haven't heard before, and I like it.

"And isn't that what really counts?"

We reach Lawson's truck, and he comes around to open my

215

door for me. I lean back against it. The metal's warm on my skin through my sundress. I reach out and gently take Lawson's book and hold it away from him. "Keep away. You gotta kiss me if you want it."

He smiles, puts one hand on my hip and one hand on the book, and presses into me. It makes me ache.

"Oh no, anything but that," he says softly, leaning in.

And now we're "that couple" in the parking lot, but who cares?

Here's what it feels like: he's the first days of summer, when I would play outside until my heart pounded with hot blood and sweat plastered my hair to my face and I'd come inside and watch TV and sit by the air conditioner and eat lemonade pop-sicles so tart they'd make tiny beads of sweat well up on my eyelids.

And while we're kissing, sweet melancholy wells inside me. The kind you get when you're already reaching the end of a beginning.

I don't want to grow up.

I want to keep living in this moment forever. With Lawson. With Delia. Take the hourglass and lay it on its side.

"I still can't believe where Bermuda is," Lawson says, pausing the kissing.

I'm about to say, "I know, right?" But his lips are back on mine before I get the chance, and it doesn't seem that important anymore to say anything, even if I could.

Delia

"You're depraved," my boss Trish says. She takes another bite of baked potato.

"Am I, though? Baked potatoes taste like wet toilet paper rolled up in a wet paper bag. They taste like a hot mop," I say.

"False. Put some butter and cheese and sour cream and bacon bits on one and get back to me."

"Like, if you're going to bury a hot lump of mud-flavored white starch in twenty delicious things, sure, maybe you can choke it down."

"I should fire you right now."

"But look how efficient I am." I lean against the shelf I've just finished inventorying.

"Are you seriously done already?"

"Yep."

Trish eyes the calendar. "So you're gone this weekend."

"Correct. ShiverCon."

"Fun. You back by Monday morning?"

"Can be."

"Good, I'll need you."

I give her a thumbs-up.

"Okay, I can finish up here if you wanna clock out," Trish says.

"I'm gonna hang out for a bit. Josie texted me and said she's getting dropped off here, and I'm giving her a ride home."

Trish takes another bite of baked potato and talks around it. "Some good stuff maybe gonna happen for your show from going to this con?" Trish watches us sometimes. It's one reason she hired me.

"I heard back from Jack Divine's assistant. We're meeting him Saturday afternoon."

"I spent many a drunk Saturday night in college watching SkeleTonya with my roommates. You gonna quit on me if you get big?"

"If I get big, I'm going to use all of my money to arrange improbable animal encounters."

"Like . . ."

"Baby elephant meets baby dolphin. Chimp feeds bottle to baby sloth. Baby kangaroo and baby hippo take nap cuddled on pile of straw. Et cetera, et cetera."

"I went to a state fair once where they had monkeys dressed as cowboys riding dogs like horses," Trish says casually, like it's a normal thing to have witnessed.

"Get. Out."

"Swear."

"Well, that goes on the list."

"Trust me when I tell you that you haven't lived until you've eaten a fried Snickers bar on a stick while watching monkeys in tiny cowboy hats race around a track riding dogs."

I feign offense. "You're telling *me* I would love eating a fried candy bar while watching cowboy monkeys ride dogs? Literally, that is my personal brand."

I don't have many heroes, but Trish is one of them. She

started a comic-book shop in Jackson, Tennessee, that has not only survived, but has done well enough to employ me and another guy. There's something inspiring about people who stay in just-okay (or even not-okay) places and build things that make those places better.

I pick up a volume of *Harrow County* and read for a few minutes, until Josie appears at the glass front door, Lawson watching protectively behind her in his truck to make sure she gets in. I hurry over and unlock the door and open it, waving at Lawson, who waves back and drives away.

"Hey," Josie says.

"Hey," I say.

Trish nods in Josie's direction and wipes her mouth.

"I need you to weigh in on baked potatoes," I say to Josie.

She shrugs. "Love 'em."

Trish hee-haws like a victorious donkey.

"Traitor," I say.

"What? Put cheese and sour cream on it? Delicious."

"Thank you," Trish says.

"Answer me this, both of you: if baked potatoes are so great, why did humanity ever advance past them?" I say.

"Huh?" Josie says.

"I assume the baked potato was the first way potatoes were ever made. Why keep going past that to fries and mashed potatoes and hash browns and potato chips? If baked potatoes are so good?"

Trish and Josie erupt, talking simultaneously, their words blending together in an unintelligible cacophony. "Sorta like, 'We have this perfectly good Earth to stand on, why send astronauts to the moon?'" Josie says, breaking through the outraged clamor.

"Humanity has a restless spirit of exploration," Trish says. "We always seek something better."

"Maybe we should *hash this out* on this week's show," Josie says, winking.

Trish and I groan loudly. "And on that sour note," I say, "we're gonna jet." We walk out to Mom's and my battered yellow Ford Focus. Josie brushes some chip crumbs off the passenger seat and gets in.

"How was your day?" I ask.

"Slept in until eleven. Applied for a couple server jobs."

"Ugh. Where?"

"Cheddar's. Logan's Roadhouse."

"Worst."

"Seriously."

"What were you and Law-dogg doing? Besides tons of smooching, of course."

"Went to Books-A-Million, got his new G. M. Pennington book." Josie suddenly seems nervous. She brushes her hair back and looks at her feet. "Hey, so . . . while Lawson and I were at the bookstore, I maybe . . . invited him to come with us to Orlando?"

I start churning inside, like when you're stirring a big bowl of something but suddenly change direction. My first impulse is to anger and jealousy, that she would invite along Lawson—who I can't compete with in certain areas—to be our third wheel, especially without asking me first.

But then another thought: *If Lawson comes, your biggest excuse for not going to visit your dad—not wanting to leave Josie on her own—is gone.* A thin film of sweat rises on my forehead as I turn it over in my mind, trying to decide if the out is even something I want.

"DeeDee? Say something. We good? I can disinvite him."

I hear in her voice that she doesn't want to disinvite him.

"No," I say softly. "It's cool."

"You sure?"

"Yeah."

"Totally? Because—"

"Totally. Don't worry about it." Adrenaline is splashing around inside my chest, burning like acid where it lands. I have a nervous-twitchy-lower-intestine feeling.

"He'll be a good bodyguard if we run into creepers at the con. And we can make him carry our bags and stuff."

I nod.

"Plus," Josie continues, "he really is fun to be around."

We drive for a bit in silence. Finally, I say, "This trip is starting to feel like Frodo taking the Ring to Mount Doom."

"In that—"

"A lot is riding on it, you know? Feels like our destiny."

"Like the universe wants us to do it."

"Exactly."

"What if we make something huge happen?"

"We might make it so that *this* is our job. Hanging out together. While people go and become accountants and stuff."

"Imagine us in a TV interview, telling how we got our start. This is gonna make such a good story."

"I'm so glad I have you," I say, the anxiety over whether to go see my dad softening into a far more welcome buoyancy. "I could never have done this show without you. What are the odds of us finding each other in Jackson, Tennessee, and making such a good team?"

Josie shakes her head. "It's amazing." But she suddenly seems to have taken a dip of her own, troubled in the way I just was. As if we swapped places.

"What?"

"Nothing." She shakes her head again and smiles wanly.

"Can you believe what we've made together? We built a *TV show*. That people in other cities *watch*."

"I never imagined I'd already be on TV by the time I was in high school. This has been my dream since I was old enough to remember."

"I mean, this is how people get their start in the entertainment business, right? You get a lucky break."

I'm getting so excited and sidetracked thinking about it, I have to slam on the brakes to avoid running a red light.

"Oof, DeeDee."

"Sorry."

"You are the squirrelliest driver."

"I said sorry! So are you and Lawson going to make out in front of me the whole way down to Orlando?"

"*What?* No."

"He has no idea what he's getting into, being trapped in a car for twelve hours with the two of us."

"Is that how long the drive is?"

"Yep."

"Whoa."

"I know. We need to start working up playlists."

"Poor Lawson. This is gonna be the test of our new relationship."

"If it survives this, I guess you're meant to be." *And please be meant to be. Please be one more stake in the ground that ties Josie here.*

I wonder a lot if I've made a mistake by letting myself need Josie so much. Life would be so much simpler if we didn't allow ourselves to need anybody. We wouldn't go through this world so easy to wound, our hearts beneath some paper-thin layer of skin.

The light turns green, and I go.

"So you heard back from Divine's assistant?" Josie asks.

"Yep."

"When are we meeting him?"

"Saturday afternoon around lunch."

"We're gonna be so tired by then."

"Exhausted."

We sit for a moment in our blossoming jubilation.

"This *could* happen," Josie says. "This could make us big."

"I know."

"Like this could determine the entire course of our adult lives."

"I know."

"If we get big, I'm going to be really smart about money. I won't be one of those celebrities who you hear about going broke."

"If we get big, I wanna pay off my dad's house. Make him feel super guilty." I say it out my window, almost to myself.

"That would be the most amazing burn ever in the history of mankind," Josie says.

"But the catch would be that he has to paint a mural across the entire front of it that has me as this benevolent queen."

We laugh and laugh. It's not all that funny, but that doesn't matter. We like the sound of our laughing in harmony.

"We're the worst," I say, sighing through another peal of giggles.

"The absolute worst."

"If we blow up, we should buy mansions right next door to each other."

"With a tunnel connecting them that you get to by pushing aside a grandfather clock or a suit of armor."

"So basically one huge mansion."

"More or less."

"And a big movie theater behind our houses where we screen our movies," I say.

"Better yet! We just park you and your mom's trailer behind our houses, and we'll screen our movies there like the old days. To keep it real."

I clap quickly, making the car swerve, and squeal. "And even though we could walk over to each other's mansions through the tunnel, we should still text a lot, for old times' sake."

We sigh in unison. Envisioning this life gives me so much pleasure, it's terrifying, thinking about how much it'll hurt if it doesn't come about.

Josie

"That's a wrap," Arliss calls. "Another completed masterpiece. Another piece of my legacy to the world. Another couple of hours closer to death."

"Let's go!" Delia yells. We race off the set to the restroom and frantically scour off our spackled-on vampire makeup, then jump out of our Rayne and Delilah costumes into long-road-trip clothes. We fold the costumes neatly. The plan is to possibly wear them at the con, depending on how we feel.

We hurry out. "Go!" I call to Lawson, who's still picking up random board splinters. "Get changed!"

"Okay! Damn!" Lawson grabs his bundle of clothing from a chair and rushes into the bathroom.

Arliss winds up a cord. "Why y'all acting like you got burning spiders in your panties?"

"Remember that con we got invited to?" Delia says.

Arliss grunts and shrugs.

"ShiverCon? You're the one who gave us the invite."

Grunt and shrug.

Delia rolls her eyes. "Anyway, we're going to ShiverCon and meeting Jack Divine to talk about the show's future."

"Is there a possibility this will lead to my getting fired?" Arliss asks.

"I mean . . . maybe?" I say.

Arliss nods and picks up the end of another stray cord. "In that case, good luck. Where is this thing?"

"Orlando," Delia says.

"Y'all are leaving here and driving to Orlando, Florida," Arliss says.

"That's why we're in a hurry," I say.

"That's a twelve-hour drive. Have y'all lost your damn minds?"

"Lost our damn minds like a fox," I say.

"How'd you know that distance off the top of your head?" Delia asks.

"Toured with a band for enough years that I can tell you the driving distance between any two cities in America. Also did it long enough to know that people stay falling asleep at the wheel, so you two goofballs be careful."

"Aw, Arliss! You don't want us to die!" I say. "Delia! Arliss cares if we live or die!"

"Don't get carried away. Why didn't y'all leave sooner?"

"Because we know you set your work schedule around the show," I say, "and we both thought the other one had told you about our trip, and we figured if we told you too late to change it, you'd be pissed and/or possibly try to murder us."

Arliss looks off, thinking. "You're right. But if y'all die in a car wreck on some godforsaken sixteen-lane highway in Florida, I'll eat a bunch of asparagus, dig you up, and then piss on your corpses. If there's anything left after the gators have had their way."

"I'm gonna cry," Delia says. "It feels good to be loved."

Arliss isn't done. "Don't drink any of that Five-Hour Energy snake oil or anything else invented by the Nazis and now sold in little plastic vials at truck stop counters along the great American highway. It'll all give you a stroke."

"Okay," I say.

Arliss catches my eyes and points for emphasis. "Good honest coffee."

"What about lying coffee?" I'm pushing my luck here, and I know it.

"Don't sassmouth. And take turns driving." Arliss nods in the direction of the bathroom. "Make Jean-Claude Van Damme carry his weight."

"Oh, we will."

"And speaking of, you said y'all are meeting with showbiz types down there?"

"Right."

"Keep Jean-Claude with you for every meeting with those guys. They think they can do anything. I'd like to see them get kicked in the head if they try. I don't want any Hollywood creeps messing with you two."

"Okay." I'm genuinely moved a little bit. Arliss probably comes across as a cranky loser to someone who doesn't know him. And certainly neither of us knows him well. But I've always sensed a world-weariness in him that makes it seem like his advice has come at the cost of hard experience, so it's more valuable.

Lawson leaves the restroom at a sprint. "I'm ready. Let's roll."

Arliss opens the back door for us. "Y'all be safe." He sounds almost paternal. Or maybe like a prison guard wishing a long-time inmate farewell. "Remember that Florida is a land of weirdos and bizarre happenings, and conduct yourselves accordingly."

• • •

Hour One

I've gotten my car somewhat less looking like a troop of baboons makes its home there. But still, with three people in it and all of our luggage, it's cramped.

"You can have shotgun," Lawson says to Delia.

"I mean, obviously," Delia says, getting in.

Lawson folds himself into the back seat. He's about six feet tall, so it'll be a long ride for him. Fortunately, he loves pain and suffering.

"Get some music going," I say.

Delia plugs in her phone. "Okay, first up, I have this playlist Jesmyn made us. It's like ninety percent Dearly songs."

"Who's Dearly?" Lawson asks.

"Listen and learn," I say, setting my phone's GPS for the convention center in Orlando. I put my car in gear, and we start to drive. "He's from some hick town here in Tennessee, so he should be right up your alley."

"If we run out of stuff to listen to, I have a bunch of music on my phone," Lawson says.

"Wait," I say. "Like Lawson-trying-to-impress-me music or Lawson-left-to-his-own-devices music?"

"The second one. Probably. I think."

"Dude, we are not listening to Carrie Underwood."

"Not Carrie Underwood."

"Or Dierks Bentley or Kenny Chesney or—"

"Groat Scroggins or . . . Pam . . . Weenus," Delia says.

"I've never heard of Groat Scroggins or Pam Weenus," Lawson says.

"Because I made them up. You get the point."

"The point is that at no point in this trip will we be listening to any music that sounds like someone hollerin' into a pair of jean shorts," I say.

"We will not be listening to any music that sounds like someone walking angrily down the street in flip-flops, holding a cigarette between their lips with their hands free, *sir*," Delia says.

"We will, at no time, be listening to any music that sounds like a sentient John Deere hat trying to have sex with a duck call, *sir*," I say.

"In no way, shape, or form will we be listening to any music that sounds like going barefoot into a Walmart to buy a new pair of panties because a possum made off with your last clean pair, *sir*."

Lawson claps his hands over his ears in good-natured exasperation and surrender. *"Okay, okay, okay!"*

Delia and I cackle.

"Have you noticed that if you switch the first letters of every country singer's first and last name, you end up with an amazing Star Wars name?" I ask. "Like, Slake Bhelton. Prad Baisley."

"Barth Grooks."

"Rhomas Thett."

"Belsea Kallerini."

"Are you two *sure* you aren't sisters?" Lawson asks.

"No," we say simultaneously, giggling.

Lawson facepalms. "Lord almighty, what have I signed up for?"

"You have no idea what you've gotten yourself into, going on a road trip with us," Delia says. "Hope you like Beyoncé songs."

"And gas station nachos," I add.

"And stopping to pee a lot," Delia says.

We talk as though we're seasoned road-trippers. In truth, Delia and I went to Memphis once for a concert and Nashville once to go shopping. I've driven to Atlanta to visit my aunt. That's the extent of it.

"That's all right," Lawson says. "I won't regret coming."

I glance in the rearview mirror and catch his eyes. He gives me a little smile that tells me he isn't lying about no regrets. I give him one back, and a glowing rush passes through me.

Hour Two

The sun dips completely below the horizon, leaving the sky a lavender gray, and we roll down our windows and let the magnolia-blossom-and-warm-asphalt-scented wind buffet our hair around our faces, making our eyes water and forcing us to yell to hear each other over the road noise and the music we've turned up. It's uncomfortable in the best way.

I'm reverberating with so many different emotions; they echo inside me like sound in a cavern, blurring into each other until I can't distinguish them. Fear. Hope. Love. Anxiety. Sadness. Anticipation. Some I can't name. Maybe there's a great German word for them.

You don't always know at the time when you're experiencing one of those random memories you'll carry all your life. When nothing momentous happened other than driving a little too fast in the direction of Florida, at dusk, with your best friend by your side and, at your back, a guy who's really good at kissing you. Still, you remember it until the day you die.

But this time I know.

Delia

Hour Three

The volume of the music has inched slowly downward as conversation has overtaken it.

"Okay, so would you rather fight one horse-sized duck or fifty duck-sized horses?" Lawson asks, sticking his head between our seats.

"You got that question from the internet," I say.

"So? It's still a valid question."

"I could sense you mining the deepest reaches of your mind for something weird enough for us to be interested in talking about," Josie says.

"I'm trying to keep up here."

Josie pulls his head onto her shoulder and nuzzles it. "Awww."

It's sweet how hard he tries. I'm fine with people who love uninteresting stuff as long as they go in for interesting stuff too. Plus, he and Josie are good at not making me feel like a third wheel.

"So?" Lawson says.

"Obviously the fifty duck-sized horses," Josie says.

"Same," I say.

"Why?" Lawson asks.

"Well, a goose is a goose-sized duck, so—" Josie starts.

"No, it isn't," Lawson says. "A goose is a goose, and a duck is a duck."

"They're both birds that make honk noises and live in the water. They're both ducks. Geese are just big ducks."

"Is this like how basset hounds are grown-up beagles?" Lawson asks.

"No, that's stupid and weird."

"Oh."

"Anyway, geese are goose-sized ducks and they're really mean and scary, so a horse-sized duck would be *terrifying*."

"You know what a horse-sized duck is?" I say. "A dinosaur. That's what. I'm not fighting a dinosaur."

"Duck-sized horses are basically squirrels," Josie says.

Lawson shakes his head. "What?! No. Chihuahuas, at least."

"Whatever. Anyway, I'll fight fifty Chihuahuas. What do you pick?"

"Horse-sized duck."

"Come on," I say.

"For real. I could use my striking skills to keep it at a distance and wear it down. But those skills aren't as useful against fifty opponents. Plus, I'm not scared of a duck bite. It's not like they have huge teeth."

"I'd say the winner of this debate is the God of Death, who's now several minutes closer to claiming all of us," I say.

Hour Four

Lawson's taken over driving. I'm in the back seat. Beyoncé sing-along, as promised. Lawson is a good sport as he sings (badly) along (a bit behind us). Gas station nachos, as promised. We pass

Chattanooga. None of us have ever been to Rock City. But we all think it sounds fun. Josie and I watch makeup tutorial videos on Dollywould on our phones until Josie gets carsick.

Hour Five

We've just gotten done talking about which celebrities we would eat and why, if we were shipwrecked with them. Josie and I watch a YouTube video of a girl listening to "All Star" by Smash Mouth and taking a bite of onion every time the song says "star." Then we watch a video of a dude singing "All Star" but one beat behind the rhythm.

Josie takes a sip of the drink she bought at our last gas stop because it had a hilarious name—Dr. Fizz. "This honestly tastes like at the factory where they make garbage generic sodas. At the end of each day, when they clean out the pipes or whatever, it all goes into the Dr. Fizz vat."

"I can only imagine. Even Dr Pepper tastes like *everything*. Like literally every flavor known to man," I say.

"I am not enjoying this," Josie says. "And yet I can't stop drinking it."

"Sometimes you have to see a generic soda through to the end," I say.

Josie takes another sip and winces. "What's weird to think about is how there's probably someone in this world who's rich because of Dr. Fizz."

"Oh, I know! Like how there's someone who probably drives a Lexus because they own a candy-corn company," I say.

"A candy-corn magnate!"

"A *monocle-wearing* candy-corn magnate!"

233

Josie hands me her bottle for a sip. "You gotta. So you don't die never having tried Dr. Fizz."

"Shouldn't one of you be sleeping so you can drive next?" Lawson asks, still behind the wheel.

We laugh and repeat back 'Shouldn't one of you be sleeping so you can drive next?' in mocking, high-pitched voices.

Lawson grins and shakes his head but bears our torment with stoicism. This ability, more than anything else, gives me faith in his future with Josie.

Hour Six

"No, but listen," Josie says.

"Uh-oh. When Josie says 'No, but listen,' that's always trouble," I say.

"I'm just saying, it's sweet how humans are animals too, but we wear clothes and drive cars. We're like dogs in sweaters and chimps in tuxedos."

Josie seems nervous about something. When she is, she talks a lot about nothing. I probably seem jittery too. I am.

But the thing with a best friend is that you're never talking about nothing. Even when you're talking about nothing, it's something. The times when you think you're talking about nothing, you're actually talking about how you have someone with whom you can talk about nothing, and it's fine.

We pass Atlanta. At this hour, the traffic is light. The air gets heavier and thicker as we travel south. More lush and tropical. The landscape changes. Dense forests of towering, ruler-straight pine trees line the highway like the world is raising thousands of index fingers with a good idea.

234

It makes me wonder how Dad got to Florida. Maybe he drove this route. Maybe he had a heaviness in his heart to match the weight of the air. Or maybe his heart skimmed the tops of the pines. I wonder if it felt like he was shedding something as the miles fell away beneath his feet. Like he was pulling off a jacket that never really fit him.

This is, as far as I know, the closest I've been to my dad in ten years. Every minute brings me closer.

I still don't know what I'm going to do about that.

Josie

Hour Seven and a Half

We stop at a gas station outside Vienna, Georgia. Delia and I run
in to pee. Lawson gases up my car. I beat Delia back out. Lawson
has moved my car away from the pumps and is leaning against
it. He smiles as I approach.

I stop short of him. "Hey."

"Hey," he says.

"I'm tired."

"Me too."

I close my eyes and pretend-snore, falling toward him, knowing he'll catch me. He does, dipping me like we're dancing. I
give a quick yip of a laugh. It's louder than I expect over the
distant ocean-wave wash of cars on the highway behind us and
the riot of crickets, cicadas, and frogs—the only sounds at the
sleepy gas station.

I genuinely want to fall asleep in his arms, but even more
than that, I want him to kiss me, and he does as he pulls me back
upright.

Being alone with him for this brief moment feels like going
to the freezer and eating only one spoonful of ice cream.

"Hey," I say.

"Hey," he says.

"Hey," I say.

He kisses me. "Hey."

"I like you," I say.

"I like *you*."

"I'm glad you came."

"I'm glad *you* came."

"Stop copying me," I say, resting my head on his chest.

"Stop copying me." He interlaces his fingers on my lower back.

"My name is Lawson Vargas, and I believe that changing your underwear gives you the flu."

"My name is Lawson Vargas, and I believe that changing your underwear gives you the flu."

"I have a hot, genius girlfriend," I murmur.

"I have a hot, genius girlfriend," he says. I can sense his face opening into a radiant, triumphant grin. "I love it when you call yourself my girlfriend."

"You lose."

"Do I? Oh no. I hate losing." He puts two fingers under my chin and gently lifts my head, and we kiss for a couple of seconds.

I rest my head back on his chest, listening to his heartbeat. It's strong and a little faster than I would have expected. His T-shirt smells like dryer sheets. It's a welcome, comfortable, and safe smell. For the last few hours, I've felt like my future is a tiny, hard planet deep in my chest, its gravity pulling every thought into its orbit.

Lawson reads my mind. "I really hope this trip is a success for you guys," he murmurs into the crown of my head.

"Me too." *You have no idea how much I hope that, you beautiful new complication, you.*

He rests his lips in my hair, and we listen to the summer night's symphony until Delia finally returns.

Delia

Hour Eight

"Why did I not listen to Arliss?" I moan.

"How did drinking something called Cobra Venomm Energy Infuzion—spelled with two *m*s and a *z*—seem like a wise plan?" Josie asks.

"*I don't know, I don't know, I don't know.* I can feel my hair. Like each individual hair, I can feel. This is meth in a little plastic bottle." I drum my feet on the floorboards, pound on the steering wheel, and throw my head back and howl, "*Wooooooooo!*"

"We should pull over and get her a branch or something to chew on," Lawson says.

"Let's talk about something. Anything. My brain is going bananas," I say.

"Uh," Josie says.

"Uh," Lawson says.

"*Come on,*" I say.

"It's hard to think of something to talk about on the spot! And also, it's like four a.m. and none of us have had more than an hour of sleep."

"Let's list words we hate!" My mind feels like it's in a blender. "*Puberty! Fungus! Gumption!*"

Josie fumbles around. "Uh . . . *squish, mucus, spork.*"

"Go, Lawson!" I shout.

"Uh."

"Okay, new game. I'm tired of this one," I say. "What's the hardest thing you've ever done? Josie, go!"

"DeeDee, my brain is moving at like one-eighth the pace of yours right now. I gotta think. Come back to me."

"Lawson! Go!"

He shakes his head. "I don't know." But it's an *I don't know if I should say,* not an *I don't know what to say.*

"Come on, Lawson."

"Do it," Josie says.

"Maybe another time."

"No time like the present!" I say. I start chanting, "Law*son*, Law*son*, Law*son*." Josie joins me.

"It'll sound stupid."

"No, it won't," Josie says.

Lawson doesn't say anything for a couple of seconds, and then gives a rueful-sounding laugh. A surrender. "Y'all really wanna hear this?"

"Yes!" we shout in unison.

He turns down the music. "Um. Okay. I guess I was eight or nine. My mom had this, like, porcelain cat. She got it from her dad. I guess it had gotten passed down, like an heirloom or something. Anyway, I liked it because it was old and kinda cool and special. So I ask my mom if I can take it to show-and-tell at school. She doesn't want to let me, but I beg and beg and finally she says okay. I take it to show-and-tell, and I'm super excited.

"School lets out and I'm walking home. I have the cat in my backpack, and I run into this group of sixth graders who loved to pick on me. I mean, they picked on everyone smaller than

239

them, but I guess I was convenient. Anyway, they chase me and catch me and push me down and pull off my backpack and start kicking it like a soccer ball. I'm crying and screaming and telling them not to because they'll break the cat. They don't care. They open the backpack and sure enough, it's busted up. They laugh and start meowing.

"I pick up the pieces and put them back in my bag and walk home. When I get there—"

Lawson pauses for a second. It's silent in the car. He clears his throat and again laughs a little. Like he's covering something. "When I get there, I pull the broken pieces of the cat out of my backpack and show my mom. All my brothers were there. Asking me why I didn't fight back better or run faster. My mom tried to act like it was okay, but I could see it wasn't. Her face. Anyway. That was the hardest thing I've ever done. Telling my mom I'd let her down. In the exact way she was afraid of."

You know how they say something is a buzzkill? This story was that in the most real sense. But it was exactly what I needed. "Wow."

"Geez," Josie murmurs.

"Yeah. Anyway," Lawson says.

"You should look them up. See if they're available for a re-match," I say.

Lawson tries to sound cheery. "Hey! That's an idea. I should do that."

"Because now you're really good at fighting," I say.

"No, yeah, I got it."

We drive on for a couple more moments.

"Your turn, JoJo," I say.

"Oh, great."

"You still don't have yours?"

"No, I do."

"Well, then."

"It sucks compared to Lawson's."

"Not a contest."

"All right. So this one time I had to go pee in a port-a-pot and I was wearing a one-piece romper."

Josie

Hour Nine and a Half

Delia's gone eerily quiet. I don't know if it's the Cobra Venomm wearing off, exhaustion, anticipation over meeting Divine, or something else entirely. She's staring out the window almost purposefully. Like she's looking for something. Or someone.

"You okay, DeeDeeBoo?" I ask softly.

It's a moment before she answers. "I'm good. You good?"

"Yeah. My ass is crying out for mercy. Any time in our lives when we were not in this Kia Rio is but a distant memory."

"We have always lived in this Kia Rio."

Delia

Hour Ten

Dawn is breaking, and we can finally make out the Florida land-scape. I thought it would look a lot more tropical and exotic. More palm trees and parrots. It looks disappointingly like west Tennessee. Endless miles of green foliage cut through with blacktop highway. Rows of pine trees. Lots of pickup trucks with Confederate flags.

I wonder if this disappointed my dad too, or if he accepted the reminder as some sort of penance.

Hour Twelve and Forty-Seven Minutes

We arrive at the Convention Center Days Inn. We check in, set an alarm for two hours, and fall on top of the beds without even taking our shoes off. I plummet into a dreamless sleep.

Josie

We buy our tickets and enter the convention center. It's a buzzing hive of nerdery. Dude cosplayers as Freddy, Jason, Pinhead, Michael Myers, Heath Ledger's Joker, the Babadook, Leatherface, White Walkers, Daryl Dixon, Beetlejuice, lots of generically creepy clowns, and zombies. Girl cosplayers as Samara from *The Ring*, Harley Quinn, SkeleTonya, Ripley, Wednesday and Morticia Addams, Lily Munster, Eleven and Barb from *Stranger Things*, Lydia Deetz, Buffy, and creepy clowns and zombies.

There are also these guys and girls called sliders, who wear kneepads, metal caps on the toes of their shoes, and gloves with metal plates on the palms and fingers and take running starts and slide on their knees and bellies on the convention center floor. There don't seem to be any standards as to what constitutes good or skilled sliding, so it's sort of like watching kids sliding in their socks on a newly waxed floor. But they look like they're having fun.

Booths sell masks; busts; DVDs; posters; comics; bobbleheads; Funko Pops; jewelry; homemade perfumes, soaps, and candles with labels in Papyrus font; intricately decorated replicas of human skulls; custom Ouija boards; makings for spells; knives and swords; corsets; animal bones; taxidermy; vintage toys, lunch boxes, and medical instruments; pulp paperbacks; and art prints.

Long, snaking lines of people await pictures and autographs from cast members of *The Walking Dead, Buffy, Penny Dreadful,* and *American Horror Story.* There's a joyous, childlike, infectious air of good-natured goofiness all around. I've seen no fewer than three Jack Skellington tattoos.

Delia seems more in her element than I've ever seen her. She's taking it all in with the broad smile and buoyant wonder of someone who suddenly feels a lot less alone, who sees new possibility in who she is. It makes me happy. She points out people who had bit parts in obscure grindhouse flicks, other horror hosts, directors, writers, and artists. I didn't grasp the depth and breadth of her knowledge. She must spend close to every minute we're apart acquiring more arcana.

The thing is, I don't feel like I quite fit in. Even though lord knows I've seen my fair share of awful horror movies. Even though I've devoted hours of my life every week to horror hosting. Somehow I feel like I'm watching people through glass.

Delia and I are costumed and made up as Delilah and Rayne. I actually feel *more* comfortable dressed this way here than in my normal clothes. Lawson appears to have gone (hilariously and adorably) with his best notion of bodyguard chic: a black T-shirt, black jeans, and black Vans. All he's missing is sunglasses and an earpiece. He's taking his role very seriously—hovering behind us, silent, stoic, and on high alert for any threat.

We've been there about an hour, wandering aimlessly around the convention floor booths, in a fog from exhaustion and sensory overload, when someone shouts, "Rayne Ravenscroft! Delilah Darkwood!" in a strong upper Midwestern accent.

We turn. It didn't occur to me for even a second that someone might recognize us. What a silly thing to be surprised by, though. If there's *one* place on earth someone might know who we are, it's here.

The shout came from a man who appears to be in his late forties, with a graying goatee, wearing an Indiana Jones hat, an olive-green short-sleeved button-down shirt, a tactical kilt with a cell phone clipped to the waistband, and those goony dad sport sandals that are illegal to wear if you're not at least a forty-two-year-old man with nightmarish hairy orc feet. They're at least a size too small, and his toes—which look like they were pedicured by lowering them into a tank full of piranhas—extend over the edge. He saunters in our direction unhurriedly. He walks like how a tuba sounds. "Rayne, Delilah," he says again in a tone of vague irritation.

"Hi. Rayne Ravenscroft," I say as he nears. The earthy bouquet of mashed potatoes precedes him by a few feet. I extend my hand. He shakes it with a large, meaty, warm-yet-somehow-still-clammy butt cheek of a hand.

"Delilah Darkwood," Delia says, and shakes his hand too.

"Larry Doehnat."

"Larry *Donut?*" Delia asks.

"Doehnat. There's an *h* in there. Huh-huh. Doe-huh-nut."

"It really sounds like donut," Delia says.

"Doe-huh-nut."

"Donut."

"Doe-huh-nut. H. Huh."

"Donut."

"Your friends call you Dunkin?" I ask. Not my A game, but listen: I'm tired.

"I do not subscribe to the antiquated notion of 'friendship,'"

246

he replies in a grandiose tone. I've never heard such smugness over being friendless.

"Oh," I say.

"I need signatures from you two." He says it like we have to sign for the load of chicken manure he's dumping in our front yard.

"Yeah, definitely," Delia says. She fumbles around. "Do you have a—"

He's way ahead of her. He pulls out a tattered, grease-spotted journal, opens it to a page, clicks open a pen, and hands it to Delia, studying her through round glasses that look like he washed them with sausage gravy. "Please sign on this line right here. Kindly take care that your signature not encroach onto other lines."

"Okay, cool." Delia signs carefully and hands the journal to me.

"Same instructions for you," Larry says. "Please don't—"

"Yep. Got it, no encroaching," I say. I sign carefully for the most part but definitely encroach a little bit on purpose. *Encroach*. What a dumb word. I'll croach; I don't care.

"So, where are you from, Larry?" Delia asks sweetly while I sign.

He looks at her for a second like it's a stupid question. "Milwaukee."

"We air in Milwaukee?" Delia asks with an eager lilt.

Larry snort-laughs. "Heavens no."

"Then how did you know us?" Delia sounds deflated.

"Well, it wasn't easy, I'll tell you that. You're rather obscure."

"Oh. Cool," I say, not trying too hard to tamp down the irritation in my voice.

247

"I'm the one who introduced you to the Obscure Horror Hosts subreddit."

"How can we ever repay you?" I mutter.

"I'm collecting autographs and getting photos with all of the active horror hosts in the United States. I never thought I'd bag you two so quick." Larry gives a turkey-choking-on-a-grasshopper chuckle at his good fortune.

"That's a . . . fun way to put it," Delia says, the sweetness dissolving from her like cotton candy sprayed with a hose.

Her tone, like mine, is completely lost on Larry. "All right, let's get a picture." He unclips his phone from the waistband of his kilt and shoves it at Lawson. "You here to make sure these two behave?"

Lawson doesn't smile or respond. He takes the phone. Larry pushes up his glasses and stands between Delia and me, wrapping his pale, sweaty, hairy, squid-tentacle arms around our waists. His hand is on my ribs, right below my boobs. He's doing the same to Delia.

"Um, yeah. This is—" I say, fidgeting.

"Could you just—" Delia says.

We squirm and wriggle to put some distance between us and Larry. I buy myself a few centimeters. *How does a human smell this much like mashed potatoes? Is he using a mashed potato–infused bodywash?*

"Okay, hold still for the picture," Larry says.

Lawson, clearly seething, takes a couple of pictures and hands back Larry's phone, still without a word.

Larry gives us one last unnecessary squeeze into him. "Mission accomplished!" he crows.

"Well, it's exciting to meet a fan," Delia says.

Larry snort-laughs again. "I wouldn't call myself a *fan*, per se. I'm not a great *fan* of that term." He gives us a *see what I did there* smirk.

I point at him and click my tongue. "*Rock*-solid joke, Larry."

"I consider myself more a *connoisseur* of horror hosting. A chronicler of it, good and bad."

"Oh," Delia says.

"Right now, you guys . . ." He makes a high-pitched *meh* sound. "But I think in time, you'll improve somewhat," Larry says, magnanimity dripping from each word.

"Cool, thanks," I say icily.

"You two could definitely ad-lib less."

"Duly noted," Delia says.

"Call your Frankenstein puppet Frankenstein's Monster instead."

"Oh, totally. *Never* heard that before," I say. Delia, Lawson, and I begin our drift away from Larry, but he's not taking the hint.

"You could also turn up the comedy on the show," Larry says.

"Oh, *do* tell. What do you find funny, Larry Donut?" Delia asks.

"People falling down and internet memes."

"Fantastic," Delia says flatly.

"I think that's about it for feedback," Larry says.

"*Nooo*, keep going," I say under my breath.

"Oh! And don't be afraid to dress a little sexier. Spice things up. Take a page from SkeleTonya's book."

"We graduated from high school like one week ago," Delia says.

Larry shrugs. "Congratulations."

"Okaaaay," Delia and I say almost simultaneously. We cut off Lawson, who started to weigh in too. We pick up the pace.

Larry walks more quickly. "Whew, walking this fast is hard in my Utilikilt. Not much support down there, if you know what I mean." He starts to say something else—more helpful advice, I'm sure; maybe that we should smile more—but I cut him off.

"Anyway, Larry—"

Then he cuts *me* off. "Oh, also it wouldn't kill you two to smile more. The show is mostly fine there, I'm talking about in person now. Makes you seem friendlier."

"All right, Larry," I say. "This has been fun the way holding in a fart is fun, but we need to be going," I say over my shoulder.

Larry stops trying to keep up and bleats after us, "Word to the wise: it's not a terrific idea to hold in farts. Does liver damage."

Delia

"So, I guess *that* happened," I say.

"We just met an anthropomorphic ingrown toenail," Josie says, throwing a quick look behind us to make sure Larry was indeed thoroughly left in the dust.

"Larry is human broccoli."

"He has the charisma of mysterious public stickiness."

"He's a gift card with thirteen cents on it."

"He's as charming as a burp that stinks up the whole room."

"He was a dick," Lawson says, interrupting our bit. But he's not wrong.

"Still, exciting to meet someone who watches the show," I say.

"Oh, totally," Josie says.

My phone buzzes. I check it. "Aw, man," I murmur.

"What?" Josie asks.

"Instead of meeting us in a little bit for lunch, Divine wants to reschedule for a dinner meeting."

"Ah, that sucks. I wanted to get that over with. I'm nervous."

"Same."

As we return to wandering, I settle back into my churning stew of emotions. There's a healthy shot of irritation with Larry Donut, sure. Definitely a dash of leftover exhilaration at being

251

recognized in public. But then . . . something else. Something deeper and bigger than both those things.

Then I place it: when I heard my name (sorta) being called, it made me wonder for a split second (even though the voice and accent were all wrong) if my dad was around this convention somewhere. It's only a few hours from where he lives now. It's a horror convention, so that fits. I can't remember him ever going to one when I was little, but . . .

The thought sets my pulse thrumming and makes me feel sick with nerves. I somehow managed to put him out of my mind, with all of the distractions of the con.

You're so close to him. Closer than you've been in years. I keep looking for him in the crowd. Just in case. I have no clue what I'd do if I actually saw him. Freeze. Cry. Who knows?

My jitters mount as the day wears on and I add being apprehensive about meeting Jack Divine to the mix. If it weren't for all of that, I'd be having a ball. We attend a couple of panels. Watch some amateur short horror films. Someone from Little Rock recognizes us. She's a lot cooler than Larry. We sign her autograph book.

I get an autograph from Sick-ola Tesla, a web-only horror host I'm into. We talk a little shop. He praises us for keeping the tradition of public access TV horror hosting alive. He's weird but nice.

At one point, I strike up a conversation with a director of independent horror films who lives in Birmingham, Alabama, and works at the public access station there. I give him one of our DVDs. We exchange phone numbers and promise to stay in touch. I sense friend potential.

Lawson and Josie make goo-goo eyes at each other. He carries her heels for her while she wears more walking-friendly flip-flops around the con. Honestly, I'm glad they're keeping each other occupied, because I can tell Josie would be massively bored otherwise, and I'm in no state of mind to entertain her. I keep thinking how much my dad would love this convention. How it should be him and me here together.

We're now scheduled to meet Jack Divine at 5:00. By the time 4:45 rolls around, I feel like puking. *You went to all that trouble to get your dad's info. You hired a PI while you and Mom barely had money to keep the lights on. You've chickened out every time you've tried to write him. When are you going to be this close to him again? You can't afford to just up and travel to Florida.*

My stomach winds around itself. I chew on my thumbnail.

"DeeDee?" Josie says, eyeing me with concern.

"Huh?"

"You okay?"

"Totally."

"You look a little . . . ghostly."

"Just, you know, tired."

"Same."

"And nervous."

You won't get another chance. You're a few hours away. You know where he lives right now. You can do it. You can go and ask him why. You can finally exorcise that question from haunting your life. You have to leave by noon tomorrow to get home for work. Josie has a job interview on Monday. Lawson has to be back too. It's tonight or never.

I start literally wringing my hands.

"It'll be fine," Josie says.

I swallow hard and nod. "Josie?"

"Yeah?"

I pause for a beat or two. "Nothing."

"What?"

I gnaw on the inside of my lip. "Remember how I told you my dad lives in Florida now?"

"*Here?*"

"Boca Raton. A few hours away."

"Did you think you saw him here?"

"No . . . but . . ." The words catch in my chest. "I'm thinking of trying to go see him."

"DeeDee," Josie says quietly, in almost a gasp.

"I know. I can't decide if I should."

"Part of you must have wanted to, or you wouldn't have tracked him down."

"I know, I know." I make my hands into fists to stop them from shaking.

"If you want to go, you can take my car. Lawson and I can handle the meeting with Divine."

I stop and look up at the ceiling. "Arrrrrrrgh. Why did I put myself through this?" I ask through clenched teeth.

"Because you had to. Go see him."

"Should I?"

"You'll torment yourself forever if you don't. I know you."

"You're cool handling our meeting?"

"I definitely don't know horror stuff like you do, but yeah, I'm cool."

I believe her. If only one of us has to handle this meeting, it should be Josie. She's got an easy confidence that naturally draws people in. Better that than my knowledge of horror film and hosting history and culture. "I don't think he's going to quiz us or anything. You're better at dealing with people than me, anyway."

"So. Confronting your dad."

I cover my face with my hands. "I know," I say from between my fingers. "I'm fully freaking out here."

"I mean, yeah." Josie hugs me. She must be able to feel me trembling.

"Like I think I would be useless to you if we met with Jack Divine. I'd be obsessing over how I'm missing a chance to visit my dad."

"Do it. Go see him."

"I'm doing it." I try to say it with enough resolve to convince myself.

"Are you gonna leave now?"

"I came all this way. I have to at least meet Jack Divine first. Then I will."

"We're still wearing our show clothes," Josie says. "I'm so tired, I didn't even think about it. Do we have time to change?"

"I think it's fine," I say. "I've been reading up on Jack Divine, and he definitely seems like the type who'd be okay with costumes. Might even help."

We go to the meeting place I planned out with Divine's assistant, in the lobby of the convention center. We wait in apprehensive silence. Five o'clock comes and goes. Then 5:05. Then 5:10.

"Should we . . . contact him?" Josie asks.

"I don't know." My stomach feels like a burlap sack of baby spiders. "Let's give it a few more minutes." It's 5:15. *Come on. Come on.*

At 5:19, we spot him. He's stalk-thin and maybe five-foot-three. He looks to be in his sixties, but he has a shoe-polish-black pompadour that gleams purple-blue under the harsh convention-center lighting. His skin is gas-station-hot-dog orange from some industrial-grade fake tanner. A thin black worm of a mustache sits just atop his upper lip. It looks penciled on. He's clothed in a shiny red suit that he does not so much *wear* as he is *festooned by*, a lemon-yellow dress shirt with the top three buttons undone, and white alligator shoes with black tips.

Behind him lumbers a hulking slab (also slob) of a man, who's grizzled and gray in every way—his buzz cut, his skin, his teeth, his watery eyes, his dour facial expression. He looks like he's made of scrap iron smeared with Crisco. He's probably six-foot-three and 275 pounds, wearing a long leather jacket (that appears to have been slapped together by the makers of my skunk pants) with cheap-looking black dress slacks and those old-man dress shoes that are sorta sneakers. Elaborate tattoos of stars, skulls, and some big, ornate Russian-looking church with a bunch of onion domes peek out from under the cuffs and above the collar of his yellowed-white dress shirt.

We stand at attention and try to smile as they approach. They walk right past us.

"Mr. Divine?" Josie calls after him.

He holds up his hand without turning around. "Can't. Meeting someone." He talks with that weird old-timey radio accent from the 1940s that doesn't exist anymore.

"I think we're who you're meeting?" I say.

He and his henchman turn and eye us.

"I set up this meeting with your assistant, Celeste?" I say.

"Celeste?"

". . . St. James?"

He still looks flummoxed for a moment. Then, "Ahhh, haha, yes! Celeste. Of course. Dear Celeste."

We laugh nervously. *He forgot his assistant's name? Weird.*

He walks up. "Jack Divine, as you obviously know. And you are?"

"Josie Howard. It's nice to meet you."

"Lawson Vargas. Good to meet you."

"Delia Wilkes, sir. Pleasure. My dad and I used to watch your show. And *SkeleTonya*, obviously."

"And what about my more recent work?"

"Um." I gulp.

"Love it," Josie says. "Of course."

He's all too happy to not call her bluff. His face glows with pleasure. "Well, well, I think we'll get along fine. Oh! Where are my manners? This is Yuri." He gestures at the Gray Hulk. Yuri grunts. "Yuri is my . . . associate?" He looks to Yuri for approval.

Yuri nods. "Associate," he says in a heavy Russian accent. "And financial planner."

Jack Divine giggles strangely.

We all murmur hello to Yuri.

I have no idea how this sort of meeting works. I guess we might as well get to the point. "So, we were hoping to—to talk to you about our show. We're—we're horror hosts," I stammer.

"Are you, now? I certainly haven't heard of you," Divine says.

"No. That's why we wanted to meet with you," Josie says.

"Where did you say you were out of? New York? LA?"

"Jackson. Tennessee," Josie says.

Divine gasps. "Jackson, Tennessee? Where on earth is that? Wherever it is, Jack's-a-not going there! Get it?"

257

"Yeah, that's fun," Josie says, forcing a laugh. "Wordplay."

Divine puts his hands on his hips and affects a broadly stereotypical Southern accent, the worst I've ever heard. "I *do* declayah, Miss Scahlett, these-uh young ladies have-a come all the way from the Land uh Dixie and *Deliverance* to become stahs! TV stahs! They want ol' city slicker Jack Divine to make them-a famous!" He looks to Yuri for approval.

Yuri grunts and smiles (?). (It's clear he's not terrific at smiling.) "Kenny Rogers," he says, like he's challenging us to fight. We wait for him to finish the sentence or connect it to some larger idea, but no. Just "Kenny Rogers."

Josie and I shoot each other an *oh boy, this could be really bad, but maybe he's just an eccentric Hollywood type . . . those Hollywood types can be really eccentric, right?* look that Lawson joins.

I figure this is probably as good a time as any to make my exit. The adrenaline over meeting Jack Divine has been replaced with adrenaline over seeing my dad. Divine seems like something of a kook, but the sort Josie and Lawson can handle without me. "Anyway, Mr. Divine, I have to go to another engagement, but Josie and Lawson are going to talk with you about our show. It really was a pleasure to meet you." I hand him a DVD from my tote bag. I've been handing them out all day. I saved two. One for Jack Divine.

"Do yuh have tuh go and slop the hogs now?" Divine says in his grotesque Southern accent.

Wow, is that ever not my favorite. But I humor him with a polite laugh and step away. Josie follows.

She hands me her keys and hugs me. "I hope it goes great," she whispers.

I feel myself teetering. "Get us a TV deal, okay?" I whisper, although I probably didn't even need to. Divine seems to be scanning the crowd for people who recognize him.

I can't believe I'm really doing this.

"Hey, good luck," Lawson says.

"Who needs luck, am I right?" I say. I try to sound jaunty and confident, but I miss the mark by a wide margin.

Maybe it's the stifling heat and humidity that feels like trying to breathe through a wool sock soaked in hot tea, or maybe I'm so preoccupied I'm forgetting to breathe. Whichever it is, I'm thoroughly breathless and panting by the time I get to Josie's car and start it. My hands quake, and I drop my phone twice while I'm pulling up the email with my dad's address. I finally get a grip and punch his address into my phone. A little under three hours' drive.

I take a deep breath and ask the universe—this once, just this one time—for a little bit of good fortune, and I drive off.

Josie

We stand there for a moment, staring at each other awkwardly after Delia leaves. I really wish she were here too. At least I have Lawson.

Divine claps twice to break the silence. "Let's not talk business on an empty stomach. I'm famished." Then, in his Southern accent (which is not getting at all tired and grating), "What say you we get some victuals, missy?"

"Sure, that sounds good."

"Okay, why don't you call us a car?"

"Uh . . . we actually had a car, but Delia took it, so . . ." I'm feeling like a naive kid, out of my depth. I guess I need to get up to speed with how TV types are.

"We'll drive, then." Divine starts striding away, snapping for Yuri to follow. We hurry to keep up.

We pass a girl with blue hair, a Linda Blair tattoo covering her whole upper arm, and several facial piercings, wearing knee-high black leather boots and a black vinyl dress and carrying a rolled-up poster under one arm and texting with the other hand. She makes the briefest eye contact with Divine and smiles politely before looking back at her phone.

He stops, sighs, and rolls his eyes. "Yes, I'm him."

The girl responds with a stunned expression and glances behind her, as if to say, *Me?* "Sorry, I don't—"

"You needn't apologize, dear heart, but I am in a bit of a haste, as I'm sure you've figured. Have to talk some business. So let's get to it, shall we? What am I signing here? No body parts. I jest, of course. Body parts on a case-by-case basis. All right, then. This?" He snatches her poster from under her arm with one hand and reaches out to Yuri with the other hand. Yuri slaps a Sharpie into it like a surgeon's assistant with a scalpel. Divine unrolls the poster and smooths it on Yuri's back.

"Mister, I'm not sure—" the girl says.

"I would've preferred to sign a poster of one of my own works, obviously, but I understand that you may not have expected to encounter me," Divine murmurs as he signs.

The girl is still too flabbergasted to react. She looks to Lawson and me. I give her an apologetic shrug. She mouths, *Who is he?*

I mouth back, *Jack Divine.*

She shakes her head, perplexed. *I don't know who that is.*

I shake my head. *Neither did I until a few weeks ago.*

Divine finishes signing, rolls up the poster briskly, and hands it back.

The girl takes it. "Um . . . thanks."

Divine sighs again. "All right, I'll take a picture with you. I sense your reluctance to ask, so I'll cut to the chase for both of our benefits." Divine seizes her phone and hands it to Yuri, then stands beside the shell-shocked-looking girl.

Yuri fumbles with the phone in his bear-paw hands. "Cheese," he commands grimly, as though ordering a firing squad to shoot.

Divine smiles radiantly, the girl uncertainly. Yuri snaps the photo and hands the girl her phone.

"All right, you got what you wanted," Divine says. "I'm in room fourteen-eleven of the Hyatt Regency if you think of anything else later. The party generally goes between midnight and three a.m. Or until the hotel shuts us down. Do not bring any cats. You may bring glazed donuts but not cake donuts. You may bring cake but not pie. Southern Comfort but not Jack Daniels. You may come dressed as a DC character but not a Marvel character. You may bring a well-mannered ape but not a monkey. If you're unsure of the difference, Google."

"Yeah, definitely don't worry about *any* of that," the girl says.

"Right then, I really can't tarry any longer," Divine says.

"That's fine."

Divine starts to walk away. He turns back. "What?"

"I didn't say anything."

"I thought—"

"Nope. Didn't say a word."

He points at her, eyebrows raised. "Room fourteen-eleven!"

"To be clear: I will not come."

"A firm maybe, then!" Divine claps at us. "Posthaste!"

I mouth *I'm sorry* at the girl, who shakes her head again. Lawson and I look at each other. "What just happened?" I whisper so quietly, I'm almost mouthing the words.

"No clue," Lawson whisper-mouths back.

This Jack Divine guy is a real trip.

Yuri stands there for a second and turns to us. "Kenny Chesney," he growls. He walks away, not waiting for any sort of response. Not that there is one.

· · ·

We follow Divine and Yuri out to the parking lot.

"You just witnessed the downside of fame," Divine says to me, heels clicking on the hot asphalt. "Everyone wanting a piece of you. Me, me, me! Let me touch the hem of your garment. It's tiresome, but it comes with the landscape. I'm grateful. Truly, I am. Blessed, if you're into that sort of thing. I don't mean to suggest otherwise. But it would be nice to be able to leave the house, you know?" He mops his brow with a silk handkerchief.

I say nothing and just nod.

"You don't know what that's like. Maybe someday you will," Divine says magnanimously.

"Sure don't," I say. *Except for Larry Donut.*

We arrive at a black Cadillac Escalade. Yuri gets in the driver's seat with a groan and a wheeze after opening the back door for Divine.

"I hope you two don't mind squishing in the far back," Divine says.

"That's fine. Or we could sit in the middle row and you sit up front," I say. "Whichever works."

"Far back."

"Far back it is."

Lawson helps me gather my dress (which I'm beginning to feel pretty ridiculous wearing) and cram into the far back seat— not an easy task in my dress and heels. He folds himself in next to me. The inside of the Cadillac reeks of expensive cologne that smells like cheap cologne.

"AC, Yuri!" Divine moans. "I'm sweating like a pig in line at a whorehouse."

Yuri grunts, and air starts blasting from the vents.

"You a country music fan, Yuri?" I ask.

He grunts.

"Lawson here is," I say. Lawson gives me a *thanks for throwing me under the bus* nod.

Another indecipherable grunt from Yuri. So much for small talk. He puts the Escalade in gear and peels out of the parking lot, pressing us back in our seats.

"Well, I once had a rather lively evening with George Jones, Willie Nelson, and Waylon Jennings in Tijuana," Divine says. "Let's just say it involved some exceedingly pure amphetamines, more racehorse tranquilizer than anyone really needs, several bottles of Jim Beam, a sextet of American strippers with a quintet of teeth among them, a cactus, a live hand grenade, about a dozen Mexican police officers, a chimp dressed like a priest, a priest in a chimp costume, a helicopter, a jug band, and a lemon poppy-seed Bundt cake."

Lawson shows me his phone, on which he's typed, *Or as I call it, another Saturday night.*

I squeeze Lawson's leg. I'm so proud of him. I've turned him into a level-three smartass.

Yuri leads us on a sphincter clencher of a ride through the streets of Orlando. At one point, Lawson puts his arm around me and hugs me into his side to keep me from being tossed around. I could not be doing this on my own. And if, instead of Lawson, Delia were here but wigging out about her dad, I would effectively be alone. So I guess things worked out.

I wonder if I should be taking advantage of the time to talk about the show. I decide to let Divine take the lead tonight and try to play it cool. I'd meant to Google "how to get a TV deal" before our meeting, but it slipped my mind.

We arrive at a place called Linda's Jim Steakhouse. There's a valet stand at the entrance. Pimpy-looking old men in white suits and orange fake tans with their considerably younger wives/girlfriends/mistresses gather around the entrance while valets whisk away their midlife/endlife-crisis mobiles. Dread seeps through me. My budget does *not* allow for a place like this. But what did I expect? Some big Hollywood type to hold a dinner meeting at Arby's? Using my phone camera as a mirror, I hurriedly wipe off some of my makeup, so I merely look eccentric and not professionally bizarre.

"Glad you're here," I whisper to Lawson, gripping his arm.

"Especially after you only recently went to your first restaurant," he whispers back, squeezing my hand on his arm. It takes me a second to remember my own joke. I love that he remembers my jokes even better than I do.

We walk inside the restaurant. It's all dark wood and leather and bottles of expensive-looking alcohol and signed headshots of old-timey famous people and Frank Sinatra playing while pissy-looking middle-aged waiters in white shirts and bow ties hustle around like snobby ants.

"Table for four, and do be as quick as you can," Divine says in an imperious, dismissive tone.

The host eyes the four of us with a wary mix of consternation and contempt. "Let me see what we have available." He gives Lawson the up-and-down. "Sir, I'm afraid our dress code does require a blazer for gentlemen. If you don't have one, I can offer you one to wear while dining."

This is going to be a fun, fun dinner. Did I mention fun?

"Sure," Lawson says tersely. "Hope I don't spill."

With a sour smile, the host walks to a nearby rack, selects a blazer, and hands it to Lawson. "I have you at a thirty-eight chest."

Lawson takes the navy-blue blazer with a little gold crest on the front pocket and puts it on. It fits perfectly.

"Now then," the host says, studying his reservation book. "It will be a few moments before we can seat you."

Divine sniffs. "A few moments? I give myself another hour before I turn to cannibalism."

The host leans in and, in a hushed tone, motioning at the four of us with his index finger, says, "Sir, if this is some sort of situation where—"

"She is *not* a prostitute, sir, if that's what you're implying," Divine says noisily and indignantly, drawing stares. "Well . . . at least I don't know her to be one. In any event, that's not the capacity in which she's here with me."

The host's face goes vermilion. "Sir, you misunderstand me. I wasn't—"

"I'm *actually* standing right here," I murmur, blushing to match the host's shade. No acknowledgment.

Divine draws himself up to his full five-foot-three like a cartoon rooster. "Do you know who I am, sir?"

"I'm afraid memory fails me, sir. Forgive me."

"Well, sir, get on your smartphone or whatever it is you use to inform yourself about the world and look up the name Jack Divine. You'll see I certainly don't pay for sex. Don't need to. And what sort of prostitute dresses like this?" He flicks his hand at me.

266

I want to dissolve and turn to vapor. Even though I am dressed as Rayne, I'm not *too* self-conscious, since the black Hot Topic Victorian-style dress I am wearing looks only a little cos-tumey when you take away the makeup and accessories. Plus, it's Florida, so come on. But now? "Right here," I say. "I am standing *right* here." Nothing.

"*Sir,*" the host says, as though speaking with a toddler, "what I was *going* to say is if this is some sort of double-date situa-tion, we might be able to seat the two couples at separate tables sooner, if time is of great concern."

Divine guffaws. "Yuri? Oh, heavens, I would aim higher than Yuri if I swung that way. He was bred for brawn, not beauty."

"Am standing right here," Yuri growls.

"Yes, yes, fine, forgive me, Yuri," Divine says. "Obviously yours is more of an inner beauty."

This is going to be a long night. Please, God, make it worthwhile. Let me deliver this for Delia. Let me save our show.

Lawson reaches down and squeezes my hand.

And let me save this.

Delia

For a while, I listen to music, loud enough to try to jar the thoughts from my head like pounding on the bottom of a ketchup bottle, but for some reason, I can't stand it. So I try one of my favorite true-crime podcasts. Nope. It sits with me like petting a dog the wrong way.

So I listen to the hum of the tires. I think about Josie and Lawson with Jack Divine. I hope they're doing well. I think about how this is the longest I've ever driven on my own. And I try to plan out what I'm going to say to my dad.

Hi. Maybe you recognize me. I'm the daughter you abandoned.

Hi. I'm Delia Wilkes. Remember me?

Hi, "Derek Armstrong." Bet you never expected to see me again.

And every one of these greetings—each of which rings more tinged with bravado than the last in my mind—ends the same way:

I came to find you because I need you to tell me to my face why you left. I need to know why I wasn't good enough to stay your daughter. Why you couldn't stay my dad.

I need to know why.

The landscape changes as I head southeast toward the coast and take I-95 South. There are more palm trees. I've never seen palm trees before this trip. From the look of my phone GPS, I'm only a short distance from the ocean. I've never seen the ocean either. I've always wanted to. I imagine loving it the way I love storms—things that are so large and powerful, they make me feel like it's okay to be small. I roll down the windows and let the sultry wind buffet my face. Maybe it's my imagination, but there's a salty softness to the air.

If he wanted to pick a place that wouldn't remind him of Jackson, he did well.

I start seeing signs for Boca Raton, and my stomach kneads and froths like it's doing a load of laundry.

This is nuts. You could get off the highway, drive until you hit the beach, kick off your shoes, sit and watch the ocean, and drive back. You'll meet up with Josie and Lawson, and they'll tell you about the amazing deal they worked out with Jack Divine, who, in spite of his obvious quirks, is still a well-connected TV professional.

You'll all change into your swimming suits and romp in the hotel pool until management kicks you out. You'll celebrate your bright future, having finally buried your dad. You'll have shown yourself you have nothing left to prove. Then you'll all drive home in triumph, singing along with Beyoncé at the top of your lungs. It'll be great.

But I'm in the pull of some gravity, and so I keep driving.

· · ·

I sit in front of the address for Derek Armstrong, aka Dylan Wilkes, aka Dad, listening to the engine of Josie's car tick as it cools and listening to my heartbeat throbbing in my ears. There's a Jeep Compass in the driveway, parked behind a Nissan sedan. He drove a Jeep Liberty when I was little. Other than that, I see no outward indication that this is where he lives. His house is small and unspecial, in a part of Boca Raton that seems to be full of small and unspecial houses. But the palm trees lining the street make it seem like an exotic destination. A window AC unit hums and drips. I think I see a flicker of a TV from deep within the house.

My dad might have rebuilt his horror movie collection and is maybe watching one right now. He could be watching my show at this moment for all I know. Maybe he got his hands on it somehow, like Larry Donut did.

I'm dizzy and breathing fast—almost hyperventilating—to the point of growing faint, and my heart is thrumming with more energy than it did when I drank the Cobra Venomm. I catch my eyes in the rearview mirror and try to psych myself up. I notice I'm still wearing my Delilah makeup. I rub most of it off. My dad will already have a hard time recognizing me.

No one would fault you if you left. No one would think less of you. Now you've seen him again, sorta. You've seen for yourself that you share the same planet and breathe the same air.

But that's not what you came for. You didn't come to see if he was still alive. You came to ask him why.

So ask him why.

A part of my brain outside of my conscious control takes over. I open the door and get out, almost collapsing immediately on legs that have taken on the consistency of biscuit dough.

I walk to the front door and stand on the porch. My life feels like it's been leading up to this moment. I suddenly have the most intense focus. I'm noticing everything. That Dad's doorbell is cracked and I can see part of the lightbulb inside. The paint on his screen door is chipped. There's a hole in the screen. The muted sounds permeating from inside.

270

I ring the doorbell and hear footsteps. The space between each footfall is a thousand years. I live a lifetime between each heartbeat.

A man opens the door. "Hi," he says tentatively, not making eye contact. "I'm sorry, I'm not—"

I am looking at my father's face. Dark spots swarm my field of vision. I feel like I'm going to black out.

He looks up and meets my eyes. The color drains instantly from his face, and his jaw hangs slack. "Are you—" he whisper-gasps. His eyes widen, and he steadies himself with a hand on the doorframe. "You can't be—Oh my lord. *DeeDee?*"

And then I look him in the face and I ask him why.

Why he left me behind.

Why I wasn't good enough.

Just kidding! I go to speak and promptly yak all over his front porch.

Josie

They seat us and hand us menus. I open mine like it's a Kleenex someone with Ebola has sneezed into. Oh, fun. Seventy-dollar steaks. Ninety-dollar lobsters. Twenty-five-dollar appetizers. Twenty-dollar salads.

Divine studies the menu. "Mmm, mmm, mmm, everything looks so tasty! Who can choose? So, tell me about your show," he says without looking up, like he's wondering out loud, *Now, what exactly is raclette cheese?*

In fact, I almost miss his asking about the show, that's how nonchalantly and seamlessly he tossed it in. "Um, okay, I'm not totally sure what Delia's told you, but—"

"Am I in the mood for something heavy like a steak?" Divine interrupts. "Or something lighter like lobster? I don't know." He taps his lips and waves at me to continue, still not looking up.

"Uh . . . so . . . we're horror hosts of a show called *Midnite Matinee* on TV Six in Jackson, Tennessee. We air from eleven p.m. to one a.m. on Saturday nights. We've been doing it for about a year and a half. We do a show a week, for the most part—"

"I might do both," Divine says.

"Sorry?"

"The steak and lobster. I can't decide, so I might do both."

"Oh. Anyway, we're syndicated in Little Rock, Topeka, Des Moines, Greenville, Macon—"

"I'm going to do both. The ol' surf 'n' turf. Isn't it strange how good lobsters and beef taste together when lobsters are just giant insects of the sea?"

"It always weirded me out to see ants eating beef, ants on a hamburger or something. It's like, *You couldn't have gotten that beef on your own, ants. Have some respect.*" I'm nervous-jabbering.

Divine's face squinches. "What does that have to do with anything?"

"I mean . . . insects and . . . beef?" I blush. "I thought we were talking about—"

"Very bizarre thing to bring up at dinner. You'll put me off my food." Divine snaps his menu shut. "Horror hosting, you say? You've come to the right man."

"So I understand."

"No one's achieved more in the genre than me. I'm the pinnacle. The top dog. The big cheese. I did well on my own, but with SkeleTonya . . . let me tell you, I took horror hosting to the mainstream. No one has achieved what I have before or since. I made her into a cultural icon. A household name. She owes me her career. Her life. How many other horror hosts do you think most Americans can name? That's right. None. Zip. Now—Oh my." Divine stares.

"What?" I look up. A stunning, Brazilian-looking woman in a sleek black dress is approaching our table.

Divine pretends to look at his menu, but his eyes follow the woman as she passes. She doesn't so much as glance in our direction.

"*Va va voom,*" Divine murmurs. "Yuri, did you see that?"

"Pretty girl," Yuri says, sucking at a tooth.

Divine nods at Lawson. "What say you, young man? Fine specimen, eh?"

"I didn't notice," Lawson says tersely.

Divine slowly lowers the menu. "Now, how am I supposed to concentrate, with Helen of Troy prancing around this steakhouse?"

"Um . . . try really hard?" I say.

"Yuri, when that young vixen comes back this way, do be a prince and get her number for me, won't you?"

Yuri shrugs. "Okeydokey."

I could count on one hand the number of things I would find more unnerving than Yuri asking for my number. "Is that a good idea? I . . . would maybe be weirded out if I were her."

"What am I thinking?" Divine says. "Of course you're right."

"Yeah, I mean—"

"I'll get her number myself. She'll have a much harder time turning me down than Yuri."

"Um."

"No! Better yet! *You* get her number for me. Woman to woman."

"Yeah," I say. "I don't know if I feel comfortable doing that."

"What's your plan, then?"

I pretend to give the matter deep consideration. "I would probably leave her alone. But that's me."

Divine starts to respond, but the waiter comes, drawing his attention, just as the woman is on her way back from the restroom. I'm grateful on her behalf. "Have we decided, ladies and gentlemen?" the waiter asks. "Yes? I'll start with the lady, then."

I'm not sure how this works—if we're paying for ourselves or if he's paying for us, and I'm on a tight budget. I order the baby kale salad. Lawson follows my lead.

"Salads? Here?" Divine asks incredulously. "Boy, are you missing out! I'll start with the crabmeat cocktail and the crab cakes, with the prime porterhouse and the three—no, four-pound Newfoundland lobster. Yuri here will have the same."

"Anything to drink, sir?" the waiter asks.

"You know, we're talking some important business, and I'd say nothing helps lubricate the gears of the free market like . . . a Pappy twelve-year-old. One for me, one for Yuri."

For a second, I wonder if I misheard and Divine actually ordered a "happy twelve-year old," who the waiter would hook up to him with blood transfusion lines. This seems like the kind of place that could accommodate a request like that.

The waiter *glows*. "Yes, *sir*! Impeccable choice, if I do say so myself!"

"I rather thought so! Now, can I get that with a splash of RC Cola?"

The waiter tries not to look aghast but fails.

Divine winks. "I'm joking, of course." He and the waiter share a hearty laugh. I guess it was a great joke?

We make (weird, uncomfortable) small talk while we wait for our food to arrive. I excuse myself to go to the restroom. While I'm in there, I text Delia. Love you, DeeDeeBoo. Thinking of you. When I exit, Lawson is standing outside the door.

"Hey," he says.

"Hey. I'm sorry."

"Don't be."

275

"I am. Dragging you along tonight. For this insanity. I had no idea it'd be like this."

He shrugs. "I would not want you dealing with this dude alone. Plus, I'm spending time with you. All I care about."

I hug him. "Right answer."

He hugs me back. "How you doing?"

"You mean besides that I'm about to sit down to eat a sorry, expensive salad while watching a person whose ego is the size of a sack containing every human sorrow and his Russian mobster bodyguard eat two thousand dollars' worth of steak and lobster?"

"Besides that."

"Besides that every time I try to talk about our show—which is my whole reason for spending an evening with this actual loon—he finds some way to talk about how amazing he is? And meanwhile, my best friend, who arranged this, is on a potential collision course with virtually certain heartbreak three hours away?"

"Besides that."

"Besides that part of me is terrified about where this night is heading, but I'm also feeling weirdly compelled to see it through to the end?"

"Besides that."

"Oh, then great, thanks."

We smile and quickly kiss.

"I've been hanging back," Lawson says. "I have a lot I could say, but I don't want to mess in your business."

"Yeah, let me handle it."

"If you need me to step in at any point . . ."

"I got this."

"Hang in there," Lawson says. "I know he seems like a nut, but maybe he can help y'all."

"I sure hope so because—" I almost slip and tell Lawson what's riding on tonight. But right now is not the time or place. "Otherwise we'll have wasted a perfectly good evening that we could have spent playing in the pool and kissing."

Delia

Dad jumps back to avoid getting his feet splashed.

"Sorry," I wheeze in a *just hurled and might still hurl a little more* voice, doubled over with my hands on my knees. I had the presence of mind not to say "Sorry, *Dad*."

"It's okay, hang on." He slips on a pair of shoes beside the door and leaps clumsily over the pool of barf on his front stoop. He uncoils a hose in the front of the house. "Okay, stand back." He sprays the puke into the bushes, thoroughly diluting it.

I'm hearing my dad's voice again. The same voice that told me to go to sleep. That asked me what I wanted for Christmas. That told me to pick up my toys. His voice.

I watch him in the fading light. He's wearing a polo shirt with *SynergInfo* embroidered on the chest, tucked into khakis. He's got a little belly paunch. He has a gentler slope where his jaw meets his neck than I remember. Fine lines surround his eyes. His hair is thinner and shorter than he used to wear it. He's never looked more like *a* dad. He's never looked less like *my* dad.

While he works, I see him stealing glances at me. He has a stunned expression. There's something else mixed in. Guilt? Anger? Sadness? Wonder? All of the above? He keeps moving his mouth like he's about to say something but stops himself.

"Derek?" a woman's voice calls from inside the house.

Dad leaps up the steps. "What, sweetie?"

Wow, it's weird to hear my dad responding to a new name.

"Everything okay?"

"Yep! I got called into work, and as I was leaving I saw Boomer had puked on the front porch."

"Has he been eating grass again?"

"Probably. I got it handled. Go back to sleep."

The sound of the woman's voice burns my ears. *And he lies so well and so easily.*

He coils the hose. "Hang on," he says quietly. "Let me get my keys." He runs inside and comes back a moment later with keys, some Kleenex, and a cold bottle of water.

I'm standing there, shell-shocked, the bitter stench of puke in my nose. He goes to hug me. "DeeDee."

I put out my hand to stop him. "I—Please just—"

"Yeah, yeah, right. Got it," he stammers. "Okay, we gotta leave. Then we can talk."

I nod and follow him to his Jeep. We get in and he pulls away. He hands me the bottle of water and the Kleenex. I blow my nose and drink half the bottle. We're silent for a second.

I'm being driven somewhere by my dad. I never, ever thought that would happen again.

"You used to spit up a lot as a baby. Your stomach got tougher as you got older, but you still . . ." His voice trails off. Several seconds pass. "How?"

"I hired a PI. Who was that woman?"

"That was, um, Marisol."

"Are you guys—"

"My fiancée."

"Wow." I have that sensation right before you slip on ice. "When's the big day?"

"September."

"Wow."

"She's . . . pregnant. That's why she was asleep when you arrived."

"Wow." (I'm having some vocabulary issues.) "Boy or girl?"

"Girl."

"*Wow*. So I'm going to have a half sister?" I'm reeling inside. I feel like a billy goat just butted me in the stomach.

Dad thinks it through for a second. "Yeah. You are," he says softly.

"A half sister that I would've *never* known about if I hadn't tracked you down."

Dad opens and closes his mouth a couple of times. Finally: "I don't—I—I don't know. Maybe not."

"Lucky little girl." I almost ask what her name's going to be, but I can't go there. *What if it's Delia?*

Dad winces like I kneed him in the nuts. He rubs his forehead.

I turn my face away and look out the window so Dad can't see the tears welling in my eyes. "Does Marisol know?"

"About you?"

"Yeah."

"She . . . does."

"That sounded very tentative."

"It's so weird that you know words like 'tentative' now."

"Does she know or not?"

"She sort of knows. She doesn't ask many questions. I don't think she really wants to know."

"So no."

"Sort of."

I keep looking out the window. "This is so weird."

"She knows it's a painful topic for me and I have a hard time talking about it. She has her own past anyway."

"Does she know your name isn't Derek Armstrong?"

"It *is* Derek Armstrong."

"Does she know you weren't born Derek Armstrong?"

"No." Quiet for a few seconds, and then he asks, "Are you hungry?"

My stomach is technically empty, but it's not sending me any signal as unambiguous as hunger. It has other things on its mind. But I say, "Sure."

"Still like pizza?"

"Do people generally outgrow liking pizza?"

He smiles thinly. "Not usually. I know a place."

· · ·

We sit and order.

"I was hoping it would be Cicis," I say, looking for some hint of recognition of the reference.

"Really?"

"No."

"Because I bet we have one."

I can't tell if he gets it. "No, I'm good."

I'm sitting across from my dad. I'm about to have pizza with my

281

dad again. I feel the tingle of tears gathering in my eyes. One falls in spite of my best efforts. I quickly wipe it away.

"Delia," Dad says softly.

"I'm fine. This is . . . a lot."

"You sure?"

"Yeah." I dab another tear with my napkin.

"I can't believe how big you are. When did you get—" He motions at the bottom of his nose, where my septum is pierced.

"Last year."

"What'd Mom think?"

"She took me to get it."

He laughs. "Sounds right. I can't stop looking at your face."

I guess I don't need to wonder anymore if my show ever somehow reached him. Nope. "Didn't you ever, like, Instagram-stalk me or anything?"

"A couple times. But seeing you . . . from that distance—it broke my heart. I couldn't handle it." Tears well up in his eyes. "Wanna tell me about your life?"

More than anything. And also no. But I do. A little. "After you left, things were hard for a long time. Mom wasn't doing well at all. Me neither. It sucked. For years. But we survived. We each got on medication that helped us a lot with our depression. And—" I realize I'm about to tell him about the most important thing in my life. The thing I made to try to get him back. My sacred thing. "I started a show with my best friend, Josie. Called *Midnite Matinee*. It's on TV Six in Jackson and some other public access stations around the U.S. We're horror hosts, like Dr. Gangrene or SkeleTonya."

"Are you serious?" he says, awestruck.

"That's why we're in Florida. For ShiverCon. Josie is meeting with Jack Divine in Orlando right now."

"Jack Divine? As in Jack-O-Lantern? He did SkeleTonya's show?!"

"The very one. He's talking to us about working together on our show."

Dad sits back. "Wow. *Wow*. DeeDee, that's amazing. Good for you."

And now he knows. It feels strangely anticlimactic. I think about all the times I sat there, Arliss counting us in, waiting for this. The moment he knew what I had done with my life. Now he knows. *And nothing is different. The earth is unmoved.*

"Josie's pretty great," I say. "She wants to go into TV professionally, so she makes our show a lot better than it would be otherwise. She's super funny."

"She sounds awesome."

"Do you still watch horror movies?" I ask.

"Sometimes. Mostly newer stuff. Marisol isn't a horror fan. She gets too scared."

"Do you ever watch horror hosts anymore?"

"No." He stares at the table.

So you were never going to see me anyway. Great. Excellent plan, Delia.

Our pizza comes. After the waitress leaves, Dad says, "The reason I couldn't watch horror hosts anymore is because they reminded me."

"So you ran from something you loved."

Dad doesn't say anything for a while. "How is she?"

"Mom?" I say through a mouthful of too-hot pizza. Per usual, I've burned myself.

"Yeah."

I shrug. "She's Mom. She's a manager at Target. She earns extra cash doing palm and tarot readings at our house and selling jewelry she makes on Etsy. I have to stay on her to take her medication. When she takes it, she's good. When she doesn't, she's bad. We're thinking about getting tattoos together."

Dad laughs. "Of what?"

"Don't know yet. We also go thrifting and watch a lot of horror movies together."

"You need a buddy to watch horror movies. Your mom was a good buddy for that."

"Yeah."

"You know that's how we got together, right?"

"No. You didn't tell me that when you were around, and you're not Mom's favorite topic of conversation now."

"I guess not," he murmurs. He takes a deep breath as he remembers. "Your mom and I met in sophomore year of high school. Became best friends overnight. Couple of weirdos who loved weird stuff. Your mom started making jewelry out of animal bones and discarded cicada shells in high school. Did you know that?"

I smile with one side of my mouth. "No. But I'm not surprised. That's still pretty much her jewelry-making vibe."

A look of nostalgia comes over Dad's face. "It was the two of us against the world. We would go over to each other's houses after school and watch MTV and smoke pot. Which you shouldn't do."

"(A) I don't. But (B) you don't really get to boss me anymore."

He looks away in embarrassment. "Fair enough. Anyway.

On Friday and Saturday nights, we'd drive to Videoville in my 1990 Ford Tempo and rent horror movies. The rule was neither of us could have even heard of it. Then we'd go sit on the couch at one of our houses and watch it. Well, that was the rule until we'd watched every horror movie Videoville had. The other rule was that we couldn't make out during the movie. We had to pay attention. Afterward was fair game. Oh, and our favorite snack during the movies was melted cheese over Doritos. We were both sad and mad all the time when we weren't together."

He speaks with the tone of someone delivering a eulogy. Maybe he is.

"So I'm sort of a genetic superhero."

"You look like her."

"I know."

"People tell you that?"

"I have eyes."

"Your mom would have loved the way you dress when she was in high school."

"I'm wearing basically what I wear for the show. We went to the con in character, and I came right here. But how I dress normally isn't super far off from this."

"She'd have loved it. Me too. Am I telling you stuff you already know?"

"Like I said, Mom doesn't ever talk about you and gets mad if I do, and when you were still around, I was a bit young to hear about you two getting high and dry-humping as wayward teens."

"What about you? Boyfriend?"

"Nice segue."

"Yeah."

"I went out with a guy for a few months when I was a sophomore. He was a ferret guy."

"Ferret guy?"

"He had like six ferrets and would hide them in his coat at school and feed them during class."

"Ah. There was a ferret guy in my high school."

"Of course there was. Anyway. After him, not really anyone. I'm tied up every Friday and Saturday night with the show, so I'm not big on dating." I'm still not sure how much of my life I want to tell him about. It doesn't feel like he's earned it.

"What about your mom? She ever find anyone?" He says it with an odd sort of gingerliness, like it's going to hurt him if he discovers she did.

It weirds me out, telling him about Mom, knowing how hard she'd freak. But . . . "When I was twelve, she dated a guy named Joey. He was nice. I guess maybe they were pretty serious. Seems like they were together until I was thirteen? Fourteen? I dunno. She'll go on a date here and there, but nothing serious."

"Where are you in school?"

"Do you really not know that?"

"I don't know if you skipped a grade or something."

"Nice save. Just graduated from high school."

"Good job!"

"Well, barely, so don't go nuts with praise. What's with—" I motion at my chest, where the embroidered words are on his shirt, the way he did with my septum piercing.

"SynergInfo? They're a data storage company. I'm a computer database administrator there."

"That's a new direction for you, from what I remember."

"Yeah, I got my database administration certificate from University of Phoenix a few years back."

"You turned into a real grown-up."

He laughs hollowly.

I arrange my pizza crusts into a frown on my plate. "I remember you being a lot older. If you'd asked me as a kid how old I thought you were, I would've said forty-seven. Because you could drive a car. Which automatically made you forty-seven."

"I was nineteen when we had you. Your mom got pregnant in the last few months of high school. We got married that fall."

"So you're not even forty yet."

He shakes his head.

"Your summer's almost over."

He looks at me quizzically.

I toy with a scrap of pepperoni. "So, like, say humans live to be eighty. I always think about how you can divide human lives into the four seasons. From birth to twenty is spring, from twenty to forty is summer, from forty to sixty is fall, and from sixty to eighty is winter."

He wipes a smudge of pizza sauce from his elbow. "So you're almost done with spring."

"Yep."

"And I'm almost done with summer."

"Got it."

"You're a deep thinker, DeeDee. You always were."

"You've had a pretty wild summer, huh?" I say.

"Yeah."

"I've had a pretty wild spring."

We sit for a while, not talking, only eating. We alternate studying each other's faces for too long and looking away bashfully.

"What if Mom hadn't gotten pregnant with me?" I ask finally.

"What do you mean?"

"Would y'all have gotten married?"

Dad looks at me for a second, then looks down at the table. He toys with a bit of straw wrapper, twisting it around his finger until it snaps. "Um," he says quietly. "I don't . . . know."

"Did you want to marry her?"

"I—I think so."

"You think so?"

"There was definitely part of me that did."

"So part of you didn't."

"I guess that's what that means."

"Did Mom want to marry you?"

"She did marry me."

"That's not what I asked."

He sighs and fiddles with his fork. "I don't know, DeeDee. I think so. I think she did."

Momentous information has a way of turning time into a syrupy, delirious crawl. I always assumed my parents definitely wanted to get married. It never once occurred to me that they only did it because of me. I'm the only reason my dad was around to leave me in the first place. It gives me that snake-eating-its-own-tail feeling of looking in the mirror too long or saying my name too many times.

I'm trying to make sense of my current tumult of emotions (a kind of storm I don't love!). Anger. Disappointment. Sadness.

Longing. Triumph. Wonderment. Hurt. It's all there, like spokes on a game show wheel that keeps turning and turning, while I wait to see where it lands.

I wonder how much of me is him and how much of him is me.

I wonder who the man sitting in front of me would have been if I had never existed.

I wonder if I'm fixing something inside me at this moment or breaking something that can never be put right again.

Josie

Divine gesticulates with a fork. "So I say, 'Hey, Cher, honey, maybe you could *share* some of that Bolivian marching powder, and while you're at it, we better find your unmentionables because I think Sly Stallone's pet dingo carried them off. And then Nicolas Cage comes in, and apparently he's gotten ahold of a hot-air balloon and a pilot. . . .'"

If the measure of success of a TV industry dinner is picking at your sad, tiny, egregiously expensive salad while the person across the table regales you with an unceasing litany of stories about how famous he is and how many celebrities he knows, while you trade *please let the sun turn the Earth into a scorched globe of ash this moment* looks with your boyfriend, who is also glumly picking at his sorry salad, then this dinner has been a smash hit.

I slip off a shoe and run my toe down Lawson's calf under the table. He grins quickly. Hey, if I'm going to be sitting at a goony restaurant, dressed like a vampire, listening to a goony dude tell goony stories, I'm pulling out my goony rom-com moves.

Yuri and Divine finish their dinners and lean back in their chairs, picking their teeth. Yuri gives a somewhat more jovial grunt.

The waiter comes by. "Madam, sirs, was everything to your liking?"

"Delectable," Divine crows. "Please give my compliments to the chef."

"Can I tempt any of you with some dessert? Perhaps our tiramisu or crème brûlée?"

"I couldn't possibly," Divine says. "Watching my figure. But do be a prince and package me another one of those four-pound Newfoundland lobsters to go. In case I get peckish in my hotel room later tonight. You know, there is *nothing* worse than being hungry in a hotel room."

I can actually think of some worse things.

"Very good, sir," the waiter says with a bow-like nod. "And then the check?"

"Please."

The waiter leaves.

Divine turns his attention (I use the term *attention* very loosely) back to us. "Speaking of getting peckish in hotel rooms, I was in Joshua Tree in 1979 with Stevie Nicks. Now let me first say, frying eggs on a hotel room iron is not an ideal situation, but with Stevie Nicks, there is a sense of infinite possibility. Anyway—"

My consciousness exits my body and I become a soaring being of pure light and energy, throwing off the cruel shackles of this world's gravity. I run through green meadows and flowered pastures. The sun is warm on my face. Lawson and I hold hands under the bracing spray of a waterfall. Jasmine and hyacinth waft on the air. Now I swim in a warm ocean under a moonlit sky. On the white sand shore, a harpist plays—

The waiter approaches with a box and what looks like an old-timey leather-bound, riveted ledger book from *A Christmas Carol*. He places the box by Divine and starts to set down the bill as well.

Divine motions at me with his head, mouths *Thank you,* and makes a namaste motion with his hands pressed together. The waiter sets the bill by me. It happens in slow motion. Falling like a sawed-through tree.

"Take your time, no rush," the waiter says, clearing a couple of plates.

I laugh awkwardly. Divine has not shown a great sense of humor up until this point, but there's a first time for everything.

Divine smiles and crosses his legs.

Okay, he's going to play out the gag. All right. This is a very stressful joke, but fine, I'll play along. A little hazing, Hollywood style. Good clean fun.

I open the bill and look at the total.

I feel like I've been impaled on a spear of burning ice.

$764.26.

I have to read it twice to make sure there isn't a decimal in the wrong place. Don't get me wrong, $76.42 would still be a *hell* of an expensive dinner for me, but it wouldn't be about eighty percent of my total net worth, including all the blood plasma in my body. *Time for the joke to be over. I'm not laughing anymore.*

I look up again at Divine. He smiles serenely, beatifically, his face betraying no hint of the joke.

"Uhhhhhhhhhhh," I say. It's finally sinking in: this might be real. I want to pass out. I'm frozen. I don't know what to do. For as big a turd as Divine is, he could still be our show's only hope. I think about Delia confronting her dad right now. I can't sell us out over $764. I can always get a job and make back the money, but I might not have another opportunity like this. I never want Delia to think I wouldn't pay $764 (plus tip . . . oh dear lord, I forgot about the tip) to help keep our show.

"Is something the matter?" Divine asks.

"Nooooo, it's just . . . wow."

"Welcome to showbiz, my dear. Wining and dining the people who can make things happen for you is as important as anything. If you learn nothing else, let it be that. And I am well pleased with how I've been wined and dined."

"Uhhhhh."

"And trust me," Divine says with a salacious eyebrow shimmy and speaking out of the corner of his mouth, "there are people whose wining and dining needs go far beyond mine, if you catch my drift."

I have a sensation like a cockroach crawled up my spine.

Lawson, whom I can feel seething next to me, starts to go for his wallet. "Here—"

I pinch his thigh so forcefully, I feel guilty. *This is my mess. I've got this.* He takes the hint and backs down.

I swallow hard. "What if we go halfsies?"

Divine chortles and claps. "I like your moxie, young lady. I do. But no, I mustn't. You have to know your value."

"You pay," Yuri says gruntily and more-to-the-pointily.

The waiter walks by. "Excuse me," I squeak. "Is the tip included in the bill?"

He looks at me like I've just told him I've never been to a restaurant. "No, miss. A *recommended* gratuity of eighteen percent is not included."

I get out my debit card and run the numbers on my phone. A tip of $137. Total: $901.26. When last I checked, I had a little over $1,200 saved up, which included my birthday money and graduation money from my grandma.

Think of it as an investment. Think of it as an investment. Think of it as an investment. Maybe he'll make you so rich you'll sneeze at thousand-dollar dinners.

"We should really do this again sometime," Divine says.

"Oh, for sure," I say, almost puking a little in my mouth.

We rise to leave, with Divine leading the way and Yuri bringing up the rear. Lawson hands the snooty host back his loaner blazer.

"Reba," Yuri grunts as Lawson holds the door for him.

"I don't know what that means," I say. "I don't know what it means when you do that."

• • •

We pile in the Escalade. Divine turns back to us from the middle row. "And now it's brass tacks time! Rubber meeting the road time! Let's go get a television program made! Yuri?"

Yuri grunts and puts the car in gear.

Could this really be happening? Did I just pay almost a thousand dollars to get our show made? Could this night have been worth it? Is this going to be an amazing story someday? I'm far too distracted by these visions and reflections on my recent financial ruin to pay attention through the limousine-dark windows to where we're going. We wind through streets and highways for about twenty minutes until we get to a nondescript, decidedly unglamorous part of town. We pull into a strip mall anchored by a Dollar Tree and a payday loan servicer. We park in front of a storefront that says Disme Entertainment in Comic Sans font. A vape shop and a dry cleaner flank it. This does not look great.

The tide of anxiety rolls in again. But a tiny ember of possibility still glows in my mind. *Maybe this is how shows really get made. Maybe it'll be a step forward for us.*

Yuri gets out and opens Divine's door, and the two stroll quickly toward the entrance. Lawson and I stumble out.

"If this is a porn studio . . . ," Lawson says under his breath.

I laugh, but not because the notion is at all implausible.

Divine rings a bell and mugs for the security camera. Someone buzzes us in. The air-conditioning is screaming, and it smells like moldy carpet. It's as humid as outside, but (conservatively) thirty degrees cooler. Every surface feels slightly damp, like a layer of condensation and/or despair covers everything.

This place is so unpromising, it feels like a mass grave for promises.

"Back office," a hoarse, high voice calls. We follow Divine to the back and walk into a cloud of cigar smoke that smells like someone burned a pile of dirty underpants to cover up the smell of a camp latrine. A man clenches a fat cigar between his teeth and types, hunt-and-peck style, on a wheezing slab of a laptop. A giant painted mural of some sort of rodent-like cartoon character covers the wall behind him. It's an attempt at cute that landed squarely on terrifying. The man at the desk appears to have been made by some blindfolded god. Despite the damp chill, he's somehow still sweaty, and his mustache looks like he glued a drain clog to his lip with spirit gum.

He does not look like a successful man. He does not look like one who brings success to others.

He starts to say something but instead coughs. And coughs. And coughs. He holds up a finger. More coughing.

Finally, Divine says, "Is your brother in the back? We have

some business to talk with you, but first a little"—he makes a motion like he's pulling a cord for a horn—"*toot toot*. To aid digestion."

The man nods, still coughing, and waves Divine and Yuri into a back room. They close the door. And it's Lawson and me with Coughing Man.

His coughs subside. He pounds his chest and hawks a loogie into a garbage can by his desk. "You working with Divine?" he croaks.

"Possibly?" I say.

"What's your name?"

"Josie Howard."

Coughing Man looks at Lawson.

"Lawson Vargas."

"I didn't catch your name," I say.

The man sticks his cigar back between his teeth. "Wald Disme."

"Wald Dis—like Walt—"

"ANY RESEMBLANCE MY NAME MAY BEAR TO ANY PERSON ALIVE OR DECEASED IS PURELY COINCIDENTAL AND NOT TO BE CONSTRUED IN ANY WAY AS INFRINGEMENT UPON THE INTELLECTUAL PROPERTY OF HERETOFORE MENTIONED PERSONS ALIVE OR DECEASED WHOSE NAME MINE MIGHT COINCIDENTALLY RESEMBLE," Disme says with great force and energy. It sounds like something someone made him read off a card verbatim until he had it memorized.

"Okay," I say, "so it's a kooky coincidence your name sounds almost exactly like—"

"ANY RESEMBLANCE MY NAME MAY BEAR TO ANY PERSON ALIVE OR DECEASED—"

I give him two thumbs-up. "Yep, yep, got it."

"So what'd old Jackie-boy tell you? He gonna make you a star?" He says the last part in a pretty passable Divine impression.

"We're just talking. I don't know if—"

"You got a nice face. Good cheekbones. Probably do all right in front of a camera."

"Um. Thanks. That's . . . cool of you. Anyway, like I was saying—"

"Did Jackie-boy tell you we worked together in the nineties?"

"No."

"I was the head of Wald Disme Studios. We were in the straight-to-video market." He points with his cigar. "We were Netflix before there was Netflix."

I take a closer look at the cartoon character painting. "Is that the mascot for Wald Disme Studios?"

Disme grins. "Rickey Rat! The rat with ratitude! 'Ratitude' like 'attitude.'"

"Yep. Got it." I squint. "Is he . . . smoking a cigarette?"

Disme wiggles his ears. He's *really* good at it.

I study his face, perplexed. I motion at my ears. "What does—"

Disme wiggles his ears more furiously.

"Yeah, I don't get it."

Disme rolls his eyes and throws his hands up in exasperation. "It's my thing I do instead of winking."

"Oh. Cool. So, your mascot is a *rat smoking a cigarette.*"

"Kids like edgy. It's the Wald Disme brand."

"Huh."

"Disney would release one of their goody-two-shoes, yawn-fest mermaid movies, and we'd get on the stick and pound one out in a few weeks, get that sucker in video stores. Beat Disney to the punch."

"Pound one out," I murmur.

"So people rent ours instead. It's cheaper. You can watch it at home. And it's better."

"Better? How?"

"Well, for starters . . ." Disme makes a circle with the thumb and forefinger of one hand and pokes his cigar in and out several times, making a slide-whistle noise with his mouth. "Sex. You looked confused."

"I was, but more about why enticing parents to rent a cartoon mermaid movie with boning in it for their kids to see is a wise idea."

Disme shrugs. "Sex sells."

"Obviously," I mutter, glancing up at a huge urine-colored water spot on the ceiling.

"Plus, kids'll find out sooner or later. Sex is natural."

"I guess so? But also *highly* weird to have in a kids' cartoon movie."

"You do you. I'll do me. Di*sme*." He points at me and wiggles his ears.

I sigh.

Disme stares off with a faraway nostalgic expression. "We even started to build DismeWorld. Like Disney World, only better. But that was not to be."

I brace myself. "*Please* tell me the difference wasn't sex."

"Rides were more dangerous."

"Incredible."

"Kids like edgy."

"So I'm told."

"Anyway, didn't happen." Disme takes a long pull on his cigar and blows the smoke skyward. "Hornets," he says finally, in a tone bespeaking deep reluctance.

"Do what now?"

"Flying bugs. Stingers. Buzzy. Like bees that make sadness instead of honey."

"Got that part."

"At the build site. They worked well as a team." Disme's look of blissful nostalgia morphs into the thousand-yard stare of a battle-weary soldier. "They seemed almost . . . sentient." He doesn't sound like he's joking.

"But . . . they weren't," I say. "Sentient. Obviously."

Several seconds pass. "No . . . no . . . of course not. That would be . . . ridiculous," he eventually murmurs, sounding unconvinced. "I'll never forget the *buzzing*. A room goes quiet? I hear the buzzing again. Like there's a giant vibrator at the center of the world."

"What a thing to imagine constantly."

"I did battle with the hornets one night. A storm was coming in. There was lightning on the horizon. We met in the field, me versus them. Mano a . . . whatever hornets have instead of manos. Sting-os. Just as we began combat, it started to pour down rain. I was wearing armor I made out of duct tape and cardboard boxes, and the rain made it fall off me like meat from a rotisserie chicken. They stung me on the lips and eyelids. My face looked worse than the time I got Botox while stopped at a red light. It was a long time before I regained my dignity."

"But you definitely did regain it," I say.

He snaps out of his pained reverie. "I had to wear a white porcelain mask every time I left the house for the next three weeks. I drank Benadryl chilled from a crystal wine goblet. . . . Anyway, it's good to see Jackie-boy developing new projects after his thing"—Disme waggles his fingers in the air—"with the Russians."

"Pardon? Lemme just pump the brakes for a sec."

"Oh, he owes the Russian mob a pretty penny for financing one of his flops. Hence Yuri."

"Yuri isn't his bodyguard?"

"Oh, Yuri *is* his bodyguard." Disme wiggles his ears again.

"Even though I know now that's your way of winking, may I suggest you just either wink or say very clearly what you mean? Easier for everyone. So, about Yuri?"

"His job is definitely to keep Divine alive from the others so Divine can pay Yuri's bosses back."

"The *others?*"

"Jackie-boy's always approached showbiz with the motto *You can't make an omelet without making some people want to murder you execution-style, tie your body to an engine block, and drop you off a bridge.*"

My guts feel like a moray eel is dragging them into a frigid undersea cavern. If you want something enough, you'll lie to yourself and lie to yourself and lie to yourself. And that's what I've been doing. I got conned. I feel like I'm waking from a NyQuil slumber to find I've been sleeping on my neck funny.

I meet Lawson's eyes. *This is not going to happen.*

His eyes agree.

What am I going to tell Delia? What am I going to tell Lawson, for that matter? Delia. I pressured her to go see her dad. If that doesn't work out and then this is a debacle too? Oh man. I begin planning how I'm going to ask Divine to take us back to our hotel.

The door bursts open, and Divine practically skips out. Yuri follows behind, also with a little more spring in his step.

"Jackie-boy!" Disme says.

Divine is sniffling and radiating this live-wire, electric, jittery energy. He gives the vibe that he'll melt down if he stops talking. "Well, well, well, that is much better. I was practically nodding off on my feet! We stuffed ourselves like debauched Roman emperors at Linda's Jim."

"Good place?" Disme asks.

"Good would be an understatement."

"Wouldn't know. Never been to a restaurant," Disme says. "I keep a little truck bread on hand in case I get peckish."

Divine claps his hands and rubs them together. "All right, folks! Who's ready to talk a little business? Who's ready to make some sawbucks? Some cold, hard cash? Some dead presidents?"

Disme chomps on his cigar and leans back in his chair. "Whattya got for me, Jackie-boy?"

"I happen to have the finest show in development for you . . . thrills and chills abound . . . *Monster Midnight Mash!*"

"It's *Midnite Matinee,*" I say. "And I think now, in your current state, might not be the best—"

"*Midnight Monster Mash,*" Divine crows. "Horror hosting for a new generation. Hashtag hip. Hashtag edgy. Hashtag young. Hashtag sexy. iHorrorhosting. Like iPod."

I have never desired more to be spontaneously vaporized. For my body to return instantly to the stardust whence it came. I had no idea cocaine made people this much more embarrassing than normal.

"And we will bring you in for a mere ten thousand cash on the barrelhead for an executive producer credit and the usual cut of back end. What say you, sir? Many people are interested."

Disme sighs. "Jackie-boy, I don't—I'm not sold. Lost my shirt on the last venture. Got something I could look at?"

"Everyone, hang on a sec—He doesn't own—" I say.

Divine gives Disme the same chiding glare he gave the host at the restaurant. "What? You don't trust my judgment now? A run of hard luck and all of a sudden you need to put your peepers on something I bring you before you'll invest? I have producers lined up, *begging* me to take their money. But okay, seventy-five hundred *cash*. Because I like you. Final offer."

"Jackie-boy."

"Gentlemen," I say, "we are not going to s—"

"Shhhhh," Divine says to me, putting his index finger to his lips and then making a *slow down* motion with his palms. Then, back to Disme: "Five grand. *Final* offer." He has a pleading, wheedling tone, all of his salesman bluster gone. "Come on, Wald. You know in your heart it's the right thing to do. You know I'm due for the winds to start blowing warm again."

"GENTLEMEN, BEFORE YOU GO ANY FURTHER—" I yell. But Disme cuts me off.

"Uh-oh," he says, squinting at one of the security monitors. "Oh, Jackie-boy, we got trouble. We got company."

Fantastic. Now whoever's after Divine is going to murder all of us.

302

Which would honestly be like the third worst thing that's happened tonight.

Divine goes volleyball-colored. "What? Who?"

Disme turns the security monitor toward us. A woman who looks to be in her fifties—with a mane of blond hair that puts Dolly Parton's to shame, wearing a glove-tight snakeskin-print dress and thigh-high boots—is *shrieking,* crimson-faced, into the security camera. The camera doesn't have sound, but no need— you can faintly hear her from inside. Veins are bulging on her neck and forehead. She has chiseled, thickly muscled arms and shoulders.

"Good gravy, it's Ulrike!" Frantic sweat boils up on Divine's forehead. "How did she find me?"

"Must've heard you were in town and figured you'd end up here," Disme says.

"Who the hell is Ulrike?" I ask. She's holding a lit cigarette lighter up to the camera and pointing at it furiously. Her nails resemble titanium claws.

"Ex-wife number four, seven, and nine, and Austrian Olympic women's shot-put bronze medalist." Divine moans. "Oh, she's got the lighter. She'll burn us out. Don't think she won't. Trust me, I speak from experience."

"Can Yuri—" I say.

Yuri holds up his hands in front of him as if pushing me away. "No. Not this one. Strong like hippo."

Lawson moves in protectively, our skin barely touching. I'm really glad he's here.

"Okay, okay, okay," Disme mutters quickly. "Here's the plan: you four make a break for the back door. When you do, I'll buzz her in the front. Once she's in, you run around the side, get in your car, and burn rubber, okay? I'll try to buy you some time."

"Owe you one, Waldy," Divine says.

"More than one," Disme says.

I kick off my shoes and pick them up, and Lawson and I rush for the door, Divine and Yuri at our heels. On our way out, we pass a bewildered man who appears to be a clone of Disme. We make it out the rear just as we hear a livid roar in German from the front. We rush for the side of the strip mall, sweating and panting, coming back around the front. A yellow Hummer H2 is parked haphazardly next to the Escalade.

"Ulrike's car," Divine says, panting. "Alimony well spent. The alimony I paid, anyway. That may be why she's here."

We pile, helter-skelter, into the Escalade and peel out of the parking lot, the g-forces pressing us into our seats like we're being sat on by a giant.

Delia

We stare silently at the empty plates in front of us. It's not that we've run out of things to talk about. It's that we have too many things that are too big to say out loud.

"We're pretty near the ocean, huh?" I say finally.

"Yeah," Dad says, clearing his throat. "About seven minutes away."

"I've never seen the ocean."

"Never?"

"You know how when you were around, we never took fancy vacations?"

"Yeah."

"That situation did not improve upon your leaving."

Dad grimaces and averts his eyes. "I guess it wouldn't. So, never seen the ocean."

"Not even once."

"Want to?"

"Who wouldn't?"

"Let's go, then."

"Yeah?"

"Yeah. Marisol is sleeping. When do you have to be back to where you're staying?"

"Dunno. Whenever."

Dad pays, and we leave. *Your dad just took you out to dinner. Like the day he took you to Cicis for your birthday. You never thought that would happen again.*

In the car, Dad says, "I keep wanting to ask you to tell me everything that's happened in the last ten years."

"I keep wanting to tell you, but I wonder if I should."

"I can handle it."

"I was talking about whether you deserve it."

He doesn't answer, only nods. We drive on until we arrive at a parking lot. It's dark. Up ahead, the sky fades to an inkier black, with no city lights to illuminate it. When I open the car door, I hear the rush of waves. It stirs something buried deep in me, something wondrous and briefly hopeful. It's windier and cooler here, and the air smells like salt and seaweed. I pause at the grassy area on the edge of the beach to take in the scope of what I'm seeing. The waves crashing white on the shore feel like some organic machinery. Like lungs inhaling and exhaling.

"I've never gotten used to it," Dad says, reading my mind. "How it keeps going and going whether we're here to see it or not."

That's right, Dad. Things keep going whether you're there to see them or not.

"I want to get closer," I murmur. "So I can feel the water."

"Sure." Dad slips off his shoes and socks and rolls up the bottoms of his khakis.

I take off my black Delilah Darkwood ankle boots and hold them, with my socks stuffed inside. I can't roll up the bottoms of my black vinyl pants very well, but I don't care if they get wet. I walk tottering in the cool sand toward the water, approaching cautiously, like it's a wild animal that could devour me. I get right to the edge of where the waves are washing up. Cool water nibbles the tips of my toes. Dad is to my side, a couple of feet behind me. I inch forward. The water floods over the tops of my feet. The vastness and emptiness of the expanse in front of me makes me light-headed.

"I literally tracked you down to the end of the earth," I say over the crash of the surf.

Dad smiles sadly.

"Why here?" I ask.

He takes a few steps to stand beside me, the waves rushing over his feet and ankles. He puts his hands in his pockets.

"Did you hear—" I start to say.

"Yeah, I'm thinking." After a moment, he says, "Because it seemed like a good place to start over. A place where no one would care who I was or what I'd done in my life. That wouldn't judge me. I guess that's my best explanation."

"You know what the worst part is about your dad leaving you?"

He murmurs something, but I can't hear over the waves.

It was a rhetorical question anyway. "It makes you scared to trust anyone or anything, because if your dad can leave you, who won't? What won't?"

"I know," he says softly.

"Where did you get the name Derek Armstrong?"

"Well, the Armstrong part comes partly from Neil Armstrong. I was always fascinated with the idea of people standing on the moon. I'd look up into the night sky, and I couldn't get my head around it. It seemed like such a brave thing to do, and I wanted to start over, but braver. And part of it was that if I had another shot at the name thing, I wasn't doing the end of the alphabet again. It was a good, solid last name that made me feel like I could be strong in my new life and better than I was before. And Derek was the name of one of my best friends growing up. I always liked his name better than mine. And I had a choice."

"I thought maybe you'd become a secret agent, or you'd joined the Mafia or something."

"Nope. Just became a database administrator."

"You really wanted to make sure I'd never find you again." I bend over and let my fingers trail in the water. I touch a fingertip to my tongue. The ocean tastes like thin blood.

When I glance back at Dad, he's hanging his head, his face pinched. In the darkness, it's hard to tell, but it looks like tears are streaming down his face.

"I, um . . ." His voice quavers. "I wanted to be someone else. Very badly. I hated myself. I had to change my name because I couldn't stand to say my old name."

"So it wasn't to keep me from finding you?"

He shakes his head. "I've thought about you so much in the last ten years. Had dreams where we did this very thing. Talked about our lives. I tried to imagine what you were like. Who you'd become. But every day that passed, I was more scared to seek you out."

And then I steel my heart and I ask him why. I ask him why.

"Pie?"

"No, *why*. Why did you leave?"

"Sorry, I thought you said 'pie.' The waves were too loud."

"*Why?*"

He takes a deep breath and holds it for a while before exhaling. And another. "Because your mom got sick and wasn't getting well, and I was scared. I was afraid to have to take care of two people. All that responsibility terrified me. I felt like in the cartoons when a character runs out over water and does fine until he notices he's over water, and then starts sinking. I kept thinking how much I wished my life was simpler and someone could take care of *me,* or at least that I only had myself to worry about. I hung in there as long as I could with your mom, but I was sick too. I was depressed and drinking a lot because of it. I couldn't be strong enough for all three of us. I started thinking nonstop about how great it would be to be dead. It was leave or die. So I chose leave. I wanted to succeed. I wanted to be a good father to you. Or at least a present father. But I was a coward. I wasn't up to the hard task. And in my frame of mind then, it was better to leave you than to stick around and be a terrible father and have you remember me that way. So that's it."

I take it in along with the sound of the waves. *You thought wrong,* I want to say. But my tongue is paralyzed.

Dad continues. "I've pondered a lot since, and I've realized there was more to it than I thought at first. I never told you this, but my dad—your grandpa—left our family when I was young. And he was my example. I wanted *so badly* to be better than him. More than anything. I have a half brother and a half sister I've never even met. But I couldn't shake this feeling that I was made out of the same weak stuff he was made of. I convinced myself that it was unavoidable. Wilkes men leave and start over. It's what we do. It wasn't even in my plan to become a dad because of that fear. Then it happened. So I guess that's why. Maybe I could have come up with a better explanation if I'd known I'd be giving it tonight."

That's it. That's why. It's so anticlimactic. This is the question I drove fifteen hours to have answered. The question I wanted answered for more of the time I've been alive than not. The question that made me put myself on TV week after week. The question that tortured me, the ghost that haunted the margins of my self-identity. And the answer was basically *It's not you; it's me.*

Maybe I *wanted* him to say it was me. Maybe, for some reason, I needed to hear it was some fault in who I was that made me unable to keep him. Maybe I wanted his answer to do more to heal a decade-old wound. I don't know what answer I was expecting or hoping for. I didn't armor my heart for any of this. If I even could have.

"DeeDee?" he says.

"Sorry, I'm processing. It's been a long—" I crumble, weeping, my hands over my face. Dad comes over and hugs me. He's so much smaller, weaker, and less substantial than I remember him. We're almost the same height. It's like time has worn him away. Made him less. He smells completely different now. This is not the same man who held me in his arms under an October sky alive with the moon and stars.

I wonder if I unearthed more things than I've buried by making this trip, by stripping away the mythology I created. You want closure, but there are things you can't repair. Hearing him tell me why didn't fix the ten years of hurt. Not even when the reason was different from the assumption that had caused me so much anguish.

All at once, the immense, empty ocean makes me feel too

puny and lonely. The shifting sand under my feet makes me feel too unmoored, like I could be swept away at any second and lost forever. I've spent enough of my life feeling small and alone, and like everything I have could be taken from me in an instant.

"Thanks for showing me the ocean, but I think I'm ready to go now," I say between sobs.

Josie

I'm turning over in my mind what a calamity this night has been and my ever-deepening guilt about having prodded Delia to go see her dad. I hope that has been a success, at least. I somehow doubt it was. But . . .

"Well, that was a close one," Divine says, even more jittery than before, blotting sweat from his brow with his silk hankie. "Let's circle around for a while and maybe we can drop back in on old Wald when Hurricane Ulrike has passed. I'll tell you, this reminds of the time when Scott Baio, an alpaca, and I—"

I cut him off. "Mr. Divine, I'm grateful for your time, but I don't think we're going to be able to work together. I'm sorry."

He dismisses me with a scornful wave. "Now, see, that's quitters' talk, is what that is. If you throw in the towel when the going gets tough, you won't get anywhere in this business. Believe you me."

"I never said I was quitting. Just that I don't think we're a good fit to work together. So if you guys would please take us to our hotel, that'd be great."

Yuri turns sharply into a parking lot, almost making Lawson and me bonk heads. "Not yet. Make money first," Yuri grunts.

This is bad. My palms start sweating. I'm not a fan of the idea of even temporary hostagedom.

Yuri throws the SUV into park near a clothing donation bin, gets out, pulls a blanket and a box of DVDs from the back, spreads the blanket on the ground, and starts arranging *Skele-Tonya* DVDs on the blanket. He clearly has a system; he's almost done before Lawson and I even manage to get out.

Divine looks on sheepishly, scratching his head.

"Here's the deal," I say to him. "We need to get back to our hotel. Please take us. I have no idea where we are."

"Even though I disapprove, on principle, of quitting, far be it from me to compel anyone to do anything. So if it were up to me, we'd go. But Yuri seems hell-bent on making a little scratch tonight, and he's rather stubborn. 'Like hippo,' he would say. Come to think of it"—Divine nods at Yuri, who's walking around slowly, scanning the donation bin—"Yuri uses the hippo a lot as a point of comparison. Strong like hippo. Stubborn like hippo. Hungry like hippo. Thirsty like hippo. Peed like—"

"Are you listening to me? I don't care what Yuri wants. We're not your prisoners or employees. I want you to take us back *immediately.*" I wasn't having fun before, but now I'm really not having fun.

Yuri walks over, shaking out a garment he picked up by the bin, holding it aloft to study it by the orange parking-lot lights, pressing it to his nose to take a deep whiff. "Good shirt. No holes. You sell."

"Oh, heavens, Yuri. How do I sell that?"

He shrugs. "Say is from famous movie star. Maybe Tom Cruise."

Divine rolls his eyes and snatches the shirt. "I'm supposed to tell people that Tom Cruise owned this"—he squints at the

313

tag—"women's blouse from Ann Taylor Loft that you got out of the garbage?"

Yuri shrugs. "Maybe Johnny Depp."

I try to keep my voice calm and even but commanding, in spite of my now being very afraid. "Yuri, we would like to go back to our hotel now. If you and Mr. Divine want to stay out until three a.m. and hawk DVDs and discarded shirts from a blanket in a parking lot after that, please, go nuts."

Yuri looks at me impassively with hooded, bleary eyes. "You help sell."

Lawson starts to say something, but I cut him off. "Yeah, me helping you sell DVDs and used clothes? That will *not* happen. I promise." I look to Divine for assistance, but he's over at the donation bin, craning, reaching his arm in.

"Um," I say.

"This isn't stealing," Divine says. "You can't steal something people have willingly thrown away."

"Kinda you can. Also, *this is not stealing* is never the way you want to start a phrase."

"If I have to sell clothing on the street like some sort of Dickensian ragamuffin, I want to see what my options are," Divine says, jerking at his arm. "I seem to be . . . stuck here. Caught up on something. Can one of you—"

"Good luck," I say. "We're leaving. Come on, Lawson." I pick a direction and start walking, Lawson at my side.

"Wait a minute!" Divine calls after us. "What about my honorarium?"

"Hono-what-ium?"

"My honorarium. My fee. You don't think I go around dispensing show business advice and knowledge for free, do you? I have to make a living."

"If you're legitimately asking me for more money, you can blow your honorarium out of your assholararium. As if I even have any money left after your little dinner."

"You owe me!"

"For what?!"

"Imparting showbiz knowledge. Connecting you with an executive producer. That warrants a finder's fee."

"You told weird stories about making fried eggs on a hotel room iron with Stevie Nicks and doing cocaine in a hot-air balloon with Nicolas Cage and took us to talk to some loser in the human-hornet wars. We're good here."

"You ingrate! Typical millennial!"

"I'm not a millennial, and also that's a dumb thing old people say. Anyway, this has been as fun as holding in a fart, but we *really* must go."

"Should not hold in poots. Is bad for liver," Yuri says.

I clench the sides of my head and say through gritted teeth: "THE BODY'S FART TUBES ARE NOT CONNECTED TO—"

"Is my opinion," Yuri says.

"You know what? I'm not doing this. I refuse." I turn and keep walking. Lawson puts his hand on my back protectively.

"Yuri! Collect my honorarium!" Divine hollers.

Yuri starts toward us. I turn and point at him. "Do. Not. *Touch* me. I will call the cops on you so fast."

Yuri only moves more swiftly.

Lawson gets between Yuri and me, holding out his arm. "Bro, not one more step, or I will straight-up knock you out."

I have my phone in hand, ready to dial 911. Yuri reaches past Lawson and swats my phone. It sails away, flipping end over end.

I'm not even able to register vocal disapproval before Lawson strikes, punching Yuri in the face with a meaty *thwack*. He assumes a fighting stance. Yuri stops, momentarily dazed, puts his fingertips to his lips, and pulls them away, checking for blood. His face hardens, and he raises his fists. I would feel a lot better if Lawson's punch had done more damage.

"Get him, Yuri!" Divine hollers. "Fisticuffs time!"

Yuri moves with shocking nimbleness. He throws a punch; Lawson ducks. I almost feel the wind from it.

"*Stop!*" I shout, but to no avail. And this doesn't look like the sort of neighborhood where shouts of "stop" are uncommon.

Yuri throws a vicious uppercut that Lawson dodges. But Lawson catches his heel on the ground and falls onto his back.

Yuri is on him in an instant.

Delia

We sit in Dad's driveway. Not a word passed between us on the ride back.

"So," I say.

"So," Dad says.

"I guess I don't really know where we go from here."

"Me neither."

I struggle to say it. "Do you . . . want to stay in touch?"

He folds in on himself, looking away from me, out into the darkness filled with chirping frogs and buzzing insects. He rests his elbow on the windowsill and bows his head into his palm, covering his eyes. Seconds tick by. He looks up, exhausted and hammered down, suddenly a decade older. "DeeDee."

Anything but "yes" is "no," and "DeeDee" isn't "yes." Still, I ask, "Is that a no?"

"I . . . can't. It hurts too much."

Fresh tears, spiked with anger, replace the ones that have dried to salt on my cheeks. "You don't know the first thing about hurt."

"I do," he says softly. "I even know what it's like to lose your dad."

"And yet you did it to me."

"I had no choice."

"So you said."

"I'm trying to start a new life. I—I can't live with a constant reminder of what a failure I was to you."

"Won't live. Are scared to live."

"That too."

"You're pathetic."

He absorbs it like a punch to the chin. He stares at the floor and doesn't speak. It's fine. I didn't want him to try to argue.

I open the car door. "I have something for you. Hang on." I walk to Josie's car and get my last *Midnite Matinee* DVD. I go back and sit in Dad's Jeep. "Here." I hand him the DVD.

"Is this—this your show?"

"Yeah. I want you to watch it."

He holds it in both hands. "DeeDee, I don't think I—"

"Are you about to tell me you don't think you can?"

"Yes."

"Because it hurts too much?"

"Yes."

"Because you would prefer to forget?"

"DeeDee—"

"Because you want to *move on.*" I spit the last two words with contempt.

He opens his mouth to speak, but I don't wait. I summon all the fury I have. Ten years' worth, saved up in every cell of my body. It made me a creature of sadness to carry that around. "Well, guess what? You *will.* I built this *castle* for you. Do you get it? I made this show so you would *see me.* So you would *hurt* for leaving me. And you're going to. You don't have to ever talk to me again. You don't have to ever remember me or think of me again. But on some Saturday night when Marisol is out with friends or if you've ditched her too, you're going to put on this DVD and pretend like you discovered this show while you were channel surfing. And you're going to watch *your daughter* on TV, acting out what you left her, with one of the VHS tapes you left her, trying with all her heart to connect with you in the only way she knew how. Maybe it was stupid and desperate to hope that you would happen to watch my show, but I'm having the last laugh because now you're going to. I *win*."

He looks down at the DVD, defeated, and nods.

"Remember my seventh birthday? When I fell asleep and you took me outside to look at the stars and the moon?" I don't know where I'm going with this. My heart is no longer communicating with my brain.

His face is blank. "Seventh birthday . . ."

"Remember?"

"Vaguely?"

"Never mind." I open the door again.

"What, DeeDee? What was it?"

I make sure I have his eyes before I speak. "That was the most perfect day of my life. That's all. Thought I'd tell you."

"I'm glad," he says softly, and looks away.

I look for some evidence of loss. There is not enough. "When did I stop feeling like a part of you? When did I start feeling like a fingernail clipping you could throw away?"

He says nothing.

"Because you've never stopped feeling like a part of me."

He looks back at me with reddening eyes. "Can you ever forgive me?"

I've rehearsed this moment in my mind so many times. The moment my dad sees me on TV and calls me and asks me to forgive him. And none of that rehearsal prepared me for this. Because I never imagined I'd be looking him in the face. Sitting in his new car, in his new driveway, in front of his new house, with his new pregnant fiancée asleep inside. And with all that newness, I think he probably doesn't need the forgiveness that would cost me so much to give him.

"No," I say. "I can't. Bye, Dad. Have a good life. Take better care of your new daughter. Too bad I'll never meet her." I get out and start walking away without closing the door. But I turn and go back. "One more thing: I'm really awesome. I'm a good person and a loving daughter, and I worked hard and made a show I thought you would love. You shouldn't have abandoned me. I didn't deserve that." I manage to get the words out, but as soon as I start stumbling back to Josie's car, the wall inside me falls. It's hard to say things out loud that you haven't even convinced yourself are true. He calls after me, but I keep walking.

This may be the least perfect day of my life. Less even than the day I woke up and discovered he was gone. But I know I'll keep it stored inside whether I want to or not.

I drive off, leaving my dad standing in the street behind me. I look in the rearview mirror and see him—probably for the last time—lit up red in the taillights like something from an old horror movie.

Josie

It's exactly like one of those dreams where you're seeing something horrible and you want to scream, but your vocal cords are frozen and all that comes out is an impotent dry squeak.

Yuri crouches over Lawson and throws another powerful punch. Lawson deflects it into the ground with a sickening thud. Yuri roars in agony and curses (probably) in Russian. Lawson has a momentary opening. He could jump to his feet while Yuri shakes it off. He doesn't. *What are you doing?* Yuri reaches behind himself, for something at the small of his back. I stop breathing.

Lawson kicks Yuri's leg out from under him. He loses his balance and pitches forward on top of Lawson, throwing another punch as he's falling. Lawson dodges it and entangles Yuri's arms. Suddenly, Lawson scissors his legs into the air and clenches them around Yuri's head and neck, pinning one of Yuri's outstretched arms like he's raising his hand to ask a question. Lawson loops one thigh around the back of Yuri's neck and hooks his other knee over the shin of the leg wrapped around Yuri's neck. It doesn't look like Lawson is improvising. His motions are purposeful and precise.

He starts to constrict like a python, pulling on his foot. Yuri's face turns a deep shade of purple in the orange glow of the parking lot lights. He wheezes what's probably more Russian profanity, then jerks, trying to escape the hold, but he can't get free. Lawson makes adjustments with his hands to the positioning of his legs and Yuri's head and neck in the hold. Yuri tries to stand, pulling Lawson up, but Lawson keeps his shoulder blades on the ground.

Yuri slowly collapses back to his knees, struggles for a couple more seconds, and then goes completely limp. Lawson releases the hold and rolls Yuri's hulking unconscious body onto its side. Yuri immediately begins snoring. Lawson jumps to his feet, dusts off his back, picks up his phone, and comes to me. "Are you okay?"

I swallow and nod, still stunned, too much adrenaline sluicing through my body to speak.

"Well, now you've done it, you brute. You killed Yuri!" Divine cries. "I'd grown fond of the oaf despite his coarseness."

"He's not dead, you idiot," Lawson says.

"Oh, this is just a horrible thing for me to have to see. You dipping your hands in a man's blood right in front of me."

"Dude? I just choked him out. He's snoring. If you'd shut up for a second, you'd hear it."

"I knew you were trouble from how little you talked all night. Quiet people, you gotta keep your eye on them. If you're not speaking, you're scheming."

Lawson points at Divine. "You shut up. You've talked enough tonight." He bends down and rummages in Yuri's pockets. He comes up with the keys to the Escalade.

"You better not steal our car, you hooligan!" Divine yells.

Lawson walks quickly toward Divine.

"Don't you dare! One of my dearest friends is Steven Seagal. He's promised to visit terrible suffering on anyone who tries to get my goat!" Despite his bravado, Divine shrivels from Lawson as he nears. "Stay back, you lout!"

Lawson holds the keys up to Divine's face, then chucks them into the donation bin. He nods at Yuri, still slumped on the ground. "When he wakes up, he'll be in a great mood. He can help you get unstuck, and maybe between the two of you, you can get the keys out. You might even still sell something."

Divine nods nervously. "All right. Fine."

Lawson walks away. As soon as he does, Divine starts in again. "I'm not scared of you! You got lucky!"

My voice returns. "Lawson, give Mr. Divine his honorarium." I hope Lawson catches my drift.

Lawson gives me a knowing smile, spins around, and walks back to Divine, whose bravado abruptly evaporates again. "Okay, all right. Let's be calm."

Lawson lifts the tail of Divine's jacket while blocking Divine's impotent swats, grabs the waistband of his boxer shorts, and yanks upward with a loud rip. Divine howls. "Ow! That was an unnecessarily violent wedgie! You'll be hearing from my attorneys in the coming days. I think you may have herniated a disc in my lower back when you did that! And if you've injured my anus, there'll be hell to pay!"

I see my phone lying several yards away. I scurry over and pick it up. It seems to be working fine, but it has seven percent left on the battery. Lawson comes over to me and starts leading me away.

"Wait," I say. "One more thing." I run to the Escalade, open the door, and grab the lobster in its to-go box. I hold it aloft like a trophy. "I paid for this lobster. And Lawson and I are going to eat it."

"What if I get peckish later?" Divine wails. "There's nothing worse than being hungry in a hotel room. Oh, I don't care to work with you anymore. I don't. You don't even mind if I get peckish. I'm going to tell everyone in television not to give you the time of day."

"You do that," I call back. "Start with Disme."

Lawson and I speed-walk away. Divine's indignant clamoring fades behind us. We steal one last look back at him, hanging there like a broken, outraged marionette. And in spite of ourselves—in spite of everything—we both laugh.

. . .

My phone was at seven percent battery, but the minute I start using it to figure out where we are, it drops to four percent.

Lawson pulls his phone from his back pocket. The screen is shattered. "Aw . . . damn. Must've broken it during the fight. It turns on, but I can't use the screen."

"I think I know which way we need to start heading. It's actually kinda easy to get back to the hotel. But it's about five miles."

"Should we try to get a cab or an Uber or something?"

"I have no idea what that would cost, and I seriously can't spend any more money. I'm legit broke."

"I don't mind walking. Plus, I guess I have to buy a new phone now, so yeah."

"I'm so, so sorry about this. How embarrassing."

Lawson smiles and puts his arm around me. "Hey, I got to spend time with you. I'll never complain about that."

I kiss his neck. "Okay, explain to me what I saw."

Lawson glows, perfectly in his element. "Basically, the min-

324

ute Yuri went into his stance, I could tell he was a striker, not a grappler. I was worried he might be a Sombo guy—"

"Sombo?"

"Russian martial art. Kinda like jujitsu."

"Wild. Go ahead."

"So I could see he was pretty much a street brawler from his stance. He didn't move like he had fight training. Still, I wasn't about to stand and bang with him. I figured if I could get the fight to the ground, I could get him in an armbar or a choke. No way does he have any submission defense. But I didn't wanna try to take him down, because he was too big. So I faked a fall to lure him to the ground, and *bam!* Triangle choke. Prettiest one I ever did."

"In other words, you basically played a chess game in your head in like one nanosecond."

"A chess game where one punch could land me in the morgue."

"Wait, *seriously?*"

"It's a worst-case scenario, but . . ."

"You risked *death* to put yourself between Yuri and me?!"

"I was not about to let him lay his hands on you."

"That is *ridiculously* hot."

He shrugs, self-consciously casual. "My favorite character in the Bloodfall books is Taaro Tarkkanan, this warrior who's the personal bodyguard of the Queen of the Autumnlands. He's sworn to die for his queen."

I step in front of him and put my hand on his chest. (It's a nice chest.) "Hey, stop." I stand on my tiptoes and pull his face down to me until his lips brush mine. "I need to make you some pancakes," I murmur.

. . .

"You know what I wish I hadn't left in Divine's car?" I ask, stopping to take off my heels.

Lawson smacks his forehead. "Your flip-flops."

"Yep. I guess they'll have to be Divine's honorarium."

"They're not going to help him if he gets peckish later."

"Nope."

Lawson stops and pulls off his shoes and socks. He stuffs his socks in the toes and hands them to me. "Put these on."

"What about you?"

"My feet are super calloused from fight training."

"Your awesomeness levels are almost scary," I say, putting on his shoes.

By about thirty minutes into our walk, the adrenaline and giddiness of our close escape have worn off. What's replaced it is the sinking realization of what our failure with Divine means.

"You've been quiet for the last few minutes," Lawson says.

"I'm pretty bummed out that Divine was such a disaster. Like *legitimately* bummed out."

"I can imagine."

"I made a big bet on this."

"You'll be able to save up money this summer."

"That's not what I mean."

"What do you mean?"

I almost say, *Now's not the time. Let's talk about it later.* But that's the worst. That's not what you say to someone who just risked his life for you. But I also can't look him in the eyes. And then, out of nowhere, I start crying. I didn't mean to. But the stress, exhaustion, and defeat of the night have overwhelmed me.

"Hey, now," Lawson says gently. He hugs me to his chest, and I bury my face in it. He strokes my hair. "It's okay. It's okay."

"What's one more indignity tonight, right?" I say, half composed.

Lawson shakes his head. "You have nothing to be ashamed of. You handled tonight like a champion. You're a fighter."

I sigh and wipe away tears. "I don't know. I made a deal with my parents. Remember that internship with Food Network I told you about the first time we hung out?"

"Yeah. That your mom hooked up for you?"

"That's the one. I kinda promised my parents that if things didn't work out with Divine, I would take the internship."

"So—"

"So if I keep my promise, that means I'm headed to Knoxville at the end of summer." I look up to see Lawson's reaction.

"Oh." His face dims. Like when you turn on a light in a room and something seems weird and you notice there's a lightbulb out.

"I don't know what to do. I don't want to leave you and Delia."

Lawson is quiet for a long time. I see his jaw muscles clenching. Finally, he says, "I never want to be the reason you break a promise."

"The other thing is, after this weekend, I'm not sure I'm meant to be a horror host for the rest of my life. Walking around that convention—I'm just not a horror person. Not really. I don't feel dedicated enough. I mean, do you have any doubt that being a professional fighter is what you want?"

"None. If I had doubts, no way could I do the things I do. It would hurt too much."

"See? Plus, I know Divine was largely full of beans, but I believe him that he's achieved as much as you can in the horror-hosting world. And it doesn't look that great."

"No. It does not."

"How am I going to tell Delia?"

"It'll come to you."

"I feel *terrible*. I pressured her to go see her dad."

"No, you didn't. She wanted to go. I could tell. You just gave her permission."

"It's going to break her heart. This. We can't tell her much about how gross a time we had. Delia doesn't require much convincing that she's a bad person."

We walk along quietly, contemplatively.

"I'm gonna miss you," Lawson says. "I wish we'd met each other sooner."

"I bet they have fighting coaches or whatever in Knoxville." Hearing the words out loud, I realize how badly I want them to take root in him.

"They do."

I give him a few seconds to take the hint. "And?"

"And . . . I gotta stick with my coach. He's a great coach. He and I have been working together since I started fighting. I'm super loyal to people."

"Think about it?"

He nods. "I'll think about it."

"I regret being bratty to you on our first date."

"Part of your charm."

"You're a really good guy."

"You're a really great girl."

We walk and walk, my dejection deepening with every step. It's started to feel like a funeral march.

I get out my phone for a progress check, and I run through the last dregs of battery doing it. Which is bad, because now there's no calling for rides, for sure. And I'm completely out of gas. Emotionally. Physically. My feet have blisters. So does my heart.

I stop in the middle of the sidewalk. I feel like crying again. "I'm exhausted."

"How far?"

"Another mile."

He turns around and gets down on one knee. "Giddyup."

"Dude."

"I'm serious. Saddle up."

"You're gonna give me a horsie ride for a *mile*?"

"Yep."

"Come on."

"This weekend has been a wash, training-wise. It'll do me good. We carry each other around the gym during practice."

"Okay, but I'm making you wear your shoes."

"Deal."

He puts his socks and shoes on. I get on his back and hold on, resting my face in his thick black hair. It feels like heaven. "You are strong like hippo," I murmur. We both start giggling so hard he has to let me down for a second.

"No more making me laugh if you want this to work," he says.

"Okay. I'm really going to miss you."

"Perfect. That's the least funny thing for me to think about."

"I wasn't finished. Miss you . . . like hippo."

Delia

My eyes are so tear-blurred, I almost run off the road a few times.

There aren't enough good places to scream in this world. You can't do it in public. You can't really do it at your house, if you live anywhere near other people. Can't do it at school. It's strange that we provide so few places to do something that you really need to do sometimes. There should be padded, sound-proof rooms, like restrooms for screaming. Fortunately, a Kia Rio on a three-hour drive on the interstate from Boca Raton to Orlando is a great place to scream.

So I roll down the window and scream into the humid night. I scream until the back of my throat is raw and hot like a skinned knee. Until I can taste copper. I scream with my wounded seven-year-old heart and every year of hurt that followed. The air, weighted with water, seems to swallow up the sound, like I'm screaming into a pillow. This strange place feels like the jungle wants to devour it; as if the moment humans stop cutting it back, it'll reclaim what belonged to it. Maybe the ice caps will melt and this place will disappear completely, washed away.

What a good place for someone running from memories, where all of the world's motion is toward forgetting.

Josie

By the time Lawson gets out of the shower, I'm sitting cross-legged on the bed, my hair wrapped up into a towel, dressed in the shorts and tank top I sleep in, tearing into my repossessed lobster. I dip chunks of the sweet white meat into the little container of butter that came with it. Delia just texted me to say that she was getting gas and would be back in about an hour and a half.

"Sorry, dude," I say, my mouth full, as Lawson emerges. "Couldn't wait."

Lawson roars in mock anger, runs up to the bed, and dives on, forcing me to pick up the lobster box at the last second, squealing and giggling. He tickles me, and I squeal some more.

"I've heard there's nothing worse than being hungry in a hotel room," he says.

"What can I say? I got peckish."

I tear off a chunk of lobster, dip it in the butter, and feed it to him.

He chews and nods. "Not bad . . . It's no pancakes, though."

"Worth ninety bucks?"

We look at each other for a second and bust up. "No way," he says.

"What a disaster this night was," I say. "In every conceivable way."

Lawson gets a distant, contented look.

"What? What's that look?"

"There's one way it wasn't so bad."

"What?" I reach up and smooth an errant patch of his damp hair.

"I told you I'd win a fight in front of you someday. Tonight I did." He beams.

I set the lobster box on the nightstand and stand at the foot of the bed. "Come here. Stand beside me."

Lawson does as he's told. I grab his hand. "Aaaaaaand the winner of tonight's fight—What do I say next? Do I say your name?"

"Yep. Also say how I won. By triangle choke."

I raise Lawson's arm. "Aaaaaaand the winner of tonight's fight, by triangle choke, Lawson 'Lost in Translation' Vargas!" I yell the last part so loudly, someone thumps on our ceiling. But we don't care. Lawson does a backflip onto the bed, bouncing a couple of times, and I flop next to him, and we laugh and kiss a lot.

We may not have forever together, but we have right now.

. . .

There's none of the weirdness or awkwardness I feared when we get in bed together to sleep. Just pure snuggliness, both of us smelling like hotel soap.

As tired as I am, and as comfortable as I am, spooned into him, I take longer to fall asleep than I expect.

I imagine how tonight probably bruised me emotionally in ways I won't realize until I wake up tomorrow, like after a hard day of some strenuous physical activity your body isn't used to.

I ponder the promise I made my parents and the wisdom of leaving behind a small but sure thing for an uncertain future.

I picture Delia, driving back alone in the dark, having had either the best night of her life or the worst. There's no way it was anywhere in between. And I consider what I'm going to have to tell her.

And I think about the boy whose warm, strong, hard-yet-welcoming body I'm nestled into. The one currently being a perfect gentleman about his obvious raging boner. The one who stood quietly by my side through every moment of a difficult night. The one who casually risked death in battle for me. The one who literally carried me on his back. The one who has taken me completely by surprise in so many ways.

Delia

I try to be absolutely silent entering the hotel room, because Josie and Lawson are probably asleep. I fumble around by the light of my phone.

Josie raises her head, squinting. "DeeDee?" she whispers, in a voice thick with sleep. Lawson doesn't stir.

"Yeah," I whisper.

"How'd it go?"

I shake my head, trying not to start crying again. "Sucky. How'd it go with you guys?"

"I'm so out of it. I'll tell you tomorrow."

I can tell from her tone that she doesn't want to tell me tonight, and if it were good news, she'd want to tell me, because I'm sure she can sense that I'm having one of the worst nights of my life and I want it to be over more than I've ever wanted anything.

• • •

All night I have dreams where my encounter with my dad ends differently. The worst dreams are the ones where it ends up well, and then I wake up for a few seconds and realize it was just a dream.

We finally stir around 11:30. We basically have time to roll out of bed and brush our teeth before checkout.

Outside, we squint against the howling sun; the air feels like stepping into a hot mouth. I still have a headache from crying. Or maybe it's a fun new headache. Whichever it is, my head pounds as if someone bonked me repeatedly with a comically large cartoon sledgehammer. I can feel leftover tear tracks on my face that escaped my hurried preparation to leave.

My stomach growls. I can hear everyone else's doing likewise—a gastrointestinal symphony. But we've made an unspoken agreement to just hit the road. Get the hell out of here.

The worst part is the silence in the car. It's got the same quality as the silence when you're gossiping about someone and they walk up and go, *Hey, guys, what're you talking about?* and you're like, *Uhhhh . . . youuuunicorns? Nothing! What?*

Josie drives, her left elbow propped on her open window, her head resting on her palm. I slump to the right, my head against the window. The palpable stench of defeat hangs yellow-green in the air, like an open container of baked beans, forgotten in the back of the fridge, that now smell like they've already made their way through someone.

It's forty-five minutes before anyone speaks. It's me: "So. Jack Divine?"

"Jack Divine," Josie mutters, shaking her head.

"Didn't go well?"

Josie chuckles sourly. "*No ho ho ho.* Yeah, no, it went *poorly,* I daresay."

"It did not go great," Lawson murmurs.

"He's—"

Josie finishes for me. "A delusional narcissistic psychopath

335

who would probably get us all murdered if we worked with him? Yes."

"So he's not—"

"Nope. He's not gonna help us. He's not gonna make us better. He's not gonna give us any opportunities. He's interested in bleeding us dry to pay off the Russian mob. *Long* story."

"Well. That sucks. Would it have made a difference if I were there?"

Josie sighs. "Yeah. It does suck. It really does. And no, no difference."

"We traveled a long way."

"That we did."

I feel like a giant wad of toilet paper being flushed. I thought I might be able to at least go one for two on this trip. What a silly thing to think. I don't *win*. I'm not *lucky*. Life is gonna dick me around time and again.

We drive several more miles without speaking.

"So. Your dad?" Josie asks.

"My dad."

"Didn't go great?"

"No, I daresay it went rather poorly."

"I'm so sorry, DeeDee."

"Me too."

"You feel like talking about it?"

"Not really."

More driving. More demoralized quiet.

"Well," I say finally. "We made our show without Jack Divine, and we can go on without him. We'll take ourselves to the next level. We can always—"

Josie just nods in this oddly tentative way.

"What?" I ask.

"Nothing."

"*What?*"

She shakes her head and raises her hand. "DeeDee, just—"

"Why are you being weird?"

"I'm not."

"No, yeah, you really are."

"Yeah, no, I'm super tired."

"I'm not stupid. I know you, like, very well."

"I really don't want to talk about this right now."

"We can make our show great without him," I murmur. I look to see Josie's reaction.

She has a pained look. "Yeah," she says faintly.

"Okay, seriously? Spill. We're in this car for like ten more hours. Let's hash out whatever this is."

"That's exactly *why* I don't want to talk about this now. Also, I don't want to make Lawson uncomfortable."

"Oh, what, scared to fight in front of Lawson . . . the *professional fighter?*"

Lawson does a *hey, leave me out of this* slump into his seat.

"No, DeeDee, I legitimately don't want drama," Josie says.

"Well, I'm currently experiencing the most devastating twenty-four hours of my life, so why not put it all out on the table?"

Josie takes both hands off the steering wheel for a second and holds them in front of her face like she's gripping an invisible box—one containing whatever she's not telling me. She breathes in deep, holds it, and releases it in a rush. "*I can't do the show anymore.* Okay? I can't do it anymore. There. Happy?"

I suddenly feel like a giant, ice-cold steel claw is opening

337

under my stomach. Going down in flames with my dad was one thing. That was my past. But this show? This show is my present and future. It's all I have. It's what gets me out of bed. "What are you talking about?" I ask weakly.

Josie blinks fast, like she's clearing away tears.

"*What*, Josie? What is it?" My voice rises.

Her voice is pinched and taut. "I promised my parents. If this didn't work out. This whole *thing*. With Jack Divine. If he couldn't help us. I told them. They made me promise."

"Promise what?"

"That I'd take the internship in Knoxville."

The claw opens more. "You cannot be serious."

"I am."

"So tell them you can't."

"I promised."

"Break your promise."

"I can't do that."

"Won't do that, you mean."

"Fine. Won't."

"So that's it?" I say, laughing astringently. "You won't fight for the show?"

"I *fought*, DeeDee. My parents have been on me for months. They wouldn't have let me come at all if I didn't promise. I rolled the dice and lost."

"You're eighteen. You could have told them to suck it."

"No, I couldn't. They're my parents. I love them."

I look out the window and shake my head. Every part of my body hurts, like my emotions are spilling over and being turned into pain chemicals or whatever.

"And honestly," she continues, "I don't know if this is the kind of show I want to be on for the rest of my life."

"Nice," I say.

"I'm not roasting our show. It's that being at that convention, I realized this isn't the world I belong in for my whole life. Like, I can be at the periphery and dabble in it, the way I've done, and that's fine. But I can't invest my whole life in it. If it weren't for you and how much I care about you and love you and love making the show with you, I wouldn't choose this world."

"So you're going to just walk away from everything we made?"

"No, I'm not going to just walk away. I thought I might drive twenty-four hours round-trip to Orlando to spend the evening hanging out with a legitimately unhinged person who, I might add, *cleaned* me out. Our little evening with Jack Divine cost me almost every penny I have."

"*What?*"

"Yeah. *That's* a terrific story, by the way. But anyway, I tried, okay? I didn't just walk away. I did my damnedest to make it work so I could have my dream and we could keep doing the show."

"You just want to be famous." I can't hide the acidity in my voice. I'm being super unchill and I know it, but . . .

"Seriously? You're going there?"

"Oh, I bought the first-class ticket there."

"Y'all," Lawson says. "Maybe—"

"We've got this," I snap.

He raises his hands like I trained a pistol on him. "Okay. Cool. Sorry."

"Please don't be rude to him," Josie says.

"Please don't both of you gang up on me," I say.

"I'm butting out," Lawson says.

"Anyway, yeah, Delia, I want to be super famous. I want to have three-point-seven million followers on the current hot social media platform. I want to post pictures of myself wearing billowy white pants and drinking a big glass of red wine with some insufferable platitude like *Caring for yourself . . . starts with you.* I want to eat expensive seaweed and drink water in which all the molecules have been lined up facing the same direction. I want to tell people who love Chili's and save twenty-percent-off Bed Bath and Beyond coupons that no wardrobe is complete without my favorite pair of twelve-hundred-dollar flats and seven-hundred-fifty-dollar jeans. I want to take trips to a private island for six months to 'center myself.' This is all I want."

"You do."

"Really? *Really?* No. Sorry. That's like accusing anyone who wants to write a book or record an album of just wanting to be famous. Maybe they want to connect with people. So unfair."

I roll my eyes.

It pisses her off. I can hear it. "The only reason we're even friends in the first place is because of my dream. It brought us together. You've known what I wanted in life for as long as you've known me."

"What about me, huh?" I ask. "Do I get dreams too?"

"Of course. And I support you in them however I can."

"Well, here's my dream: to keep working at and improving our show together, until it was something we both did for a living. Like we talked about."

"I tried to make that happen. I did. I tried to support you."

"You tried a little bit."

"DeeDee, I genuinely understand how bummed out you are, and you can't believe how bummed out I am."

"Oh, really? You understand growing up without a dad and all the rollicking fun that entails and having *one* good thing and then having that thing snatched away? That's something you genuinely understand?"

"DeeDee."

"No. Do you? Do you understand that? Is that your life?"

"No," Josie says softly after a long pause.

"You're so bummed out to be leaving me behind so you can go on to bigger and better things?"

"Yes."

"Whatever."

"DeeDee, you came up with the idea for the show. How we would do it. You made all the calls to arrange for the studio and get Arliss on board. You handled the merch sales. You had all the movies. Replace me. It's your show."

"It's *our* show."

"The show can exist without me. It could never exist without you."

"That's flattering, but . . ."

"I could come home on breaks, and we could record a bunch of episodes in a row," Josie says.

"No. First off, Arliss won't go for that. Second, we need to be producing new material more regularly than that or we'll lose our slot and maybe our syndicates." *And third, this is what I look forward to every week. It's all I look forward to.*

"Get another person to help you or do the show by yourself like SkeleTonya used to. Maybe I can be a guest."

"No way. If you leave, you're gone. You're not being a guest on my show. I'm sick of people who half-ass being in my life." Saying this is anguish, like running myself through with a fireplace poker. My brain is such a maelstrom of hurt, anger, sadness, exhaustion, and something I might call disappointment (but a million times deeper), my mouth is sorta doing its own thing.

"Okay, then," Josie murmurs, barely audible.

I feel like a sack of wet skunk feces. Maybe this is why everyone leaves me.

I would give anything to be too good for people to discard. Why am I not better? Why am I never enough? If I can't keep you, Josie, then who? In fact, maybe it would save me a lot of heartache in the future to not give anyone the chance to abandon me in the first place. That'll be my new plan. I'm done loving people.

I watch Josie out of the corner of my eye as she gazes at the road. She quickly wipes away a tear. And another with the other hand. And another. She finally gives up and lets them flow. One hangs on her jawline for an improbably long time, catching the radiant Florida sunshine like a prism.

I guess everything dies eventually, even the sun someday. My life feels like a star collapsing into itself. And it was never that bright to begin with.

Josie

It randomly occurs to me while I'm crying how grateful I am that tears don't smell like pee, and I almost want to tell Delia, because I know she'd laugh under normal circumstances, but she has her eyes closed and is leaning her head on the window, away from me. She doesn't even appear to be sleeping; she seems to have just shut down, circuits overwhelmed. Honestly, if I were in her position, I would.

I feel something at my left hip. Lawson's snuck his hand between the door and my seat. I reach down and hold the ends of his fingers with the ends of mine. It brings me a little comfort. Right until I remember that I'm leaving him—*this*—behind too, and I continue weeping.

I keep trying to stop, but the sheer weight of exhaustion, guilt, and grief for the life I'm outgrowing keeps squeezing tears out of me like stepping on a sponge.

I put on the Dearly mix that Jesmyn made us. She said she got super into him after her boyfriend died, and I can see why. He sings like a fellow traveler in sorrow. The hurt and longing in his voice are all I can stand to listen to for the next few hours. Lawson's hand checks in on me periodically.

We stop a lot less on the way home than we did on the way there. We're not driving in the middle of the night, so we don't need to wake ourselves up as much. Plus, we all want to be done.

We pull in at a little gas station outside Ringgold, Georgia. One of those Mom's Country Cookin'/tchotchke-shop places. While I'm inside buying a Coke, I see something I need. I shouldn't be spending even a penny more than absolutely necessary after the way Divine shook me down, but this is absolutely necessary. I pay for it and take it outside, wrapped in white butcher paper for safekeeping.

Lawson is still inside using the restroom when I get to the car, so I wait.

When he comes out, our eyes meet and he gives me a sad smile and says, "Are we there yet?" (His jokes could still use work.)

When he gets close, I pull my purchase from behind my back and hand it to him.

He grins and starts to unwrap the package. "What's—" A small porcelain cat falls from the paper into his hands. His grin fades, as if he were a little boy seeing a present under the Christmas tree that he had completely abandoned any hope of receiving, and his brain's pleasure center is too overwhelmed by joy even to keep telling his mouth to smile.

He looks at me quickly, looks back down. Up. Down. Up.

His eyes look like firelight on polished oak when the sun catches them. I didn't notice that before. *How has a face that struck me as so ordinary the first few times I saw it become the most beautiful face in the world to me?*

His brow furrows. He clenches his fist around the cat and comes for me. I think he's going to kiss me, but instead, he grabs me up in a powerful embrace, almost squeezing the wind from me.

"Okay, tiger, don't Yuri me." I gasp and giggle.

He lets me go. He attempts to say something and stops. He tries once more and stops. He hugs me again, more gently this time, so I can breathe. Then he puts his hand on my cheek, presses his body against mine, and kisses me like he's on fire and I'm water.

Sometimes you know you're getting a fever way before you do. Days. A week. It's there, ticking away in the back of your mind. You still feel fine, but your body tells you *something's waiting to overcome you*. It's a premonition. Falling in love is like that. Like the most welcome sort of fever, a perfect delirium descending on you. You feel it coming long before it reaches you. Long before it knocks you flat.

Delia

"All right, later," I say, not meeting Josie's eyes as she drops me off.

"DeeDee?" she says in an imploring voice.

But I ignore her, grab my bag from her trunk, and walk quickly into my trailer. I know I'm acting like a dick to one of the people I love most in this world, but I can't help it.

Mom meets me inside the front door, dressed for bed. "How'd it go, sweetie?" she asks.

I shake my head and try not to look at her, but then she hugs me and I unravel, sobbing. "I love you, Mom."

"I love you too, DeeDee. Wanna talk?"

I shake my head again.

"Did someone hurt you?" Mom raises my chin to meet my eyes.

"Not in the way you're asking."

She looks at me for a second before dragging me gently by the hand over to our couch. She sits and pulls my head onto her lap and strokes my hair and tear-sodden face.

She knows. I can sense it. I never truly believed in her gift the way she does, but there's not a doubt in my mind that she knows and hurts with me.

Josie

It's almost one a.m. when I slip inside my house after dropping off Lawson. I sneak into the kitchen without turning on any lights and pull a carton of chocolate chip cookie dough ice cream from the freezer. I grab a spoon, sit at the table, and settle in for a good stress-eat. Buford shuffles into the kitchen and gives me a reproachful woof.

I shush him and scratch him behind the ears. "Someday I'm going to try to make a batch of chocolate chip cookies using only the cookie dough from chocolate chip cookie dough ice cream," I whisper.

Buford gives me a quizzical look.

"But you can't have any, Bufie Bear," I continue. "Because I can never remember the two hundred and sixty-seven different human foods that are poison to dogs, so I play it safe."

Buford gives me a forlorn look. He is aware on some level that there are things in the world he's not allowed to eat, and this causes him great sorrow.

"Jo?" My mom's sleepy voice startles me.

"Hey, Mom. Sorry for waking you up."

"I'm glad you got home safe." She pads in and sits beside me.

"Sorry. I know you hate it when I do this." I hold up the spoon and the ice cream container.

"I do. But you wouldn't be my Josie if you didn't do it anyway." She regards me in her bleary, unfocused, contacts-out way. "So? How'd it go in Florida?"

"Well, I'm eating ice cream from the carton with a spoon, which is one of the most clichéd ways writers of film and television convey that someone is undergoing emotional turmoil, so you tell me."

Mom rests her chin on her palm and strokes my hair with her other hand. "I'm sorry, sweetie."

I inhale deeply through my nose. "It feels weird to wish something had gone better but also be glad it went how it did."

"Learning what you don't want can be as important as learning what you do want."

"Yeah, well. Anyway. You and Dad win. I'm doing the internship. Congrats."

Mom stops stroking my hair and folds her arms on the table. "It was never about getting our way. We win when you're happy. That's all we want. I know it might not seem like it, but I think you'll be happy getting out and seeing more of the world."

We look at each other for a long time. "I'm worried about Delia," I say finally.

"You're a really, really good friend to her."

"I think she would disagree right now."

"She'll remember."

"People keep leaving her behind. I wanted to be better than that."

"Pursuing your dreams isn't the same thing as leaving someone behind."

I nod and scrape at the dregs of the ice cream carton. "Tell that to Delia."

"I think Delia will land on her feet," Mom says. "She seems to have a certain gutsiness."

"I hope."

Mom stands, leans over, and kisses me on the top of my head. "I'm going back to sleep. We'll talk tomorrow."

I catch her in a side hug. "I love you, Mom."

"Love you too. Put your spoon in the dishwasher." She starts to leave but turns in the doorway. "I'm proud of who you're growing up to be."

I tear open the ice cream carton and lick the sides. "And why wouldn't you be?"

She smiles and disappears down the hall. I hear the soft click of her door shutting.

I sit there for a while, too tired even to get up and go to bed, and let the buzzing of my thoughts harmonize with the hum of the refrigerator. Then the fridge goes silent and the kitchen is quiet like loneliness.

I wonder if it's how Delia feels all the time.

• • •

It's Thursday and I still haven't heard from Delia. Total silence. I texted her a couple of times but got no response. It's time for more active measures.

I'm sitting in Delia's gravel driveway. It's late enough that she should be home from work. I keep trying to think of what to tell her, what to say to make things right. But we've never been the sort of friends who make planned speeches to each other. I get out, walk up to her door, and knock.

I'm about to turn around and leave when I hear a thumping

and the door swings open. It's Delia. She looks resigned and sad, but not angry to see me.

"Hey." I wave awkwardly.

"Hey." She waves awkwardly.

"Hey," I say in a dumb-person voice and wave goonily.

"Hey," she says in a dumber-person voice and waves even more goonily.

This goes back and forth for a while until we're both smiling.

"Are we still friends?" I ask.

Delia comes outside, closing the door behind her, and sits on the front steps. "Of course, dummy."

I sit next to her. "We've never gone so long without talking. I wondered."

"Haven't felt like talking to anyone."

"I hoped it was that and that you didn't hate me."

"I'm so sure."

We watch moths flit and dance around in the light of Delia's mom's sign.

"It's not even you," Delia says. "Mostly I'm still processing my meet-up with my dad."

"Was it horrible?"

"It wasn't *horrible*. Like he didn't slam the door in my face. But it sucked in how little it was what I'd hoped it would be."

"What did you hope?"

"I don't even know. That's the frustrating thing. But whatever I wanted, it wasn't what I got."

I just listen.

Delia continues. "What I got was that he was cowardly and small. He ran from my mom and me because he was scared of the responsibility. It feels weird that something that affected my life so much is the result of someone being *afraid*. I almost wish he left because he hated me."

I put my arm around her. "I'm really sorry, DeeDeeBoo. You deserve better than that. I love you."

She lays her head on my shoulder. "I love you, JoJoBee. I'm really sad I'm losing you too."

"You're not losing me. You'll always have me."

"But you'll be far away."

"Five hours."

"Do you have to leave?" Delia asks plaintively.

"I can't do what I want to do with my life if I stick around here."

"It's what you've wanted since you were little, huh?"

"Yeah. But it still guts me to leave you."

"I get it. I wouldn't make you want less for yourself, even if I could."

"I really tried with Jack Divine, boo."

"I believe you."

"Like legitimately, if you knew what we went through that night. He's seriously a piece of work."

"How so?"

"Well, for one thing, I'm like ninety-nine percent sure his 'assistant' Celeste who you emailed with is actually him."

"Are you serious?"

"Yep. And Lawson ended up knocking out Yuri."

"*For reals?*"

"Yep. Divine told Yuri to get money from us. So Lawson did some MMA move on him and choked him until he passed out.

When we left Divine, he had his arm stuck in a clothing donation bin."

Delia snort-laughs. "Come on."

"Oh, oh! And we had just come from the office of a dude
named Wald Disme."

"Wait, like Walt—"

"NO. NOT AT ALL LIKE WALT DISNEY. He was *very* em-
phatic about that. Anyway, Disme had barely told me about
doing battle with a bunch of hornets at a construction site when
Divine's scary Austrian professional shot-putter ex-wife showed
up and threatened to burn down the building. So we had to escape."

"I *deeply* regret not being present for all of this."

"It's funny in hindsight. I can't emphasize the hindsight part
enough. Oh, and fair warning, Divine said that he was going to
tell *everyone* in Hollywood not to work with us, so . . ."

"I wonder if he's still stuck in the donation bin. Maybe he
chewed his arm off like a coyote."

"Lawson wedgied him super hard. He bid us farewell by saying we were in trouble if we injured his anus."

"As one does, I suppose."

We crack up. When our laughs subside, I ask, "So what are
you going to do about the show?"

Delia gives a resigned shrug. "Keep it going, I guess. For a
long time, I thought I was doing the show because it would be
a connection to my dad. But even knowing that's not going to
happen, the show's really all I have."

"I think you should keep it alive."

"It's not going to be as good without you."

"Dude, you'll be great."

"Think how much Larry Donut's going to hate our show if it diminishes even one iota in quality," Delia says.

"I'm imagining Larry Donut watching and fuming while eating a giant mixing bowl of melted cheese with a wooden spoon."

"*Gahhhh! My name is Larry Donut and I hate this stupid show, but I love my melted cheese bowl.*"

"I mean, Larry Donut can legit blow it out the back of his gross Utilikilt for all I care," I say.

"That's the healthy thing to do, I've heard. Good for your liver."

"That is not a thing. *Where is my anger-cheese bowl?*"

Once our laughter subsides, Delia starts talking again. "I'm sorry for what I said about you not being a guest on the show ever. *Obviously,* I want you to do the show with me any time you can."

"I'd like that a lot."

"Rayne and Delilah forever." Delia side-hugs me.

"Rayne and Delilah forever." I hug her back tighter.

"Did you and Lawson bone in Orlando before I got back?" Delia asks after a pause.

I laugh. "No. We'd had a horrible night. I didn't want to cap off our evening of follies by taking a trip to the bone zone."

"But you guys way made out."

"Sure, sure."

"I was afraid I was gonna walk in on you two bone-zoning," Delia says.

"I missed you so much the last few days."

"I missed *you*. It'll suck living in different cities."

"Yeah, it will." I stand and open Delia's front door. "Now, I believe we have a show tomorrow night to prepare for."

"You're gonna love the movie I picked. Or hate. Maybe hate."

"You knew I was coming over?"

"Of course. We have a show to do."

Delia

Summer passes like a cloud moves across the sky. While you watch it, it seems to creep along. But if you look away for a second, it's almost gone.

I work a lot. I get a second job at the new organic grocery store in Jackson. I've made friends with a couple of coworkers there and pal around with them sometimes. One of them is this guy named Dax, who's a guitarist in a halfway decent metal band. He seemed adorably overjoyed when I came out to one of his shows. He loves horror movies and started watching *Midnite Matinee* after we met. He and I have plans to do Thirty-One Days of Horror in October, where you watch a horror flick every night. I'm looking forward to it. He's easy to spend time with and nice to look at.

I hang out with Josie whenever she's not working or with Lawson. We text until the early-morning hours and we're both ready to pass out. We do our show, and Lawson helps when he can. Each week I try to envision myself doing it alone. It never gets any easier. But I do my best to step up a little more each time.

I savor the days we have left together. I hate thinking about how our remaining weeks could be counted on one hand.

Toward the end of summer, there's a big solar eclipse.

Everyone's saying it's pretty rare, and it turns out Nashville is one of the best places in America to see it. So Josie and I drive the couple of hours there and buy little cardboard eclipse glasses. We find a quiet corner of a park to watch it. As it starts to happen, the light turns a cool, flat sepia. For a while, we joke around, but as it reaches total eclipse, the world darkens and turns to dusk in the middle of the day. The cicadas and the crickets begin humming and chirping, but otherwise, there's a deep and heavy stillness, as if the world has gone inside a blanket fort. The sound of the space between heartbeats.

We stand side by side and stare up at the moon covering the sun. I feel so tiny—a cog in this immense heavenly machinery—the way I felt standing in the ocean with my dad. But being there with Josie, I'm okay with it. There are times when there's solace in smallness. It puts the bigness of problems in perspective. As long as there's someone by your side to remind you that you're not nothing.

I don't know why, but I start crying. I look over at Josie, and tears streak her cheeks too under her goofy eclipse glasses.

There's something about witnessing something holy with someone you love, because you take that sacred thing and weave it, like a golden thread, into the fabric of your togetherness.

Making something with someone you love is the same way.

As we stand there together in the moon's shadow, for that brief moment, I wish I could tell time *stop* and it would obey, as if time were the one thing that wouldn't leave me behind.

Josie

On TV, expressions of love are grand and cinematic. They happen under literal fireworks or in the pouring rain.

But in real life, sometimes what happens is you get done watching a movie with a boy who took you by surprise with the way he slipped into your heart, and you walk out to the parking lot, where he opens the door of his pickup truck for you because he's charmingly old-fashioned in all the good ways. You unlock his door for him, and he gets in. He goes to start the truck but stops, and you ask him what's up, and he says he has something to tell you and he's having a tough time forming the words. And you're a little scared until finally, he says he's gotten a job as a trainer and grappling instructor at a gym in Knoxville, and he's lined up a place to live with a couple of other MMA fighters.

And then he looks you in the eyes and says that the reason he did that is because he loves you and the thought of your being far from him made him heartsick.

You turn the fiery pink of a sunrise inside.

So you tell him you love him too, and that it would have also hurt too much to let him be far from you, so this is a pretty cool new development, to say the least. You try to think of a quip to help you deal with everything you're feeling, and you're coming up empty for once, but he saves you by kissing you, in a way both urgent and gentle, and he tastes like movie theater popcorn butter and salt, and you can't get enough of him, and because he is a very good kisser, in addition to every other good thing he is, you kiss until you fog up the windows on his truck, and a cop knocks on your window to make sure everything is okay, which it very much is—more so than it's ever been.

You maybe take a break from kissing and cry a little bit because you're so ecstatic, and it might be the first time that's ever happened to you—crying from joy—and you feel as though a massive burden has been lifted from you because you didn't realize how scared and sad you were to leave behind your best friend *and* the boy you love in order to chase a dream. In fact, you were starting to question the worth of your dream.

You ask him if he's really sure, because you know how loyal he is. He tells you he's sure—that he can be a champion anywhere he goes, under anyone with whom he trains—and the look in his eyes (he has nice eyes) tells you that you now occupy his top tier of loyalty, which is a sublime place to be.

Sometimes things are better on TV, but this is better in real life.

Delia

On TV, expressions of loneliness are grand and cinematic. Walks through cemeteries with swelling strings playing. Plucking petals off a rose while rain cascades down your windows.

But in real life, sometimes what happens is you're picking out a final movie for the show you do with your best friend (and you know it's not really the *final* movie because you'll surely do other shows with her as a guest, but still), and a rogue wave of loneliness breaks over you with such intensity that it literally drives you to your knees and robs your breath. It reminds you of the one time you stood in the ocean, with a father who abandoned you, and you felt the cool water wash indifferently over your feet.

And so you kneel on the cheap carpet in your cramped bedroom in the double-wide you share with your mom—who does her best—and you try to breathe through the crushing weight in your chest, and you wonder if you're going to be okay, and you reflect on how little dignity there is in loneliness, because by definition, it's a burden you bear alone. You wish that being lonely was something you could get good at, the way Tibetan monks can control their body temperature with their mind. Or the sort of thing you could find exaltation in, the way all sorts of monks everywhere did.

But then you think about how, to experience loneliness, you have to feel the absence of somebody, and you'd hate to have gone through life never having anybody, so you're grateful in a weird way.

On TV, things are uncomplicated, with lots of fanfare. But sometimes real life is better, in all of its complications, in all of its everyday, quiet ache.

Josie

I thought my excitement about my internship would take the edge off my melancholy over doing our last show, but it doesn't. I still have a last-day-of-sixth-grade feeling. All year you're excited for school to end so you can move on to junior high, but then the day comes and you realize that something that was an important part of your life is dying. And endings are still so new that you don't know quite how to feel.

You find an excuse not to run out the door when the bell rings and school's out. You talk to your teacher one last time. You use the restroom one last time. You take a circuitous route back to your classroom. On your way out, you look back and sigh, and you experience this deep wistfulness, and you wonder if life is just a series of endings. New beginnings don't make endings any easier.

Tonight it's only me and Delia, no guests, the way we started. The way we'll finish. I'm glad it's this way.

I keep looking at Delia. She's working with all her strength to be brave. I sense her almost chanting it to herself like a mantra. She seems like someone holding a bucket over a nest of angry wasps (or maybe hornets determined to shut down an ill-conceived theme park). They'll get out if she lets the bucket drop, and her arms are getting tired and shaky.

It's clear she's trying to step up and take the lead more in this show because she knows she won't have me around to help her. I can tell she wants me to know everything will be okay without me.

I can also feel her heart breaking, and it's breaking my heart too.

Her endings, including this one, haven't always come with new beginnings.

. . .

"Anyway, Ryan, thanks for writing! Obviously, I'll miss Rayne too. But her new blood bank internship is too good to pass up!" Delia says.

"Well, that does it for letters for this week," I say wistfully. "I wanna thank you all so much for—"

Arliss pops up his hand with Frankenstein holding one more letter. "Hold your horses! You got one more!"

"What? Frankenstein, you're normally so eager to finish up mail corner!" Delia says.

Arliss turns Frankenstein and hands the letter—a real letter, not a printed-off email—to me. "Yep. Well, I guess today's special."

I take the letter hesitantly, nervous about what Arliss has cooked up. I read the first few lines to see what I'm getting into. As I read, I put a shaking hand over my lips.

"Don't keep us in suspense, Rayne!" Delia says.

"Um." I shake my head. "Sorry, Delilah. Okay. I—Okay." I clear my throat and begin reading in an unsteady voice.

Hello, Delilah and Rayne,

My name is Jacob Waters. I live in Topeka, Kansas, and I'm a fan of your show. When I was in high school, I had a best friend named Erica. We used to love to watch cheesy horror movies together. We would make jokes about them and pretend to be scared. We both went away to separate colleges, but ended up returning to our hometown. When she was diagnosed with cervical cancer she developed after contracting HPV, I would bring my laptop to the hospital and we would watch movies. It hurt her to laugh, and she had a hard time staying awake through them toward the end. She died a couple of years ago. She was only twenty-eight. I miss her every day.

One Saturday night a few months back, when I was randomly flipping through channels, I happened upon your show, and it immediately transported me to hanging out with Erica. The goofy jokes. The way you two obviously love each other's company. The movies that are too funny to be scary. Your show felt to me like what it would have looked like if someone had filmed me and Erica. It made me feel loved and safe. It was a bright, warm fire, the way Erica was to me in—

I start to lose it entirely. My voice cracks and fails me. I look over at Delia, and tears are coursing down her face. I offer the letter to her.

"Don't look at *me*," she chokes out, cry-laughing. She wipes her nose with the back of her hand.

I clear my throat and take a deep breath. "Whew. Okay. All right. I'm going to try to get through this. Sorry, everyone. I guess there's no chance of another take, is there, Frankenstein?"

"Good enough for access," Arliss says.

"Of course that's what you'd say. Here goes nothing." I start reading again.

... the way Erica was to me in my coldest, darkest midnights. I had a hard time in high school. There were a lot of times when I felt like I wanted to stop living. There were times when I wanted to give up. There were times when my light went dim. Erica was there for me then, and I tried to be a comfort to her during her most painful days.

Randomly finding your show on public access reminded me that there are small troves of beauty and moments of human connection in the most unexpected places. So I watch your show with Erica's spirit by my side. I know she'd have loved you two also.

You don't know me, and I doubt we'll ever meet. But know that I'm your friend, and I've loved pretending like you're mine as I remember one who's gone. You have given me a great gift with this show, and I'll always be grateful.

Your fan and friend,
Jacob Waters

PS: I don't care that you call your puppet Frankenstein. I think it's fine.

There's a long silence when I finish. A silence that you can *hear.* The kind of silence you rarely see on normal TV because it's way too long and awkward. Good enough for public access, though.

Delia sighs. "Well."

"Wow, right," I say.

"Yeah, that was . . . a really great letter."

"Yes, it was. Thank you, Jacob. Truly. This means more to me than you'll ever know." I hold the paper in my lap and turn. "Frankenstein?"

Arliss pops up Frankenstein. "Sorry for making you wait so long to hear your letter, Jacob. Frankenstein saved it for a special occasion."

"You purposely made us cry, Frankenstein," I say. "You're grounded." I leave a beat for Arliss to put in some sad slide-whistle sound effect or a rim shot. "No, I don't mean we're putting you *back in the ground,* Frankenstein."

Arliss doesn't say anything but makes Frankenstein pat my shoulder. I pull him in to me and hug him hard, until he squirms and goes, "All right, enough already."

• • •

"Well, manticores and woman-ticores, banshees and ban-hees, that'll do it for this week's show," Delia says.

"Lemme say something real quick, Delilah."

365

"Go for it, Rayne."

"I wanna say thank you to all of you who've supported and watched our show, who've taken the time to write such nice letters." I'm starting to slip. My composure is crumbling like a muffin being squeezed in a fist. "Being on TV has been my dream since I was little, so doing this show has legitimately been a dream come true. Thank you." I manage to finish relatively intact.

"We're gonna miss Rayne here at *Midnite Matinee*—especially me." Delia reaches over and takes my hand. We grip tight.

"I'll still be making guest appearances," I say.

"I hope so, Rayne. So tune in next week, folks, because the chills and thrills aren't over. I'll be back along with Frankenstein, and who knows what'll happen?" She suddenly sounds unsteady and faltering.

"Until we meet again," I say, smiling and waving with my free hand.

"Until next week," Delia says, waving with her free hand.

We sit, still and quiet, until Arliss says "Cut."

But we stay seated there for a while, holding hands. I take in the small, dark studio of TV Six. Arliss, switching things off and winding up cords. Our makeshift little set. The dark camera lens. The plastic skull and candelabra on the table next to us. The knowledge that my image and voice will travel to the homes of people I've never met and never will meet, and I'll be a small part of their lives and never even know. I'm not just leaving Delia behind. I'm leaving a piece of myself.

In my mind, I say, *Remember, remember.*

In my heart, I say *Thank you* over and over. *Thank you, show. Thank you for being a part of the twilight of my childhood. Thank you for giving me my best friend and my boyfriend. Thank you for being the first step on my path to realize my dreams. Thank you for being something I helped build with my own hands and heart and mind.*

Gripping me inside too is the profound ache of nostalgia for something that's not even a part of my past yet.

Sometimes small and unspectacular things can be a universe.

. . .

We walk slowly, reluctantly, down the corridor to the door, carrying our decorations and costumes. Neither of us speaks. Arliss follows us, an abnormal occurrence.

Before he opens the door to let us out (another uncommon gesture), I set down the things I'm holding and give him a bear hug. He smells like cigarette smoke, warm cotton, and clean dog. It's a comforting combo.

He stands there for a second while I hug him. Then he awkwardly pats the back of my head a few times like I'm a cat resting my butthole on his keyboard and he's gently shooing me away. "All right. Good luck with everything. Don't forget us when you're famous."

"Thanks for everything, Arliss. I know it wasn't easy," I murmur.

"Or fun."

"Right. Or fun. Anyway, thanks for putting up with us."

He grunts kindly and gives my head a couple more quick pats. "Okay, kid. Go be a TV star."

"I'll miss you."

"Yep." He closes the door behind us.

Now it's just me and Delia. My heart slides down the wall of my chest like a raindrop down a window.

367

I was trying to think of things to say—the right way to express something I can't express—and kept coming up empty. Fortunately, I don't have to say anything. As if we planned it, Delia and I drop our things without a word, sink down together, sitting on the top step, and hug ferociously. Like a yawning, bottomless chasm has opened up beneath each of us, and we're the only thing keeping the other from tumbling down it.

I breathe in Delia's smell of incense and the kind of vaguely fruity lotion that's no one's favorite smell but that you buy in agreement with someone else because you can both live with it. I try to imprint it onto my brain, to summon up on some bleak day when it feels like no one loves me.

"I'll miss you so much when you're in Knoxville," Delia croaks. "I know you'll do great."

"Promise you'll come visit."

"I will. Swear we'll stay best friends."

"Until we both die."

"Even after that."

"Our gross flyblown corpses will be friends. We'll pick maggots out of each other's eyeholes and paint each other's yellow nails black and laugh about how we smell like dumpsters."

"Deal."

We both laugh, but it quickly dissolves into crying.

It suddenly hits me, more raw than it ever has before: everything ends. Some things last longer than others, but everything ends. Childhood feels like it takes forever when you're in the midst of it, but one day you wake up and you're eighteen and going to college. That basset hound puppy with the bow around his neck? You're going to see his whole life pass. You may find someone you love and get married. And it might last a long time, but it ends one way or another. Maybe you'll be together for fifty or sixty years, but one of you is going to get left behind. I'm glad things end, though. It forces you to love them ferociously while you have them.

There's nothing worth having that doesn't die.

Delia and I hug for a long time, our heads pressed together so hard it hurts, but not as much as it would hurt to not share one more moment of connection. We only stop when we startle at Arliss opening the door behind us to leave.

Delia

Walking into the studio feels like walking into a mausoleum, except I'd surely be happier walking into a mausoleum. I'd rather see the bones of strangers than the slow death of something I created. I'm already dreading seeing Josie off tomorrow morning. I'm doubly dreading doing the show alone for the first time.

I make it a couple of echoing steps inside when the armload of puppets and decorations I'm carrying slowly slips from my grasp. It's twice what I normally carry.

Quite an omen. It's probably not great that I already want to cry.

I swallow down the stiff knot in my throat, gather everything, and keep struggling my way inside.

Arliss has our stage ready. The end table. A solitary chair. Josie's chair sits off to the side of the stage. Empty. I feel like I'm sliding down wet grass toward a muddy pond. I don't know how I'm going to do this.

Arliss is setting up the camera.

"Hey," I say to him.

"Hey," he says.

I walk over and hand him an envelope. "I'm sorry. I only have thirty bucks today. Our car broke down last week and Josie's not around to split the cost, so—" Part of me wants him to say, *No, deal's a deal. Fifty bucks or I walk.* Then I would have an excuse to give up.

Arliss takes the envelope. Holds it for a second, taps it with his index finger, then hands it back. "Don't sweat it."

"I can get you the rest, I promise. I just—"

"Don't sweat it," he says softly but firmly.

"Take what's there."

"I don't know how many more ways I can say don't sweat it."

"Okay."

I give Arliss the cue sheet and tell him about this week's movie. He keeps setting up, and so do I. I finish a couple of minutes before him and sit quietly, jitters winding between my ribs like snakes. I check my makeup and make a few adjustments. I think about doing some vocal warm-ups like Josie used to do, but I can't remember hers. I recall some of the things I planned during my solo preshow planning session.

Arliss finishes and gives me a thumbs-up. I give him a frail smile and return his thumbs-up. He raises his hand, fingers splayed, and starts counting down. "In five, four, three, two—" He points at me.

I suddenly feel an overwhelming, palpable solitude. It's terrifying to be alone when all eyes are on you. It's like realizing you're standing on the highest branch of a tree. This is not like my dad leaving me, when at least my pain was private. Everyone who watches our show can see. *But not my dad. Now I know he doesn't watch.*

"Hey, ladies and goblins, it's time for—sorry, I mean maybe—" I stammer with forced brightness. *"Ugh.* Cut. I screwed up already. Can we—"

He nods. "In five, four, three, two—" He points.

I take a deep breath. My head swims. I had no idea how much I depended on Josie for strength until this moment. I had no idea how much I depended on the faintest glimmer of a possibility of my dad seeing me until this moment.

"Hey, ladies and goblins, I'm Delilah Darkwood. Maybe you noticed"—my voice starts to quaver—"it's just me this week." My heart feels like it got elbowed in the boob. My composure collapses. I feel my face crumple into itself. I cover my mouth with my hand and tears pour hot over it like a river flooding over a spillway. I have to keep going. This is take two, and I'm all out of takes—good enough for access, as Arliss would say. But I can't gather myself. I start sobbing. Full-on *Honey, are you okay? Do you need me to call someone? Are you sure? But are you sure you're sure?* sobbing. I look up through the blur and see Arliss walking over. I shake my head. *I can't. I'm sorry for wasting your time,* I try to say with my head shake.

He veers right, to where Josie's empty chair faces away from me. He grabs it, drags it over so that it's facing me, and sits.

I try to tell him *I'm sorry,* but I can't talk. My heart is splitting.

Arliss reaches out and puts a warm, heavy, strong hand on my shoulder. I make blurred eye contact with him but still can't speak.

He readjusts his baseball cap and slowly nods. "Let me tell you what I know about getting left behind," he says, more quietly and gently than I've ever heard him.

"That sounds like a fun conversation," I manage.

"I'll forgive the sassmouth this time." He strokes his beard and looks at the ground for a second, and then back up at me. "Woulda been 1998. You weren't even born yet. I was having a real good time. Lord. I looked cool. I had a sexy, wild girlfriend who was three years older than me and had a tattoo of a rose right above her—Well, anyway. I played a mean bass. Was on the road with Cole Conway. That's where I picked up my girlfriend. Cole was supposed to be the next big thing in country music. The next Garth Brooks, they said. I'd acquired a little bit of a heroin habit along the way, but it wasn't any big deal, I thought. Just put me in a good mood, right? I ain't always in the best mood."

I shake my head and wipe my eyes with my pinkies, trying not to smear my badly smeared mascara any more. "Hadn't noticed, really."

"So I'm flying high. Turns out, I wasn't the only one having a good time. That girlfriend of mine had been having a little fun of her own, and so had Cole. Fact, they'd been having a little fun *together.*"

"She sounds cool and nice," I say.

"You could say that." Arliss sighs long and deep. He averts his eyes, but before he does, I see the hurt flickering in them like a dying candle flame. He clicks his tongue a few times, in the way of someone trying to buy time before doing something painful. "Well, I take the news . . . hard. I start using a *lot*. We pull into a truck stop outside Jackson. I walk into a restroom stall, stick a needle in my arm, and wake up all alone in Madison County Hospital. And that's where the party ended for me. I spent a little while in the hospital, and then they transferred me to an inpatient drug rehab center so I could clean up.

"They discharged me, and I had nowhere to go. No job. No money. I'd finally realized I had a problem. Cole and his new girlfriend were kind enough to leave me my bass and amp when they dumped me at the ER, and I pawned them for a month's rent in some roach-farm flophouse in south Jackson. So here I am. No skills other than playing bass. No education other than the road. I get work washing dishes out at Cracker Barrel. And I start trying to figure out how to live a life. I see a job posting for a janitor here at TV Six. I get the gig. They figure out I have some technical know-how from my music days, so they put me behind a camera and an editing console. I wake up one day and it's twenty-plus years later, and here I am still."

He pauses for a moment. "*That's* getting left behind. And even then, you can have a decent life. You know why I'm still here? It's because I'm content. Maybe even happy. I found my path. My life is simple. I wake up in the morning. I eat my Cheerios, drink my coffee, think my thoughts. I go home after work and sit on my back patio and pet my dog and listen to music and myself breathing. It feels good to be alive and exist. Most things haven't worked out for me—especially love—but that's all right. I'm not as pretty as I used to be. More of my life's behind me than in front of me. Who knows how many years I took off it while I was partying. But I'm a lot healthier now, if you can believe it.

"I get lonely sometimes, but so does everyone else. We're all looking for some sort of salvation in something. Sometimes we try to find it in people. We find our salvation. It slips through our fingers. We find it again. We get left behind. Living is hurting, but I'll take living over the alternative any day. Consciousness is a marvelous gift. It took almost dying to make me realize that. Hell, I'm just rambling now. Anyway, having said all this, you did not get left behind."

"Feels like I did," I say through sniffles, wiping my nose with the back of my hand.

"My girlfriend left me and left me good. Josie? She didn't leave you. People who love each other never really leave each other. If I know y'all, you won't be two steps out that door before you're texting about what a pain in the ass I am."

"Wrong."

"Really?"

"Yeah, we like you."

"My efforts have been in vain," Arliss says, his eyes twinkling. "Here's the deal, kid. Josie is going out and finding her path. You gotta find yours. Sometimes that takes people in different directions for a while. But you'll stay friends and be okay." Arliss pats my shoulder. "Here's one more thing: it'd be real easy to think that you can protect yourself from hurt by just never loving anyone. Kinda like how you can keep from getting hit by a bus by never leaving the house. But that's no way to go through life. Better to love people and get hurt. No one ever says on their deathbed they wish they'd loved fewer people."

I dab a tear away with my index finger. "Arliss?"

"Yeah?"

"I think you're a really good person, no matter how hard you try to convince people you aren't."

"Let's don't get carried away."

I wipe my eyes. "Promise you won't make fun of me for what I'm about to say?"

"No."

"Thank you for being here for me. Not even my own dad was. Thanks for that, and for helping me do this for so long." I wish I had something better to say, but I come up empty—sort of the way of things tonight.

Arliss looks at the floor. He clears his throat a couple of times. "Yeah." It might be my imagination, but his voice cracks a little. He nods, stands, drags the chair back off set. "It's my pleasure," he says quietly, his back to me.

"Liar."

He turns, half smiles, and takes his position behind the camera. "I still don't want to be here all night. So let's nail this intro."

I take a deep breath that stutters as it fills my lungs and exits. I've made a decision. Arliss's pep talk has given me the sliver of courage to end this thing I created. To give it the finish it deserves. And then I'll go find my path. I thought it was this, but I'm not strong enough to go it alone.

I steel myself to kill off this part of me, the one beautiful and exceptional thing I had (and it wasn't even that beautiful or exceptional). It's run its course. I don't know what I'll say. I decide to speak from my heart, and if it's a calamity, so be it. I wish I could give it a more dignified send-off.

Arliss raises his hand one more time. "In five, four, three, two . . ."

I want so badly to cry again, it nauseates me to button it in. But I know I have this one last chance. Because even at his most patient and accommodating, Arliss isn't going to let me try this twenty times. We should have ended with Josie here instead of my limping across the finish line alone. I silently pray to get it right. *This once, let me be as good as Josie.*

"Hello, ladies and ghouls, I'm Delilah Darkwood. You may have noticed I'm by myself this week. So I guess I want to say something." I start to crack. I breathe the lump back down. "This is going to be the—"

There's a loud knock at the outside door. *Great.*

"The hell," Arliss mutters. "We're never gonna get through this." He stomps back up the corridor to answer the door.

I stay seated, trying to smooth down my latest surge of stage fright like a stubborn cowlick. I hope I haven't lost the little bit of momentum I had going. While Arliss talks with whoever's at the door, I close my eyes to concentrate on what I'm going to say. Instead, my thoughts spiral.

You're not good enough.

You can't.

You'll never be happy.

People will always leave you.

You aren't enough for the things you love.

Two sets of steps echo in the corridor over my sniffling. Arliss's heavy plod, and some lighter, quicker ones. I assume someone who works at the station left their keys at their desk, or a half-eaten bologna sandwich in the break-room fridge that they can't stop thinking about.

"Hey, kid," Arliss says.

I open my eyes and look up.

My mom is standing in front of me. She's dressed in a black satin gown she bought on one of our thrifting expeditions, and has long black gloves up to her elbows. Pale foundation covers her face and upper chest, and she has theatrical dark eye makeup. Her hair is teased up wildly and has a gray streak sprayed into it. Her look is somewhere between Helena Bonham Carter as Bellatrix Lestrange and Helena Bonham Carter as everyone else she's ever played.

I don't know how to make sense of what I'm seeing. I stand. "Mom?"

She beams. "You mean"—she does jazz hands—"Dolores Darkwood."

"Mom," I say again, my voice quavering, pleading with her not to be making some awful joke as I start toward her slowly.

She holds out her arms, and I rush into them, and she hugs me tight, like I'll slip from her grasp. I sob and sob. And I feel her warm tears on the side of my face.

"I couldn't do it alone," I say. "I tried so hard."

"And you don't have to, DeeDee. I'll never leave you on your own. I'm here for you, baby. Always."

We hug and rock back and forth.

I break the embrace and wipe my eyes. I take a deep breath and fan myself. "How did you get here? I have the car."

She wipes her eyes too. "Candy brought me after her reading. Helped me with my makeup."

"What about work?"

"I talked with my manager. I'm picking up extra night shifts in return for no Fridays anymore."

"Why didn't you tell me?"

"I wasn't sure I had the guts to do this. I didn't want to get your hopes up and then chicken out."

I glance in Arliss's direction. He's standing by the camera, waiting patiently. But I'm not about to press my luck.

"Okay," I say to my mom. "Should we fix our makeup?"

"I think our runny mascara actually looks kinda cool and spooky," she says.

"I'm good if you are."

"Let's do this. I gotta warn you, I'm very nervous. I've never done anything like this before."

We walk over to the stage. Arliss hurries and grabs Josie's chair and sets it up for Mom.

"Why, thank you—I'm sorry, I didn't catch your name at the door," Mom says.

Arliss tips his cap. "Arliss Thacker. Ma'am." He's uncharacteristically stammery and jittery.

"Shawna Wilkes. You're a fine gentleman, Arliss. Thank you for all you've done for my daughter."

He blushes. "Ain't no big thing."

"It's a huge deal to her."

Arliss smiles, showing *teeth*. This is an exceedingly rare occurrence. "All right. Follow your daughter's lead, okay?"

"I've watched every single episode of the show."

"I don't doubt it."

"But it's different being on this side of the camera."

"I don't doubt it."

"I've survived worse, though," Mom says with a deep breath. "I'll survive this."

Arliss smiles *again*. He actually has a good smile. "I don't doubt it. We survivors have a way of surviving." He and Mom share a knowing look.

We sit. Mom vibrates with anxious energy. I reach over and take her hand, which has gone cold and tense. "Hey," I say. "You'll be great."

She nods quickly and swallows hard but doesn't respond.

"It just takes practice," I say.

She nods again and gives me a thin smile. "By the way, I had an idea for a new horoscope segment we could do tonight," she whispers.

Arliss counts us down and points.

I don't even need to try very hard to sound upbeat and bright. "Hello, ladies and ghouls, I'm Delilah Darkwood, and you're seeing a new face on *Midnite Matinee*. With me is . . ."

Mom sits frozen for a beat. "Oh! Me? Dolores Darkwood." She dissolves into the church giggles. "I'm sorry. I'm sorry. Can we take it again?"

"Okay, Mom," I say gently. "Deep breath. Arliss lets us have two tries, and then—"

"It's fine," Arliss says, cutting me off, all jittery and blushy again. "We can go until you get it right."

"I don't want to tie you up all night. I promise I'll get the hang of this," Mom says.

"It's no trouble at all," Arliss says.

Man, Arliss is acting really strangely. It's almost like . . . Oh, come *on*. I can practically see my own brain with the internal eye roll I'm doing.

But also, every molecule in my body feels like the rush of birds taking flight from a field.

Sometimes you've resigned yourself to living your life in the shadow of what might have been. Looking up at happiness from some low place. You've finally accepted that your life isn't on the unbroken upward trajectory it feels like it'll be when you're a kid, when you assume every year will be better than the one before. You've said to yourself, *This is all there is for me*, and then something, some*one*, comes along and says, *Hold on, there's more*.

Maybe life isn't about avoiding pain at all costs. Maybe it's

380

about having one or two people who have signed up for the messy job of being your salvation, who make your life bigger.

I used to keep a memory in my most sacred heart of my dad holding me in his arms under October stars, the clean smell of autumn night air in my nose. A perfect day.

But now I'll keep a new one, of my mom holding me in her arms in the dim light and cool, musty-basement smell of TV Six. A perfect day.

Josie

Buford let me cuddle him all night last night. He hasn't let me do that since we were both young. I guess he just kinda outgrew it as he got old and grumpy. I was packing a few last things and he waddled into my room, slowly and painfully, the way he does now. And I kissed the top of his head and said, "Bufie, Mama's gonna be going away, and they won't let me have you in the dorms. So you're going to have to stay here." And I saw in his mournful, droopy eyes that he understood, and also he understood that maybe he won't be around anymore the next time I come home. The thought filled me with the deepest, purest sadness—the sort you can't even begrudge for its inevitability but can only accept. And so when it came time for me to go to bed, he shuffled over and let me help him onto the bed with me, and allowed me to snuggle him once more.

I see him now, in my side-view mirror, Delia kneeling next to him, lifting his paw and making him wave. She waves too and wipes her eyes with the back of her hand. I wave back out my window and wipe my eyes as I slowly pull away.

Behind me, at my back like always, is Lawson, his pickup pulling a U-Haul trailer with a mix of our stuff. He's going to help me move into my dorm, and then I'm going to help him move into his house.

His phone is full of music I picked out for him to listen to on the drive. My phone is full of music he picked out for me. We made a deal that neither of us is allowed to listen to anything else for the five-hour drive to Knoxville.

I made a big show of pretending like it was going to be some great ordeal, but the truth is that his music reminds me of him now, so it's fine.

. . .

We pull up outside Jesmyn's house in Nashville to have lunch and visit awhile, and there's a single text on my phone from Delia: Rayne & Delilah 4ever.

It's hard to see through the tears to text her back, but I manage.

Me: Rayne & Delilah 4ever.

Delia: I miss you already.

Me: I miss you more.

Delia: I love you, JoJoBee.

Me: I love you, DeeDeeBooBoo.

Delia

Dear Dad,

I've written a lot of these emails, but you wouldn't know that because I never sent them. Maybe I won't send this one either. I guess I'll see when I get to the end.

I have two stories for you. Here's the first. I was sitting in the break room at the grocery store where I work, chatting with a couple of my new friends, when Josie (my friend I told you about, who I used to do my show with) called. She said she heard some girls dying laughing in the hall outside her dorm room, and she went out to see what was up. They were watching a video clip from my show. Mom does it with me now. When Josie left for college, I wanted to quit because it was too hard to do it alone, but Mom stepped up and saved me. Anyway, in this clip, Mom and I were trying to do a sketch with marionettes and we were terrible at it, and Mom kept accidentally making the marionette do this jacking-off motion.

So we both crack up, and we can't stop. We were having so much fun, we left it in. It's not the first time this has happened on our show, but this time, somehow, people got ahold of the clip and started sharing it. It's infectious, I guess, to see two people laughing like that, being silly and enjoying being together. Anyway, it went viral. Millions of people have seen it. Maybe even you have by now. We've gotten all these invites to horror cons and talk shows. Thousands and thousands of people have subscribed to our YouTube channel, which we've started putting more work into.

All I can think about is how glad I am that Mom was there for me when I needed her the most. How glad I am that she's kept my life from being too small. And that brings me to my second story.

Ever since I saw you in Florida, I've been thinking about a memory I have from a few years ago. This one morning in late September, I woke up a lot earlier than usual. For some reason, I went outside, and it was still dark and chilly.

Then I saw a firefly blink. I couldn't believe it. I thought I was hallucinating. I'd never seen one that late in the year. You could tell by how slowly it moved that it was close to dying. I thought about it all day. How bummed I was that this lonely firefly was shining its light out into the world when everyone had left it behind. It seemed sad and desperate.

But lately I've been thinking a lot about that firefly. And not because it's September. Because I see it differently now. Maybe that firefly wasn't sad and lonely and desperate. Maybe it was okay with being left behind, and it was shining its light because that's what it does.

For a long time I shined my light for someone other than me. But not anymore. Now I shine bright for me. You can create light even when everyone's left you behind because that's what you do. It's what I do. I don't know if the world will remember me or what I did, Dad. But I'll know that I burned as bright as I could.

I'm glad I got to have pizza with you one more time. I'm glad I got to see the ocean.

I hope you have a good life and you're a good father to your new daughter.

I hope you remember me sometimes and love me, or at least remember that you loved me once. There will always be part of me that loves you.

I hope I'm braver than you when life hurts. I think I already am in some ways.

Your daughter,
Delia

I hit send.

Acknowledgments

This book would not have been possible without my amazing agents, Charlie Olsen, Lyndsey Blessing, and Philippa Milnes-Smith, or my brilliant editorial team of Emily Easton, Lynne Missen, and Samantha Gentry. My undying gratitude to you all.

Thanks to Phoebe Yeh and everyone at Crown Books for Young Readers. Thanks to Barbara Marcus, Judith Haut, John Adamo, Dominique Cimina, Mary McCue, Margret Wiggins, Kristin Schulz, Adrienne Waintraub, Lisa Nadel, Alison Kolani, Ray Shappell, Trish Parcell, and Megan Williams at Random House Children's Books.

My eternal gratitude as always to Kerry Kletter. Your writing reminds me of the possibilities of precise, beautiful language and clear insight. I don't know how I ever wrote without your friendship, brilliance, wisdom, and critical eye. Yes, I cut and pasted that from my last set of acknowledgments, but it's still as true as ever.

Deepest thanks to Brittany Cavallaro and Emily Henry. You are brilliant, hilarious, amazing writers and people who inspire me daily both with your published works and with the text message threads with which I can only barely keep up. Thanks for being such a wonderful exemplar of female friendship. I need the book you're writing together in my hands.

Victoria Coe and Bridget Hodder, another dynamic duo of friendship, an inspiration to me and this book.

Stephanie Perkins, for your phone call that day and for making me believe I could write romance. Who, after all, is more of an expert?

David Arnold, my bizarro twin. Will it ever stop surprising us how similarly we think? More to the point, it will never stop pleasing me.

Nic Stone. My Working on Excellence partner and Crown sister. I'm so excited the world finally has your books.

Jennifer Niven and Angelo Surmelis, for being the models of generosity and kindness as authors and people. Y'all deserve every good thing that's come and will come to you yet.

Jesse Andrews, for inspiring me to write a funny book.

My bosses, Amy Tarkington and Rachel Willis. I get asked all the time how I manage to write with a full-time job. You are how. Thank you.

John Corey Whaley, Rainbow Rowell, and Benjamin Alire Sáenz, thank you for letting me vent about politics in addition to leaving me in awe of your talents.

Adriana Mather, for being basically the epitome of cool and putting your head down, tuning everything out, and working. You're one of my heroes.

Brendan Kiely, for being such a welcome and familiar face on so many of my travels, and for being such a powerful voice for good in our world.

Ryan Labay, for being the raddest and most supportive.

Kristen Gilligan and Len Vlahos, for being so awesome and talented, and such advocates for my books.

Marlena Midnite, Robyn Graves, and Blake Powell of Mid-

nite Mausoleum, for creating such a fun, sweet, goofy, and bizarre show for me to randomly discover on my local public access station at eleven on a Saturday night. Josie and Delia aren't an attempt to write you, but they certainly owe their existence to you.

Cameron McCasland, thank you for the insights on the strange and wonderful world of public access. I can't believe I was so lucky to have a member of one of the all-time great horror-hosting teams right in my backyard.

Amber Addison, thank you for the MMA information.

Rose Little-Brock, for putting so much goodness into the world and basically encapsulating why I'd watch a TV series about Texas librarians.

Steph Post, for being not only a brilliant writer of books but an amazing advocate for them.

Nickolas Butler, for taking the time out of your day to hang out with a total stranger who happens to be one of your biggest fans.

The crew from Jeffz Game of Thronez Korner.

The brilliant authors who have allowed me the honor of being one of the early readers of their work: Sharon Huss Roat, Marie Marquardt, Estelle Laure, Calla Devlin, Ashley Woodfolk, Samira Ahmed, Randy Ribay, Maggie Thrash, Jared Reck, Richard Lawson, Anica Mrose Rissi, Kelly Loy Gilbert, Tanaz Bhathena, Carlie Noël Sorosiak, Gae Polisner, Kit Frick, Farrah Penn, Sarah Nicole Smetana, Eric Gansworth, Peter Brown Hoffmeister, and Susin Nielsen.

The staff and campers of Tennessee Teens Rock Camp and Southern Girls Rock Camp. Allowing me to see firsthand the magic and beauty of young women coming together to make art was a huge impetus for this book.

The readers, librarians, educators, booksellers, podcasters, book clubbers, Instagrammers, and bloggers (and every other category of book people) who have been such advocates for my books. I see you and the work you do, and I am so deeply appreciative. You make our country a better place when so many are trying to do the opposite. By sharing stories, you're giving dignity to those who are targets of those trying to strip it away. You're helping to write the counternarrative to the narratives of hate and fear that are all too prevalent now.

Mom and Dad, Grandma Z, Brooke, Adam, Steve. I love you all.

The love of my life, best friend, and first reader, Sara. I could not have written this or any other book without your love and support and the happiness you give me. Being with you turns a Comfort Inn in Jackson, Tennessee, into the Ritz-Carlton.

My precious boy, Tennessee. Nothing brings me more joy than watching you grow up, and calling myself your father is the greatest honor I'll ever know. I love that I have a book of yours on my bookshelf now. I hope someday everyone gets to read the adventures of *Mega Monster Man*. Thank you for being my son.

About the Author

JEFF ZENTNER is the author of the *New York Times* Notable Book *The Serpent King* and *Goodbye Days*. He has won the William C. Morris Award, the Amelia Elizabeth Walden Award, the International Literacy Association Award, and the Westchester Fiction Award, was longlisted for the Carnegie Medal and the United Kingdom Literacy Association Award, and was a finalist for the Southern Book Prize and the Indies Choice Award. He was a *Publishers Weekly* Flying Start and an Indies Introduce pick. Before becoming a writer, he was a musician who recorded with Iggy Pop, Nick Cave, and Debbie Harry. *Rayne & Delilah's Midnite Matinee* is his ode to people who try hard and come up short. He lives in Nashville with his wife and son. You can follow him on Facebook, on Instagram, and on Twitter at @jeffzentner.